ROTARY SPOKES

FIONA COOPER

ROTARY SPOKES

BRILLIANCE BOOKS

This first edition published by
Brilliance Books / Plain Edition
14 Clerkenwell Green London EC1R 0DP England

Copyright © Fiona Cooper 1988

ISBN 0 946189 22 6

Printed and bound by Woolnough Bookbinding, Irthlingborough,
Northants

This book is dedicated to Barbara, with love, thanks and laughter.

Special Acknowledgements to : Calamity Jane, Edith Massey, The She-Hulk, Divine, Theodora of Byzantium, Maureen Schorr, Moll Cutpurse, Karen Ingall, Virginia Woolf, Stella Gibbons and the Chicago Ladies Garden Club.

PROLOGUE

*"Preacher man, don't tell me heaven is under the earth
I know you don't know what life is really worth."*
(Bob Marley, Stand Up for Your Rights.)

It was the terminal half- hour of a forensic p.m. in Anywhere, Middle America. Any attempt at a hard day's work had died of natural causes before noon. On the porches, in the shade of pick-up trucks and cactus bushes, the good people of Anywhere flapped newspapers, limp handkerchiefs and fans of damp paper or bleached cane, pushing the air around their humid skin and sweating with the effort.

As the heat skulked away over the horizon and the backdrop of night slumped into place, a hum of excitement began.

This night was The Night.

For weeks beforehand, posters had prepared the Way of The Mouthpiece of the Lord, the natural Son and Heir to Jesus Christ, one Reverend Thomas Pateman of the Church of the Salvated.

Alleluia, Jesus, comin' to our town tonight!

Purraise the Lord!

The posters were full of Divine promise:

An end to misery!

A cleansing of ALL our wickedness!

A place in the Eternal Mansion!

Salvation!

In smaller letters, the posters held out a more practical lure:

Real Domestic Bliss in the love of Jesus Christ!

The Guiding Light of God in all our Earthly Transactions!

A Divine Ear of Love for All Our Worries!

Door-to-door hand-outs promised the Scourge of the Temple for the Wicked, and forgiveness for even the basest sinner. Better than all this, the Reverend Thomas Pateman had had a TV series coast-to-coast for a number of years, and had deigned to step out of the magic box, out onto the road, to be with Ordinary People and share his Ministry, personally. The good folk of Anywhere surged out of their homes into the dusk, trembling with Sunday-best awe. As one, they moved along the road out of town towards the huge marquee where canvas billowed around the Inner Light like a spaceship tethered in the darkness. Thomas Pateman would vouchsafe an appearance at 8.30.

Feet shuffled in the dust, fingers unfolded dollar bills, lips whispered their hopes and fears; hands clutched elbows, swatted starched children, smoothed skirts and trouser creases, and opened the hymn sheets. Throats were cleared, and voices rose past the spotlights through the canvas to the sparkling stars above. Already tears oozed from wondering, wet and weary eyes.

Backstage, Thomas Pateman checked his watch. The minute hand was a bolt of lightning, the hour hand was the finger of God: 9.17. Billed for 8.30, he would let the heat and guilt build up; he would wait for at least three fainting conversions; he listened for the spontaneous testifying of the Chosen, who would burst onto the stage to be fielded and soothed by his inner temple of acolytes in their white, sexless, neo-classical robes.

He had as little personal contact with the Unrighteous as possible; early in his ministry he had made the mistake of trying to have a dialogue with his congregation. In one redneck town he had promised them a green hill far away . . .

'Yaaasss! It's called Lynchin' Hall, preacher . . . clear across the plain.' sneered one ungodly heckler, waving a coil of rope.

Shortly afterwards he had decided to take up with the new boom of TV salvation: Jesus Christ coast-to-coast. His targets were the ungodly, the unwashed, the unrighteous, and the Un-American. He paraded these monsters of iniquity throughout his sermons clad in the shameful scarlet of Sin, and the purple prose of Evil.

But in the halls of media hype and the corridors of mass communication, he had witnessed a new spectre bare its slavering jaws: a personification of Unnatural Abomination eroding the Family and Life As We Know It. He shuddered at the scope of its lusts; he trembled at the way it stalked the streets seeking whom it could devour and pervert to its desires. He covered his eyes against the rock stars and actors who admitted their wanton evil; he stopped his ears against the pleas for compassion, tolerance and understanding. He flew to the granite bosom of Saint Paul, and blessed the day that he had written:

'The women exchanged natural relations for unnatural, and the men likewise gave up natural relations with women and were consumed with passion for one another. They were filled with all manner of Wickedness, Evil, Covetousness, Malice.

'Full of Envy, Murder, Strife, Deceit, Malignity . . . they are Gossips, Slanderers, Haters of God, Insolent, Haughty, Boastful, Inventors of Evil, Disobedient to Parents, Foolish, Faithless, Heartless, Ruthless.

'Those who do such things deserve to Die!'

God had tried them and found them wanting.

They had tried Thomas Pateman.

It was more than the Man of God could endure.

The trials of Thomas Pateman came in three stages.

First was the appointment of an un-masculine and un-American religious programmes coordinator. He darling-ed everyone, caressed everyone, and was given to silk cravats and pastel slacks. Thomas Patemen decided to stay and beard this gelded lion in its den. The next stage was when he realized that the new sound crew included several women who displayed no respect, Christian principles, or wedding rings, and clearly preferred each other's company to the lofty wisdom of his conversation. He invited Anita Bryant onto his chat show and was truly humbled when she accepted. And then this trio of perverts blacked the programme. He hurtled around to the sound technician's apartment and, in a fit of moral outrage, burst in.

And there they were, lying on their couch, lustificatin' and laughin'! The sight horrified and haunted him into a chill sweat of revulsion.

And so the Reverend Thomas Pateman was back among the ordinary people, that mass of humanity in whom he had an absurdly unswerving faith. He saw himself as the floodgate against iniquity, his arms outstretched as if crucified, holding back the licentious torrent.

From TV he had gained considerably: his voice was amplified by 'Let 'Em Hear!' religious audio engineers; his slight figure was illuminated by Paraclete Presentation, 'Lights for the Enlightened', (Profit for the Prophets).

3

He spoke with Authority: he had seen the Evil, his shoulder had burned where its producer had touched him; his eyes had seared with the unrepentant wickedness of those unnatural women – but he had never broken bread with the Evil, he had never supped from the same cup!

And thus spoke Thomas Pateman in the plains of America:

'My dear friends, my brothers and sisters, I come to you in Jesus' name, as one running ahead of wildfire scattering the waters of Righteousness that you may be saved; that your homes will not be razed to the ground!

'Evil are their ways and they would besmirch us too!

'What is our Life for? I will tell you. Life is for good, clean, natural, normal American Love, in God's name. Life is not for cheap thrills and indulgence in the transitory pleasures of the Flesh! Life is not for polluting the Temple of our body with drugs and unnatural lustin'!'

At this spoint his acolytes would hand out buttons saying 'Normal or Damned!'

There was no other choice.

He finished each oration with the awful thunder of the Red Sea on Pharoah's troops:

'WASH THEM OUT! I SAY WORRRSSCCHH'EM OUT! Fornicators, thieves, commies, faggots, hippies, veg-eye-tarians, lesbohemes, those breakers of marriage, those who would blast the innocence of our children, those who deny God's love – WORRRSSCCHH'EM OUT! Toss'em on the smokin' trash heaps of Eternal Damnation to writhe and suffer in their unnatural FILTH!

'For there is only one way to fulfil his purpose, my friends. This is the path of Celibacy, or the bed of Holy Matrimony! This is the path of the Normal American Citizen. This is the Way of GOD!'

At this earth-shaking moment, the Reverend Thomas Pateman would collapse in a pool of celestial sweat and crumpled linen, clutching the microphone to catch every heartfelt sigh. The lights would go from pale gold to white to dazzling. And out of the blinding centre of the stage, Thomas Pateman gasped his final message:

'Let my words mingle with this fruitful earth on which we stand . . . let them be seeds . . . seeds, my friends. Seeds of His righteous retribution throughout the world . . .'

And even as he spoke, his words drifted down like fallout, coating the shoes, hems and heels of the faithful. And behold, from that one tent, a nuclear sparkler, the Word spread in great rings, surging through the land, with the fearful bloodless heartbeat of hatred, ignorance and fear.

CHAPTER
ONE

"Gee, what a dump."
(Bette Davis)

As the spectre of holocaust and moral decay bestrode the land, there was one small town which would not have agreed with Thomas Pateman. It was a town of one street. A mile or so up the red dust road, beyond where the developments were never even started, there was a sign stuck in the dirt. And the sign said:

NORMAL

Buildings shimmered vaguely ahead. The road lurched on and finally dribbled into the street. Some myopic optimist named it 1st Street. Now it is divided into 1st Street East and 1st Street West. Divided by three stores, one cafe, a dry water trough, social expectation. If there had been a railroad it would have made the same split. 1st Street East was undeniably the wrong side of the tracks.

People in Normal had never heard of Thomas Pateman. The idea of a Normal Revival would have brought sneers and disbelief. They had only had electric for fifteen years or so. There were only two TVs on 1st Street East. The reception delivered either sound or picture. Had Lorie-Kay Squash seen Thomas Pateman through the blizzard of static, she would have thought he was a soap-powder commercial. Had she heard him, she might well have thought the same. Such things are sent to try one who is forced to use a washboard and green soap in the late twentieth century. One whose washing remains slightly grey or dust-red, no matter what. But there it was. And, true, in the eighties occasionally good sound and picture would come together. But by then, Thomas Pateman had left TV.

Life was hard, hot and slow. Everywhere outside, heat and dust. Everywhere inside, heat swirled by slow-swimming fans, and dust damped down by handfuls of tepid water sprinkled through the day. The dust rose near as soon as damped, and steamed into the air, coating boots, toes, chair legs, cats, children and dogs.

In Schlumberger's Hardware, you could buy hooks and hoses, picks and pails, rake and rugs, insecticides and instant fertilizers, wheelbarrows and whips, garden chairs and barbeque grills, mosquito flares and mosquito nets, snap-traps for lizards and guila monsters, and safe-to-pets Rat Suicide pellets.

If you had the money.

Or you could shift next door, to Grodzinski's Grab Palace, and buy candy and cotton, cigarettes and sugar, coffee and cake, cabbages and cornmeal, tostadas and tobacco, bacon and beans. The store oozed with milk and molasses; flies dozed, pinned to sacks and sills in the heat.

In the post office combination corner store, you could buy newspapers and notepaper, string and stamps, hairnets and horror comics.

Or, wore out with looking and hoping, you could shuffle next door into Dino's and buy sodas-n-shakes, pizza-n-pop, fries-n-frozen seafood, beer-n-burgers, sandwiches-n-snax, eat here or to go.

Although there were thirteen bleached shacks along 1st Street East, on the long road to Hook Airs, there were only four or five households. Left there because they didn't have the money to fix the truck to get out. Left high and dry with no truck to fix as the canning works closed; the mine was found to be empty; the thrill of the oil well turned out to be an overflow from a gas station that had subsided into the sand before anyone could remember there ever had been one.

Most days, you could find Gooseneck Squash down 1st Street East sitting on his brand-new roof. Waaall, the timbers for the brand- new roof. Waaall, let's be exact – sitting right on the spot by the road where he would pile the new timbers when he had the money to buy them. Meanwhile, there was some planning to do. He scratched his neck, pulled his ear, pushed his hat up from his eyes, coughed and spat. Such a lot for a man to be doing. He unfolded his unattractive length and shambled across the street and settled in a doorway.

The door where he leant was somehow hopeful. The wood was new and fitted the frame. It bore two new brass locks. Around it, the shack was painted matte silver, and the whole had signs of being cared for.

Rising from the ground were great dragon tails of flame spurting from the wheels of a huge motorbike which filled one side wall. A fabulous creature wrought in metal.

From the roof of the shack a heavy electric cable stretched towards the power line in 1st Street West, one solid guy rope this side of the stores. Spindly and illegal wires straggled from here to the other four inhabited shacks.

A black and silver sign hung from the eaves:

ROTARY SPOKES. M'T'R REPAIRS. E.S.P. BIKES

Everywhere else in 1st Street East, the dust shifted and sighed around inertia and exhaustion. Here, tools clattered, a hissing flame arced through metal, engines roared, exhausts PHOOW-PHOOWed, and, most miraculous, money regularly changed hands.

All the burn-ups for miles around ended up here, to be unmeshed, untangled and re-made. All the old country boys heaped their wrecks onto ancient flatbed trucks and rattled to a stop here. If ever the proprietor of this one flourishing business had another name it had been lost. She was, simply, Rotary Spokes.

She was six foot four in her boots. Had never been seen out of them. She could shoot, play pool, spit and fight better than any man around. She favoured black leather. Only they wasn't too many places to go in Normal. Just Dino's.

1st Street West didn't like her looks, but had to admire her faultless work, and pay the bills. For 1st Street East the prices would drop to near nothing. Only they wasn't presently no call for repairs. There being no vehicles here. It was legend in Normal that some uppity bachelor-type from 1st Street West had once told her:

'Your work's damn near as good as a man would do, sweetheart.'

Followed a brief silence in the workshop, then a splintering crash as a pressed-linen bum hit the sidewalk. His bill included a new door and locks, and he had paid it.

'You some smart-ass . . . she made your ass smart!' said the town wit, Dragnet Hornwinder. To do him credit, it was the funniest joke he had ever made. Mr Smart-ass didn't lose the name and moved out of Normal, courtesy of the well-repaired engine, and got all the way to L.A., where he sold life insurance. Peppered with ulcers, he headed pressure groups against Hell's Angels, hippies and women. He wore a

'Normal or Damned' button, and ended his days in a room papered with photos of Jerry Falwell, Thomas Pateman, Anita Bryant and Ronald Reagan. He died unfulfilled, but hopeful. There's a new day comin' Lord, yeah.

Rotary Spokes had started off living in the workshop, sleeping under the bench in a sleeping bag. She had got there about the time of the oil-well and stayed. Over the years she had earned a reputation for mechanical genius. She spent little, but after a few years had ordered good seasoned timber and built onto the back of the workshop. A huge room, a kitchen and a shower. She had built herself a hybrid chop from the death throes of a Hell's Angel's burn-out that had half the boys put away for years, and the rest maimed or hospitalized. The tattered remnant of the chapter had willed her the bizarre metal sculpture in the desert in return for making their two bikes road-worthy.

On the wall she had a Samurai sword over a rack of rifles she was holding till the Hartville Ranch was on its feet again. The rifles had sat there for seven years. There was a wolf skin on the floor and motorbike pennants along the ceiling beams. By her bed was a scale model of a Harley Electraglide.

Of an evening, she would sprawl on her bed with a can of Blue Stripe, and listen to a record from the Country Club catalogue. She liked Doris Day, Brenda Lee, Sweet Sue's Rhythm Band and so on.

And her household had class. She shared it with an aristocratic cat, whose real name was Princess Henrietta Maria II. From the cat's point of view, the workshop was a proletarian dump and Rotary Spokes an oafish minion. The squalor was made bearable by the TV permanently on a station that showed old movies, Hollywood's Europe. There was also the frequency of meals. Rotary Spokes liked to eat well, in her terms, and had been well trained over the years to provide liver, heart, salmon steaks, cream and milk.

The Princess' mother, Queen Alexandrovna, had been a stowaway on a midnight boat out of some mad Eastern European dictatorship some years before. She had given birth amid the oily swells and Atlantic mists and unfitted all five daughters for the New World with a flow of stories about the glory of the Old. The fresh salmon! The coursing hare! The white-columned mansion! The bear-skin hearthrug! The blazing logs ... by the time the wheezing station wagon bearing the family and their protectors – the Liebesteins – had broken down two miles out of Normal, each kitten knew what she was entitled to, although they had only ever felt these things through their mother's silk-furred tummy. And when the Liebesteins had despaired at the *cuisine ancienne* at Dino's and found only an enormous wordless young woman, with a permanent cigarette, to repair the station wagon, Frau Liebestein had donned a black-veiled toque and refused to speak until they rolled into Hook Airs, lighter by many dollars and two kittens.

Princess Katerina went west, wore ribbon and slept in a basket.

Rotary Spokes seduced Princess Henrietta Maria II east, with fresh fish and liver. Beneath her aristocratic disdain for this loutish foreigner who called her Fluffy, she realized that she could do well here. A sweatshirt on a workbench in the sun was hardly a bear skin, but it was better than shared rags in a station wagon. She approved the wolf skin and allowed Rotary Spokes to serve her. On a cold evening, she would honour her by sitting solidly on her hard thighs and gripping holes through to her knees.

Damn! It was hot! Rotary Spokes opened the door and nudged Gooseneck Squash off the doorstep, like an old mattress.

'Git,' she said.

'Aw, jist a while . . .' he said.

It happened most days. If there was a work bus, somehow Gooseneck never managed to scramble into it. He would always wind up on her doorstep, belly-aching for a smoke to wrap around breakfast. She made him a cigarette.

'You bring the mail?'

'Ah been in,' he lied. 'Ain't nuthin' in yit.'

'Waaall, mebbe you can go up there later.'

'Yeah, ah do thet,' he mumbled, dozing in heaven.

She slammed the door on him.

In the workshop a bike lay, one wheel crippled to a painful angle. Rotary Spokes walked around the tangle, pictured the wheel round and perfect, and started to strip off the useless metal. A ton twist-up. Some crazy boy in plaster to the hip. Ah well. Her hands were smeared with oil, her nails ground and short and flat with metal shavings. 'I want mah baby!' growled Rotary Spokes. She called it singing. 'I want my baby . . . All I want is a little baby, so I kin call 'em mine . . . Make my dreams come true with you – GODDAM!', she spat out tobacco strands and scarlet blood oozed through black oil on her thumb.

The cat shrugged into the moving path of the sun and wrapped her long tail over her nose.

'Ollviss ven she is sinkink iss coming blood and goddam,' she thought in Hildegard Knef's voice. 'Baby, baby, baby . . . iss meanink man friend. Bot ven iss coming man into ze place, mensch, she is tritting him like it vas dirt under her feet. Snip, snap, like a little mouse.' She stretched her splendid claws.

Rotary Spokes spat oil and blood into the sink.

'Lieber Gott,' shuddered the cat, and summoned beautiful thoughts of kittenhood in the icing east-European Castle. 'Zis place iss altogedders vidout hisstory or dignity . . . but the food comes more often.' She fell asleep, thinking shallow aristocratic thoughts. Throaty purrs.

A knock at the door, muffled through flabby knuckles and dust. Rotary Spokes drew spit into her mouth and stood still.

'Ro . . . ho . . rodry?' a voice slithered under the door, rising blindly towards her ankles. Thwat! The spit knocked the voice into the floor.

'Damn! Whuchuh want there, Goosenick?' said Rotary Spokes. Her voice stripped a little more varnish from the door.

'Uh . . .'

The door creaked, the voice creaked, and Gooseneck Squash, pale shadow, oozed into the sun-dusty workshop.

'Damned if I ain't forgot, Rodry . . . mebbe ah just set there an' it'll just come to me.' Goosenick started to sit.

'Damned if yuh do!' snapped Rotary Spokes and shoved him back outside. She liked the workshop hot and steamy, dusty and hot, sweltering, and on her own. She breathed slow and deep until the heat built up and the oil smell rose around her with her own smell of sweat pouring down her back and arms.

From time to time, Rotary Spokes swaggered along the houses for 'cawfy' and a cigarette. She didn't know it, but Lorie-Kay Squash and Mar'Ann Springer and Dor liked her coming in.

'She ain't let herself go,' they said.

Then they would think of her house, just like theirs almost, only husbandless and with a good income.

'She ain't had to!' they would decide.

'And she alwiz seems so damn happy.'

Lorie-Kay Squash shredded out the next words, grated them through her unhappy lips.

'And why do he spend all his time on her workshop door, like a dawg . . . why?'

Life had dealt Lorie-Kay Squash, nee Higgle, a bad hand from a pack with no aces and too many jokers.

'I bless the day a Higgle do become a Squash!' her grandmother had wept on her wedding day. But why? Why? Dutiful years in inept marital embrace had left Lorie-Kay confused and irritated, and she met his humid poking with heavier and heavier sighs.

It was the same as the schoolyard fumbles, the frantic scrabbling on hard pick-up seats, one ear numb on the door handle. At least that had the thrill of being forbidden. And the tense days until she knew she wasn't . . . *you know*. Only now she had been twice and Darlene and Gooseneck Jr. were the evidence – pale, thin, addicted to TV and always hungry. Life left Lorie-Kay cold; her hug-less life a round of whining to Mar'Ann or Dor, trapped like her, in Normal with no prospect of living or leaving.

The tired round of housework never led them anywhere near the magazine or TV or radio perfection ladled to them daily: it was a drug they had never tasted, and it was losing all its kick in twenty or so years of dry waiting in Middle America.

Daily they thrust their feet into tatty hostess Christmas slippers, relics from when there had been a Christmas to celebrate. They made something of a Mother Hubbard breakfast, and stood accusingly as their 'men' ate, rose and slunk out of the house, unshaven.

'Lookin' for work . . . only they ain't none here.'

They all knew it, but just occasionally there would be a work bus, some rush job needing extra hands.

Then there were the kids. Darlene and Gooseneck Jr. looked . . . well, not sweet, but better when they were asleep. The minute their pale eyes opened on the world, their thin lips parted and their scrawny necks stretched. And tweet tweet *tweeeet* all day long, food, food, food, toys, toys, games, TV, food. Lorie-Kay had a high opinion of schooling. It got the kids out of the house.

In Mar'Ann's house, it was Beau and Shirley-Anne's turn to be nagged and screamed at as soon as their father had gone. Lucas J. Springer at least would get a day's work if the bus turned up. He was, relatively, a good man.

The kids bundled off to school in Hook Airs, or out to play if it was a vacation, Lorie-Kay and Mar'Ann did the house. They banged thin rugs on peeling walls, raked house dust onto street dust, sprinkled water on bleached boards, and then Mar'Ann would flap over for cigarettes and cawfy. On the TV they sneered at women who told them that cawfy and cigarettes were bad for you.

'And when your Special One comes home, will he want to kiss lips that owe their fragrance more to *nicotine* than *Dentokleen?*'

Lorie-Kay Squash rubbed her teeth with a rag and salt. Mar'Ann left hers in a glass of water.

No Special One. Gooseneck? Hah! Lucas? Hah! No house on the hill, no white picket fence, no car, no steak, no candlelit evening for two, no love, nothing. Sure was no place like home, except just next door. They heard the radio talk about deepfreezes, orgasms, planned parenthood: city talk. The radio and TV people might have been living on a different planet.

And they ain't no passenger space shuttles outta Normal.

The silken web of life had let Mar'Ann Springer down, strand by strand. Just when she'd adjusted herself to the humiliation of married life in a trailer park and started to hold her head high as she raked her three square feet of gravel, the trailer had been repossessed, Lucas having been laid off. Then came the advert for able-bodied men for an oil development in Normal. She had pawned her wedding ring and all the china for a down payment on an ancient wagon to get them there, the promised land.

When the oil failed to gush, she had decided to leave Lucas and Normal and the wooden shack with its corrugated roof. And then she fell for Beau, who burst into the world needing clothes and food every damn day. She watched the shacks around her empty one by one, was three bucks short of bus-fare, and then she fell for Shirley-Anne. And here she was, wife and mother of two and blue as Monday.

There were just the three shacks left with people in them. Not what you'd call company. Not what you'd call a good influence on little Beau and Shirley-Anne. That Spokes woman, with the loud mouth and leather, swaggering around like no woman had a right to. And the other one was Dor, who said she was a widder woman, and shook with laughter.

You'd never of thought she was a widder from the bright clothes and the clanking earrings. Her door was never shut and she never did appear to do a hand's turn. Cars parked up the empty street from her place. Conspicuous. Shameless. Mar'Ann sang loud to block out the licentious laughter and music blaring from the curtained windows.

Beau and Shirley-Anne gleaned the facts of life, despite having been forbidden to ever go near Dor's place. Besides, she gave them ratafias, candy, liqueur chocolates:

'For mah figure, honey lambs,' she would say, laughing and patting where her waist would have been.

Beau hadn't realized in any way that Rotary Spokes was a grown-up *girl*. He wanted to be a mechanic, just like her. He sat reverently in the dust, cussed to a distance by Rotary Spokes when she was working outside. Shirley-Anne used to sneak into Dor's place and play house among the shawls and strong perfumes, the feather boas and spangled high-heels.

Long as they was out of the house between breakfast and supper!

Neither one of them would have dared to go in the workshop or touch the regal cat.

Then, one day, 1st Street East was altered. The monthly bus from the city squelched to a halt outside Dino's, in the autumn week of rains. It only came by if someone was getting off and they hadn't seen it in nearly a year.

When the bus ploughed away again, there were four figures standing there. Gooseneck, Lorie-Kay, Darlene and Gooseneck Jr.; they called him Gozo. The Squash Family. Beside them, a heap of straw suitcases, newspapers, thin mattresses and blankets tied with string.

What the hell was they doin' in Normal?

It is the way of a Squash to be just a little later and more useless than any other living creature. In the Great Flood, Squashes would have been flailing along in the rising water, lookin' for some fella calls hisself Noah.

So now they had come to Normal for work. Not even in the oil field which had been abandoned the year before – no; Gooseneck had the five-year-old newspaper cutting seeking labour in the canning factory, four years empty. They had been stunned at their good luck when some other itinerant family had sold them number 15, 1st Street East, Normal for their last fifty bucks.

'Who says America ain't a land of opportunity? Seems to me we oughtta do this in style. Git us a porter fer the luggage, darlin',' said Gooseneck.

Lorie-Kay waited. Nothing. She banged into Dino's.

'Can y'all give me directions to number 15, First Street East?'

Dino took her in at one glance. He grinned broadly. Never had thought of no-one having an address in 1st Street East.

'Down the street,' he said. Then, as she turned to leave, 'You folks come for the oil strike?'

'Oil strike? You mean they's oil work here too?'

'The strike is struck and gone.'

'Y'all got a porter we kin borrer?'

'Lady, you don't got but two hunnerd yards to go.'

'My man ain't too good for liftin' and carryin'. Thank you kindly.'

Outside Darlene sneezed. Gooseneck Jr. coughed loud and high.

'T'ain't but two hunnerd yards, Goosenick. Pick 'em up an' let's git.'

'Waaall, ah cain't carry nothin' Lorie-Kay. Mah spine done relocated in that there bus.'

'Pick up them beds and walk.' said Lorie-Kay flatly.

Darlene humped two cases, Lorie-Kay humped three, Gooseneck Jr. was jammed with newspaper parcels up to his chin. Gooseneck Squash dragged along behind them, grimacing, one hand on his relocated spine, the feather-light, featherless mattresses high on one bony shoulder.

Through the evening, Darlene and Gooseneck Jr. scampered up and down to the store with precious handfuls of nickels for the bare necessities. Lorie-Kay swept and raked and pulled things around a little. Gooseneck fumbled the string undone on the biggest mattress and crawled under a blanket.

Dor and Rotary Spokes watched the whole thing from between Dor's lilac net curtains. They were having a girls' evening, which involved brandy and bragging and Dor trying to persuade Rotary Spokes she'd be better off with a man. A clean date, Dor called these evenings.

15

'What the hail they want here, Dor?'

'Beats the bahoolas offa me, honey. Gimme some a that brandy.'

'Y'all reckon we oughtta be neighbourly?'

'Waaall, sure. What you got in mind, dearie?'

'Waall, take 'em some beers and a good meal, huh?'

A meal for Rotary Spokes was hamburgers, fries and every kind of relish she could find.

'Yiz . . . Git that skillet heated and I'll go over. I never was too hot in the kitchen.'

In the door of number 15, Dor appeared. Her stilettoes were muddied and Lorie-Kay, bent double, looked up along the fishnet tights, the hot-pink polyester skirt, the black satin blouse, the ample rouged face, the sparkling junk earrings, the teased dyed hair.

'Hi, y'all, I'm Dor . . . one a your neighbours.'

Lorie-Kay pushed back a strand of dull hair.

'Hi.' she said.

'Mom, she smells funny,' hissed Gooseneck Jr.

Dor threw back her head and laughed brandy fumes into the room.

'Nice, ain't it, honey lamb,' she said, and pinched Gooseneck Jr's waif's cheek.

'Anyhow, we was wonderin' if you folks would like to come over and eat with us, when you're straight. AAAAAAARRRRGGGHH!' Dor screamed, as the thin blanket in the corner writhed upright and the hideous pallor of Gooseneck Squash's face appeared.

'It's my husband, Gooseneck Squash. Don't you mind him none.'

'I'm a widder woman,' said Dor. 'Y'all step over when you through.'

'That's right nice of you.'

Dor left.

Lorie Kay stared at Gooseneck.

'I believe we landed on our feet, Goosenick. What with the factory work and neighbours. Just you lie there and don't say nothing to spoil it while I straighten up.'

Two doors down, Mar'Ann was raking through the cupboard. Nothing. She sent Beau up to the store with Lucas's tobacco money. She'd make them a stew.

At last – neighbours!

In that hour, Lorie-Kay received more invitations than ever a Squash had before. Not just one set of neighbours, but two! She accepted both – of course! Life had taught her never to say no to anything free. It was beyond her how to arrange it all.

Darlene took over.

Over the road, she found Dor boogie-ing absent-mindedly to Earl Hines, and Rotary Spokes growling over a pan of hamburgers and a mountain of french fries.

'Don't you worry none, honey. This side of the street's adaptable. We got a moveable feed here. We'll come over to Mar'Ann's house,' Dor drawled reassuringly.

When the pale child had whisked back into the night, Rotary Spokes stopped Dor in mid-wiggle.

'Dor! Listen to me, crazy woman. Ain't you or me been neighbourly with Mar'Ann since she been here. You think this is gonna work out?'

'Are you the woman as knocked Mr Jesus Smart-ass through your door, or are you a little gopher goofball? If she don't like it, we kin leave.'

'Anyway,' demanded Dor, 'The damn woman oughtta consider herself honoured! Hah! Ain't I turned that damn Lucas of hers offa my doorstep, seeing we was neighbours? Yes, I did. Woman gotta have standards.'

Mar'Ann was setting the table, with what remained of a cutlery set. She wondered grimly if she'd ever have anything matching, like in the catalogue.

'Wash up!' she spat at her family, plastered in terror around the walls. 'We got Company.'

They washed.

'I oughtta git some tobacco in. Maybe a few beers.' said Lucas hopelessly.

'Hush your flappin' tongue. This is a Meal. Not a *barroom*. Anyways, the tobacco money's gone to pay for the meal. And don't you say or think a word against it.'

'I never do argue with you, dear,' said Lucas winningly. At least now there'd be another man around. Nights in a bar again. Lucas dreamed on. It was what he did best. Maybe even set up in business.

A dream that was shattered as soon as Gooseneck Squash shuffled in. Never seen such a no-hoper, Lucas thought to himself. It was a pitiful six foot a nothin' with a raggy muffler round his neck. Goddam walleyed stringbean. Mar'Ann would be mightily disappointed if this was the Company. He flinched.

For Mar'Ann, another silken strand of hope frayed and twanged. Look on the bright side – it was another family. A married woman with kids. She didn't have to pay no account to the man. They were all useless and a burden.

Lorie-Kay apologized for her dress, her hair, her ripped cotton shoes, her children, her life. Mar'Ann forgave her, with dark looks at the two critters who had brought them this low.

Lucas discovered that Gooseneck had no trade, a weak back, and high hopes of the canning factory.

'The cannery's closed. Years now.'

In the bleak silence, Gooseneck Jr. started his desperate hacking cough. Darlene sat mute. Beau and Shirley-Anne looked at each other.

There was a knock at the door.

It could have been the avenging angel.

It was Rotary Spokes and Dor who sashayed and swaggered into the void, bringing the rich scent of brandy, hamburgers, french fries, tobacco, leather, a musky perfume and rouge.

'Evenin' Miz Springer,' said Dor. 'Seems like we all had the same idea here, ta be neighbourly. So we all thought we'd bring ourn over, seein' as it ain't but hamburgers. Hi theer, big fella!' she added to Gooseneck Jr. in mid-cough.

Rotary Spokes grinned and winked at Beau and Shirley-Ane.

'We brung yuh some things.' she said.

'That's real nice of you,' Mar'Ann managed to say. 'I'm just finishin' up here.'

Lucas was sweating. Surely Dor would say nothing. He caught her eye.

'Maybe you men could git out and git us some beers,' she said, 'Have a few up there. Go on, git.'

She gave him a couple of bills and he and Gooseneck slid out into the night. No place for a man in the kitchen.

'Waaall,' said Dor, brightly. 'Now we got rid of them men, hows about a little drink?'

Mar'Ann clutched the stew spoon. She had no drink to offer. Damn the brazen woman!

But Dor unclipped her huge handbag and flourished a brandy bottle – Nappa Valley '81, and four glasses.

'Don't wanna waste the good stuff on them as won't appreciate it,' she said, jerking her head towards the door.

Mar'Ann faced her.

'I thought you was kinda fond of men,' she drawled.

'We all gotta do what we can, honey,' said Dor softly, with no hint of apology. Rotary Spokes had never given a heap of thought as to how Dor got her money, beyond wondering how she could put up with it. That was business. This was socializing. She poured out brandy and handed it round.

'Nice tuh meet you, finally,' Rotary told Mar'Ann. 'That boy of yourn gonna be a real mechanic.'

She had hit on the only line that could have touched Mar'Ann.

'You think he's got a future?'

'Waaall, certainly. If he's prepared to work hard. You don't git nowhere without work.'

'There's always been hard workers in *my* family.' said Mar'Ann.

'I kin see that.' said Rotary Spokes looking around the spotless room.

Mar'Ann nudged the children off the chairs.

'You kids wanna watch TV?' asked Rotary Spokes. 'Git over to my place and give your mom a break. Git now.'

'I'll be hog-swallered,' said Lorie-Kay. 'You got TV?'

'Yiz-ma'am. Kinda shame-making', really. I got two.'

'Two!' Lorie-Kay's loose jaw dropped.

'I ordered the one and they brung me two. Y'all kin borrer th'other one, if you want. I don't reckon they gonna pick it up, not now. It's been there eighteen months.'

Lorie-Kay was speechless.

One: she had never tasted brandy before, and after the burn, it sure was good. Two: she had never dreamed she would have a TV.

Life could be good, she thought, sucking the rim of her glass.

Mar'Ann sniffed. Huh! Walks into town and sets up as a charity in less than an evenin'!

'A course, y'all kin watch any time,' Lorie-Kay told her. 'Do we got electric?'

'I kin fix that,' said Rotary Spokes.

Dor wisely poured brandy, especially for Mar'Ann.

After a while, Mar'Ann relaxed. Them two was odd, and sinners with it. But they didn't have no airs about 'em. And they was women. Waaall, she reserved judgment on Rotary Spokes.

CHAPTER
TWO

"There's no place like home."
(Judy Garland)

And whenever Rotary Spokes came in for cigarettes and cawfy, she had the good sense to bring cigarettes and cawfy with her, and generally leave them behind her. And, as they weren't her own, she was good with the sprawling, brawling children. Somehow from one chair, she could handle the whole heap of them climbing all over her, roll a cigarette, and hold a conversation at the same time. The kids adored it: she'd give them rides from time to time, and even take them to the movies in Hook Airs. She and Dor were lavish with the kind of upmarket gifts the TV plugged all the way through children's programmes; gifts that neither Lucas nor Gooseneck had a hope in hell of buying.

'Darlene, you sure you're wantin' a Barbie doll?'

'Ye-e-e-e-s!'

'I'll git this one, honey,' said Dor, laughing. 'Quit whining, Darlene, and we'll see, huh?'

But when she'd had enough, Rotary Spokes would stand up, shake the children off like clinging cats, and tell them to Git. Which they always did.

'Maybe they should call yuh auntie?' said Mar'Ann, one day. 'Auntie Rodry?'

'Aw, sheee-it, Mar'Ann, it ain't needful fuh them tuh call me nothin' yit. Let 'em sort it out when they want to.'

Dor had taken on the coiffure of 1st Street East. Mar'Ann and Lorie-Kay, that was. Rotary Spokes hacked her hair herself. Dor's fictional widowhood kept her apart from Mar'Ann and Lorie-Kay, and she marvelled at how they put up with it all: one man and, she gathered over the years, no technique at all. But she wasn't about to hand out advice. Mar'Ann would have called it sinful, and Lorie-Kay would not have understood – rather, there was no point if the man was Gooseneck Squash.

Rotary Spokes always sat in the best chair, just like a man would, but years had dulled Mar'Ann's hostility. No-one after all could accuse Rotary Spokes of being one of those devil women – unmarried, approaching thirty, and making a play for the 'Special One'. She was more likely to spit a scathing comment at any 'Special One' who had the nerve to be home in the day.

So she sat and listened to the endless grind, from her own planet, conceived and piloted by her alone. She heard the daily string of complaints: the children, the money, the food, the money, the house, the sex. She thought of their pale limbs cardboardly arranged for the cut-out mechanics of Normal sex, which was usually allowed just on Friday evening, unless it could be avoided.

But this particular day, clearly, something had happened. Mar'Ann was furious, narrowing her eyes, and almost clawing her chair.

'I got *things* to tell you,' she threatened.

Rotary Spokes kicked the kids out.

The women arranged themselves over their cawfy. Dor fingered the neck of the brandy bottle. Might be required in a while.

'Mar'Ann,' said Lorie-Kay, 'you ain't smokin', gal.'

Mar'Ann drew the smoke in and streamed it through her nostrils.

'*We* ain't smoking,' she said. 'It's me and Lucas ain't smokin' for three months now, and you know why?'

She lit another cigarette from her first and ground out the stub.

'"We ain't been smokin' for ow health," Lucas said. "Ow health and the money," Lucas said.' She gave a bitter cackle.

'Listen to me good,' she said, 'you ain't gonna believe it Rodry, you ain't never gonna believe the Evil that lurks in the hearts of men. I don't want no interruptin' me. You see that tin? That tin up there?'

Eight eyes swivelled to a tin on the shelf. It was pale blue with a spray of flowers on the side. 'That there tin . . . that tin is my hopes and dreams. Me and Lucas been puttin' all the cigarette money in it now for three months. I ain't never looked in it. I thought if I looked, I'd surely find something the kids needed. Lucas said to me: "This town's a dead town, and we're turnin' into the ghosts as lives here." Took him all these years to know what I knew the minute I put my foolish foot to the earth of Normal. Ghosts! Anyways, the other week, I decided I would count the money and get me a bus timetable and work out how many months till we could git outta here. No offence to you all. You are the only friends I ever had, but I got life in me and I can feel it draining outta my body with ever; cursed breath I draw here.'

'Waaall?' said Lorie-Kay. 'How much did you got?'

'Hush you mouth and listen to me. I got the kids outta the house. I got Lucas outta the house, and I got that tin offa the shelf, and I tipped it out on the table.' She paused.

'They was a few nickels on top. Underneath, they was washers, screws, nails, nuts . . . any kinda metal trash you kin pick up in the street. It weighs like money, it sounds like money, but it ain't money.'

'Waaall, shoot me fer a fool galoot,' said Lorie-Kay.

'Where'd the money go?'

'If you all kin quit your brayin', I'm gonna tell you. You know how I been kinda cheerful these last few months?'

They didn't, but nodded anyway.

'Waaall, all along account of this here tin. So when Lucas come in, I set him down and said: "Lucas, I always been a fool for you. Fool to know you, fool to marry you, and fool to lie in the same fool's bed we made together. But I ain't no more your fool. Where's my money?"'

Another pause, another cigarette.

'Lucas stood him up and put his arm round me. "Honey," he said, God blast his wicked soul, "Honey, don't you worry. There's work here soon. I kin feel it." Him who couldn't feel a needle of pain no more than a wallerin' hog. "I took *our* money, darlin', and I invested it in somethin' that's gonna make out lives so good and full, I do wonder why I never thought of it before." And thats the last thing he'd say. I cussed him, and kicked him, and done ever'thin' a good woman can do with a blind pig of a man, and not one more word.'

'Waaall, what you gonna do now?' said Dor.

'I ain't finished yit!' yelled Mar'Ann. 'Gawd's sake, hear me out! Yuh know what happened four days ago? Course you don't. That's what I'm tellin' you. Now hear me. Lucas got a letter. A big brown letter.'

Consternation. No-one in 1st Street East ever got a letter bar Rotary Spokes' catalogues and Dor's mail-order fun garments. It would have to be a death . . . or what?

'He brung in the letter, and he said to me, "Mar'Ann, come through here. This is my investment." Grinnin' like a yaller dawg just found somethin' dead. "Set down," he said. I set. Then he tears the envelope and out comes . . . a magazine. A subscription magazine. Seems he's put up the money for a subscription magazine.'

They looked. They thought. A get-rich-quick magazine? *Set Yourself Up In Business* – they had all heard Lucas bragging and dreaming fit to beat the band.

Mar'Ann shook her head to every suggestion.

'I'll show you all,' she said significantly, and scooped up the dusty family Bible.

Out of Maccabees, she pulled a glossy production, called *Feast Your Eyes*. All over the cover there were peroxide smiles held on carmine lips, held on bronzed faces, topped by *haute coiffure*. Further, not one of those people had a stitch on their back. Or anywhere else. The magazine had no text, only cartoon captions saying things like "OOOOOOH!" "YES!" "AAAAH!" "NAUGHTY!"

The pictures were of men fucking women and women fucking men. Sometimes the man on top, the way it ought to be if it had to go on; sometimes the woman on top. Sometimes like a pair of dogs! Sometimes hanging on a swing. And one with the both the wrong way up and no faces showing.

'He calls that *sixty-nine*,' said Mar'Ann grimly. 'I call it a sin and shame, though I disbelieve there's a God above to allow such wickeness. Lord knows I have endured that man and his dirty ways for years. They supposed to go offa it, ain't they? Waaall, it seems this new hope and joy is if we make a goddam freak show outta that stuff, we're gonna be happy. HAPPY! Jesus Christ!'

'What did yuh do?' asked Lorie-Kay, shuddering at the pale spectre of Gooseneck erect crawling over her like a bug.

'I got my period four days ago. I'm gonna bleed for the rest of my life. That'd better hold him offa me.'

'Gimme the magazine,' said Dor, who liked fucking.

'"Feast Your Eyes" it's called. "Feast Your Eyes"! Waaall, he kin feast his eyes and I hope they bust blind *feastin'*.'

Dor flipped through the magazine.

'Ain't nothin' new to me here,' she said.

'Is that what yuh do to git rid of them,' shrieked Lorie-Kay, feeling daring at the '69' page. 'You near suffocate 'em between yuh laigs?'

Dor laughed.

'They leave breathin',' she said, 'Breathin' heavy.'

Rotary Spokes took the magazine, though it sure as hell didn't belong on her planet. The blonde, bronzed, gold-furred men, the pale-gold shaven women, the parted lip-gloss faking ecstacy, the capped teeth. It didn't do nothin' for her.

'Waaall?' said Dor, accusingly. It was years since she'd lectured Rotary Spokes on 'How To Get A Good Man'. Like showing paintings to the blind.

'Nothin',' said Rotary Spokes. 'Damn hairy asses.' But she felt something. Not to do with the pictures. To do with her. An unusual throb. Then she looked at Dor's wicked little twinkling eyes, her pointed tongue laughing at the whole shebang. Had she been a man, Dor would have fielded her glance, patted her hair, sashayed into the street and told her to drop by later. As it was, Dor didn't see it, and Rotary Spokes wasn't even clear what she meant.

Someday I have to sort this out, thought Rotary Spokes, swaggering out with exaggerated nonchalance, back to work.

Mar'Ann and Lorie-Kay and Dor pored over the magazine. In the back four pages they saw – what was this – a WOMAN with a WOMAN? They looked again. No doubt about it.

'Hell!' said Mar'Ann, 'That don't happen.'

'Sheee-it!' said Dor, who had never thought of it.

'Wimmin don't do that,' said Lorie-Kay, decidedly.

In a mausoleum in London, England, a dead Queen registered a rare smile. She was singularly amused.

It wasn't that Rotary Spokes had never been touched.

Hell, there had been plenty of old boys from way back. Plenty of bruises, and even one broken jaw. But she didn't think that was what it was all about. So that evening, she locked her door, put on a record of Doris Day doing her best to be Calamity Jane with a bunch of rat-shit men around, opened a can of Blue Label and sat on her bed to think.

And she'd been hugged too. But not the kind of hugging and touching which made her feel that throb she'd felt, looking at Dor. She blushed and lit another cigarette. I'm smokin' too much, she thought automatically. But a woman has to think clear.

There was the Thanksgiving hug Lorie-Kay gave her. She closed her eyes and recalled it. It was a sad, timid hug; they touched cheeks, touched shoulders, and then Lorie-Kay's hands firmly held her body away at the shoulder. There was this no-go, no-touch area, this no-woman's land which went from shoulder to toe. It was a sad, sad hug like a written description of a scent or texture – technically accurate, but with no real warmth. It was a waxen hug, etiolated like a plant forgotten in some dark cupboard, creeping its arid length instinctively towards a chink of light.

At the other end of the scale was The Hug that Rotary Spokes hardly dared dream of. This Hug would be warm like a chord out of heaven in a movie as the clouds part; a Hug which strides the hill tops with the sunrise and cradles the sky at sunset; a Hug to start the night with and – dare she even think it? – a Hug to go to bed by.

At the thought 'bed' she blushed again.

'You cain't get a man with a gu-hun!' trilled Doris Day.

'But,' thought Rotary Spokes, 'never have wanted me a man.'

She closed her eyes. A Hug. An all-body, head-spinning, toe-tingling Hug that occupied the space where it happened forever. It was a hologram of a Hug, glinting rainbows off all your eyes can see.

Rotary Spokes woke with the dream of The Hug, swishing a leonine tail over the hills and far away. She lay in the warmth as the morning spilled over the windowsill, and the sunlight caught the smoke eddies of her first cigarette and played shadows through the coffee steam. The Hug burrowed under her skin as she thundered water over her body and felt like a tropical rainstorm. She stood steaming dry on the floor, like an exotic and undiscovered plant, feeling muscles tingle and tighten, blood course through her body, already thinking ahead to the workshop heat and the familiar weight of her powerful metal tools, ranged and waiting in dust-swirling perfection.

'I have a dream today.' she thought.

The phrase crescendoed through her house with the golden trumpets of spring daffodils and Jericho, the pounding hooves and clashing chariots of Hollywood at its heels.

'I have a dream of a Hug. And I ain't never been hugged that way. And I have a dream of a woman. And I am a woman. And what the damn hell can I make of that?'

She hitched on her overalls and strolled into the workshop.

'I make engines roar where the spark was dead, and spanners spin where the pins was rusty. I make an opera and symphony outta trash. But I cain't make no sense outta this feelin'.'

She made breakfast.

'Somethin' is missin' here,' she decided, spooning up egg yolk and ketchup, chilli sauce and oven-ready fries.

'And she iss not yokking,' shuddered the cat, smoothing cream from her fine whiskers. 'There iss no manners in this place, all togedders.'

Rotary Spokes gulped scalding coffee and belched.

'I must find what's missing. I must sling my worldly goods in a red-spotty handkerchief on a pole over my shoulder, and I must walk outta Normal.'

The Hug went – thattaway – over the plain.

'For a vacation,' she was saying by mid-morning. 'For a long trip across the continent of America.'

The Hug growled, dissatisfied, thunder in the foothills, and leapt back to paw up dust on the workshop floor.

'Waaall,' she said at lunch time, massaging grease from her enormous hands, 'Mebbe a week.'

A leonine tail skewed a can of oil over the floor.

'Holy St. Mary of Liepzig,' growled the cat, 'She iss inviting in here a zoological garden or *vat*?'

By the evening she had decided to maybe take a day off sometime. You cain't jest drop everything and go on a dream. Can you? She had worked here every day, bar Sundays, Christmas and Thanksgiving since she could remember and felt itchy at the thought of change.

The Hug crouched on the roof all night and directed a plate to fall at 3 a.m.; the door to blow open at 4, and Rotary Spokes to stumble blearily around the yard at five, watching the stars spatter the sky. At 5.13, there was a shooting star.

'See it!' roared The Hug.

'That's nice,' said Rotary Spokes, unaware of the panther shadow on her roof, waiting to spring.

When the sun rose, The Hug was growling across the windowsill, twitching at her blankets, curling a cold draught into the bed, pulling her to her feet, nagging like a dog: walk me, walk me, and I'll be so good to you!

She looked at her bank book. More money than she had thought. More than she could spend in a whole year's vacation.

'I'll give it a month or so,' she decided. 'Then I'll take a week and go to Middlesville. Then I'll see what's what and what all this here is about. Sure as hell ain't nothin' to do with Normal.'

The Hug bounded away down the dusty road to raise hell in Middlesville and cast palm fronds beneath her 1000 c.c. Harley wheels.

CHAPTER
THREE

"Went out last with a crowd of my friends,
Musta bin women cuz I don't like no men."

Some months later, Rotary Stokes strutted down a municipal boulevard in Middlesville. She felt she oughtta been kickin' at cans. Hell, Middlesville was so damn clean! The dust was smooth on the sidewalk slabs and there wcre no cans to be seen: the meticulous ministrations of the municipal refuse disposal expert saw to that.

He was Moses Jeremiah Fitzgerald. For years he had been receiving all of society's benefits grudged through red tape: he was one-legged, partially-sighted, hearing-impaired, asthmatic, bronchitic, of mixed and anonymous parentage. He was the town geek, and for years had subsisted in a street which had officially been cleared and demolished. The street had no name. He did miserably O.K. until the late-twentieth century hit Middlesville, a decade or so after almost anywhere else. Suddenly there were discos, a shopping mall, housing projects, minority group agitation (chaired by majority interests), equal opportunities, employment rehabilitation programmes: a society which had been hastily legislated to Care.

He was sitting on his doorstep one late morning, one aching limb ahead of him, the day's possibilities playing slowly through his weary mind. It was damn near summer, and whut the hail, inniways.

A foreign sound intruded. Large tyres with a full tread, bearing a Mercedes Benz of legendary horsepower. The engine was enshrined in chrome of a liquid sheen; the smoked windshields would repel bullets as successfully as they now made searchlights of the white, noon-high sun. Out of the dazzle, burning into thc scarred retinas of Moses Jeremiah's eyes, came four silhouettes.

'Glory,' breathed Moses, 'Glory.'

He had seen nothing so awesome since the radioactive incandescence of the Fifty-Foot-Woman strode the thirty-foot screen at the drive-in back of the derelict alley. He had seen hundreds of movies over the years, all silent and back to front. The showing of *The Attack of the Fifty-Foot Woman* had been followed by a series of black-outs in Middlesville as no-gooders hurled metal debris, cars, and themselves at the pylons striding across the plain and through the city.

One moment of glory for a lifelong deadbeat! A resurrection! A charred rebirth on a wire hung over an unlit street of sliding tenements.

Moses Jeremiah Fitzgerald had seen one of the cars leap and cling, sparking like a bug on the wire. He had squinted critically and walked on by, past molten metal spattering the pavement, muttering with contempt. He thought they were shooting a sequel to *The Attack*, and a sequel was never as good as the first time. Look at *Godfather VII* . . . chickenshit!

'Ef yuh askin' mah opinion, fellas,' mumbled Moses.

Nobody ever had.

But now, today, the movie people had come to the alley. Finally, they were casting a movie starring Moses J. Fitzgerald the *First*!

They used all his names, several times, clicked their tongues and shook their heads as they looked at him. They walked around him, saying:

'Well, this is perfect!'

'I feel truly humbled, you know?'

'I really feel confident that we are changing things.'

They handed him paper . . . a contract! You had to read all the small print, that he knew. Trouble was, he had problems with any kind of print. They ran manicured fingers under each line and read it to him. Trouble was that he couldn't hear too much, because they all talked too fast and at the same time. Something about an electric car . . . he played a character who was to scour the streets. Hot dog! Something else about *indebted*. Who to and what for . . .

'So, finally, fellas . . . and ma'am,' brayed Moses in the voice of the partially-hearing and seldom-speaking, 'so, finally, you guys gonna take me uptown to the bright lights.'

'You could put it that way,' said one of them, the one with the gold chain across his chest – in fact, the mayor of Middlesville. Showbiz people, thought Moses . . . the man talked like he was giving gold dollars away.

They all shook hands, haw-hawed, and dusted themselves back into the car.

And so it was that the crazed Moses was duped into becoming municipal refuse disposal expert, under the impression that every lamp post and tree housed a camera and all the people on the streets were extras. He made the town feel real good for the next few weeks, as self-congratulatory headlines sprawled over his inane grin, captioned as 'Glowing with Gratitude', or 'A Smile from our Shameful Slums'.

In *The Middlesville Chat*, and the more serious *Middlesville Echo* (the voice of your town), the reporters got inspired and carried away by the True Life element in the story and went to press with borrowed biographies of their one and only Moses Jeremiah Fitzgerald.

If the *Chat* could produce a tear-jerking personal testament from an aged mother – he had no mother – the *Echo* could find a burial plot in the Eastside cemetery filled with Fitzgerald bones, a smudged photo under the banner 'NO MORE A PAUPER'S GRAVE!'

If the *Chat* unearthed a warm reminiscence from a school pal – Moses had never been to school, there being no school for coloured in those distant days – the *Echo* responded with a photo of a winsome, toothless old lady who claimed to have been his first love. No-one had ever loved Moses. J. Fitzgerald. The interviewees lived on the distant planets of Chicago; Poetic Licence; New York; Deadline Expedience; San Francisco and Fevered Imagination.

Everybody in the late twentieth century had this romantic idea about Roots – everybody bar the breadline handful scratching a living from the ungiving polluted soil. All the city dwellers were like hothouse cuttings thrust into a chemical earth-substitute compound, thriving on electric sunlight and carcinogenic fertilizers. How they wanted Roots! To crumble bare earth between thumb and forefinger and drawl 'My great-granddaddy was born and raised here!' And what a privilege to feel that there *were* real Roots, in the store-bought compost of a city. Their city.

Whose roots? Who knows and who cares.

It became fashionable, briefly, to slum it on the wrong side of the screen. This was Real Life with mud and smells finally found in Our City.

But in the alley they found only a charred shell and no Moses.

The City Hall had hushed-up the hot story of how, shortly after the mayor's visit, the refracted sunbeams from the Mercedes Benz windscreen had smouldered on the rag-stuffed roof of Moses' hut and burned everything burnable, leaving only smoked and blistered corrugated iron. Moses' employed respectability stopped him from simply shifting in with the bum next door – he was provided with an apartment in the Housing Project. Two-years-old and half empty, it would give him, they said, a fine view of Middlesville. He found the stairs difficult, the lifts out of service. He found the sky-topped blue from the window made him dizzy and the glass, floor to ceiling in the living-room, made him sweat with the fear of falling.

When he deducted carfare, the clothes necessary for work, and the food he suddenly craved after years of doing nothing at all, Moses Jeremiah Fitzgerald was $6.95 better off per week, and this $6.95 went soon enough as he travelled across town to the alley and back to the Project late at night when the dark hid the awful, gaping windows which he couldn't afford to have curtained. When he asked about leaving the film set, he was told he would get no benefits for six weeks if he did, and after that, his ingratitude would mean that his benefits would be drastically reduced.

So Rotary Spokes had to kick at cans that weren't there, and chew gum that had lost its flavour: she couldn't very well spit it out onto the immaculate sidewalk. She could only add another stick of gum to the grey mass in her mouth. What the hell was she doing here? She longed for Normal and the easy routine, but between her throb and The Hug she could do nothing until there was some kind of resolution.

Before she had come to Middlesville, Rotary Spokes had sneaked addresses from the back of *Feast Your Eyes*, answered any advertisement mentioning motorbikes, leather or women. What a weird bunch of stuff she'd gotten back. Didn't they know there was *women* out here into bikes and leather? Goddam, there was some stuff illustrated that she couldn't figure out where the hell you was meant to put it. She trashed all the lip gloss, tit-and-ass bike shit; cussing, she gum that had lost its flavour: she couldn't very well spit it out onto the publication: *Dyke's Delight*. Truth to tell she had to read it as *Byke's Delight* but she sure as hell wasn't complaining.

For *Dyke's Delight* put a name to her feelings. *Dyke's Delight* assured her that there were other women who felt as she did.

'There is a growing scene for women who are woman-identified. Dykes. Lesbians. Dare we say it – let us proclaim it: we are one in every ten!'

One in Ten! That was something else!

It went on:

'In every city, sister, you will find a bar or cafe or club where we can meet and share our lives and *much more*. Knowing that everyone there is One in Ten. Free from the Patriarchy! Free to *be*.'

There was no 'patriarchy' in her dictionary, but whatever it was, she'd handle it. She knew that *Dyke's Delight* would hit her doorstep in its plain brown wrapper every month for the rest of her life. She *was* a dyke. In every way they talked about, bar one. She was a celibate, which she pronounced Keel-Eye-Bait, a little unsure of what that meant and with no-one to ask – well, she had asked Dor, who had said:

'How the hell should I know? Somethin' ta do with fishing'?'

She was a solo-dyke and after fourteen years of building muscles, dreams, bikes and frustration in her workshop she was more than ready to Hit Town.

So where was the action? Middlesville was the biggest city in the state. Where was the bar, the cafe, the club and all that?

It's O.K. to be ready to hit town, only there was nowhere immediately obvious to snuggle her leathered fist in its belt-bulging complacency; no flashing disco floor for her black-booted legs to stroll across. Rotary Spokes was getting twitchy.

'Look out, world, here I come,' she had thought, roaring through the desert. The only response seemed to be cluster after cluster of shoppers parting before her; the respectful swishing aside of elbows at countless bars. She was worlds away. She felt like she was in a bubble – seen, but mouthing an unheard plea.

'Excuse me.'

She almost missed it.

'Excuse me.'

The voice came from a woman clad in green linen, immaculately made-up, and pushing a folded leaflet into her hands.

'Read. Enjoy. Come.' she said breathily and dove through the crowd.

Rotary Spokes looked around quickly, stuffed the leaflet into her zippered sleeve pocket and shoved into the next bar. Damned if it twarn't dark in here, she thought as she slid her mirrored shades onto the table. That was better. She gulped her beer and started to read the leaflet.

The Magdalena Janus Ladies Society

'... *from the Fount of Energy, we gush ...*'

There was a circular conglomeration of symbols underneath: a triangle, a star, a flower, a bolt of lightning through a cloud, an open thick-lashed eye, and some matchstick figures – women, certainly, going by the vague wisps of material: women holding hands.

'Ha!' though Rotary Spokes, 'They put all that other stuff there to hide that women were holding hands!'

She was jubilant at the thought of even hand-holding. A little wary of the chiffon skirts but not about to get too picky at this stage.

Around the symbols was a ring of words, each one in a different writing style:

Oneness • Fulfillment • Directed Energy • Karma • Unity • Hope • Joy • True Personal Liberation •

Inside, the text was in the kind of type that looks like it's been handwritten, and Rotary Spokes certainly read it as a personal message. And the message read:

'The Magdalena Janus Ladies Society presents a Medial Confrontary Introduction for *all* women, from every path in life, every nationality, every star sign, and every persuasion ..... our female energy binds us.'

It was the ..... that seemed the most clear and inviting part. Damn! Every story in *Dyke's Delight* had plenty of them. She thought of the best one:

'Rosanna looked deep into Billy's sea-grey eyes! The woman with the man's name but very little else about her to go with it! They moved closer together and merged as one ..... "Rosanna!" breathed Billy ..... "Billy!" sighed Rosanna .....'

Yeah, the ..... was the best bit of that story. Rotary Spokes gulped Blue Label and read on.

'We are a synthesis of some 5,000 women from every continent, pursuing every kind of calling. We are doctors, nurses, dieticians, psychologists, journalists, herpetologists, data analysts, urbanologists, taxi-drivers and toxicologists. Whatever our calling, we have been drawn together by the sure knowledge that there is Something Else in our late twentieth-century existence, pulling us forward, driving us on a hungry quest, with questions we can hardly verbalize . . .'

Hungry quest? Rotary Spokes ordered a meatball sandwich and tore into it with her strong white teeth.

'We in the Magdalena Janus Ladies Society have developed *The Ladies Way*. Do you feel an answering throb in your pulse? Stop and see. Let yourself align with the Forces.'

Rotary Spokes chewed more slowly – throb? She felt it.

'Are you aware of the Karmic flow of Woman Energy?' Waaall, some kinda flow.

'Have you experienced your true aura, vibrating from your centre?'

Made you think of earth tremors. Damn, if this weren't real subtle! Talkin' so's no-one would pick out the *real* meaning. Rotary Spokes flicked back to the jumble on the front and read on. Matchstick ladies, she thought, here's to you all!

'Do you know the magic of your cycles?'

This was clearer . . . it was a personal message.

'The perfect alignment of Cosmos and Terra and Karma . . . now you can confirm your true being, discard old chains' (what the hell else do you do with old chains?) 'and dance – free on the wheel of *The Ladies Way*'.

So there was a women's dance-hall in Middlesville! This was where it was happening! Damned if they wasn't smart! They knew she was One in Ten. She'd never have guessed that lady in green linen was one too! But maybe she used the suit and wedding ring as disguise. Rotary Spokes had few illusions about how popular dykes were. And if they had to put out this code sort of shit to meet each other . . . life was more complicated than she had imagined. Now, where was this dance place? The Al Marquisa Motel Lounge, 7.30. She drained her can, belched and strode back to her hotel room. Better take a shower, shine the leather, grease her hair real good. Better look her best. Best to be straight out!

Dyke's Delight currently had several correspondences raging about things she'd never heard of before: Butch and Femme; monogamy and non-monogamy; co-parenting and creches. She didn't know what any of these terms meant, but she sure as hell would find out at this here

Magdalena Janus Ladies Way Dance Hall.

She slapped her hard stomach, and looked head to toe in the mirror.

Damned if she didn't look good!

She blushed.

Rotary Spokes was not the only one to whom the lady in green linen had excused herself. There was a child psychologist called Mavis, from Detroit, whooping it up in Middlesville after her mother's funeral. Gnashing a monogrammed menthol cigarette, she read the leaflet and thought of her own chains, now welded to a coffin deep below the ground. She thought of her mother's last words:

'How come you see them screwball kids so good and you all are such a mortified mess?'

Karma, Smarma, Aura Flora . . . anything was worth a go.

There was Lilli-O, a willowy wisp of a violin player, who threw a hat down in the Middlesville Mall five days a week and played Mozart, the Inkspots, Satie, and The Supremes to embarrassed shoppers. When she had skimmed through the leaflet: Freebie munchies! thought Lilli-O.

There was Reen the Bean, ex weight-trainer, running a little to fat and now a bouncer at a pool hall near the drive-in. Reen carolled obscenely in the tub, gargling a Dos Equis beer, trimming her dainty toenails, shampooing her thick Mediterranean hair.

'Brrrossa fa cupola! O sodomiso!'

Reen would go to anything if asked. O.K., she'd had to hustle the lady in green linen a bit . . . what the hell. It was a invite.

There was Diz Darling, your friendly neighbourhood dope dealer, who was whisking last night's little number out of her rainbow apartment, with sincere lies that she would call him later. Well, she would. What she would call him or when – well . . .

'Nobody does it like you, lover,' she whispered, sliding him out of the door with a tender kiss. It was the one true thing she had said in all the long seventeen hours of their deep meaningless relationship.

Her now ex-lover, Blissful Ignorance Jr., floated down the street.

There was one woman who came to the word Motel and threw the leaflet in the garbage-shredder.

And there was Leonora Hendriksen, a European immigrant who had fled her marriage, mortgage and mother on the way to the

Tandoori take-away in Earl's Court, London, England, three years before.

She was just knitting together the smithereens of an ego, and didn't hide under the table much any more. She did laugh rather high, loud and often.

And then there were Leslie, Trixie, Belinda and Clarabelle, who moved as one and shared out their brain cells in endless conference about 'How to Get a Good Man'. 'How to Make Him Think It's His Idea'. 'How To Keep Him'. 'How to Make Him Keep You'. They shared all the magazines on these burning questions, and toured the cocktail lounges with their expertise, prospecting.

The lady in the green linen was married to the owner of the Al Marquisa Motel. She was Karen Schuchter, petite and glowing, constantly away at conventions and effusively the *married* Mrs Schuchter, when Al was around. He had given her the use of the lounge.

'My little petal,' she had crooned and patted his nose. Then flittered away to print the leaflets. What a doll, thought Al.

He was all tuxedo-ed, aftershaved and dentally irrigated to welcome the party of business women. And only mildly upset when Karen pinned him behind the bar and confined him with a cooing:

'Nobody does it better, lover baby. Keep your hands on those bottles!'

Good Normal citizen that she was, Rotary Spokes arrived at 7.15 to have a beer before the meeting. She ordered a Blue Label. Al thought that she was the vanguard for a Hell's Angel chapter, and squeaked:

'Do you travel in leatherwear, ma'am?'

Rotary Spokes cracked her knuckles and smiled.

'Alwiz,' she said.

'Hey, Al!' a contralto bellow hit his churning gut.

'Lookit what blessings I have . . . hiya, Reen!' Al came round the bar to play-punch Reen. Shame about the doors last time.

Rotary Spokes took a furtive look at Reen. One in Ten? Butch? Monogamous? Femme? How the hell could you tell?

'Have a beer, Reen. Whaddaya doin' here?'

'I come to the Ladies meeting.'

Al drew his head close to hers. They were wearing the same

aftershave.

'Reen, you ain't no bidnisswoman.'

'Damned if I ain't!' she clenched her bouncer's fist. 'Do I mean bidniss, Al, or do I mean bidness?'

'Hell, yes, Reen, don't mind me,' said Al, wincing as he looked at the new glass doors.

He mixed a martini cocktail for Mavis in dove-grey.

He mixed a long cool drink for long cool Lilli-O, nibbling peanuts and snacks from every tiny bowl on the bar.

He mixed a Daiquiri for Diz Darling, and pretty soon two more.

He mixed a lethal Lone Pine for Leonora Hendriksen.

He made a Royal Smile – on the house, mah pleasure, ma'am – for Rotary Spokes.

He shook a Rip-it-up Boomerang for Reen the Bean.

And unctuous with unconscious alliteration, greasy with goodwill, when Leslie, Trixie, Belinda and Clarabelle swanned in, dressed to stun, the 'Good Man' Al gave them a Lady be Good, a Tequila Mockingbird, a Button Hook, and a Cara Sposa.

'You goin' it some, Clara*belle*!'

Clarabelle, who occasionally surprised herself with a private reserve of independent thought, smiled, surveyed the room and sat poised to strike.

At 7.45, Karen tippy-toed from the lounge, smiled in a way she had heard was warm and appealing, and said:

'Ladies?'

The bar cleared into the lounge, and Al polished glasses and swallowed Alka Seltzer.

Karen gambolled up to the bar.

'Drinky-poo for darling?' she murmured.

Al grinned foolishly and piled the ingredients of a Queen Bee in a glass. He topped it with a ridiculous amount of fruit and vegetable slivers.

Karen sipped, pecked the glistening cheek, and crossed the room. She locked the doors and the radio started to play a froth of Muzak greats. This was Ladies Night, after all.

Karen had practised her opening phrase all week. The tone was to be friendly but brisk. Depending upon who came, levity could filter in here and there.

'Well, ladies, thank you all so very much for responding to The Message. I'm Karen Schuchter and I'm married to that very talented soul out in the bar there.'

Reen cackled and whooped, tossing ash wide of the ashtray. Karen waited for silence and continued, ruling out the light approach. Three hundred and fifty bucks that door had cost. And the no-claims clause in the insurance.

'I expect you all wonder what my little invitation was about. I am certain that we all have our own intuitions and ideas though, don't we?'

Gracious heavens! That other . . . 'type' . . . with the greased hair and shades was growing a grin like a . . . surely not!

Married! thought Rotary Spokes. Married! That was one helluva cover-up!

'Let us start by sharing our names, shall we? Not our *true* names, of course, we don't know *them* yet, before we have travelled some distance on The Way . . . let us share the names we have carried with us so far, and let us say a little too about the essence of Who We Are, our directions thus far . . . in Life.'

She smiled around . . . nine; ten, with herself. Pathetic really with all the treasure to be found on The Way, but for the first meeting, for Middlesville . . . excellent.

'Maybe we will start with . . . YOU,' her smile hit Leonora between the eyes. Leonora almost dropped her glass. Always this! Always picked out! Always the first to be ridiculed. Leonora swallowed the dregs of her Lone Pine down her elegant and misunderstood throat.

'I am Delia Schreiver,' she lied in her ice-pick accent. 'I am a writer,' she ad-libbed, appalled, 'I am widely published in Europe,' she gabbled. 'I have never been married. I have no family. The idea of owning property revolts me –'

Karen's danger light flashed. This was commie talk. She cut in.

'Thank you so much, Delia. So frank; ladies, let us greet Delia, make her feel at home.'

Home! That word again! Leonora a.k.a. Delia shuddered as the room murmured Hi, Delia.

She sat amazed . . . who had said all those things? It was like a shield to hide behind. You couldn't dive under a table here, she decided. Delia asked Reen for a cigarette. Leonora sat smoking, shocked to silence.

Karen decided, the worst next. Reen she already knew the worst about. She smiled at Rotary Spokes. Anyone who still wore the skins of dead animals and polluted their lungs with nicotine was more to be pitied.

'Perhaps you'll go next . . . and tell us your business concerns.'

'Motorbikes . . . uh, cycles, jest like you said in that there leaflet. Hrrm,' said Rotary Spokes. 'Um, I'm Rotary Spokes, outta Normal . . . over there in the desert . . . Rotary Spokes . . . glad to meet you all.'

'Now let us all say Hi to Rhoda; remember, Normal is a long way from here. We welcome you, Rhoda.'

RHODA? Shee-it! Rotary blushed, feeling like a kid back at school.

'We're Leslie, Trixie, Belinda and Clara*belle*.'

Each woman smiled at her name, and sat back inspecting nails, bracelets, shoes. No Good Men here. They would wait for a break and drift on.

'Let my fiddle speak for me,' said Lilli-O through a mouthful of corn chips, and played a few bars of *I'm Nobody's Baby*. There was a polite smattering of applause.

Damn, thought Rotary Spokes. They is ten women in this room, and I'm One in Ten, so if it's me, and there's just the ten of us . . .? No way could she buy the quartet of Leslie, Trixie, Belinda and Clarabelle being 'woman-identified'. *Whatever* that was.

'I'm Mavis from Detroit.'

'And holidaying here? How nice,' said Karen, clutching at the ordinary grey of a good suit.

Mavis smiled. Later she would corner Karen and confide, and began to select phrases. No. This was something her analyst had told her to avoid. Be spontaneous! Be yourself! Her subconscious rehearsed spontaneous phrases.

'I'm Reen, Maureen, I got bidiniss near th'East Side, near the drive-in.'

'Do be specific, Miss Bean,' purred Karen. 'What business do you have? I never saw anything flourish near the drive-in.' Karen injected a microgram of humour into the last two words and a wave of educated indulgence flowed around Reen and skirted the feet of the misnamed Rhoda. Reen heaved up, stared at Karen and got more beer. Goddam uppity woman. She never *meant* to break the goddam door.

Diz skipped down from a mauve cloud and tried to focus. 'I'm Diz Darling.' (This surprised Karen. Probably an actress.) 'I really relate to all this cyclic shi . . . stuff, I mean the aura is so well . . . ah! And the whole cosmic rhythm number, I mean it's essential . . . like, of the essence, if you can tune in, and drop all this life Trip . . . ah, I mean, like my whole being is dedicated to the trans-spatial synthesis process, like every breath you, uh, take . . .' The mauve cloud was now turning pink and irresistible, and floated tantalizingly above her centre. She swam back to it, while her voice continued on another planet, like, light years below.

Karen wondered: as Diz waved her languid arms, there was that sort of *smell* again. Well, you couldn't be too choosy, not out of ten. Maybe Diz could redesign the logo . . . it had taken Karen several weeks to include all the relevant symbols, but somehow it wasn't *clear* enough. Diz looked the artistic type. Red eyes from irregular hours, she decided.

By the end of the evening, Karen and Mavis were organizing another meeting and saying slow 'yeahs' through the menthol smoke about their mother/funeral stories. Clarabelle was nowhere to be seen. Reen was promising Leonora a.k.a. Delia a night she'd never forget. Rotary Spokes was royally drunk on Royal Smiles: she'd agreed to look at Karen's little car, meet Lilli-O at the Eat-All-You-Want Pizzeria, play pool with an amused Reen, and fix Diz Darling's faucet:

'It, like, you know . . . leaks? Can you get your head around that? You *can*? All right!'

She had been totally avoided by Leonora a.k.a. Delia who had had a nasty experience with a gang of greasers in Mill Hill some fourteen years ago.

'Time to find your beds, girls,' leered Al, chucking Karen under the chin with his ring finger. The group broke up on the chill doorstep.

Rotary Spokes kicked her magnificent bike into life and fell over.

'I'll drive,' said Diz, making a snap decision. Hell, why not. It goes on. With Rotary Spokes a deadweight giggling down her neck, Diz skeetered and lurched back into town in first gear.

'You better have some coffee,' she said and hauled Rotary Spokes up the stairs.

'Waaall, I'd better git on,' said Rotary Spokes, three coffees later.

Diz lay back on the couch and sent her a searing blue gaze.

'You better do what you came here to do,' she said, wriggling her versatile tongue.

What? Oh, yiz. Rotary Spokes stumbled into the kitchen and stared at the three faucets till they became one. Which dribbled.

'I'll need my tools,' she said.

Diz laughed.

'Come on over here,' she said. 'I think you will find I have everything you might require.'

Jesus Christ! This was the planet of . . . . . and the rarefied air made it hard to breathe. Rotary Spokes' hands walked out on her, leaving empty rubber gloves paralyzed in Diz's smooth, warm, soft caress.

On the rug, The Hug lay purring like a mountain, and as Rotary Spokes' hands came burning back to collect her . . . one feline spring, and for the first time in twenty long years, Diz Darling whispered, cried, gasped and screamed an express train of truth to a lover.

Rotary Spokes woke for the first time with another woman and The Hug lying over them like fur. 5 a.m. She slid out of bed and rubbed her bare feet on the Indian cotton mat. Diz's place smelt of perfume. Real different to Dor's too. She liked this. Diz had Chinese silk kimonos and Thai caftans strewn around the room, and she liked them too. Diz woke up and held back the covers.

'Come back here,' she said. 'You ain't going nowhere. You better fix this faucet, honey.'

She arched her lovely body against Rotary Spokes who thought, reverently:

'If I die this minute, I will be one happy woman and a angel of paradise.'

Diz was so small and soft and thin, she loved her like a piece of porcelain; Diz was so wiry and clawing and howling, she loved her like every kind of wild animal.

'You're like a tree,' sighed Diz, and fell back on the pillows.

And here I could put down my roots, thought Rotary Spokes, blushing.

'You want to smoke?'

Rotary Spokes nodded. One of Dor's Get-A-Man lectures had stressed that you should never smoke in bed on a first date. She guessed it was different with women. She rolled a cigarette with one hand. Then two for Diz to laugh at, then three to laugh at herself and finally thirteen and all her tobacco was gone. She breathed smoke, rubbing her thumb idly around Diz's shoulder, and thought, Butch? Femme? What the hell, they was both the same, her and Diz.

'Now, honey, this is now I make a cigarette.' Diz made a long cigarette in a paper printed with rainbow stripes, and smudged some brown dusty stuff into it.

'Wrap your lips round that, lover,' she said, and proceeded to blow Rotary Spokes' mind.

She called at the hotel at the end of the week to pick up her bag, and roared back to Normal with a silly smile on her face, The Hug clinging like a fur banshee to her jacket.

She would wind down the shop, and go back to Middlesville, Dizville, and never get out of bed for the rest of her life.

And special delivery letters hit her doormat every day for a week: magenta, pink, gold, leaf green, sky blue, silver, pearl grey.

So she went up to the store and bought a pen and paper, locked the door to her house, put on Fats Domino and sat down to write her first love letter.

The words came as hard as the voice grinding out of the speakers. *Ah foun' mah thurrrillll . . .*

Dear Diz,

On blehewhewhewberriii Heee-ll . . .

Sheee-it.

Darling Diz,

This is me Rotary writing to you (this was so Diz wouldn't throw it away as a circular – but who the hell else would be callin' her Darling? Rotary Spokes pushed the unwelcome thought away).

I am writin' to let you know how I am gettin' on without you . . .

She changed the record to the Andrews Sisters . . . *you are my hoochi coochi hoochi smoochi cuddle buddle baby o!*

I have been thinkin' about that meetin'. Not that I recall much, but I am tryin' to put it together.

Baby baby boohoo, maybe you love me trrooo hoo . . .

If you don't want I won't shut up the shop now like we talked about, although I am so sure I don't need no time, and there is plenty of space around Normal, sometimes it gits me down, nuthin' but sky. You should come here and see. I would like that.

Take me in your arms/show me all your charms/it's alarming/how disarming/you can be.

I have put up a new sign with them letters we bought. It looks real smart.

Bring me to my knees/I'll always want you please/you're my little teasy weasy funny honey bear.

Since I got back I done some clearing up and I had a good idea. I warn't gonna tell you for a surprise, but here it is. You know that life's journey you was talkin' about, well I got just the thing out the back. It is in my shop now, and I am rebuilding it. Diz you will love it, it is a old Harley, one of the best, some long hair greaseball left it here a good while ago. I don't guess he will want it, he is in the state pen for life for first degree, I hear he were a real no-good, you know, he never looked after the thing and it is a beaut, the best, carrying 1,000cc.

Fly away with me in Spring/fly away with me in summer/don't you fly without me/I am your lovin' momma.

I worked on that bike for him for three weeks and then he said he din want it and ask me to buy it offa him, and damned if I din wait for him in Dino's three Saturdays and then Dragnet – he's the guy here who alwiz kin tell you everybody's business – Dragnet told me he had gone down. A lot of the ole boys is gone down these few years, Diz, it's mainly cars and trucks these days now so it is real good to be workin' on somethin' proper for a change. And I think of you every time I work on it, and how we will ride and ride and I'm sure it will take us anywhere you want.

Rotary Spokes stared at the last sentence, blushing . . . that was only the start of what she wanted to be saying. But Diz wrote backwards forwards upside down, in circles, through rainbows, in hearts, in flowers, she wrote I love you, I want you, I need you, I adore you, she rhapsodized Rotary Spokes' fingers, her skin, her neck, her earlobes; she traced in metallic and multicoloured felt tip pens the glories and graces of Rotary Spokes. And sitting in the hot dust of Normal, Rotary Spokes blushed, sweated, giggled and grinned, reading and re-reading and kissing the rainbow sheets and thinking to herself: Who the hell needs *Feast Your Eyes*?

On the third day of the week, she went up to the store and picked a fight. Hell, she never meant to, it was the way Dragnet Hornwinder leered at the satin stuffed heart on a card: 'To My One True Love'.

'Has my luck changed then?' he asked her.

No wonder that man left town, thought Dragnet Hornwinder as the seat of his creased slacks hit the sidewalk still full of his bum.

'Now who's Mistah Smart-ass?' cackled Dino behind the counter. Well, it certainly wasn't Dino. Oh, aeroplanes fly, eggs crack and water gushes, but today in Normal, Middle America, chairs, windows, milk, tables, doors and bottles did all these things: Miraculo? No. Just Rotary Spokes gone demented and Dragnet Hornwinder being his natural self.

'Damn', said Gooseneck Squash, as two frozen steaks hit the dust at his feet.

'What th' *hell*?' he said, as frozen strawberries hailed around his ragged shoulders. He stuck his head round the door, and smiled unappealingly.

'Y'all got inny french fries or cream there?'

An avalanche hurtled him into the street: frozen bricks of spinach, onion rings, two-minute pizzas.

'Don' you mind about th' cream . . .' he called, shambling down the street with more food than he had ever had before at any one time.

Later, Lorie-Kay smiled at him over a laden table. He warn't so bad for a man . . . once in a while. Hell, she'd let him do 47, uh 71, whutever it was, if she had to. But Gooseneck's belly stuck out like a frog's throat and he slept after the meal.

Just as well, thought Lorie-Kay, digesting.

And so Diz brought rainbows, and unknowingly, manna to 1st Street East.

But on the eighth day there was no letter, and Rotary Spokes welded and oiled and hammered and cursed, so that Princess Henrietta Maria II, replete with salmon steaks and cream, shuddered in the sunshine and wrapped her fabulous tail over her dainty nose and buried one ear in her belly, the other under her sleek paw.

And the ninth day was Sunday when the good Lord and the Postal Service have decreed no man shall labour.

And on the tenth day came a letter in a plain white envelope which read like this to Rotary Spokes' chilling heart:

Darling – it was such fun wasn't it? I will never forget you – you have given me so much – my wonderful tree-woman baby – but – the skies change, the seas change, the earth changes – and so do I. I have gone away, maybe for the short ever of my present incarnation – who can tell – the wind blows, the rain falls, and there is something out there saying – Come.

Ever together where it really counts –

Diz.

Rotary Spokes' fingers shook as she read the bleak words six, seven, a hundred times. She looked along the rainbow letters on the shelf. Glorious sunshine every day, lazy and lush. She felt her heart thunder against this monstrosity. Frost stung along her arm. 'Together where it really counts!' Where the hell does it count but here, now, me, her, us? Snow blasted into the seismic rift in front of her. She knew there was no crossing it: this road was at an end. She set her jaw grimly, and like a robot, went into the workshop. The paper stuck to her fingers, burning like metal in mid-winter. The half-built Harley stood there like a wounded bird.

CHAPTER
FOUR

"I remember Sam, he was the village idiot,
And though it seems a pidiot,
He was swell. . . "
(Tom Lehrer)

All morning Gooseneck Squash had been shuffling and scuffing near the front of the workshop. Once or twice he had half-lowered his patched jeans towards the doorstep, and fallen forward off-balance, as if kicked. Inside he heard crashes and curses, grinding of metal, gnashing of teeth. The door shuddered as metal, wood, and china were hurled against it. Gooseneck stood on one leg for twenty minutes and then on the other. What to do? When Lorie-Kay started ragin' like this, he came over here, but Rotary Spokes?

'Nevvuh thought she'd have these wimmin's tahms,' mumbled Gooseneck, desperate for a cigarette or a familiar curse, or even a pellet of spit.

No point shuffling back over the road: no men could come in the house during the day, work or no work. He wavered towards getting the mail for her, but Rotary Spokes had been getting special delivery to the door every day these past weeks. Weeks? Never a word about what the letters said. Life was changing. Last week she had a damn holiday and that she never did.

Or was it the week before? Gooseneck stared at his lumpy fingers, tried to count, and gave up.

'Yuh wan' some cawfy, there?'

What the hell? That was surely Lorie-Kay, and he was surely the only person in the street.

Cawfy? In the *house*? In the *day*? He heard himself say no – wouldn't

47

know where to put himself, and wandered up to Dino's.

At Dino's something was wrong too. Dino was wearing a Stetson two sizes too big, and a new bandanna, and the cafe was swept . . . different walls? Gooseneck balanced in front of a cup of coffee, on the house.

'What's happenin'?' he said. 'What's happenin' heah?'

'We gonna have a rodeo,' said Dino, 'Yee-ha, Gooseneck. Yee-ha.'

'Yee-ha?' said Gooseneck.

'Yee-ha,' said Dino miserably. 'The owner come in th'other day and said we gotta change the image. We're on the Old West Trail an' we oughtta draw the tourist trade. He been readin' them cussed trade magazines. *Cost effective. Maximize the potential.* Movin' into th'eighties. Local colour. Lure 'em offa the freeways back to they natural heritage. Here Gooseneck, boy, have ma hat, it's hotter than a whore's bloomers back here . . .'

The Stetson settled above Gooseneck's eyes.

'Lookit that,' said Dino.

'That' was a new jukebox, chromed and studded and hologrammed with scenes from the Old West. Dino went over to it and punched the numbers. Above the holograms was a three-foot-square screen, where the *artistes* sprang to life as their music blared below.

The Mountain Blues Boys sparkled onto the screen and belted out the Mountain Blues Boys True-Blue Blues: *Plinketty Plink yeeeeeeee-hi*!

Then came the Middle Plains Grass Stompers, with lime-green fluorescent waistcoats: *Ricketty-hicketty ping yaaaa hooooo*!

The the High Hills Hillbilly Blasters: *Tinketty picketty yackety hacketty yah yippee ooh ya ya*!

'Who these boys?' said Gooseneck, thinking to himself, hell, he weren't no musician. He thought they was so damn bad, they was probably real good.

'They's our newly-discovered culture and heritage, boy,' said Dragnet Hornwinder in shiny spurred boots, hooking newly-ringed hands in a tooled leather belt with forty-two bullets, fastened with a chrome horseshoe.

'Times changin', Gooseneck,' he added importantly. Gooseneck felt the Stetson slide onto the bridge of his nose. He pushed it back to make an unlikely halo.

'Out of the backwater, boy,' said Dino, with all the joy of a toad whose swamp has been stomped into a six-lane highway overnight. He spoke in a croak from his dust-filled throat. Someone would write that in a song soon, as part of the revival.

Then the High Hills Hillbilly Blasters bowed out and Norah Natchville, Lady of the Wagon Trains, filled the screen, and some jerky camera work closed in on the most expensive dental job ever seen in Normal. Norah's throat wobbled with real feeling, and her wet eyes gazed into the cafe.

I yah neeed Yoooo hoooo! she told Gooseneck and Dragnet and Dino.
I need you like a otter needs the wotter
I neee heeed you like a fly-hi neee-heeeds a swotter
I yah neee-heed you like a berry needs some cream
a-a-ah-hand!
I neee-heeed yoo-hoo like a piller needs a dream!

(She made an unconvincing pillow from her jewelled fingers and scarlet-spiked nails, and swayed a little, before the camera dived once more towards her glistening parted lips.)

I need you like no-one ever done before
I nee-heeed you like a woman neee-heeeeds to wax her floor
I yah neee-heeeed you like a snake nee-heeeeds to coil
e-e-ey-yand!
I neee-heeed you like a engine neee-heeeeds some oil!

The jukebox was the brainchild of Whipcrack Ah-Weh. 'Gems of Real American Talent!' claimed the brochure. 'The world is a galaxy, and there are many stars Man has never known. Their meteoric passage through the universe has gone unrecorded, save perhaps by some lone astronomer, in the wild. As bright as the Pole Star or some unnamed planet, the songs and talents of our Stars are as diverse as the multifarious pebbles on the beach of time. Who is to say that Smokey Joe Bilton and the Bilton Boys are lesser than the Stars of our screens? Who would affirm that our own Norah Natchville, hitherto undiscovered among the Wagon Trains, sings songs less poignant than the Lady with the Gardenia?'

And so it went for ten or so glossy pages dotted with cactus silhouettes and gaudy sunsets.

It was just what Mr Luigi Tertiorelli had been looking for. He had half a dozen struggling cafes through the state, leased to Dino in Normal, Mario in Hook Airs, Lorenzo in Champagne, and so on. The brochure plopped through his door among the teetering accounts, bills and apologies which nourished his ulcers and migraines. He read right through, and felt with relief that This Was It: the turning point, the Holy Grail – solvency – even profits!

Whipcrack Ah-Weh had a passion for country and western music that had got him sacked from every Chinese restaurant he had ever worked in. He was a chef of mediocre talent and it was felt that enthusiastic flat ballads destroyed the atmosphere of Eastern refinement among the crimson flock wallpaper and hand-painted lanterns.

'No-one want hear *Mississippi Mudflat Boy* when they eat Poo-Poo Platters or Nanking Chow Mein.'

'Customer don't want "Howdy Pardner, how you saucy inkfish balls, fine and dandy", they want hear customary Chinese greeting: Good evening, honourable Sir and Lady. Very sorry, Ah-Weh.'

He had even written a song of his own which had done little to improve East/West relations. It was whined to a tinny guitar and electric organ in a rent-by-the-hour studio.

Don' go kickin' my Chinese bum!
A thousand miles along this road I've come
I cook you chow mein and garlic prawn
An' you make me cuss the day I born!
American Yank, don' kick my Chinese bum!

Finally Ah-Weh had ditched his unpronounceable surname, planning to root out wasted talent like his own, and create a blaze of glory: Whipcrack Ah-Weh would show them! But *Chinese Bum* had been dropped from the final selection and Ah-Weh now sat on a balcony in Santa Monica, rich and disillusioned, collecting royalties on his idea amidst demo tapes of his own returned from every recording company in the States.

In Dino's cafe, a revelation was imminent. There was a significant click as Norah Natchville drained the last note to death.

It had been felt that some 'real' stars should be added to the dim galaxy. 'Real' being proved by good solid record sales, coast-to-coast recognition ... just to cushion the 'raw talent'. No self-respecting agent of the millionaire-category singer would jeopardize their client's names. The only ones which could be used had to be posthumous greats whose songs had outlived their copyrights. The inimitable Patsy Cline, wiped out in a plane crash some seventeen years earlier, was ideal. And they had used many of her songs, the greatest being *Crazy*.

'This town gone crazy,' fretted Dino, unaware.

And time stood still for Gooseneck Squash, as the jukebox pumped breathily:

Cru-hu-hazy,
I'm cru-hazy for feelin' so lonesome . . .
Cru-hu-hazy,
I'm cru-hazy for feelin' so blue . . .

Hallowed centuries tip-toed through the dusty halls of Gooseneck's mind, until:

I'm cru-hazy for tru-hying
And cru-hazy for cru-hying
And I'm cru-hazy for lu-huvin' Yooouu!

Gooseneck slid Dino's Stetson onto the bar.

'Who was that?' he whispered from a throat gone dry with feeling.

'Lemme look, Goosenick,' said Dino, from another time. 'Uh, that's Patsy Klein.'

'She's mah angel,' said Gooseneck. 'Dino, Dragnet, gimme a nickel, gimme all the nickels you got, I need 'em like I never done before . . .'

When Gooseneck reeled down the street two hours later, Dino said:

'You hear that? Din' I say this town gone crazy? That tune's called "Crazy", and damned if we ain't all gonna be crazy, time this here rodeo's finished.'

Uniquely, Dragnet had no words. Gooseneck Squash, no more brain than a bandicoot's baseball cap, had been *silent* and *concentrating* for two hours. Two hours next to each other. Two hours in the same day. Not a damn-fool babbling word out of him. And this, lessee, Patsy Klein, the card said, had sung a marathon of *Crazy*, forty times all the way through.

When the lightning strikes and the heavens open, what does a man do? One way or another he consults the oracle, whether it lies, like a baby's china frog, at the end of some drinking vessel or in the discreet pink pages of a financial time-server, he goes to the oracle, reads the entrails, falls to his knees . . .

51

And so, in Normal Middle America, Gooseneck Squash floated gracelessly down the only street it seemed he had ever known and stood in the workshop doorway, with the smile of a beatific turtle which stopped Rotary Spokes' legendary biceps, her arm in mid-fling. She tapped the hammer against her knee and said:

'What?'

'Rotary, you the finest woman I know. You know a lot of stuff, wimmin stuff and that . . .

The longest thought of Gooseneck's life paused, wavered and recovered itself.

'You been to the city, Rotary, who's Patsy Klein? How do I meet her? Where is she?'

'What is this shit?' asked Rotary Spokes, stirring shreds of white paper with her toe. 'What the hell you talkin' about, Goosenick?'

'Dino got a new juke-box, Rotary and ah just heerd a angel.'

Cursing, kicking, and glad of the distraction, Rotary Spokes walked up to Dino's and filled the jukebox with nickels as Gooseneck mechanically punched H12, H12, H12.

Three minutes later, she turned to him.

'Waaall, she's a damn singer, yuh doodlebrain, that's what.'

'Yeah, yeah, yeah, but where is she now? I gotta see her. I never felt this way before.'

'Gimme a beer,' said Rotary grimly. Serious bidniss if ya never felt that way before. The beer stung her lips. Goddam wimmin, she thought, sitting heavily by Dragnet Hornwinder, who edged over with respect.

And so the finest sages, onions and wits of 1st Street East, discussed a simple heart's desire.

'We'll send the boy to th' library,' said Dragnet excitedly, 'In Hook Airs.'

'And?' said Dino

'And?' said Rotary Spokes.

Gooseneck Squash sat blissful, eyes shut as his fate was decided. They'd know what to do. Hell! Rotary Spokes could do anything, Dragnet Hornwinder knew everything, and Dino had lots of money: with talents like this in your friends, you couldn't lose.

'And,' said Dragnet Hornwinder, impressive to anyone who didn't know him, 'Evvah library in the United States of America has evvah name of evvah person in evvah town in evvah part of these here states . . . in evvah *telephone directory*.'

'Bullsheee-it,' said Rotary Spokes, 'Ain't no book big enough for that.'

'It all in different books,' said Dino, 'Eh, Dragnet?'

'Uh-huh,' said Dragnet, 'hunnerds of books and they cain't be too many Kleins in 'em. P. Klein, that's what the boy gotta look up. Take a while, but it's gonna be worth it to him. He ain't doin' too much these days, eh Rotary?'

'Ah can spare him,' said Rotary, paying lip-service to the idea that Gooseneck ran errands for her.

'So . . . we gonna send him to Hook Airs, an' ease his mind.'

Alas, the bored clerk who had typed the cards for the jukebox had not been chosen for scholarship or accuracy or enthusiasm, but simply for low-price availability, and so the piece of paper in Gooseneck's pocket as he waited for the weekly bus read PATSY KLEIN, Klein as in the drugstore over the way from the typist's office. Not Cline.

More alas – Gooseneck Squash had all the privileges of an average American rural education, and only the haziest idea of whereabouts a 'K' might sit in the threadbare tapestry of the alphabet. But, over the years, this would improve.

Yet more alas – the library in Hook Airs shut half-days on Tuesdays, when the librarian played bridge, and the bus from Normal ran late mornings on Tuesdays. And so a communal twelve dollars and forty cents were squandered on the sight of a closed library door, and a siesta for Gooseneck on a different set of steps, his back against a Grecian-style pillar.

Back at Dino's on Wednesday, Gooseneck slumped once more in *Crazy* bliss as his three good fairies bent their mental powers as if over a checkerboard, moving the pieces of the library, the bus, the bus, the library, in puzzled silence.

'It ain't right,' said Dragnet. 'Stands to reason you want to talk to someone, they oughtta be there. And what if we was wanting some Education?'

'What about it?' snarled Rotary Spokes, who knew too well that a phone number doesn't always magically summon the loved one.

'Waaall, if we people here in Normal was wanting an Education we couldn't git none.'

'Ah guess it ain't happen before,' said Dino, guessing right.

'Waaall! Howdy, howdy and good day to you folks, gents and lady,' bellowed Luigi Tertiorelli, the cafe's owner, flinging wide the door screens and looking happily round the sepia photos on the evenly-peeling Kwik-Kleen Saloon Bar Vinyl. 'How's bidniss in the eighties?'

Rotary and Dragnet ordered another beer and paid for it. Dino would slide it back later. 'Yeee-*hi*!' whooped the owner 'Yippee-o-ki-yay, git along liddle dogies, that's what we need here – time's changing,' he boomed in his oil-magnate voice, deep and slippery. 'What the hail *he* doin' here?' he kicked Gooseneck Squash, who could have lowered the tone of the Park Lane Hilton.

'He's really sad, Mister Tertiorelli,' said Dragnet Hornwinder, winking at Dino. 'He got a chance to improve hisself with a college place . . . a correspondence course.'

'*Whut*? said Luigi Tertiorelli, awed by the opportunities still available in the land of opportunity.

'He gonna do a study of, uh, etymology of the state,' said Dragnet.

'Yes, indeed,' said Dino, 'Eatin' habits, ain't it?'

Dragnet looked at him with utter contempt. Then wondered. Etymology . . . never mind.

'Huh,' he said, 'this proves my point. This town full of blind ignorance. Fact is, Mister Tertiorelli, we have a problem . . . he has a problem, and he is our friend.'

Half an hour of old baloney and windy flattery later, Luigi Tertiorelli had ben conned into taking Gooseneck Squash weekly to the library in Hook Airs, while he checked on one of his other thriving business concerns, Mario's.

'You doin' a service for education, Mister,' said Rotary Spokes, collapsing into her sixth beer with laughter as he strutted into the street, imagining a brass plate forever embedded in the sidewalk in front of his house.

> **HERE LIVED**
> **LUIGI TERTIORELLI**
> **PATRON OF EDUCATION**
> **AND GOURMET RESTAURATEUR**
> you asked for it, you got it.

CHAPTER
FIVE

"When you wander round this world, babe
You might find out, honey, the road don't end in Detroit,
The road don't even end in Katmandu."
(Janis Joplin)

Once upon a time there was a sky-blue bus trailing pink clouds, windows covered with sun and sunflowers. It was driven by the bare and filthy feet of Dave the Deep Sea Diver, peering through mauve shades and luxuriant flaxen hair, careering the highways and lowways of untracked America. It was fuelled by a healthy flow of uppers and downers, peyote and pills, handmade earrings and woven bags, translated into thousands of miles of Life's Journey, manned in the late sixties, personned in the eighties by the Caravanserai commune, drop a few here, pick up a few there – roughly a mystical seven or mystical nine or, as at present, a mystical eleven.

The Caravanserai would continue forever . . . it was so *Organic.* It's main function was . . . functioning. Had anyone asked, they might have guessed that, yeah, anarchism was, like, a pretty strong unifying, like, theme. It was committed to self-perpetuation. To this end, it summoned new beings from the Eternal Now, through Fucking and Meditation. For the first few years, the fucking had been a communal, giggly, higgledy-piggledy, doped-out humpaty-dumpaty thing. Babies had spilled more or less happily around in the back of the bus, wriggling from one hug to another, with no one-biological-set-of-parents trip. Free to commune. Then in the mid-seventies, Dave the Deep Sea Diver drifted along with the bus.

He had strolled off a beach somewhere and sat still and smiling over brown rice and tofu for a few days. His void blue eyes were either sensuous, sinister or psychotic, depending on your point of view.

Between the Silences, where he sat with one ear on the Cosmos, Dave wove a tapestry of words that came to be the destiny and direction of the Caravanserai. He said Fucking was a one-to-one, specific Yang energy-sharing process, and, of course, the male, being like, more yang-balanced, should be the initiator.

So although ultimately, sharing Yang was a communal, like, Prayer to the Life Force, only two star-beings had been summoned from Eternity since Dave arrived. Astra had inherited his vacant blue gaze and Sikita's hair gew long, thick, straight and flaxen. And secretly he taught them to say Daddy Dave.

'Like, where are we, Dave?' said Fender Rhodes, crystal mother of Astra.

'Skyways, byways,' said Dave, forcing the bus around a cactus bush.

'Uh, I really don't want to be heavy, man,' said Fender, licking a licorice-flavoured paper around some Panama Red. 'I mean *where* are we?'

'It's cool, cool,' said Dave.

Fender wiped sweat from her unfurrowed brow, lit and inhaled. She centred on her mantra and gazed through the dusty windows. Sand, sand, cactus, tumbleweed, clumps of red rock, Chevvy trucks honking out of dust clouds ... like, schedules, such an unreal reality, destinations ... man, timetables. For Dave, there were only the seasons of his destiny, the maps of the soul. Fender could drive; Riverboy could drive; Yolanda could drive, on the right, the wrong side of the road; even Sikita aged seven and Astra aged nine could drive. Jaanethi could drive; Musky had driven to India for years in the Skybus and probably Horse Paul, Spark Mark and Asteroid Aruel could drive.

But the only fingerprints on the sweating steering wheel belonged to Dave the Deep Sea Diver. Fender had tried to raise this point at many of the daily communications which gave the temporal directionals of the Caravanserai, and it had transpired that Dave knew, cosmically, that he was the steersman, the guru, the father and the facilitator, the yang of the commune and would continue to drive the bus. And for Asteroid Aruel, Spark Mark and Horse Paul, it was much easier to lie among the Hopi blankets, Tibetan prayer rugs, Nepalese meditation shawls, Sears sleeping bags and contemplate the revelations swirling in gold and silver and black on the sunset ceiling of the bus:

Wow
Been down so long it looks like up to me
Fear and loathing in the universe
Mother mother
Our children are not our property
The enlightened one walks silent, the stupid one chatters.

The bus roared through Big Bend, the Grand Canyon, Yosemite, Ojai, and broke down in Baltimore, Detroit, Chicago. The directionals revealed – through Dave – that cities had bad karma, as garages paid in advance changed corroded plugs and ripped out rusted wires. The bus broke down in deserts, and suspicious mechanics were lured from miles away by Yolanda's gutteral urgency and Aruel's roll of bills. And one day, on a road rising unnoticeably over thirty miles, the bus coughed and died at the top of an empty plain and coasted towards Normal, Middle America.

It lurched past the sign saying Normal and past a new sign sponsored by Luigi Tertiorelli, saying: WELCOME TO ONE OF THE FRONTIER OUTPOSTS OF THE OLD WEST

'Wow,' said Fender Rhodes, peering through ragged curtains.

Horse Paul waved one hand in the air, searching for words. 'Like, this is nowhere, man. Normal, nowhere . . . yeah.'

Sikita and Astra hung out of the back of the bus. They loved towns, arcades and jukeboxes, TV, movie houses, hot dogs and Coca-Cola.

Yolanda leaned against one of the bunks, sweating a little from a tiny pink dot of something on a piece of blotter paper. She would regard all of Normal as a Devic judgment from a previous dark incarnation. A town with lilac emus at the water trough? She shuddered and wrapped her head in a Diana von Furstenburg towel. She felt suspended in a gelid zone of no time, silence without the engine's roar. The blood-stained murals of the Catholic church where she had knelt still and cold as a child, hearing about her culpability from the manic Catholic monsignor . . . it was like syphilis . . . she writhed against the sheer poison of her body . . . Father forgive me . . . outer darkness . . .

The bus wavered as it hit 1st Street and skeetered left down 1st Street East. It juddered and stopped on its old pillow tyres, right outside Rotary Spokes' workshop. Princess Henrietta Maria II growled as a shadow stole her sun, and Rotary Spokes walked over and leaned on the doorpost.

'Damnedest thang I ever saw,' she muttered. And then her heart started to pound. Could it be? The sunflowers brought back Diz's ceiling, the hangings at the window said Diz. She was sure that every piece of fabric in Diz's paradise wonderland was unique. Patchouli and myrrh wafted from the bus . . . it had to be. All she had understood of Diz's last letter was that It was over, that Diz had gone away from her, that she, Rotary Spokes, ex-virgin queen and solo-dyke was, as she had always been, alone in Normal: a life sentence with no hope of appeal. And now Diz had come back to her and would never go away again. She moved forward with a radiant smile, blood tingling from head to toe.

The Caravanserai swayed and spilled and jumped out of the bus. Dave the Diver swung from the driving seat and snorted fresh air and dust. Rotary Spokes' hands numbed and chilled, winter stung her. Eleven of the mothers and no Diz. She spat her smile into the dust. But Fender Rhodes had seen it and nodded in a stunned stoned way at the sneer now frozen on Rotary Spokes' face.

'Sunset, sunrise like, arctic night,' she mouthed.

Astra and Sikita eeled through the open doorway and started grabbing and wrecking as seven and nine-year-old free spirits will do.

'You damn kids git your asses outta my place,' yelled Rotary Spokes. Fender Rhodes' crystal perception shattered. Even celestial star children hear rage and will duck out of the way of an avalanche.

'I swear,' said Rotary Spokes, cussing, 'I swear I'll take y'apart . . . cain't you keep them damn kids witchuh?' she snarled, unfortunately at Yolanda, who had just worked up the nerve to look at Hell with one eye through the towel. She fell to the ground and lay twitching and writhing. The rest of the commune hummed peace to the place, and Astra and Sikita sulked in the bus, unravelling rugs and tearing alternative magazines to shreds.

'Like . . .' said Dave, grinning and licking his lips like an emaciated monitor lizard. 'Like, I mean, no sweat, yeah, like, uh, man . . . the bus just did a real like no-go. I mean, it is totalled, it's really dessicated-out . . . like the summit, man, above this *living* place, and . . . zody-pody, baby, no way.'

He waved a long and skinny arm around the sky, bracelets jangling.

'Yiz?' said Rotary Spokes in a voice of H2SO4. This was just Gooseneck Squash with earrings and a pretty shirt. No more sense than a muskrat's asshole. But where Gooseneck would have deflated from within, whined, cringed and finally shambled off, Dave nodded and more-or-less stood his ground and drew out a Moroccan tobacco pouch.

'Like hostile,' whispered Jaanethi. Fender Rhodes' bare feet walked her to the edge of the minefield mushrooming around the workshop door.

'You could really help us,' she said, head bobbing, chanting her mantra in her head.

'Yiz?'

'I mean, this is really intended – you know. We're here, and you're here . . .'

'And there's no *spark* . . .' giggled Dave.

'In the engine, yeah,' said Fender hastily.

'No spark in the engine,' said Rotary Spokes.

No one moved bar a little swaying. Dor and Mar'Ann and Lorie-Kay stood on the other side of the street, chewing the spearmint silence.

'Wheeee, High Noon,' said Aruel, with a graceful skip and giggle.

'He has really bad karma to work out,' said Fender.

'He your mechanic?' asked Rotary Spokes.

'Whee, no, man, like, I mean . . . spanner . . . star-spangled banner, uh-huh,' said Aruel.

Rotary Spokes looked round the group. Fuckin' screwball raggedy-ass mothershits. Dave yo-yoed at her heels as she strolled to the red and blue engine flap.

'I would really, like take-off, yeah, if you would look at this . . .' he flashed, low and earnest, and squeezed, or tried to, her arm. Her muscle burst his grip and she shrugged him away.

'Open it up,' she said.

He babbled the engine's history to her. She christened him Banana. She poured contempt over the cowboy-patching in what had once been a damn fine engine. She poked the cracked casing off the wires and spun rust-ochred plugs from the scarred guts of the bus.

She wanted to fix him. Say, 'Banana, your big end's all fucked.' That would screw him. Screw all his money and limp him across the desert. But the big end, by a miracle, had not gone. And he wouldn't know what a damn big end was. Sheeee-it.

'Don't you nevvah maintain this engine?' she demanded indignantly.

'I, like, really read that,' said Fender Rhodes. *'Zen and the Art of Motorcycle Maintenance* . . . yeah.' Her damn head would fall off with all that noddin' that stalk neck.

'This ain't no motorcycle' said Rotary Spokes, with scorn.

'Yeah, no, yeah,' said Fender. 'But it's all the same thing.'

'Just a different groove,' said Dave, wondering idly about screwing Rotary Spokes. She'd really dig it, he decided.

'Gonna take three days,' said Rotary Spokes. 'I have to git parts. Ah'll git 'em tumorruh . . . cost ya three hunnerd-fifty bucks.'

'In advance?' asked Dave the Deep Sea Diver, winningly.

'Yiz,' said Rotary Spokes. Fucking Banana. 'In God we trust, all others pay cash.'

Aruel gave her three hundred and fifty. She counted and stuffed the money deep into her overalls.

'Like,' sparkled Fender, 'like we have to eat, huh?' Rotary Spokes would offer them hospitality, the directionals buzzed into the circuits of Fender Rhodes' brain. They sent her a picture of an iceberg floating south, snow crystals melting into a pure turquoise seat.

'There's Dino's, down the street,' said Rotary Spokes, trudging through her ice age, and went back to the Harley in the workshop.

'Heav . . .eee . . .' said Aruel, exhaling bad air yogically.

'Heav . . . eee.'

In the gutter, Yolanda moaned and sweated. The Caravanserai moved down the street, supporting her, to check out Dino's.

Rotary Spokes polished rich chrome in the workshop, speechless, and with only a red and black cloud raging in her mind. It was just too damn familiar – the damn scents of the bus, the damn pattern of the fabric, the way the wind lifted the thin cotton and silk draped around the lean tanned bodies of the Caravanserai. Shee-it, she had been O.K. for weeks now, even happy a couple of days ago, testing out the Harley without even thinking of Diz. Somehow, she felt they knew all about her and Diz and she felt like she always had at school . . . dirty, big, clumsy, stupid. *Sheeeeeeiiiiit* on the goddam trash-heap bus; *double-sheeeeit* on the goddam pigfuckin' Banana driver, might's well've walked around with his goddam dick hanging out; shit and shit and *sheeit* on the goddam jeeraffe-necked woman wearing Diz's caftan and massacring her memories. Same colour eyes and the same serene smile . . . listen, you know, and I know, and the drugs investigation officer of every country knows that there are a million such smiles jogging and surfing, singing and rebirthing, dancing and weaving, according to location, all over wherever there is sun and dope. But to Rotary Spokes, only one person should be wearing that smile. Fender Rhodes was blasphemy and even her stinking voice was about as come-hither as a turd in a swimming pool.

'Where there is discord, we must spread peace,' said Fender Rhodes, nodding. She blessed her minute pizza; all the exploited pickers of red and green capsicums; the heedless kneaders of processed dough; the evil dairy farmers; and the dollar-deadened operators of cheese blenders and graters.

Dave swallowed his pizza slice in one gulp and picked the sacred crusts from Fender Rhodes' plate.

'I get a really heavy vibe, Fender,' he said, pouring deep blue into his large pale eyes. 'No harmony.'

She fixed his with her watery blue eyes.

'These people are dead, Dave,' she said. 'The Caravanserai has life, man.'

To Yolanda, the chairs were tombstones, Dino a cursed ghost, condemned forever to make coffee, heat pizza, open beers, wipe tables. For ever and ever. Dino thought so too but had a growing bank balance. For him life would start when it hit five figures. Meanwhile:

'Fahve beers comin' up!' said Dino.

Dave felt his pure system freak out at the poison he was putting into it, and then accept it: monosodium glutamate. E 102, D 785, processed sugar, refined flour, reconstituted egg yolk – yuuu-uum!

'I mean,' he said, 'if this person is going to life-blood the metal, like, she really oughtta join with us, unite. Yeah, mingle, or man, the Hostility is going to live on in the engine. I mean, that is obviously what has happened and then the city and the death trip come out into the desert and all the beautiful places.'

'Unite?' said Jaanethi, who was currently the chosen one sharing yang with Dave to invite star-being number three. Dave felt the finger of jealous reality poking aside the veils of unity. He started to roll a joint.

'You can't smoke that stuff in heah,' said Dragnet Hornwinder, excitedly. Dave took in the tooled leather boots, the rhinestone-studded belt, the check shirt, the rawhide Stetson.

'You the *lawman* . . . the sheriff?' he asked, inhaling.

'Hell, no boy. Just a citizen of Normal. A real fine town. But you cain't smoke that stuff in heah. This *is* Normal.'

Dave giggled weakly and passed the joint to Dragnet Hornwinder. Fender Rhodes drowned him in spaceship blue, and told him:

'Suck, man, suck deep.'

Damn! What nahce people they was! What real purdy earrings that boy was wearin'! What a gorgeous shirt that gal had on! How tuneful was they voices! Weren't they simply bruthuhs and sistuz, an' Damn if that boy couldn' swaller pizza like he was starved!

Dragnet Hornwinder moonwalked to the distant bar, only them spurs that jingle jangle jingle keeping him on the dusty surface.

'Get all mah frenz a beer!' he told Dino.

'You ain't got no friends,' Dino told him.

Tears oozed out of Dragnet's pink little eyes. 'These are mah frenz,' he said, waving at the rainbow raggletaggle lolling over the Wipe Kleen redcheck tables. Maybe there was miracles, Dino decided. Dragnet Hornwinder never bought anyone a beer. Dino leaned over to hear what they were saying. Damned if he could make sense of it. And there was Dragnet patting the women and the men and now he's saying WHUT?

'You are all mah house guests whaal you here in Normal,' said Dragnet. 'Hospitality along the highway of life, mah frenz.'

'Hey . . . let's catch us some sounds,' said Horse Paul, suddenly caught by the holograms on the juke box.

'Uh?' said Dino, automatically reaching in the till for nickels when handfuls that had been bulging Dragnet's pockets for weeks were fed into the machine.

The volume went past the usual three to a glass-tingling eleven.

Is you or is you ain't mah liddle prairie gal? asked Buffalo Pat Hildreth.
It's all ah want t'know, and ah sweah you done me w'all
If you ain't mah liddle gal of the prairie . . .
Ah'm gonna make me a wish on a fairy
Keep it a secret in my hay-id
Till you come back to my home spread!

Iz you, iz you aint' mah prairie gal.

'Spread?' said Fender.

'Airhead,' said Astra.

'Gross,' said Sikita, who adored only Tina Turna and Frank Zappa.

'Grody to the *max!*' giggled Aruel.

'Shove it, asshole,' chorused the pink-lipped cherubs.

'This song . . . this song here . . . this song's how I feel 'bout y'all . . .' said Dragnet, as Norah Natchville and her dental wonders loomed on the screen.

'So, like, yeah,' murmured Fender, running her mantra by again and again.

'Whutchuh mean, you ain't got the right leads?' Rotary Spokes sweated in black leather, face stung with seventy five miles of Harley 1000 desert riding.

'I mean we ain't got 'em. Have to order 'em.'

'Sheeeit . . . how long?'

'Mebbe a week, Rodry, ah'm real sorry.'

Rotary Spokes laughed.

'Ain't you or me sorry, boy – it's the goddam Salvation Hornwinder Army hostel gonna be sorry.'

'Hi, is this Patsy Klein?' squeaked Gooseneck, 'The singer?'

'Shove it up your ass!' yelled Paula Klein of Baltimore, Maryland.

Gooseneck put a dot against her name and dialled New York.

CHAPTER
SIX

Dear Auntie Deborah,
I am worried about my friend who doesn't seem at all
interested in boys.
Dear Worried,
You do not say how old your friend is. Many young
girls go through a phase where girlfriends are very
important. If she is more than a young teenager, urge
her to see a psychiatrist. She is probably as worried as
you!

Lorie-Kay and Mar'Ann fretted about how to get Rotary Spokes over for coffee. She'd been mightily busy since her vacation, and there was questions they were dyin' to ask about that. And *this*. What the hail was with that damn bus? What was with them people? Was they a circus? Was they *furrin*? What did they have on Dragnet Hornwinder – mean as a one-eyed rattler – that they could stay in his house for five days? Why was his eyes so red? Did he suddenly git religion, or what?

'Bunch of drop-outs,' said Rotary Spokes.

'Them kids been around, askin' for money. Whatzit, trick-or-treat in *July*?'

Not even Dor had the nerve to ask about the vacation. And all them letters – they had decided that Rotary Spokes had finally got herself a man and now she too was one of the sisterhood who knew it weren't up to much. A broken heart, thought Dor, her fust man an' he broke her heart. She trickled a little brandy into all their coffees and snuffled with the tragedy of it all.

'Hi, people, greetings, ladies . . .'

Dave the Deep Sea Diver zippetty-doo-dahed in and sat down unasked, feeling like a sultan come home from the wars to a harem starved of his presence. There was outrage, contempt, curiosity and anger in the room, but Dave's planetary influences guaranteed him immunity from criticism. Hail to thee, Proud Leo! And the vibes were vitriolic and getting worse.

He fixed his lean keen gaze on Rotary Spokes.

'We wanted you to, you know, break *bread* with us,' he told her, in a dark-brown voice.

'I don' eat *bread*,' she told him acidly.

'You will, you must,' he murmured grabbing her hand. 'We usually, you understand, commune at star-rise ... unfinished business ... lifeblood.'

And he was gone. Lorie-Kay sniffed.

'Waaall, don't look at *me*,' said Rotary Spokes, rubbing raw Nappa Valley into her contaminated fist.

'What's yuh *unfinished business*?' leered Dor, her jigsaw pieces interlocking in all the wrong places.

'*I* wouldn't lay under *that* if all the other men was turned into swamp frogs,' announced Lorie-Kay.

'What about page twenty three?' jeered Mar'Ann. 'Ah hear that's yuh favourite position, Lorie-Kay Squash.'

She should never have told 'em that, sure as hell wouldn't git forgot in years. But it was better sitting on top. Meant yuh could breathe, and yuh din have to do no kissin'.

'Waaall?' said Dor. 'Waaall? You meet him on yuh vacation, Rodry er what? He followed yuh here, uh?'

Hell! She had to tell 'em. She'd bust wide open if she tried to keep it to herself much longer!

'Gimme that *Feast Your Eyes*,' growled Rotary Spokes. Lorie-Kay opened the Bible at Job.

'She's goin' to show us what she done with that damned hippie!' crowed Dor.

Lorie-Kay tossed the magazine over. It fell open at the last few pages, women grinning at the camera as they faked it with other women.

'That ain't it!' yelled Dor. 'Is it *this*? Or *this*? Er, Gawd save us, Rodry, you ain't done 69, have ya, yuh fust time?'

Rotary Spokes was appalled. How to tell 'em, if even Dor felt like that! They was so damned sure it was a damned man – *Banana*!

'He's the type to send all them coloured envelopes!' screeched Mar'Ann.

'You went out 'an spent two bucks on a sateen card for *that*?' squawked Lorie-Kay.

'THINK WHUTCHUH DAMN WELL LIKE, I AIN'T TELLIN' YUH SHIT!' roared Rotary Spokes, flinging herself to her feet. How *dare* they! Friends! *Goddamighty*!

'Hey, keep yer rag on, precious,' soothed Dor. 'We just been dyin' a curiosity these past weeks, Rodry, and be fair, have we asked yuh any questions? Sugar, if he's what yuh want, we sure as hell got no room to criticize yuh. Y'ever see me or Mar'Ann or Lorie-Kay walkin' out with Clark Gable?'

'Hail,' said Lorie-Kay, 'the thang I got at home, waaall, you know Goosenick . . .'

'I wanna tell yuh,' exploded Rotary, 'I'd love to tell yuh, on'y . . . on'y I just cain't find the right words.

'GODDAMMIT!' she shouted finally and stomped back over the road.

'Ah'll find out,' said Dor, patting her hair maternally and slopping her satin mules over to the workshop's slammed door.

The Princess wrapped her nose in her own perfect fur. She despised cheap perfume, cheap brandy and loud voices. Dor's could strip paint at five hundred paces, and turn complexions purple at the top of her range – usually aimed at a happy nuclear household in 1st Street West, whose doting poppa had sidled East to sample fleshly delights.

'YOU FUCK WITH ME PADRE AND I'LL SANCTIMOAN WHAT LITTLE YOU GOT!' drowned out '*God is our love and salvation*' and amplified '*Lyin' in my bed with me*' from an assembly horrified to blushing silence.

But now Dor was using her close range, the bedroom, barroom tones, luring dollars, coaxing erections and now, confidences from Rotary Spokes.

'Tell me, baby, tell me, I kin keep a secret. It's just you and me. Tell me, you're hurtin'.'

Rotary Spokes knew why them men came back time and time to Dor's comforting arms and warm breasts. She felt a distant and all-too-pleasant shiver. No! That shiver belonged to Diz. Even if she didn't want it. Never gonna use it nowhere else, whimpered The Hug, licking its flesh wounds. Rotary Spokes snorted back tears and poured out her aching heart.

Half an hour later, Dor backed out into the street and flip-flapped her satin and feathered mules back over the road. So *that* was it. Her mind and heart gawped at the new vistas ahead.

'Ah sworn ah'd say nuthin'. It's private,' she told Lorie-Kay and Mar'Ann. 'Nuthin'. She'll have to tell you herself when she's ready. Give her a break, poor darlin'. She's really been through it,' she added mysteriously. Neither brandy, nor pleadin', nor cussin' would part her carmine lips.

Dor leafed through *Feast Your Eyes*.

'Can I borrer this?' she said innocently.

'Ah though they was nuthin' new to you in there!' said Mar'Ann accusingly.

'Just about,' said Dor. 'Ah'm gonna do me some homewuk, gals. Wuk,' she said, copying Rotary Spokes' swagger. Lorie-Kay shrugged and Mar'Ann poured the rest of the brandy.

Lorie-Kay tried to look worldly-wise. 'Thay is one thing in this world more ornery 'en men,' she pronounced.

'And whut is that?' sneered Mar'Ann.

'Wimmin', said Lorie-Kay.

They sipped in bemused silence.

'Oi've had weirdos like you call me up before!' raged Miss Perdita Klein in her triple-locked Manhattan apartment, into Gooseneck's unattractive ear. 'Poivert!'

'Beg pardon ma'am?' said Gooseneck.

'Why don'cha go through the book? Call up some other helpless lady? Make her throw away eighty bucks a week with carfare, schlepping to some analyst? Make *her* paranoid?'

'Ah'll do thet, ma'am,' said Gooseneck Squash politely, hanging up in Hook Airs.

'How's your *thesis* going, sonny?' bristled the librarian, who had been listening in.

Down the road where everything in sight is Normal, Fender Rhodes wafted in to collect Rotary Spokes for the breaking of bread.

'She'll come,' Dave had assured her. 'I, really, you know, *touched* her.'

Recalling Dave's yang touch that had summoned Astra from infinity, Fender Rhodes had decided to reinforce it with her own yin. Fascinated, anyway, by that woman's like, *venutian* smile.

'You're really like a hermit,' she told Rotary Spokes. 'Wow, I can't get in your circle, can I?' She danced around Rotary Spokes, dispensing Karma. 'I mean, there you are and I can't get in, you *know?*'

She was like a hooded cobra, now nodding, now swaying. Damn right! Wouldn't let you near me, thought Rotary Spokes morosely tapping the bottom yoke into place on the Harley.

'You know, you're so yang . . . and so yin . . . yeah, like, I mean, it's really cool.'

Whatever she was twitterin' about, it pleased *her*, though Rotary Spokes, tense against the textures, the colours and the patchouli oil.

Half an hour later, suspicious and miserable, Rotary Spokes' dark figure strode along beside a shifting blue neon aura, purpling as it touched her. But neither she nor the rest of the town, gasping cooler air on their doorsteps and balconies, were in the space to perceive it.

At 8.00 p.m., a sluggish brown aura soaked in *California Honeymoon* and the dregs of Nappa Valley '81 brandy leaned against the door of her empty shack. Dor shook with anticipation and nervous giggles brought on by an afternoon with pages 47, 48, 49 and 50. She pictured Rotary Spokes' blonde head nestling between her thighs, Rotary Spokes' full breast teasing her lips . . .

Where was the damn woman?

Shit! She humped her greying aura back to *Lover's Paradise* with Ella Fitzgerald, and lay on her pink polyester quilt in radiant apricot nylon, planning. Maybe . . . a little dinner for two? Lawd!

It's only a paper moon, crooned Ella in 1st Street East.

But a moon made of rock reflecting sunlight shone full outside and nowhere more bright in Normal than on the bouncing candlelit porch outside Dragnet Hornwinder's house. Dragnet now lumbered round in an orange kaftan and had parted with more dollars in the last week than in many a long year. This was what he had been saving for. The peace of mankind flowed from his Buddha-like smile and the drugs of India and Pakistan flowed through his body like anaesthetic. He poured wine, broke wholemeal bread, and munched nut rissoles and mung sprouts. Sometimes he swigged tamari and slapped asses, but the Caravanserai were forgiving. Their forgiveness cushioned him, finally at home in his own house.

Fender Rhodes murmured 'nonsification' to Rotary Spokes, who found herself nodding inanely. Mebbe that was why *she* did it – she didn't unnerstand a word she said neither! Rotary Spokes' present incarnation giggled, what-the-hailed through more joints than she could count and felt pleasantly numb.

Fender Rhodes left to expel fluid poisons, and became transfixed by the way the water thundered in the closet. Some great revelation was winging towards her and she flushed again.

'*Wow,*' she thought. Yes, she really thought: 'Wow'. Outside, Dragnet was being eased into a lotus position.

'Mind mah best parts, boy,' he told Asteroid Aruel.

Dave shifted next to Rotary Spokes. She had come, yin yang to yang yin.

'Yang and yin,' he whispered, 'the sun and the moon, Harmony and Discord, Krishna and Arvati . . .'

'Popeye and Olive Oyl,' said Rotary Spokes, willing to join the game, 'Laurel and Hardy, Fred and Ginger, Tonto and the Lone Ranger, um, Bugs Bunny and Elmer Fudd . . . I cain't think of no more.'

Dave smoothed his long hair and asked:

'Can I touch you?' It never failed. He prided himself on the *basso profundo*, the slight hesitation.

'Screw you, Banana,' Rotary Spokes splattered his unreality. 'I'm goin' home.'

Her long shadow shortened towards her house.

Dazzling through the dark, a midnight-blue shape followed its own peculiar destiny.

'Are you all right?' gasped Fender Rhodes, catching up with her. The communications had told her all: Dave's scarlet aura seething on the porch, the first time Rotary had smoked . . .

'I feel so responsible,' she said.

'You better come in.'

Rotary Spokes kicked the fire alive, sat on her chair and popped a can of Blue Label. Fender Rhodes found herself holding her can gingerly, as if it was a martian missile – all this pollution. And when Rotary Spokes lit a cigarette and put on a record of Doris Day with evident pleasure, even her mantra stopped. Jesus fucking God, she thought.

'I mean, I feel we really upset your space, Rotary. Can I call you that? I mean, it isn't your *name*, but it is the name you carry . . . until you get out on the way . . .'

'I already heard all that shit,' snarled Rotary Spokes.

'Wow, I'm so, like, glad, you hear me . . .'

'Nah! I heard all that trash at a goddam motel, at a goddam ladies meetin'.' The memory, the beer, Fender . . . it was all too much and Rotary Spokes' tears of desolation gushed down her cheeks.

How yin can you get, thought the business side of Fender Rhodes, which had wheeled and dealed the Caravanserai out of gaol for five years – and that had taken some genius.

She summoned vague platitudes and wraped her long thin arms round Rotary Spokes' head. The Hug crashed through its iron cage.

Rotary Spokes woke at 4.00 a.m., already making love with the body beside her.

'Diz,' she whispered, 'Diz, darlin' Diz.'

Then her hands told her different, and horrified, Rotary Spokes explored this unwanted stranger, last night seeping into her mind. No, no, she thought, as her hungry hands mutinied and did their duty.

And on the third day, Rotary Spokes looked round her room and through to herself, damned if it ain't real nice, the spinnin' wheel in the corner, Fender and her silly face playin' with th' cat, a fine mess of beans cookin' on the stove, the Andrews Sisters whoopin' it up on th' stereo. Nice and homey. She started to like the idea, oh dear, she did. And like most ideas, it fed itself through the night and filled her heart and then the house.

Fender Rhodes was confused at the sudden warmth, the Ah lerve yuh, Fender; the tenderness; even a shadow of that smile of Rotary's she had seen at first (which had been for Diz.) Fender never said I love you. It was a political decision, that was all such a heavy trip.

'Ah lerve you, Fender,' said Rotary Spokes for the fifty-third time that morning.

'But, Rotary, what is love?' said Fender Rhodes, om-ing silently, to centre herself.

'This is lerve,' said Rotary Spokes, lighting a cigarette, and stroking her shoulder.

'I have to meditate,' snapped Fender, and hummed into the ashing fire.

Miles away in the black hills of Dakota, the beautiful coveted Indian country that the sons of America stole, Thomas Pateman, Jesus' natural boy, frothed away to a packed stadium:

'They will lie in they beds an' take pleasure, sinful pleasure of they cursed flesh. And they will laugh as they lust as they lie in the sheets of abandonment, and the satin pillows of shame. THIS IS NOT THE BED OF HOLY MATRIMONY! This is the bed of perverted lustin' and animal desire! They offspring will be damned and their houses will fall down around their monstrous heads!'

And thus it was – in Normal – only Rotary Spokes' womb did not conceive and her house stood firm around her inquity. Damn . . . she'd built the house with her own hands.

On the fourth night of the absence of Fender Rhodes' agile body, Dave the Deep Sea Diver left the harmony at Chateau Hornwinder, and walked around Normal under the stars, his mantra vainly trying to blank out how horny he was feeling. Since she had conceived Astra, he felt she was his. But her home-birth midwife had cautioned against another child, and although the Caravanserai had an esoteric antipathy for allopathic medicine, she had been fitted with a coil, and the tiny thread nestled in her womb.

Dave was also feeling panicky as he had not in a long time: not only was Fender preferring another bed to his, but Rotary Spokes didn't even have a prick. Dave had spent many hours meditating over his prick and marvelling at its, and his, incredible power and beauty. A tiny doubt was mushrooming in his unflawed ego. When in doubt – when the heavens were dark – when his quicksilver tongue was mute – Dave followed his prick.

Tonight it took him down the street to the back of the matte-silver workshop and the glow of the fire through the curtains. He stood still for an hour or so, listening to the sounds and chilled by the vibes.

Fats Domino, murmurs, soft laughter, sighs. Dave waited in confusion; the elements had clouded out the stars, and his crystal hung motionless round his neck. He thought of Rotary Spokes and could only summon pictures of Olive Oyl, Popeye, Yogi Bear, Bluto, the cartoon trash she had flung in the face of his tantric love.

Finally the light switched off and something switched on in Dave's dim mind. He lifted the latch and crept in. Oh, what a farrago for the flaxen-haired boy! Fender Rhodes (who he'd had), and Rotary Spokes (who he wanted) gently nibbling each other's lips with delicious concentration. Oh what a dilemma for Davey-boy and his seven-league rosy prick . . . a hard decision. Dave snaked into a lotus position and gazed ahead of him, four feet from the back of Fender's cradled head. Who, when she turned, was entranced. Here was the *gegenschein*, the male and the female, her guru and her woman lover.

'He's so leonine,' she murmured ecstatically to Rotary Spokes, somewhere around her navel.

Rotary Spokes muttered 'Unnh.'

Then heard, and looked up.

'Wha'!'

'What the!'

'What the damn hail!'

Goddamn Banana, sittin' stitchless in *her* house. Pink and gold flesh in *her* firelight, and with a goddam HARD-ON!

'So . . . leonine . . . like a lion,' rhapsodized Fender.

But to Rotary Spokes, who lived with a savannah-stomping Hug gradually becoming a part of her body; to Rotary Spokes who had ridden into the teeth of a wind at 140 mph on a Harley with a tiger banshee Hug clawing her back, Dave was as much like a lion as an old fur collar or a red-eyed ferret. She lashed out and flung Fender Rhodes onto the floor, leapt out of bed, scooped up Dave and his jester's rags and Fender and her tatters and dumped the lot out in the clouded light.

'Enough is enough,' raged Rotary Spokes, hurling the spinning-wheel after them, ripping the sheets and pillows off the bed and stuffing them into the dying fire.

Tomorrow she would *decontaminate*! Tomorrow she would get the bunch of dickhead assholes on their bus and out of her life!

Tomorrow she would call Reen the Bean, 90% hamburger and good beer, in Middleville, and GIT!

After all, tomorrow, already two hours old, would be another day.

CHAPTER
SEVEN

"Everybody loves my baby
But my baby don't love nobody . . ."
(Fats Waller)

'Reen?'

'Yeah?'

'Reen?'

'YEAH?'

'Uh, umm, Reen, this is Rotary Spokes . . . ah'm real sorry to call yuh so early.'

'SHUDDUP YOUR NOISE,' yelled Reen into the poolhall already humming at 8.30 a.m.

'Who the hell is this? Y'all gonna have to shout.'

'ROTARY SPOKES FROM NORMAL. I MET YOU AT THAT DAMN MOTEL MEETIN'!'

'RIGHT!'

'YOU SAID CALL UP SOMETIME AND PLAY POOL.'

'RIGHT!'

'WAAALL, I'M CALLIN'. I THOUGHT I'D COME OVER TODAY, ANY GOOD?'

'YEAH!' Reen sounded really pleased. 'Great, good, fine, I kin hear you now. I'll be here all day and we kin kill a few balls and a few beers!'

'I'll see you then,' said Rotary Spokes.

She was shaking as she put the phone down. Hell, Reen spoke the same language as her. She showered, towelled her hair dry, slicked a little grease through it, and zipped on black leather.

'Dor'll take care of you, Fluffy,' she said to the disdainful raised eyebrow snuggling in the chair. 'I'll see you soon.'

She rubbed the cat's head, who waited until she had gone to stretch and shake.

'Der hass been alltogedders too motch off dis totch and strock dis vik vid der noddink lonkhair,' she thought fastidiously.

Rotary Spokes took the keys to the bus, the *Every Day is The First Day of the Rest of Your Life* keyring already an old cracked tune. She stuffed the lot into an envelope and pinned it to the door. She locked up, and kicked her magnificent engine into life.

9.15 a.m. Nobody about. The day was hers alone. She spat down the side of the bus and took the road at sixty, eighty, ninety, then a hundred wind-stinging m.p.h.

'Yuh mean tuh tell me, yuh went off with *Diz*?' yelled Reen the Bean over the click of balls and the growl of Pat Benatar. (Ah chose the whole jukebox mahself, Rodry.)

'Yiz,' said Rotary Spokes, mellowing through her fourth afternoon beer. 'Ah went off with her, and she went offa me.'

'Yuh try ringing her?'

'Yiz. The direct'ry said the number was discontinued and no new number under that name.'

'That woman has more new numbers and names than she bin laid,' said Reen.

This sounded like sacrilige . . . real ass-kicking blasphemy.

'Whuchuh mean? Yuh know Diz?'

'Sheee-it, Rodry, lookit that guy over there.'

Rotary Spokes looked. He was tall, unshaven with a luxuriant moustache; long pony-tailed hair, originals over a leather vest sporting a gothic-lettered 'Brotherhood of Satan' through the stains. His bleached denim crotch bulged through a nest of scarlet stitching, and a thin cigarette manoeuvred round his lips like a toothpick.

'That's Lemmie, the guy Diz blew into town with eight years ago. Give her tequila and she gits nostalgic. He was her world record – seven months. Ah bin her *significant other* mahself, three years ago. Can ah pick 'em, or can ah pick 'em?'

'*Sheee-it*!' It had never occurred to Rotary Spokes that Diz was anyone's but hers, or at least, that she had been her first woman. And now Bean, gurgling beer and puffing Marlboros had been there before, and that goddam screwball, a meatier twin of Banana, had been the best, the longest.

'What she tell yuh? Nah. Nah. Lemme guess.' Reen recited: '"You are the one, Rodry. You really press mah buttons. You have taught me so much" . . . and what was the killer? Awiz used to make me cry? "My wonderful baby."' She camped Diz's breathy California accent.

'Yiz,' said Rotary Spokes. 'How did yuh know all them things?'

It turned out that Diz had a surprisingly practical streak where lovers were concerned. She showed an admirable economy of meaningful phrases; significant music – "This is the song I'll play and think of *you*", and "This is *your* colour notepaper". She gave the impression to each new lover that all these things were spontaneous emanations from the sunshine of their love. Bean had even stopped drinking for two weeks when Diz had sighed her heart-felt worries into the fond, impish ear.

'Sheee-it,' said Bean, 'Ah knew a real nice woman here; she met Diz, fell in love . . . you know the rest. On'y she wouldn't go away, and Diz had her commit herself to the state asylum to sort her haid out . . . git rid of paranoid delusions, lahk caring for someone . . . and git out of Diz's life – "You really must shed this heavy number" – '

'But, I really loved her,' Rotary Spokes snuffled into her bourbon.

'Yeah, and ah love Steamship Dutch's ice cream. On'y th'ain't no use puttin' it on no damn statuette pedestal, Rodry. It's gonna make a mess on your bric-a-brac shelf. Fawgit her.'

Three hours later, an off-duty Bean proved her love for Steamship Dutch's ice cream: three scoops of rocky road and maple walnut, doused in marshmallow sauce, pineapple krush, Chok-o-lait cream, burnt almonds, and strawberry slush, the sunset goo at the bottom of the glass swamped in soft pyramids of more marshmallow sauce. Bean hitched her enormous Levis, belched, hicupped, said 'Pardon me' coy as a southern belle, and waddled into the street.

'That's mah baby,' she told Rotary Spokes.

The 'baby' was a silver Ford truck with purple metallic flake streaking each side. Over the windscreen was a green light strip saying GOD over the driver seat and THE VIRGIN MARY over the passenger seat. There was a white sticker on the windscreen saying: 'Repent, oh ye foolish, Jesus is your Personal Saviour. Call *Our Lady of the Thousand Miseries* – TODAY.' Reen scraped at it, swearing.

'Damn church mafia, thcy awiz stickin' that shit on me,' she grunted, heaving into God's driving seat. Rotary Spokes put one toe on the Virgin's running board.

'Guess ah better git along,' she said. (Better not to overstay.)

'WHAAAT?' hollered Bean. 'Yuh on'y just got here – saddle up under the Virgin Mary, Rodry, we gonna hit town.' Rotary Spokes looked embarassed.

'Ah don't ride cars,' she said. 'That's mine.' Reen took in the fabulous Harley cresting the sidewalk in desert dust and gleaming chrome.

'Ah know,' she soothed, 'but you visitin' with me and ah got a bodacious stereo in this honeybunch here. Sheee-it, ah'll put your big baby back of the hall. Bite the nuts offa any motherfucker who touches it.'

She straddled the saddle, kicked and roared into the poolhall, scattering players and raising a few eyebrows.

'This mah friend's bike,' she howled over Aretha Franklin, 'touch it, yuh bastards, and yuh don't shoot no more balls in *heah*!'

Rotary Spokes climbed into the truck, pushing her shades on.

'*And . . .* ' Bean told her, roaring into a backward arc, 'this ain't no *car*. This here's a TRUCK, and it's *mah* truck.'

'Sorry,' mumbled Rotary Spokes.

Reen roared through the town, leering at the traffic policewomen, hurling obscenities at the policemen deaf in their storm-trooper helmets; jerking to a screen-shattering halt when any woman wanted to cross the road; luring men onto pedestrian crossings with a lessening of speed, only to jump them back onto the sidewalks as her dainty foot hit the gas. She careered to a stop.

'This's mah place,' she said, puffing up eight flights of stairs, and:

'*Babies!*' she screeched like Bette Davis, as she flung the door wide and two slender white-furred bodies clawed up her legs and boa-ed round her neck. 'Marlita, Fifina, babies,' she crooned.

'You'd like my friend Dor,' said Rotary Spokes.

'She another dirty mouth fat-ass dyke?'

'Hell, Reen, no . . . she ain't no dyke,' she said, unaware of the brown-auraed vigil outside her distant door the night before. 'Hell, she really likes fucking with men . . . but she's real nice. She's the only one I told about Diz – till today.'

'Watch yuh ass, gal. Nuthin' lahk knowin' it's there to bring 'em runnin'.'

'Naaah. She wouldn't even know what to do.' Rotary Spokes was also unaware of the 'homewuk' Dor was doing, back in Normal.

'Did *you* know how to do it? Did yuh? When yuh jumped in the sack with Diz?'

'Waaall,' Rotary Spokes was scarlet.

'It just come natural to you?'

'Yiz . . . ah guess.'

'That's the way of it. Sheee-it, ah'm gonna shower. You wanna scrub mah back?'

Rotary Spokes wandered around the large room while the water hissed and splattered next door. Did Reen . . .? There was a poster of two women kissing on one wall. Did Reen want to . . . ? A picture of Reen in the bath with, undeniably, another woman. Lordy, Lordy, a lifetime of nothing, and then Diz, and then damn Fender . . . ah must just be a natural degenerate, she thought.

'When ah said, yuh wanna scrub my back,' said Bean, rubbing her thick hair with a daffodil Elena von Hechtenstein towel, 'Ah wuz not tryin' to git into your pants. If you was worried. Ah lahk yuh, Rodry, let's keep it that way.' Rotary Spokes was relieved. She knew, since Fender, that she could fake it, but it left a sour taste. Bean rolled a joint. Rotary Spokes took it.

'Where yuh git this stuff?'

'Just cuz ah don't fuck with Diz don't mean ah don't deal with her. She got a little "arrangement" with the sheriff. Best bet.'

'Is this against the law?'

'Rotary Spokes, where yuh been all yuh lahf? Yeah it's against the law. And so is what you done with Diz. It ain't on no statute books, but it just as well might be. Cuz you ain't gonna git no civic recognition for it. If you was St. Theresa of Avila, it would knock yuh halo offa yuh haid. Mary Magdalene got forgiven for whorin', but you an' me . . . they ain't no Resurrection or Heaven for us, dear heart. And ah figure, fine – no Heaven, no Hell. Where yuh want to go tonight?'

'I leave that to you. I don't know nuthin' 'bout –'

'About birthin' babies?' finished Reen. 'You never seen *Gone with the Wind*?' she said, full-volume incredulous. 'NEVER?

'Damn,' she said, 'You got a lot of educatin' to do. Ah was kicked outta fourth grade, wrong attitude and a bad influence, but I kin show yuh around. Yuh wanna see Diz?'

'No!' Rotary Spokes jerked back.

'Git the lovelight outta your eyes. Cold light of a few weeks after? Never mind. Later,' said Bean, sucking the dear so dear and miraculous drug into her tortured lungs.

'Thass better.'

The night was young and through its childhood traumas, Bean and Rotary Spokes toured all the bars where Bean had taken a shine to one or more of the waitresses. Tottering along the sidewalk around nine o'clock, they were noted by the busy pastel-clad Karen Schuchter, the leaflet lady, who happily skipped to the wrong conclusion: like attracts like, and she might have guessed Bean was *one of them*. She dithered over letting them know about the second, booster meeting of her 'baby', the Magdalena Janus Ladies Society. Well, we are all God's children, and all God's children got – rhythm? Swing? She checked herself as the pair lurched into a garbage can. But all God's children got dee doo dat dee doo … dollars, and Karen mentally pencilled them onto the mailing list: dollars fit snug into pockets in Middlesville and she was a woman whose dream needed every buck she could raise.

As the evening neared its difficult adolescence, Reen and Rotary Spokes chomped their way through some four pounds of hamburger and two Caesar salads. This was observed by a wraith-like figure, pale eyes masked in dark spectacles corrected for acute myopia. Leonora Hendriksen had never had that night on the town with Bean, and decided to shadow the pair to see what she, the eternal outcast, was missing.

'Yuh gotta eat good,' said Bean, topping ninety degrees of a fourteen-inch black cherry cheesecake with Simulo Supa-Krem, which in her stomach mulched with red wine. In her booth, Leonora pushed a slice of cucumber around her plate and sipped Perrier.

'Well, pumpkin, where to now?'

'Yuh doin' a real good sight seein' tour, Reen. It's up to you. I don't mind.'

'Waaall, Miz Scarlett, y'oughtta mind,' Reen splintered her fist into the table. 'Yuh on'y got one life and yuh oughtta mind, Rodry. Tell me and we'll find it.'

Rotary Spokes thought, tuning into the piped blues. It was *Mr Bojangles*, 'the old soft shoes' and suddenly, overpoweringly, she wanted to see Diz. The beer made her invincible, romantic, horny as hell. She swept aside the silent telephone, the chill white letter. She could overwhelm Diz, light the fire again.

'Nah,' said Bean, 'you're pissed as a tadpole in a puddle of moonshine, Rodry. You think she's gonna fall over backwards for somethin' stinkin' like an empty sherry cask? Come on pumpkin, you're here to have fun . . . screw *her*!'

That struck Rotary Spokes as hilarious and her guffaw had them thrown out into the sophisticated, perfumed middle age of the Middlesville main drag. Rotary Spokes stumbled, her head at ninety degrees to her body as every shawled, kaftanned, sandaled, scented woman loomed mistily Diz.

'Aw-right, you grade-A dingleberry, we'll go there. But watch yuhself. Sheee-it, ah'm never wrong, and ah don't like this one bit.'

Somehow, Reen navigated the Dizless wastes across town and Rotary Spokes started to sober up or at least, realize how drunk she was, as she recognized the corner store, a street lamp, a sacred crack in a paving stone.

'Mebbe not, Bean,' she said.

'Make up yuh mahnd, woman!'

So they spilled back and forth around the street, while the dogs began to bark and the hounds began to howl. Yiz. No. Mebbe. NO! YIZ!

Finally they negotiated the iron stairs to Diz's rainbow door. George Benson charmed the night, and they knocked and stood, doubting for several reasons that their legs could support them much longer. Below, Leonora Hendriksen hovered in the street, her strikingly European mac turned up at the collar for anonymity. Diz opened the door.

'Well, wow, Bean!' she flirted, and then stopped. 'Rhoda . . . what a surprise.'

Down the foaming rapids of feeling, Diz paddled her feather-light skiff, laughing and bubbling like froth on Californian champagne. Rotary Spokes was struck dumb, sitting smoking on the, she now saw, faded cover of their and everyone else's bed. Diz perked decaffeinated coffee, poured bourbon, flipped records, lit incense, and swayed around among the multi-coloured hangings.

'You know the Caravanserai?' said Rotary Spokes suddenly.

'No, Rhoda . . . does it feel good?' arched Diz from the other side of Reen. Rotary Spokes stumbled to the toilet.

'Get her out,' hissed Diz suddenly to Bean.

'Hell no, Diz, that's my friend *Rotary* Spokes. I do believe you been toyin' with her affections. I ain't gonna clean up your mess,' said Bean, pinching Diz's lean thigh.

'Get her out! Why did you bring her here? She's so . . .'

'Unbalanced?' finished Reen. 'So was I. *"Maybe you'd better see a therapist, Bean."* Everybody's unbalanced when you finished with screwin' em. Get *yourself* outta this one, Diz Darling.'

Diz ushered them out rapidly, with lies about meeting Rotary Spokes to *talk* the next evening. Oh Diz, oh dear, never light a spark of hope in a fond and drunken brain. Rotary Spokes was almost sober with joy as they took an hour or so over the twelve blocks back to Reen's place.

'She's gonna talk to me! She does care! She said she *values my friendship*! Oh, Reen, and I been thinkin' such terrible things. She's gonna talk to me!'

They collapsed on the sofa, to Siamese yowls and lively scarves of white around both their necks.

'Talk about somethin' else – I'll talk about Diz after breakfast,' mumbled Reen.

Talk about something else? What else was there to talk about?

'I got a cat. Fluffy,' she managed, casting around for small talk.

'No shit, ain't they just the best?'

Rotary Spokes thought of the scornful silken creature, currently disdaining Pukina Cat Chow as Dor wolfed fresh fish and cream.

'I guess,' she said, slumping sideways. Diz was like her cat, she thought. Soft, warm, and real proud. What a woman!

'Yuh wanna sleep in my bed? C'mon, no shit, Rodry, sometimes it's just nice not to be alone.'

The Hug warily consented, sheathed its claws and dozed over them for the rest of the night. Rotary Spokes woke, no regrets, and curled around Bean's hot 224 pounds in the back-broken bed. Reen cupped her hand around one melon breast, and so the sun found them.

'I slept like a baby,' said Rotary Spokes.

'Woman, you got some heart in you,' said Bean. 'I'll be down the pool hall when y'all want to raise your sweet self.'

Two pints of black coffee and a megavitamin pill sent Reen out into the white heat of 8 a.m., amd Rotary Spokes dozed in the great warm cavern, Fifina and Marlita curling over her.

'Ah'll tell yuh what,' said Bean, as she watched Rotary Spokes preening, preparing with fluttering heart to speak to Diz. 'Wash the grease outta yuh hair.'

'What? I wanna look my best, Reen,' she said, stroking her slicked back hair.

'Waaall, grease is out, Rodry. A real no-no. Sheee-it, ah stopped wearin' grease soon's I seen what it does to the piller cases.'

'I don't alwiz wear it, Bean. Just when I want to hold my head high . . . I was wearin' it at the motel, and she liked it just fine.'

'Am I yuh Guardian Angel or what?' demanded Bean. 'Wash your goddam hair and blow it dry.'

'Sheee-it,' Rotary Spokes was about to say: *Girls* blow-dry their hair.

'Yuh see!' said Bean a half hour later, 'Yuh got real good thick hair, and it stands up swell.'

'I might as well put on a damn dress!' grumbled Rotary Spokes, blushing at the short blonde cloud around her face.

'Brings out your eyes real nice, dearheart. You are a damn fine-lookin' woman, Rodry, and I seen enough to know.'

Rotary Spokes remembered fourteen and fifteen when she had long thick plaits and needed to fight off the boys scrabbling at her blouse and skirt. She hadn't worn skirts since, and had slashed the whole mess of hair off with kitchen scissors. Kept it almost the same way ever since.

'What yuh got under your jacket – apart from your bodacious ta-tas?'

Reen howled as Rotary Spokes blushed again. 'Like a goddam virgin,' Bean chuckled.

'I got my Harley T-shirt, Bean. What's wrong with that?'

'You borrer mah seduction shirt, woman,' said the Guardian Angel, pulling a purple silk shirt from the closet. 'Yuh wear that and a nice thin black tie and if she don't love you, it just proves she's got no damn taste. Which I personally have suspected ever since she got rid of *me*.'

Rotary Spokes slouched into the fine soft folds, tight as an onion skin on Reen, and stared savagely at the definitely sexy, definitely feminine figure in the mirror.

'Fuck you, Bean,' she exploded. 'I feel like . . . I don't feel right.'

The heavenly body slugged bourbon into a crystal glass.

'Drink that,' she said and put on a record. 'Now yuh dance a little and git yourself in the mood.'

Crazy came through the speakers. Rotary Spokes choked on laughing and told Bean about Gooseneck Squash's quest for Patsy Klein.

'The woman's been dead twenty years.'

Rotary Spokes looked at the cover.

'What, oh lawd, Bean no! Damn, what can I tell Goosenick?'

'This is Ladies' Night. We can talk about that tomorrer. Now, check yourself out. Your billfold? Tobacco? Papers? Your fancy gold lighter? Now your Angel Gabriel's gonna complete you.' Bean dabbed perfume onto Rotary Spokes' startled neck, and pushed a small plastic package into her pocket.

'What's that?'

'It's Acapulco Gold. Bit like takin' oil to Texas, but ah bin savin' it for a special occasion. And you are that occasion. And the perfume – that's Paris perfume. From Paris, France. The best. Ah'll be here all evenin' if it don't work out. Don't want yuh roamin' the streets with a broken heart, wouldn't be fair to the good citizens of Middlesville, and y'all so gorgeous. Now. Go to it, gal, git.'

Rotary Spokes strode but tentatively down the street, sure that everyone could smell the 200-dollars-an-ounce perfume and see through the black leather to the clinging silk. Too embarassed to take Dutch courage at the humming neon bars en route, she climbed the iron stairs, stone-cold sober. Diz looked surprised and distant.

'Oh, you. You better come in, I guess,' she said – promises come easy and so does amnesia in the world of Diz Darling. Rotary Spokes' blood reached 170 degrees as she slipped off her jacket, waiting for laughter. Diz said nothing about it, gave her a drink, rolled a joint.

Diz curled into a chair, thinking rapidly. Simeon was due back at 10.00. It was 8.05. She juggled desire, minutes and seconds in her buzzing brain.

'How long are you in town?' she asked casually. Simeon would be away for two days soon.

'I don't know. Just a few days, stayin' with Bean.'

Diz lied. 'Ah, darlin' little Bean. I really love her.' She compounded the lie. 'She's one of my oldest friends, you know?' she confided through her long, long lashes. She decided to stall . . . get her out by 9.30, and make another meeting time. Her tongue flicked along her lips, apparently unaware of the growling, pounding heart four feet ahead of it.

But something feline must have charged the air. In the pampered menagerie of Diz's heart a cream-fed kitten awoke, and flexed its dinky needle-sharp claws. It rated Rotary Spokes as an unusually large, loose-woven ball of fluffy mohair, and began to pat and play.

'Well . . . ' mewed Diz, 'we weren't exactly thunder and lightning between the sheets, darling.'

Rotary Spokes recalled an Amazonian rainstorm . . . but the kitten had tired of that easily-teased strand.

'There's always something *different* with women,' dallied Diz.

Allowing another tender strand to unravel.

'I've never felt the need to commit myself either way.' The tiny claws were shredding near the centre now.

'They's never been no question for me,' mumbled Rotary Spokes. Should there have been? Should she have faked something with a guy? The Hug snarled, loathe to unleash the power of unsheathed claws.

'Have you ever done it with a man?' The kitten sat back, licking one tiny paw.

'Well, I, Diz, you know I haven't. I never did feel that way about any man. I never did feel that way till I met you.'

Feelings! The kitten wrinkled its pink nose at the shreds and strands littering the floor between them, yawned a tiny rosebud yawn fringed with dagger teeth, and snoozed again in Diz's heart.

Diz was left with the whole untidy mess – tedious, grossly uncool – and hardly *her* responsibility. What did *she*, curled neatly around iced tea, have to do with the stripping and clawing of Rotary Spokes? *She* would never have done anything so ferocious. She swept the whole painful bruised and bleeding nuisance into a sterilized package – emotional involvement; commitment; and – Lord Jesus over easy on a raft – LOVE, whatever that was supposed to be; she sealed the package with her wide-eyed, chill smile, and deposited it at Rotary Spokes' feet.

Briskly she yawned, stretched and feigned weariness. She suggested that tomorrow would be a busy day for her, and she had better go to bed. On the word, her eyes drooped suggestively, out of habit, and she purred 'alone' to the open and gasping heart in front of her. Perhaps

Rotary Spokes would like to come back for a *real* talk before she left town. In fact, she, Diz, would really like that. There was surely a lot to say.

This was all wrong. Rotary Spokes had been checked, castled, captured; all her tiny stalwart pawns, the 'do you remember' the 'didn't you really like?', the 'wasn't it fun?' and 'oh, darlin', let's do it again!' – all swept from the board, this precious board of Time With Diz. Everything had been decimated by knowing and bored smiles; annihilated by almost unremarkable sighs; nuked by wide blue incredulity.

The feeling came over her that Diz had never been in all those shared and precious places, the sacred shrines of memory. But there was nothing she said or did that you could pick up and throw back at her.

Rotary Spokes felt as though she had lost when she had not been playing to win. When she didn't even know what game Diz had elected to play.

Diz flung open a window to the street, where once she had giggled while Rotary Spokes rolled cigarettes one-handed.

'I've passed the equinox of my experience with nicotine, Rhoda. I mean, it really invades my life space, you know?'

No, no, . . . but I'll sure as hell learn, thought Rotary Spokes wildly, stubbing out her cigarette.

Queen captured, king checkmated in talk of fulfillment with men, at 9.45, Diz taunted her with a bodylong hug at the open door. For Diz, this meant *I'm keeping you on ice, you flattering baby*; for Rotary Spokes, it could mean only one thing. Her bruised lips met Diz's so gently, lingering, warm, soft . . . oh Jesus, why'd we waste time *talking*? Her heart would burst with longing, and then Diz's strong lean hands led her shoulders towards the doorway, and her blue-green eyes stared deep . . . and *cold*? YES, spat The Hug . . . deep and cold . . . *Diz* . . . *cold*? Never, said the faithful heart, but The Hug knew better.

'Come and see me Friday,' said Diz, three minutes behind schedule.

After all, she had to get all the smoke out, punch the creases from the cushions and slide in her cap and spermicidal gel before Simeon and his willing prick came in. He *hated* all that stuff. Rotary Spokes walked up the street, feeling she had just fought ten rounds. What of, she didn't know. Shadow boxing?

Diz had been pleased to see her.
Hadn't she?
She had hugged her.
Hadn't she?
She had kissed her.
Had she?
She bought a quart of bourbon and strode back to Reen's, oblivious of the admiring gazes and second glances whirling around her tall figure, jacket over one shoulder, parting the crowds in the Mall.

At Reen's, Sylvester Stallone was punching his way out of *Rocky VII*. Another woman, almost a twin of Reen's as to physique, was sitting on the edge of the sofa, jerking forward with every punch, slapping her fist and shouting.

'GO ON! GIT 'IM, GO, YOU STUPID BASTARD! KILL 'IM! FEINT, YUH DAMN AIRHEAD! DUCK! SLAP 'IM AROUND THE PARK!' She flung herself back, swallowed a great gust of smoke and said to Rotary Spokes:

'Damn film man don't know how to fight . . . sheee-it, I wish I'd done these scenes mahself. ASSHOLE!' she told Sylvester as he curled his unmemorable lip and threw a wild hook.

'Waaall? Waaall?' demanded Reen, a rosy Buddha.

'Waaall . . . nuthin'. She said to come back an' have another chat before I leave town.'

'BOOOOOO!' yelled Reen.

'Whooziz?' said the other woman, mouthing obscenities at the limping fight.

'Diz. Darlin' Diz *Darling.*' said Reen.

'Diz! Jesus, she still messing good girls around with all that peace, love and bi-sexuality shit?' The woman grinned at Rotary Spokes. 'You're too good for her, honey; come an' bust your cherry with me. I'll appreciate yuh.'

'That's real neighbourly of yuh,' drawled Rotary Spokes, loosening her tie. 'Real nice.' She sauntered into the toilet.

'Where did you find *her*?' said Jo-Marie Lesenbrecht. She and Reen had been at Madame Rufflette's Academy for Young Ladies years before. They had discovered their own version of natural joy behind the gym when they were thirteen or so, and had spent the next couple of decades looking, with fond hearts and dwindling hopes, for Ms. Right.

'She's somethin' else!' said Jo-Marie, with true appreciation. Reen condensed Rotary Spokes' Normal life into three minutes. Up to the present when Normal just wasn't good enough.

Returning to the sofa, Rotary Spokes relaxed. She certainly was Something Else, thought Jo-Marie. And she was fresh in town. At one time in Middlesville there had been eight gay women. Six of them had leapt into three mortgages and might as well have been married for all they put themselves about. Friendship was one thing, and there was no better friend in the universe than Reen, but Jo-Marie had made several fruitless trips across the States looking for love. Yup, they had all come to nothing, and here she was.

She stunned Rotary Spokes with the weird and wonderful tales of her travels. Her life's journey. A few weeks before, Middlesville had seemed like a metropolis to Rotary Spokes. Now bourbon brought forth the lurid trans-continental memoirs of Jo-Marie Lesenbrecht; it was a twentieth-century gay decameron. Sacrilege soared to new and ridiculous heights.

Jo-Marie closed her eyes, swallowed bourbon and sucked smoke. She was now in a bar in Chicago. Just on her way to a fag wedding in The Scorpion, – where you could be guaranteed of some kind of sting in the tail.

'And when I got there, the guy who was marryin' Bruce and Wayne was sayin' "Do you take this man as often as you can, for as long as it lasts?" Then he leant over to Bruce and said "Say it, you fascinatin' monster, say I do, else, goddamit, I'm gonna do it for yah!" He was a minister of the Order of the Sisters of Perpetual Indulgence. It was all weddings that year. There was an open-air one where the preacher started dancin' on the tables, and flashin' his robe up – not a stitch under it – and it turned out *he* was a woman – Reverend Meretricious Delicious!'

'Waaall, I'll git me a one-way to Podunk!' said Rotary Spokes. 'So what was *her* leanin's? I'm real confused.'

'No more 'en she was! She was just one of them women who adores gay men, a real fag-hag. I've met quite a few.' said Jo-Marie, 'Reen, you remember Alleluia Alison. She wound up marryin' Maxine L'Aureole, the big, and I mean *Big* Brazilian drag star so as he wouldn't be deported. They used to have immigration officers round to their place to check 'em out, and everything did appear to be in order – dresses, nightgowns, pants, make-up and pyjamas. Only all the make-up and dresses belonged to him. She sure as hell wore the pants in that marriage!'

He, she, he as she, she as he; women who liked women; women who liked men dressed as women; men who even had operations to be like women *and* like women . . . or men . . . Rotary Spokes began to feel that she was relatively uncomplicated. Damn! she felt Normal. And she was not referring to her adopted town.

'And my mother, in River Bend, Wyoming,' continued Jo-Marie, sucking air through her teeth. 'She said, when we was all hippies, you can't tell the boys from the girls with all that long hair. Then when I cropped mine, she said: "You cain't tell the girls from the boys! Why cain't you be like your nice friend Dolores, with nice clothes and a elegant way of sitting? And lacquered nails, and a nice permanent?" Trouble was, Dolores used to be Jeremy, and when my mom met him, he'd just about finished with the injections and the operation. "Nice to meet a well brought-up gal," my mom said. Dolores was about delirious, he was so flattered!'

Rotary Spokes hooted.

'What about your mother, Rodry?' said Bean.

'Waaall,' even Rotary Spokes' silk and leather-clad confidence faltered at the thought of the gaunt and ravaged woman who had raised six of them and buried five more, driving a wastrel husband out to work with a fury that would have made Lorie-Kay and Mar'Ann look soft, even indulgent towards Gooseneck and Lucas.

'She had a tough time, what with the farm goin' to rack and ruin.'

She recalled the piercing grey eyes though the bus window when she had left, years before.

'Never darken this land with your ungrateful feet again,' she had said. 'You ain't no natural child of mine, and I've thought it for many a year. No natural child leaves her mother, without she's got a good man as can care for her.'

'Waaall,' she said to Jo-Marie and Bean, 'she said I'd never find the man as would take me on. She said I didn't have no feelings for my kind. Hell, I ain't seen her in years. Could be dead. I dunno.'

'And don't git no ideas 'bout motherin' her,' Bean told Jo-Marie,

'Josie's speciality is motherin'. Y'all don't need no t.l.c. that way, Rodry.'

'Yeah,' said Rotary Spokes, putting her mother out of her mind in a cloud of smoke, the way the bus exhaust had blotted out her black, unwavering figure in the featureless landscape.

'What about your mother, Bean?'

Bean smiled and blew a kiss into mid-air.

'She said "Anything you want to do, my baby Maureen, remember your mother's always here for you. I gave you birth and I ain't gonna live to regret it. Call collect if you need to, and there is dollars here if you need 'em and I got 'em. If you find happiness with women, then I wish you the best. Cuz nothin' in this life is easy. Particularly if you don't run with the herd." She'd like it if I went to church, but she don't push it none.'

'My mother still asks me when I'm gittin' married,' said Jo-Marie, snorting. '"Is they anything you should tell your mom? I do wish you'd do yourself up purdy when your cousins is here. Herb has a real flourishin' law practice now, and your sister Nona Ruth is settin' her cap for him, but he alwiz was sweet on you."' She mimicked the tremulous hope.

'Mebbe I'm better off 'n you,' said Rotary Spokes. 'Least mine ain't got no way of gittin' in touch with me.' But she felt wistful for the warmth Bean had spoken of. No matter. That was life. And this here, with friends, bein' herself, that was life, too. Like she'd never dreamed it could be.

'So, when are you goin' to *chat* with Diz?'

'Friday, Bean, Friday for sure. I'll call her up, though.'

'She know you're stayin' here?

'Yiz, I guess.'

'Waaall, let the goddamed piranha call you up. She has a telephone, doodle-brain. Let *her* chase.'

'And if she don't?'

'Child, they is a lot of livin' to do in Middlesville, without moonin' around about Diz Darlin'. Put yourself out a bit, we'll find a party or two. See who else is around and let 'em see you too! Not every dyke here is a life-size inflatable like me an' Josie, though I always have said, "If you got it, flaunt it," eh, Josie? She ain't seen nuthin' yet! Give her a chance!' Bean said, and then, turning to Rotary Spokes, she added:

'Jo-Marie has this habit of falling in lust with every pretty face that comes along.'

Jo-Marie play-punched Reen, and mumbled: 'Call yuh tomorrer.' She crushed Rotary Spokes and let herself out, saying: 'I guess that's the nearest ah'll ever git. Bean knows too much about me to let her precious baby get corrupted. Ah, waaall, fuck you, Bean, you're too good.'

'And fuck you too, darlin',' said Bean blowing kisses all the way down the stairwell.

'Bed,' said Bean. 'Jo-Marie's been drinkin' since ten this mornin'. She ain't even gonna remember her own name in the sweet dawn light.'

Rotary Spokes woke on Friday, feeling like Boudicca. Only she wasn't the type to take no mean advantage with knives on her chariot wheels. The morning she mooched around boutiques in the mall, waiting for The Shirt to leap off the rails. Hell, she and Diz were going to *talk*, she knew, but Jo-Marie and Bean had delighted in warning her how important clothes were. She still felt best in black leather and a Harley T-shirt, but now she was looking for a fabric which would leave her invincible. But somewhere at the heart of her unrequited Hug, she knew that no leather, silk, linen, velvet or sateen would proof her against the invisible venom darts that had festered since the last time she saw Diz.

Goddam! It was easy for the Big Bean to talk!

'Stand up to her, Rodry! She ain't the finest thang in the universe. The heart you got in your body is bigger than the whole of her, girl!'

She couldn't explain how Diz made her feel. Helpless? Exposed? Bean could never have been In Love with Diz, she told herself desperately, buttoning wild silk and scowling in the mirror. If she had loved her, she thought, frowning over velvet shot with gold, she'd never have left her.

'Aw, Jesus!' said The Hug, pacing, 'Look at yourself! She loved you in your Harley T-shirt and leather. If she don't love you now, they ain't no fabrics on this earth – and particularly in the Middlesville Smooch-O-Boutique – gonna make her love you again!'

But Rotary Spokes believed in love eternal. Hadn't Dor said:

'If you find it, girl, hang on in there, tooth and claw.' But what if tooth and claw is offered the unflawed surface of indifference?

surface with no purchase? She had snuffled over enough movies with Dor to know that if you tried hard enough, then love would be yours. It was always the holding back that stopped you winning through. Never let it be said that I could have won if only I'd tried harder, thought Rotary Spokes, grimly ignoring the price tag on a batikked silk tunic. That was the sort of thing Diz went for. She looked into her own troubled gray eyes. Was that the sort of thing Diz went for?

Half a pint of bourbon assured her that it would be. She sped home, showered, washed and blow-dried her hair. She dressed herself. The damn tunic was unlike anything she had ever worn. Well, if Diz was tired of the way she looked, she ought to love her this way.

Bean hummed the *Dead March*.

'Cut that shit out, Bean!'

'Ain't no shit. Ah'm just givin' a intro to suit the look you got on your face. Come on home if it ain't no good. Better still, don't go.'

'But, Bean,' Rotary Spokes plastered a mask of happiness over her face, 'it'll be fine.'

Reen the Bean stared at her while she dialled a number.

'Jo-Marie? Rotary Spokes is just goin' over for a special meetin' with Diz. I'm fulla forebodin'. What do you think – hey, bye, Rodry – remember we're here, best of luck, honey – Jo-Marie? She's just gone. What do you think that damned woman do have in her mind?'

'You want me to come over, Reen?'

'Sure as hell do, Josie dear. I give it three hours and then they's gonna be a fine mess to wipe up. Bye.'

Lovin' is the thing I crave,
For your love I'd be your slave,
You gotta give me some . . .

Rotary Spokes chugged the blues nervously through her mind. Bad news! It was the same blues Dor played when she was waitin' for what she called a late riser.

She knocked at the rainbow door.

'Rhoda! What a surprise!'

Surprise? Rotary Spokes allowed herself to laugh.

'Simeon, Jalna, this is Rhoda E. Spokes, from Normal.'

The air in the room was fighting with patchouli, joss-sticks and dope. On the rug, Simeon, unbuttoned to the waist, leered over a bong. Jalna sat half-lotus at his side. Goddam! Another nodder!

Another scarlet-stitched fly! Will I always have this problem, thought Rotary Spokes, that all men look the same to me? And over it all, Diz was grinning like she was delighted about something. Rotary Spokes stood awkward, her bottle of Cold Duck welded to her fist.

'Rhoda has this real hostility problem,' purred Diz. 'Sit. Join us. I must turn the soyburgers.'

Rotary leant in the kitchen doorway.

'What's goin' on, Diz?'

'Goin' on!' falsettoed Diz. 'Why, what are you being so heavy about?'

'I thought we was goin' to talk.'

'Rhoda, these are my oldest friends. Anything you have to talk about can be shared with them. We have this real, like, indefinable rapport. Simeon and I really ground each other. Yeah. Like, earth-contact. And *Jalna*, I'd realy like to share Jalna with you – we have this whole vibe going for us – you know, energy, yin, music, you know?'

'She your lover?'

'Oh, Rhoda! You're so, like, *yang*. About everything! Relax. *Be.*'

Diz bestowed a meaningless chill kiss on Rotary Spokes' set mouth.

'God, take the demons out of your eyes, Rhoda,' she said, muttering something else over the sputtering soyburgers. The bean-pulp stuck in Rotary Spokes' throat. The alfalfa sprouts and mung beans formed a trap in her mouth and she gnashed away and finally, forced the cloying mess down. Simeon nodded at Diz.

'Like, you really poison your system with alcohol, Diz.' Diz looked humbled.

'I guess,' she said and obediently sipped water.

'What's your substitute for this here libation?' said Rotary Spokes. 'You smoked three a them joints since *I* been here, and you tellin' her she cain't have a drink?' Simeon looked pained and faked humility.

'Maybe you know something I don't,' he said.

(Damned right! For a start this was supposed to be a date, a talk between me and her, thought Rotary.)

The meaningless minutes ticked away. Rotary Spokes let the joint go by. Suck smoke from where Simeon's lips had been? She thought of an evening of TV with Bean and Jo-Marie. Git yourself together, she ordered. Be sociable.

'What do you do?' she asked Jalna.

'Well,' Jalna's nods slowed significantly. 'I guess my life's direction is, uh, leaning towards, you know, uh, global networks.'

'Global networks. I'll be hog-tied. What sorta networks are they?'

Jalna paled at the direct question.

'*You* know,' she breathed, one tapering arm embracing the cosmic miasma. 'I'm really, like, *into*, the older parts of our planet. There's so much wisdom in the soil . . . the air, there. I'm like, facilitating wholefood cooperatives throughout Europe.'

'Europe,' said Rotary Spokes slowly.

'You know, we're going to get, I mean, like *buy*, purchase, an old-world ship between here and Europe, and then the *people* can, like, travel globally, without, you know, nutrition pollution, as they, uh, wander the globe.'

'Wow,' sighed Diz with glowing eyes.

'Yeah. Like, it's already happening. There's this really cool commune, like, in Bordeaux, France, right? Like – they have nothing, zero, like no water, no electricity. And they've really sweated – but the sweat is *no sweat* – like their love is the whole synthesis of the New Age. Everything . . .'

'Bordeaux; well I never,' said Rotary Spokes with an edge of sarcasm lost among the smoke.

Jalna sat with legs spread, as good as embracing Diz, as good as embracing Simeon. Simeon placed one veined and ringed hand on Jalna's knee; with the other, he massaged Diz's foot. His grin circled round to Rotary Spokes, and she stood up.

'I guess I'll be *splittin'*,' she drawled.

Diz feigned surprise. Jalna nodded. Simeon shook his head with regret. Rotary Spokes was gone before Diz was only half on her feet. She didn't trust herself to let Diz touch her, not being given to physical violence by choice. She strode home, breathing deep the clean air, swaggered into the living room of Reen the Bean and kissed Jo-Marie and Reen full on the lips.

'Waaall?' said Reen, anxiously.

'I NEVER HEARD SO MUCH GODDAM SHIT OUTSIDE OF A TEXAS LIVESTOCK EXCHANGE!' yelled Rotary Spokes, slinging her jacket on the floor, ripping the tunic from her back and sliding into her Harley T-shirt.

'Nice!' said Jo-Marie. 'Y'outta *talk* to Diz more often if we git a floor show after!'

'Any good movies tonight?' asked Rotary Spokes, grabbing the bourbon.

'I brought ya a real treat,' said Jo-Marie. '*Polyester*, on a video.'

'*Polyester?*'

'Yup. the one and only Divine rippin' apart the fake fabric of our society. You watch it, girl. And you better fall in love with Miss Edith Massey, playin' Cuddles.' Rotary Spokes' eyebrows shot up at the credits.

'Tab *Hunter?*' she said.

Twenty minutes in, she protested.

'They can't *do* this on film!'

'Just you wait!' said Jo-Marie, shaking with laughter. Reen massaged Rotary Spokes' knees.

'Shut your hick mouth and watch, baby,' she said. 'And keep your scratch-and-sniff card handy.'

Two Divine hours later, Rotary Spokes' ribs aching with laughter, she said:

'I don't think I'll ever eat pizza again!'

'Here's to Edith Massey!' Jo-Marie swayed the toast. 'She died last year in Baltimore and, from what I hear, everybody was drunk for a fortnight!'

'Edith Massey,' said Rotary Spokes, bourbon burning down her throat like a live wire.

CHAPTER
EIGHT

"I feel just like a turtle
Hidin' underneath its horny shell
But y' see I'm very well protected
I know this goddam life too well."
(Turtle Blues, Janis Joplin)

Carolee P. Hodges had been in Middlesville seven months and was o.d.ing on a reality so gross that she felt that she was tripping most of the time. Maybe they were seeding the clouds, for chrissake, or flooding the distant reservoir with mind-control drugs. And the food – you could only get tofu products at one store in the place. And the bars – hassling her for an ID, scrutinizing every word and number on her fake California driver's licence, like it was in a strange language. And that haze over the sky most of the time – an addict of drive-in 3D movies, she felt she was in The Bubble. Or Stepford. Or Amityville . . . Jesus!

Her florid pop, Abner J. Hodges, Jr., had been hand-picked to head the Middlesville Moral Revival Squad – a ripe and unwilling flesh fruit from the golden vineyards of the West Coast. There, he and his chosen helpmate Corah Hodges and their dear blessed progeny (Praise the Lord!) had been soaking up the sun and sweating his Loving Way for thirteen years. Amen Lord, the dollars came easy, the converted fell at their feet and worldly goods ornamented their split-level ranch house at the head of a dazzling blue valley.

They had not always been so blessed – the Lord giveth and the Lord taketh away – Carolee had no memory of the first four years of her life when her manicured, coiffured, tailor-made mom had been thin and patched, and her fervent, paunchy pop had been gaunt and earnest.

They had towed a trailer around the grassroots of the Lord's movement, and he had chosen to reward their toil a hundredfold. For now the movement was sweeping forty-three states with an income and style that passeth all understanding. They had little time for the commie 'Love your unworthy brother' sentiments of the Risen Christ. They held literally to the Old Testament, and the scorched earth, raze and be raised revelations of the new leader of the movement, Merry Fullwell, the widow of the founder. Divine Word singled her out for its astonishing messages as she cruised this earthly desert in her custom Cadillac, bearing the flaming sword of righteousness to the wild. Merry spoke the Word and the movement joyously did the deed, leaving in its wake wrecked lives, broken spirits and the tatters of unworthy ambitions. *Then* there was a Way for people touched by the Word to drag themselves upright again, and it came only through the guiding hands of the Movement's leaders and ministers. Celestial Inspiration had unleashed a flow of megabucks into these chosen hands, and they had set up meeting halls, churches, community centres and colleges. In Abner J.'s living room there was a map of the United States, the colour of dried blood across each state where chosen cities and towns bristled with the flags and pins of moral ascendancy.

'Amen, Lord,' said Abner J. Hodges, the new principal of the Middlesville College of Habakkuk, gazing for the last time over the azure Californian valley and trying to square his sagging chins into resolution. He turned and looked at the map with heavy heart. He faced the waste of the midwest and one particular pin topped with a Bible; it was a long way from any other pin. It was Middlesville.

The West Coast, however, had already glossed Carolee against the cleansing rain of repentance and the waters of forgiveness: she was slick as a Muscovy diving duck. She popped pills, snorted coke, smoked dope, and faked grades through faking orgasms with her teachers. She spent hours in her black-ceilinged room, headphoned to her idols, Fazio Fantini, Son of Satan, Patti Smith or Debbie Harry. If she was feeling really bombed, she'd listen to Duran Duran and know that things couldn't get any worse.

Middlesville was a real threat to her survival techniques. She had no-one to score off in the first few weeks. She had a special place at the Middlesville College of Habakkuk: her pop the principal was only just up the hall; she had fanatically celibate instructors. And prayers with every class – Alleluia for Algebra! Praise the Lord for Latin! Gymnastics in the Name of Jesus! Bless His Name for the less controversial aspects of Biology, like cutting small animals to pieces.

Middlesville's only definition of a good time seemed to be 'A liddle drive ... jest outta town' and once there, a sweaty hump on a hard truck seat: gross.

'Did yuh come, uh?'

No, space-cadet, she'd say to herself, and more of the same ain't gonna make it happen. And there was always just more of the same.

Wednesday afternoon of this particular week found her staring listlessly out a window as her Humanities instructor pounded some pearl of English literature to dull dust. She wondered how long it would take a body, her body, to hit the ground, three floors below.

She heard a hum rising to a dull roar, then a street-streaking growl as a bike to be reckoned with cruised the wide flat boulevard. The love of Carolee's life had been Road Kickin' Rufus and his CZ 850, from Santa Cruz. He had wordlessly allowed her to worship him for a year until she left the coast. He would never write: Real Men don't use words; she could never call his ripped-out phone and they would never see each other again. She had monologued misery into his sweating chest grinding away for the last time on the floor of the Santa Cruz beach hut. She had even kicked around the idea of hitching back and being his old lady but after fifty miles and a slimy octopus fuck with a trucker outside Middlesville, the idea had shed its glamour. She had slouched home, like, on the *bus*. Home, to another prayerful tear-filled lecture about her grades and her immortal soul. Middlesville was Babylon to her parents, but for her it was the place of the Pillar of Salt, as she yearned for the fire-heat and brimstone glitter of her lost home.

'Perhaps John Milton, blind in the terms of this depraved world, had true sight in his heart from God, although the sumptuous colours of his materialistic surrounds were as ash to his blistered eyeballs,' droned the instructor. Carolee stuffed her fingers down her throat, and threw at the tutor one word.

'*Gagsville.*'

She fled down the corridor.

On the street, the bike was gone. Shit. The petrol fumes were tantalizing ozone. Her instructor ogled her slight figure from on high and prayed to the Lord to purge his mortal soul. He had been appointed by a governing body headed by Abner J. Hodges Jr., more for his Christian principles than his dubious European qualifications: where is this Leipzig, anyhow?

Fervour and Ignorance had signed his contract and he had sworn on the flag and the Bible to honour their trust. He read through the remains of his plagiarized doggerel and dismissed the class.

On Thursday afternoon, Carolee was prepared. She had skipped the afternoon session: 'Flagellation – Maybe Those Medieval Monks Were On The Right Track'.

She sat cross-legged in scarlet satin shorts, waiting for the new boy in town. She despised the grinning street-cleaner on his humming trolley; she fielded the scandalized stares of the Middlesville mid-afternoon shoppers, and flung back her Blatant smile (an unholy blend of Bette Davis and Frank Zappa). They seemed to expect the wheels to come off the baby buggies, the shopping trolleys to buckle, or at the very least that their mauve or peroxide permanents should drop flat into their outraged eyes as they scuttled out of range.

Nothing. No bike. No nothing, she thought.

She gave it an hour, then mashed out her eighth turquoise cigarette and hopped the mall bus to rifle through the clothes store – the Mall Mega – Mega? Huh! Chickenshit! Friday she was wiser. Thursday evening had brought her a slug-like face-suck with some no-no in a tame go-go bar. And the knowledge that the bike boys hang around the poolhall near the drive-in.

'Little lady, you're gonna need, like, some, pertection,' leered her swain.

She left him with a lapful of crushed ice.

Friday, she walked the twelve or so blocks to, surely, heaven.

Inside the hall, there was the usual collection of slab-cases and dick-heads. *Toadfuck*! she sneered to herself. There was a huge woman wallowing on a stool at the bar. Carolee perched at the other end, slammed her licence on the bar and glared at the bartender. An hour and three Tequila Sunrises later, nothing and no-one. She slung her Gucci bag over one bare shoulder and wandered outside.

'Thought you was about to have a seizure there, Bean,' said the bartender. 'No offence.'

'Jailbait, honey,' said Bean morosely.

But, my God, merciful heavens . . .

Here He Was!

The Harley spun dust in front of the hall. Carolee's lips and hips fanfared. She swayed and plastered one hand on her upper thigh.

Nothing.

'Nice machine, big fella,' she cooed.

'Shit, yeah,' the face grinned under its black helmet. Kid prob'ly never seen a bike like this before, thought Rotary Spokes, warily expansive after a mung sprout avo-burger with Diz. Carolee slung one leg over the pillion seat. The figure in its sumptuous leather swivelled and stared. Carolee puckered up to where the eyes were blanked-out by the helmet's mirror-surface shield. Kid prob'ly never ridden a bike like this before either, thought Rotary Spokes.

She kicked the bike alive.

'Where to, kid?'

Carolee wrapped herself round her saviour's back, gripping with her thighs.

'Just drive, baby,' she wheedled.

And so Rotary Spokes obediently arrived at an abandoned gas station some twenty miles out of town.

'What's this?' *he* said.

'Nice place for a little, um, party,' squeaked Carolee. 'I've had my eye on it for some time.' No need to explain *how* she had first found it, or how many times since the first *yawnsville* fuck.

Shit! *He* was supposed to swagger ahead of her, grab her and gaze deep into her eyes. *He* just stood there – looking puzzled? Hard to tell with the helmet.

'Weeeeeell? Come ON!' squealed Carolee, running as leggily as one can at five foot four, and then posing beside one of the rusting porch supports.

He frowned, looked around, walked to the edge of the road. Carolee marched up to his bike and tried to push it around to the back. Keeps away the Highway Patrol – Rufus had taught her that. And scuff out the tracks. And this big hunk just stood there. He wasn't the type to make the first move, she decided. Right, he was just a shy guy, right?

She took his hand and led him through the broken screen doors. She posed, looking meaningfully at the stained mattress and litter of beer cans.

Nothing.

Fuck, was he a *fag*? That would be the final, the *ultimate* shit Middlesville could dump on her. A leather queen. She unbuttoned her blouse.

He turned away!

'You a fag?' she demanded.

'Nuuuh-Uhh.'

'You don't like girls? You like guys?

'Waaall – sorta, um, it ain't quite that simple.'

Ah, he was a cherry boy. Fun, fun! Carolee slipped off her blouse and catwalked over to him. She picked up one of his hands and put it over one of her breasts. Nothing. She took a deep breath and drew him towards the mattress. He sat bolt upright, blushing. She started to feel maternal. She drew down the zip of his jacket, and slipped her hand inside. So warm, so – oh Christ! Her hand paralysed around Rotary Spokes' left breast. God, it felt so nice. She let the feeling tingle all over her. She unzipped the jacket to the waist.

'I'm a woman, kid,' said Rotary Spokes. She took off her helmet.

'I realize that,' said Carolee, one hand throbbing. She moved in slow-motion and brushed Rotary Spokes' lips with her own.

And I never been kissed before

The way that you kiss me

sang her jukebox heart.

But, there was no response. Nothing. She put her hands in her lap. God, the *embarrassment*.

'You some biker's old lady?'

'Nah!' snarled Rotary Spokes, confused and yet, at the same time, rather flattered. 'I ride by myself, kid.'

'Do you . . . do you like me? squeaked Carolee.

Rotary Spokes suddenly received a warning growl from The Hug. Back! She leapt to her feet.

'Hell, kid, I don't even know you,' she said.

'Hi, I'm Carolee.'

'Fer Chrissakes! I'm Rotary Spokes. Sheee-it, I'll take yuh home, kid. It'd be best.'

'Oh, sit down,' said Carolee. She rifled through her bag. 'Anyone can make a mistake. You smoke?'

'Yiz.' Rotary Spokes sat at a careful distance.

'Well, let's get some joy out of this ride, Rotary Spokes, since, aw, it's a real shame, my body doesn't drive you wild with desire.'

Carolee inhaled and passed the joint over. And another. Hell. The stuff didn't touch either one of them.

'I don't have any more,' said Carolee.

Rotary Spokes smiled.

'I do have a little Acapulco Gold,' she said, unzipping her pocket. The gold dust was for Diz, for a *special occasion* . . . but, what the hell? Carolee gave her a packet of papers printed with the Stars and Stripes. The packet said:

100% PURE RICE PAPER

100% PURE VEGETABLE COLORING.

LOVE IS OUR LAW — TRUTH IS OUR WORSHIP — FORM IS OUR MANIFESTATION — CONSCIENCE IS OUR GUIDE — PEACE IS OUR SHELTER — NATURE IS OUR COMPANION — ORDER IS OUR ATTITUDE — BEAUTY AND PERFECTION IS OUR LIFE —

100% CHEMICALLY PURE PAPER

ONE LEAF AT A TIME

Rotary Spokes' days of singing to and saluting the flag raised their eyebrows. What the fuck. They smoked, a careful six inches apart. Carolee crossed the barrier and snuggled up.

'I'm cold,' she lied.

Rotary Spokes put one stiff arm around her. Carolee shivered. She stared ahead, mesmerizing herself in the warmth, and inched her hand onto Rotary Spokes' breast again. She started to stroke gently. Rotary Spokes' steel hand closed on her wrist.

'Kid, ah cain't do this,' she said.

'You think it's going to make you blind? You telling me you've never done it before?'

'How the hell old are you?'

'JESUS! You sound like my *mother*. And my father . . . I'm seventeen, and old enough to know better.'

'Nah, I ain't puttin' you down, Carolee. I don't know you and it would be like doin' it with my kid sister. I just wouldn't feel right about it. I'm sorry. Real sorry. I rushed into a few too many things in my life so far.'

'You could *get* to know me. I'm always hanging out. Any place. Not my place. Your place. Where is your place?'

'I don't live around these parts. I'm only here for a few days. Forget it, Carolee.'

'I don't think I want to,' said Carolee. 'Hold me.' That could do no harm. Rotary Spokes held her awkwardly from the waist up.

'Fool!' growled The Hug, ravenous. Carolee pulled her down, full length, searching for her mouth.

'Double fool!' The Hug growled, deeper. But Rotary Spokes held Carolee's head against her shoulder. And The Hug hissed, 'Kiss her, you *fool*! You can wait forever for the whims of Diz Darlin'!'

But she couldn't. Carolee leant on her elbows and made another joint. Then snuggled back, like a trusting small animal, under Rotary's jacket. The smoke curled up in silence. The Hug paced behind padlocked bars. NO! The gold dust laid them flat out in deep sleep. The moon rose unnoticed outside.

Rotary Spokes woke with Carolee baby-soft, asleep in her arms. She lay awhile. The Hug pawed the boards of its confinement.

'Carolee . . . you better wake up,' she said.

Carolee pretended to wake. She had been lying rigid, hoping it wouldn't stop. She grunted and yawned, wriggling even closer.

'Carolee, wake up. It's really late. I'll take yuh home, and tell your folks you was with me.'

'I don't think my pop would like that,' said Carolee quickly. 'Take me home with you, where you're staying. My folks don't really care what I do.'

'Come on, kid.'

'Don't fucking call me kid . . . shit, call me what you like. You didn't take advantage of me in my sleep, did you? I feel so *good*.'

'What the hell? No, I didn't! I mean, hey, Carolee, drop it, huh, it just ain't right.'

'Well, well,' said Carolee, 'I got the moral majority at home, and the moral minority in my bed! Christ!'

Rotary Spokes put an arm round her shoulder. The Hug batted the bars with one huge paw. She whipcracked it back.

'You can see me tomorrow, Rotary Spokes. I'll come down to the poolhall. You could pick me up at the corner of Soquel and Grand Scenic any time tomorow afternoon.'

'Mm,' said Rotary Spokes.

Carolee slipped from the bike two blocks from her parents' house.

She stood and held Rotary Spokes' face with a burning gaze. Rotary Spokes couldn't resist.

'Here's looking at you, kid,' she said and roared off into the growing darkness. Carolee walked home, floating, feet moving automatically. Jesus. Her hands held her secret. Carolee was gone, starry-eyed and laughing, blood coursing with ecstacy, excuses tripping off her practised tongue, and something in her eyes stopped the usual tearful intercessions that followed her late arrival.

'I don't know what possesses that child of our poor benighted limbs,' her mother said to her father.

'I guess we must trust the Lord to open her heart to Him, as He has opened His heart to her, in His love,' said Abner J., plopping down on aching knees.

Love? God's love? Whatever. Carolee's heart brimmed with a golden nectar, and she strolled the boulevard the next day, ashen with expectation. She wanted to *ride* down to the poolhall. A silver truck rolled by in Motown stereo, with a leering figure at the wheel.

'She's there,' Bean told Rotary, crouched down in the passenger seat. Yuh got yuhself a baby, yuh damn dingleberry.'

'I don't want no baby, Bean!'

'Just think how happy you woulda been to have someone like your sweet self sweep yuh offa your feet when *you* was seventeen. Who was you in love with when you was seventeen?'

'Greta Garbo, Katherine Hepburn . . . I never been properly in love till I met Diz.'

'Huh! You just lost yourself a hunnerd bucks. You ain't mentioned Diz once in, lessee . . . twenty-two hours. Twenty-four, and we was going to celebrate.'

'Anyhow, Bean, I better be gettin' back to Normal. I got bidniss t'attend to.'

'Yuh oughtta move up here, Rodry. Yuh cain't be a dyke in the desert, just waitin' for Sappho coach tours to drop by.'

'Shit, Bean! Drop me off at the house, will yuh, and I'll git right now. Anyhow, who the hell's gonna buy a workshop in Normal, huh?'

'Just pack your tools up. I'll pick yuh up in the truck on twelve hours' notice, and you can ride your sweet baby monster bike behind. You don't got that much stuff. We'll git yuh an apartment, there's plenty of work here – no plain ole asshole can fix bikes like you do.'

As Rotary Spokes hurtled through the starry evening on her way home, Carolee P. Hodges was drawn to the poolhall, a major transfusion of Tequila Sunrise, and Bean's wide shoulder.

'You know Rotary Spokes?'

'Ah've heared the name,' said Bean. Screw this for a sack of ponyturds! Goddam teenage crush! No wonder she shot outta town like a human cannonball!

'You know where I can find her?'

'She's just blown town, kiddo. Back home to Normal.'

'She's gone? Where? Normal? Where the hell is Normal?'

Bean stared at the charcoal eyes, the pale lips.

'Normal is a million light years from here, kid,' she said. 'Come home with momma, angel, and I'll tell yuh all I know.'

By the desert road, thick wires snaked their voltage to Normal. The sign, 'Normal' was now bordered in multi-coloured carnival lights, waiting for the generator spark to immortalize them.

Dino's cafe would become 'The Wells Fargo Fun Chow House' when a twelve-by-seven foot neon sign lit up. Horses and cattle had been herded from their air-conditioned vans into pre-moulded 'Plasti-Timbre' pens, with wood-effect slats, steel-cored and 'Chu-pruf'. 1st Street West had all the folks in their Sunday clothes parakeeting on newly-painted porches; the folk of 1st Street East sat on their steps, or stood in drab huddles gawping as ropes of light bulbs were hoisted above them and garlands of flags and flowers were festooned from building to building, and strung from scaffolding tacked over with an authentic 'Wild West' building front, where there were no buildings. Luigi Tertiorelli, the harassed cafe owner, had never before thought of Normal as a place of festivity and financial gain, but the rodeo idea had snowballed ahead and the bills galloped home every day. All his estimates were screwed-up pieces of paper in the wastebasket of time. And he was terrified, as the spectre of ruin snapped at the heels of unimaginable wealth.

In Normal, there was no hotel. Yet.

There were no boarding houses. Yet.

There was no cocktail lounge. Yet.

There was no dance hall, nor was there a natural arena for outdoor band concerts; the sand sloped firmly down away from the edges of the town.

So Luigi had shifted his deeds to a Swiss safety deposit box, and called his brother Euplio in Chicago to ask for that favour back. No problem, Euplio had gushed, you are my brother. Trust me. Euplio had then grabbed the throat of Homer the Weasel, a burnt-out speed freak who was fond enough of breathing to pass on the favour to Heiko Bleischtiffe, who was the end of most people's lines. Bleischtiffe listened to the rasping voice, wiped his hairless brow with silk, and ran through the international unwritten wanted list. The money for the rodeo could be got – no problem there. But it was important, in Bleischtiffe's business, to get it from the right person. He ran through the people who had owed him for longest, and who probably thought the favour would never be asked in return.

He called a meeting in his windowless attic office.

'The money,' he whispered, 'is not colossal . . . in certain circles, pfff! and there are ways around it . . . someone who has not just cash, but the right contacts, the right people . . . it's always cheaper to buy people than money,' said Bleischtiffe. 'I'll organize it myself.'

Homer the Weasel rubbed the bruised scrag under his chin.

'De only person gonna do this . . . de lights, de dance floors, de hotels. Cheezus, Euplio, yuh brudder a bigger fool else he's a genius. We gonna need Martizzio.'

Bleischtiffe looked pained.

'Think big, moron. Martizzio – phsssst!' he made a derisive hiss through his teeth.

'Who's bigger than Martizzio?'

'Euplio,' oiled Bleischtiffe, 'You must be glad to have found your way to my door. I am a man with many friends. Your brother is going to have the biggest and the best: The Phoenix of Texas!'

'Huh? *You* know *her*?' Euplio's eyes bulged like black olives.

Bleitschtiffe looked modest and patted his pocket.

'I *got* her,' he whispered. With his other hand he knocked the ten-cent cigar from Homer the Weasel's twitching lips.

The Phoenix of Texas was less than delighted with her long distance call from The Snowman, as Bleischtiffe code-named himself for dealing with a certain class of illegal activity. But ball she would have to play, and the electricians, builders and mechanics bussed out to Normal had a uniform hunted look about them, and a tendency to stammer when they heard certain tones of voice.

Luigi Tertiorelli called Chicago.

'Criminals! Luigi! This is the voice of your bruddah! Would I get you criminals for your nice little rodeo? Trust me!'

'They better not be. This is a nice town, and I want it kept that way! But they are some creepy guys!'

'Don't worry. My business partner and his partner will be with you soon.'

'What's their names?'

What was Bleischtiffe using for this one? Ah yes.

'Mr Goering and Ms Phoenix. Charming people.'

'A *lady*! To do *business*! Euplio!'

'This lady *is* business. Don't worry, Luigi. Trust me. Good night, little brother. A thousand angels sit on your shoulders.'

'Angels! To keep my troubles company. Good night, Euplio – Euplio – God bless us all.'

Luigi hung up cursing. Why me? he thought. Why do I have to have a brother who thinks an Italian name entitles you to wear a black shirt and white tie, and carry on like the m . . . – suddenly his thoughts brought a scalp-creeping trickle of sweat. Surely not the . . .! He crossed himself.

Rotary Spokes idled down the road and strode over to Mar'Ann and Lorie-Kay and Dor. Seemed like Mar'Ann and Lorie-Kay wasn't too pleased to see her. From Dor she got a sloppy brandy kiss. Dor was felling as guilty as hell. She'd blurted out Rotary Spokes' secret a few days before. How could she have known they'd take it this way?

But Mar'Ann had started subscribing to the *Normal Revival*, the misbegotten child of the Reverend Thomas Patemen. She had misread the advertisement as Normal *be* damned. But the whole idea of the slogan 'Normal or Damned' suited her as well. It confirmed her paranoia and guilt and disillusion about sex, and gave infinite scope for her bitter tongue.

When Dor just happed to slur out Rotary Spokes' big secret, this unnatural abomination festering under the noses of good Normal folk, Mar'Ann had pursed her hard lips, waiting for the Hand of God to strike Rotary Spokes down. And the Hand of God would surely have some cause to smite *her*, too. After all, she had supped with the Evil One. She had been tainted, Mar'Ann thought. Tainted. She had begun to freeze Dor out of her house, and instead of cawfy and cigarettes, she held ferocious prayer meetings with Lorie-Kay.

Lorie-Kay was less willing to damn Rotary Spokes, and not at all clear what Rotary Spokes had done to deserve it. Lovin' women? But over the weeks Rotary had been away, she had begun to believe in the monster of lust and perversion that Mar'Ann described to her daily with relish. She shuddered as Mar'Ann ripped the offending pages from *Feast Your Eyes* and thrust them into the stove.

And now here she was. Rotary Spokes.

'Blatant,' thought Mar'Ann. 'Unashamed.' She looked just the same, but now that both she and Lorie-Kay knew the Wickedness of her Unnatural Nature, Lorie-Kay wondered. Somethin' odd had happed to Goosenick recently: he was callin' out in his sleep, 'Patsy', and crooning some tuneless song all day long. Rodry musta had somethin' to do with that. And this mysterious library business. Gooseneck had never picked up a book in his life and Lorie-Kay was confused. But she had insisted to Mar'Ann that they at least take a look at Rodry before they condemned her to Outer Darkness for ever.

'Where yuh bin, Rodry?' asked Mar'Ann.

'Shakin' mah liddle bronzed body – never mind: Middlesville. Bidniss. Whut's goin' on here?'

'We havin' a god-forsaken rodeo as soon as they fix this place up. Babylon,' said Mar'Ann.

Some indignant whuffing and stamping came from the end of the street.

'Ah hate this fuckin' Chu-Pruf plastic,' snorted one heifer.

'Try the Nutri-Straw,' said another, without moving her lips. 'What the hell you think we got four stomachs for?'

Suddenly a sign flared: 'The Wells Fargo Fun Chow Palace.'

'Yee-ha!' yelled Luigi from the balcony above Dino's. The carnival lights danced like bugs around the sign, NORMAL. A sign slung high across the street, bordered in red, white and blue, said: HOWDY FOLKS!

'Girls, less have a beer,' slurred Dor.

Lorie-Kay grinned yes as Mar'Ann dug her with her sharp elbow. '*Alcoholic licentiousness*,' she hissed.

'Sure sounds good to me,' said Lorie-Kay.

Dor teetered along, clutching Rotary Spokes' arm. Lorie-Kay and Mar'Ann walked separately, looking Rotary Spokes up and down. Now you come to think of it, it made perfect sense. She never did have herself a man, if you didn't count that hippie. Mar'Ann had seen Dave the Deep Sea Diver spilt onto the dry ground and had drawn her own conclusions. Couldn't even gratify her evil flesh the natural way. She had always looked the type, and they had never thought of it. More confidence than a woman had a right to. And the size of her. And her strength. It just wasn't godly and normal. Lorie-Kay sipped beer, her eyes bulging, and Mar'Ann toyed with a lemonade. A well-greased man in a loud suit bustled up and placed a flabby hand on Rotary Spokes' wrist. He was The Press. She looked like some kind of stunt star.

'You here for the rodeo, Sir? I beg your pardon – *Miss?*'

She stared at him.

'I live here.'

'And what do you do, young lady?' Local colour, he thought. These people were suckers for print.

Rotary Spokes stood over him.

'I eat men,' she said. 'GRRRRRR!'

'You didn't have to be so mean, Rodry,' giggled Dor as he scuttled for the porch.

'I didn't have to *nothin'* . But it was fun,' Rotary smiled and tilted her can.

'What *have* yuh been doin', Rodry?' cooed Dor, who seldom gave up.

Lorie-Kay and Mar'Ann swapped looks. With what falsehoods would the Wicked One cover her Iniquity? They waited. Rotary thought a little. Diz? Bean? Jo-Marie? Carolee?

'Nothin' much,' she said, 'just bidniss. Ah might open a workshop there sometime.'

Down the stret, two hours on, Mar'Ann and Lorie-Kay went their scandalized way.

'Ah don' believe ah can walk these last few steps,' lied Dor, falling against Rotary like an old mattress.

'I'll carry yuh,' said Rotary Spokes and slung Dor in her arms. The world spun for Dor. Her willing heart pounded. Rotary Spokes kicked open the door.

'Jeez, Dor, stinks like a soap factory in here,' she grunted, dumping Dor on her polyester quilt. Dor leaned back. At last? At last? She closed her eyes for the kiss.

'Night,' said Rotary Spokes, 'sweet dreams.'

The screen door slammed.

Dor sat up, lurched to the sink, and scrubbed at her face.

'Ah just ain't the outdoor type,' she said to the mirror. Suspicious of fresh air, she almost opened a window, but the heart has its limits.

Around 3.00 p.m. some day that week, a carmine spot sparkled in the distance, growing bigger and more luscious through the dust and the heat haze.

A car.

The car.

A Gucci Cadillac slammed to a halt, more or less in the centre of the street, blaring Mercedes Sosa singing *Gracias a la Vida* above the hammering and drilling. Out stepped Señorita Rosarita Enchilada De Martinez Y Josephina Mañuela Tu Quiere Combaté Son Dio Y Jesus, a.k.a. The Phoenix.

At six foot, a million bucks a centimetre; she owned a thousand acres for every hair on her aristocratic head. When people asked her name, she had at first taken a deep refined breath and told them. Then she had realized that a De Martinez need say nothing and could give any damn name she pleased, and so she chose Phoenix, after her father had bought it for her when she was twenty-three – a sort of welcome-home present.

An intrepid toddler, she had been lost at sea at the age of two, and given up for drowned. She was rescued by the gentle fisherfolk of Hauizi, not even a dot on most world maps. They had called her The One From The Sea and as she grew, marvelled at her dark hair and light skin – poor sea child. And how she grew! Taller than their bravest fishers, taller than the wise woman, taller than the huts in their cozy circle. They had taught her all she needed to know in life: weaving, curing fish, how to shinny up palm trees and draw fire from sticks, how to read the face of the moon and how to dance. And when she danced, she was known as She Who is Mad As The Sun Goes Down. The musicians had made new rhythms for her, and she was destined for legend.

Then a European shipload of naturalists had landed, looking for a breed of lizard isolated, they were sure, somewhere in the Pacific. They had found a tall, muscular, aristocratic-looking young woman who seemed to pick up English with astonishing alacrity and learnt to speak it with a uniquely quaint Hauizi lilt. She had gone with them, warily, and her mother had seen her photo in one of the many glossy monthlies she subscribed to. Leafing through it languidly on the sun-kissed terrace, the photo had leapt out at her, captioned: 'Natural Rhythm of Desert Island Belle Astonishes Crew of Lizard Quest Ship.' Through a haze of margaritas, Senora De Martinez thought the face looked familiar and fascinating. Jesu-Mio! It was almost her own face – as it used to be. It was the face that looked out of a thousand photos and paintings lining every wall of her mansion. What was it doing in this magazine? Was it a hoax dreamed up by her practical joke of a husband? He, of course, was in his European hide-away in Capri – the rat! The international operator couldn't get through.

'Place a call to *Mysteries of Our Planet*', she commanded smoothly into the gold mouthpiece.

In this way she had been reunited with her daughter, who had taken to limitless wealth with the blasé ease of a De Martinez. Her first independent purchase was the island of Hauizi. They drew up a constitution which guaranteed no further unsolicited landings, and no development which had not been unanimously supported by all the islanders. Hauizi was matriarchal; 'all the islanders' meant all responsible adults – the women.

On a whim, they decided that they would like a generator to power a laser show and revolving dance floor. But her Hauizi mother scolded The Phoenix sharply when she told them about some of the achievements of civilization. How could it be *civilization* run by the oldest of the old men? Clearly, a recipe for disaster.

'I never raised you to speak like the monkeys, chattering foolishness,' she said grimly.

'But they did land on the moon!'

Her adoptive mother looked at the pearl orb.

'Don't be silly,' she said.

The Phoenix now owned a chain of discotheques with hand-built revolving dance floors, ambience bars, holographic skies full of silver spacewomen, and a clientele collectively and criminally worth zillions. She was never so happy as when she was dancing, and had taken to various illegal stimulants which allowed her the illusion that she was once again naked beneath the moon, feet high-kicking the sand, as the boundless ocean pounded on the shore. This was how she had met Bleischtiffe. He had insulated her against what could have been a ruinous court case, but now when he wanted the favour returned, he signed himself The Snowman. Curse the man, he could still stir up a blizzard if he wanted to.

And so The Phoenix found herself heading for Normal, a nothing town to help with some ludicrous scheme about a rodeo. She had no choice. And it amused her, she had to admit. Her lover had begged to come with her, but The Phoenix was in no mood for this. Hauizi had not fitted her to deal too well with hysterics in one of the stronger sex, and she was having one hell of a time unmaking this disastrous attachment. Ruth was adamant about not moving out of the fabulous beach house, and showed no sign of doing anything but singing the blues – badly – while thumping ruin into the Steinway; that, and drinking pina coladas by the cut-crystal bucketful. In business, The Phoenix was totally ruthless, and she wished she could be totally Ruth-less in love. But she had a marshmallow for a heart.

She looked around Normal. The whole place was like a tacky B-movie set, abandoned before it was half-made. Judy Garland could have had a breakdown here and the press would have sympathized. The Phoenix looked around for Bleischtiffe. In a black shirt and white tie? Probably. He was that kind of crook, so cheap and obvious that state police nationwide dismissed him as small-time or unlikely. No Bleischtiffe. She loped to the post office.

'Yup, lady, I do have a telegraph wire here. But ah do require me some I.D. before I part with this here state property. What's your name?'

She took a deep breath. Nah, why bother? She tossed a bill at him, and ripped the wire open.

'Tomorrow. Sunshine all the way, I trust.

The Snowman.'

Bastard. She knew there would be no air conditioning in the hotel.

'We don't have a hotel here, ma'am. There's trailers down the end of the street for rodeo folks. You here for the rodeo?'

'Yes, I am here for the rodeo. And no, I do not sleep in trailers,' she spat.

'Waaall, I don't rightly figure what to be suggestin'. Git along tuh the cafe, ma'am, and they all might be able to help you.'

'I do not "git along" to cafes,' thought The Phoenix. 'And' I do not get wires from little crumbs called Bleischtiffe who sell out.'

In Dino's, she ordered a beer.

'Ah cain't change this, ma'am.' Dino handed back her thousand dollar bill.

'You better open an account,' she snapped.

'Ah don't have no accounts, ma'am.'

'You do now,' she told him.

'What's the name, ma'am?'

She stared at him and curled her well-bred lip away from the misty glass.

'You like names a lot in this town, don't you?'

'Waaall, you gotta call folks somethin', ma'am.'

'Put it under Milhous.'

'That have one l, or two?' asked Dino, chalking nervously.

CHAPTER NINE

"She's so fine
Doo lang doo lang doo lang doo lang
Gotta make her mine
Doo lang doo lang doo lang doo lang."
(The Chiffons. Adapted.)

'Rotary Spokes, have yuh packed your damn tools yit?'

'Truth to tell, Bean, I ain't so sure Middlesville's the right place to go. Normal ain't half as bad now I'm back. I been helpin' with the rodeo.'

Rotary Spokes yawned and looked round the room. Hot damn, even the cat had seemed pleased to see her: a diet of Pukina Cat Chow had left her thin and furious, and she had stalked round her friend's black dusty boots until salmon filled her plate and cream drowned the pink bunnies cavorting cutely at the bottom of her bowl. She kept a wary eye on Rotary Spokes and had taken to sitting on the Harley saddle just to be absolutely certain that she couldn't leave again.

Rotary Spokes looked at the bike pennants on the ceiling, and snuggled further under the quilt. Truth to tell, she liked the simple life – bikes, beer and brawling. Bean exploded down the wire:

'Your damn girlfriend's driving me nuts! When I elected myself yuh guardian angel, I was not plannin' on takin' responsibility for yuh fatal charms . . . all I heerd this last week is yuh damn name!'

'Diz?' Rotary Spokes sat up.

'Airhead! Space-cadet!' cascaded Bean. 'Y'oughtta be locked up! Nah! *Carolee!* Rodry, Carolee done flipped over you.'

'Aw! c'mon, Bean, she ain't but seventeen. I told her nothin' doing – it ain't right.'

'Right, shmight! Is it right that I gotta sit here and pick up the damn pieces? You git your ass back here!'

'Bean, I got work to do here. I cain't take holidays all the time.'

'Aw, shit! Knucklehead! I'm comin' to give you a ecclesiastical visitation, knock some sense into you, yuh dingbat!'

'Aw, Bean, gimme a break – lemme think about it. I ain't had no coffee, no cigarette, nothin' yet – I ain't scarcely awake.'

'Break? Ah'll break yuh stoopid head, woman. Ah'm gonna waste my own time and good gas an' come an' see you an' your damn Normal . . . Ah'll be seein' yuh!'

Bean slammed the phone down. Charitable, yes; sweet, yes; loyal, yes – but, she fumed, Mother Teresa of Calcutta Ah ain't. Carolee had been mooning around and drowning her sorrows all week with Bean. She would glide, shoulders hunched, into the pool hall in lack-lustre black like a vampire bat. She would come and make Bean bizarre mountains of breakfast and cower deep in a chair, shaking over dope and coffee, tears never more than a heartbeat away.

She would have stayed there all night every night if Bean had not driven her home. Abner J. Hodges had all the saints of heaven on twenty-four-hour duty, and he and Corah wept, beseeching divine intervention.

Carolee had always made a pretence of attending college, and now, she hadn't even made the Gospel Aerobics option, which had been daringly devised with her in mind. Corah mouthed pleas to Eternity, and Eternity blew her little girl home reeking of nicotine, and that other Satanic poison: Alcohol.

Carolee was, for Carolee, living like a nun. She had taken no hard drugs since Rotary Spokes had blown town. For the first time her handful of multi-coloured pills held nothing for her: she was cold inside, and had never felt so alone.

All I want is to be in the same room as her, Bean.

All I want is to know where she is, Bean.

All I want is to see her, Bean.

I only want to hear her voice . . .

The sun doesn't warm me any more, Bean . . .

Bean snorted at the memory of the hopeless litany and stamped the gas pedal of her truck. Where in hell *was* Normal, anyhow? She cursed as she gushed lead-free into the gas tank, screwed the orange stamps into a ball, and jammed a Marlboro between her lips. Two miles out of

Middlesville, she picked up one of Bertha's megaburgers, eight relishes on a half-pounder in a wholewheat bun, and swallowed it in angry gulps.

What was right? What was wrong?

'Ain't I always lived as good a life as I knew how?' she thundered out at the cloudless sky. 'I know you ain't up there, you bastard!'

Thirty miles out, she picked up a litre of root beer, Desert Saviour, at the Last Chance Ice Bar – 'No Oases for 178 miles!' – There was a twenty-foot plastic camel outside it, rolling long-lashed blue eyes towards the sand ahead, the sign on its hump proclaiming smugly: 'I'M O.K. – I'M HERE TO STAY'. Bean bought a six-pack, 200 Marlboro, and a Freez-Blu ice pack for the beer.

'Never knew America could be so all-fired empty!' she yelled at the hot wind slapping her face and arms.

A blonde head popped up from behind the seat.

'Bean?' the voice quavered with tragedy.

'Jesus Christ on a raft!' hollered Bean, scorching her thigh with her dropped cigarette.

'I had to come,' panted Carolee, brushing sparks away as the truck careered into a cactus bush. 'I just had to. I've been in the truck all night for the last two days. I knew you'd go sometime, and I have to go with you, if it's the last thing I ever do.'

'Aw, fuck you, angel, what about your folks? They're gonna have me for child-molestin'!'

'Oh, what the hell do they know? What do they really care? They said they'd only be happy when I have a god-fearing husband and some children, to keep me on the path of the Lord, to keep my hands from the work of the Devil. I pass on that one. There's not a thing I can do to make them like me – they don't even know me. So I'm going my own way from now on.'

Her voice changed from hard to fluttering panic.

'Do you think *she'll* mind?'

'*She* being the goddam Empress of Normal? Ah, I dunno, Carolee.'

'Well, things couldn't be worse,' said Carolee, 'my mom said she wished I'd never been born.'

'Tell me about your folks,' said Bean. 'They sound really weird.'

Dusty miles streamlined by. Carolee sipped beer.

'You know Fazio Fantini? Son of Satan?'

'He the guy who eats rats on stage?'

'Yeah. They aren't real rats, I don't think. Anyway, he's amazing, right? Well, I had a record of *Hell Child*. This is my pop: he burnt it, melted it. Then I wanted to go to this gig in California last year, and my mom said rock concerts were Bedlam and Pandemonium, and Fazio Fantini was a glittering Satan roaring round the world to see who he could devour. And he wasn't gonna get to me, the blessed child of their blessed union. I mean, he gives half his money to starving children, but they said that was conscience money, and you couldn't buy your way out of the mouth of Beelzebub. Fazio Fantini is practically a saint, anyhow. If my parents met Jesus Christ *now*, today, they'd say he was a filthy irresponsible hippie.'

Carolee dribbled a few more tears. Some family, thought Bean. Carolee was in Nightmare Alley; her parents thought she was the Geek.

'Bean, do you think I'm evil? Sick? Unnatural? Or do you think I'm just being paranoid?'

'Shit, if I had your folks, I'd be paranoid, and I ain't even met 'em yet.'

'They took me to see the school shrink, and they told him I was, well, those things.'

'What'd he say?'

'Aw, nothing. I said my house was like living in the Tomb of Christ, waiting for someone to roll away the stone. He's called Astler. Astler the Asshole. All the kids have to see him if they've got a bad attitude. It's only me right now.'

'Yeah, I had a bad attitude. I used to go to Madame Rufflette's Academy for Young Ladies, and they kicked me and Josie both out, in the fourth grade.'

'Well, my pop's moving the heavens, and Astler's digging around the sick earth, to get me back to normal. But I'd rather go to Rotary's Normal a whole lot more.'

'What'd the nutcracker say?'

'Well, once he finished looking down my shirt, he was asleep most of the time, till I got around to saying I was gay. He said what had I done with women? Real creepy stuff, could I describe it, get it out of my system that way. I said "nothing – yet." I think he was disappointed. I said I'd fallen in love with a woman. He said I should give it a while to see if I readjusted – date a nice boy. If that didn't help, then I should go into the hospital for tests, and some weird thing – an e.e.g.? He said he could cure me at this stage.'

'Love ain't a disease, honey.'

'He said that kind of love was, and would never make me happy. He said I should meet a nice, steady boy, and avoid the company of deviants. Deviants! That's why I've been hanging round you all the time. I figured it would keep me together.'

'Would your parents let you go into the bin?'

'Anything, Bean, to get me back under the blessed umbrella of the church, and married to the All-American boy. Anyway, maybe if the only person I love doesn't love me, then maybe I really am sick.'

'We don't *know* she doesn't love you, pumpkin tiny,' said Bean, hastily attempting to stem the Niagara of misery and confusion. 'Give her a chance, huh, she don't even know what she thinks herself yet. The very least you're gonna find in Rotary Spokes is a good friend, and they ain't too thick on the ground, believe me.'

'You mean – what did she say? She *does* love me?

'Ah'll tell yuh what,' said Bean, 'let's not talk about it anymore now. Put on some tunes and relax. Gimme a beer.'

Carolee sipped beer and smoked shakily. It was so hard to think straight. But maybe if she could, then she could work out how to make Rotary Spokes love her back. Shit! No guy had ever turned her down and there weren't even any feelings even involved there. She sat up, swept the Garbo dark glasses off and fixed her face a little.

'How do I look?'

'Fine,' said Bean, 'just fine.'

And she did look fine, till you got to the eyes.

'Where is this Normal, anyway?'

'Over the dunes and far away.'

Bean whooped past the carnival lights, down the hill, bumping over wires, dodging scaffolding, and roared towards the main street.

'Shit,' she said, back in the desert at the far end of 1st Street West, 'it's a D.B.E.Y.M.I.T. – Don't-blink-else-you'll-miss-it-town. I'll try that again.' She took the street very slowly. Jesus Christ. It looked like they was making a Grade B movie about how they used to make movies when Hollywood first began. She saw the street-wide sign: 'HOWDY FOLKS!' and further on:

ROTARY SPOKES
MOTORCYCLE REPAIRS
THE BEST IN THE WEST

'Here we are,' she said, braking four inches from a carmine Cadillac worth more than the town.

As Rotary Spokes felt about big bikes, so felt Bean about certain models of automobile. She forgot Carolee, forgot everything, and walked reverently around the Cadillac, peering through the smoked windows: platinum, chrome, soft Spanish leather monogrammed in a whirling tapestry of gold along the low seats.

'Jesus,' thought Bean, 'might even pass up a date with Navratilova to road-test this beauty. No, I wouldn't either, I'd take her with me, if she played her cards right.'

'HEY! WHAT ARE YOU DOING WITH MY CAR?' The voice was its own characteristic blend of Hauizi lilt, Chicago big money, and New York boardroom.

Bean wheeled around and took in the tall and very expensive figure in front of her. She raised The Phoenix's left hand to her lips, and kissed it.

'Pardon me,' she said, 'I couldn't resist. I always know the best when I see it.'

The Phoenix tapped her thigh with her diamond-handled riding crop and smiled. Paddling along in her wake, Bleischtiffe stared, then inwardly shrugged.

So, a ladies' lady. That's why she wasn't any man's lady, he decided, banishing his oily charm until he could use it to more effect. With megabucks, who cares whose lady you are, so long as the bucks boogie to Bleischtiffe.

'Bean, we're here!' said Carolee urgently, ignoring The Phoenix, ignoring the leer on Bleischtiffe's crumpled face. She saw nothing but the sign by the workshop.

'You have come for the rodeo?' enquired The Phoenix.

'Rodeo?' Carolee looked at her wildly. 'Uh, no – *Bean* – come *on*!'

Bean bowed goodbye, nay, *au revoir*, and grinned broadly. Nothing like an old dyke who knows the happy rules of flirting. Ah ain't losin' mah touch . . .

She pounded on the workshop door.

Rotary Spokes opened it in overalls and a faded shirt, greased to the elbows. Carolee sprung like an animal out of quarantine and clung, burying her face in Rotary Spokes' neck.

'Y'see,' said Bean, 'They ain't a damn thing I can do about this. All week long I heard your name, and I wanted – aw, shit, Rodry, I didn't mean for her to come.'

'I stowed away,' rapturized Carolee, eyes closed, in Rotary Spokes' strong arms.

'Waaall, I'll leave you two alone,' said Bean.

'No!' said Rotary Spokes.

'Yes!' said Carolee.

Bean patted Rotary Spokes' shoulder.

'Ah'm your guardian angel, for my sins. Ah ain't your bodyguard. And I got bidniss of my own to look after.' She stepped back into the street. In the distance, she saw a certain tall figure with an arrogant stride and an apology of a human being shambling at her heels. Reen the Bean patted her hair and followed.

'HOWDY FOLKS!' She chortled at the sign. The Big Bean had just hit town!

'Yee-ha!' she whooped to Luigi Tertiorelli, who was nervously punching a calculator on his balcony. He jumped and dropped it. The figures went wild.

Yee-ha? Mama Mia, he thought.

'You want some cawfy?' said Rotary Spokes, disengaging Carolee.

'No.'

'You want a cigarette?'

'No.'

Carolee backed Rotary Spokes around the workshop. Aw hell.

'I do believe you're toying with my affections,' camped Carolee.

Helpless, Rotary Spokes stood, hands thrust deep into her pockets.

'Less go up the street to Dino's,' she said.

'I might just offend public decency,' said Carolee. 'Oh, go on and make me a coffee, you gorgeous, beautiful woman. I'll just watch you with my tongue hanging out.'

Rotary Spokes put on the coffee.

Into the seething atmosphere tottered Dor. Drunk so damn much Dutch courage, she felt like a damn windmill. But something was already going on in here. There was a pale blonde kid, sitting on a bike like she was posing for Playboy – only she had clothes on. Managed to look like the clothes was a temporary state of affairs. Dor saw two or three of Rotary Spokes, and shook her bleary head. So, she wanted a blonde nymphette. Dor wondered about breaking out the bleach and dieting. Je-*sus*.

'Ah'll see you,' she said, and wallowed out again.

'Is *she* your type?' asked Carolee.

'Hell, no, she's just a real good friend . . . I'll git some milk for this here coffee from over the street.'

Rotary Spokes escaped to Mar'Ann's.

Out of the frying pan, and into the hell fire.

'I got company,' she said, 'can I borrer some milk?'

On the TV, now housed at Mar'Ann's, Derga the Dinosaur peered around a cartoon neanderthal rock. Sterga the Stegosaurus perched in a tree, inching his scaly bulk along a bending branch.

'Git' im, Sterga,' yelled Beau.

'Git' im, Derga,' hollered Shirley-Anne.

The branch cracked and Derga side-stepped neatly as Sterga's body made a crater in the mauve earth.

'Derga's shit-hot!' screamed Shirley-Anne.

'Derga sucks!' bellowed Beau.

'You kids close your dirty mouths!' screeched Mar'Ann. 'School vacations, and nothin' but Godless trash on the TV.'

'Mom, Mom, Mom, can I have a Derga model?' whined Shirley-Anne.

'Mom, if she gets a Derga, ah wanna Sterga!' wailed Beau.

'I'll git' em for yuh,' said Rotary Spokes. 'When I go into town next. Hush up and give your mom some peace.'

'No, you won't,' said Mar'Ann. 'Anyone gits my kids them trashy things, it'll be me. And I ain't.'

'It's no bother,' said Rotary Spokes.

'Truth to tell, Rotary Spokes, I don't want you gettin' nothing' for them kids no more.'

'Aw, Mar'Ann, it's my pleasure.'

Mar'Ann stared at her. Pleasure!

'I don't want your kind havin' nothin' to do with my kids no more, Rotary Spokes,' she said flatly. 'You been *good* to 'em, but I ask myself why. And I shudder to think about it. I ain't takin' no chances with their innercent souls.'

What the hell?

Lorie-Kay sidled up.

'Same goes for Darlene and Gooseneck Junior and me,' she jeered defiantly. 'Leave us alone.'

Rotary Spokes looked from Mar'Ann's venomous triumph to Lorie-Kay's frightened sheep face. What the damn hell foolishness was this?

'What have I done? Sure, I been away, but I really like your kids, it ain't no bother, we been neighbours for years – Mar'Ann, Lorie-Kay, what have I done?'

They couldn't quite meet her eyes and started to turn away.

Then abruptly, Mar'Ann twisted back, glassily stared at her.

'It ain't what you *done*,' she hissed, 'it's what you *are*. We don't want none of it here.'

'Nah,' chimed Lorie-Kay, 'you do what you have to, but don't you do none of it round here, ain't that right, Mar'Ann?'

They went into Lorie-Kay's house, and almost immediately began to wail from the Thomas Pateman Hymnal For Struggling Sinners.

Rotary Spokes walked back to her workshop, face stinging as though it had been frost-bitten then slapped. She was utterly puzzled. She liked them kids the way she liked puppies, young cats, yearling colts.

She'd always got them treats: monster masks and Spiderman costumes for Hallowe'en; firecrackers and bottle rockets for the Fourth of July; games and books they were always husslin' for, yammerin' away at they useless pop and mom. One year when she was doin' real well, she'd even sent 'em to a summer camp for two weeks, and they'd never stopped braggin' and mouthin' off about canoeing, archery, swimming, horseback riding, ever since. Money weren't nothing to git proud about – she'd noticed that even the rodeo hadn't gotten either Gooseneck or Lucas into gainful employment. What was they so damned touchy about, here in the middle of nowhere, where there was nothing to dig for under the ground, nothing as would grow on it, and precious little to live for above ground?

'What's the matter?' said Carolee to the thunder-clouded brow. 'I didn't mean to hassle you – we'll go up to Dino's, or anywhere. Please don't be angry with me.'

'Ah ain't angry with you, Carolee. Funny thing just happened.'

She told Carolee what had been said, and Carolee nodded.

'You *understand* that?'

'Sure,' said Carolee. 'They know you're a dyke, a godless lesboheme.'

'What the hail's that go to do with this? I'm the same person I always been. And how the hell would they know, anyway?'

'Someone must have told them. It's obvious, anyway. You look like a dyke. You act like one.'

'*You* didn't think so!'

'Didn't take me long to figure. Who was it you told round here?'

'Dor.'

'Dor?'

'The one who came in here before, stinkin' like a brewery drain and a cosmetic counter. But she promised she wouldn't say nothin'.'

'Someone's been breaking their promises.'

'So? Dor told 'em. What's that to do with all this keep-away-from-the-kids stuff?'

'Haven't you heard? Where have you been all your life? Perverts, dykes, fairies, fags, deviants, they're supposed to molest children. *Do It* with kids.'

'DO IT WITH KIDS?'

'Jesus, yeah. It's Moral Majority common knowledge. Of course it isn't true – ninety-nine per cent of child abuse is heterosexual male and well within the family. But a lot of people just believe what gets put in the papers, and they think it's all the same thing. You know. If you're gay, you're wide open to being called every kind of freak and pervert under the sun. My pop says it's all a sickness emanating from Satan, and there's no line to be drawn between being gay, child-molesting, fucking dogs, screwing sheep – it's all the spawn of Beelzebub.'

'SEX with CHILDREN?' Rotary Spokes thought of Shirley-Anne and Beau and Darlene and Gooseneck Junior. They didn't even know if they wanted Wheatie-Puffs or Krispi-Krunch for breakfast. They was all the family she had, really.

'Sheeee-it!' she snarled, 'I'd take anyone apart if they molested them kids. Chrissakes, Carolee, I'd mutilate 'em. That's, well, it's disgustin'.'

'Rotary, my shrink says loving you is disgusting.'

'Well, he's fulla shit,' roared Rotary Spokes, outraged at what she had just learnt. Her! Molestin' kids! She smashed her fist into the workshop bench. 'I'm gonna talk to 'em.'

'Rotary, honey . . . they're never going to admit it! They probably think you're itching to go to bed with both of them, too. Lesbohemes have a boundless lust. My daddy told me.'

'This is crazy,' said Rotary Spokes. 'It ain't got nothin' to do with them. I've known the both of them years now, heard all their shit about their goddam dead marriages, and I never thought it was my place to say a word against it. Not wishin' to offend them. And now they pour this stinkin' shit on me.'

'I know what,' said Carolee, who was only surprised that something like this had not happened earlier, 'let's go down the street, walkin' like nothin' had happened. Let's go to Dino's and get drunk as a heap of hogs – that what you say round here?'

Rotary Spokes washed her hands, rubbed them dry and looked at them. They were good hands. Apart from fighting if some asshole set on her, she had never hurt anyone. She rubbed the cat's head so gently that she surprised a purr from the full throat of the regal animal.

'I em feelink dat thinx are changching here,' thought the Princess. 'Diss little blonde vun is talkink sense. Too motch hostilitiss. Ve vill be emikratink soon.'

'It's nuts, really,' said Carolee, slipping her arm through Rotary Spokes' elbow. 'You're too damn moral to molest *me*, and I *want* you to.'

Rotary Spokes kissed her gently on the forehead.

'Leave it, huh? And . . . don't hang on to me. I do like you, but . . . I don't want no talk. Seems there's been enough talk round here.'

Rotary Spokes laughed bitterly, and strolled up to Dino's as if she was the most casual being on earth.

'There she goes,' hissed Lorie-Kay, behind the curtain.

'Yuh think we're doin' the right thing?'

'I'm sure of it,' said Mar'Ann, nodding wisely. 'Open your book at page seventy-two.'

Their thin voices rose in a chorus of:

> *We will cast them out!*
> *The tares among the wheat!*
> *We will burn them up!*
> *And our harvest will be sweet!*

The Phoenix accepted a beer from the Bean's fair hand. Bean was playing chivalrous, and The Phoenix was playing gracious-goodness coy. Bleischtiffe sipped a mineral water, his pale eyes flicking back and forth like a sick fish.

He left Dino's, and shambled back to the site of the hotel. He sweated sourly as he watched the work.

The Phoenix was here.

Already the foundations were laid.

The men were non-union and worked all the hours God gave. The bucks were shunting into his Swiss bank account, noughts puffing like a steam train's smoke. God was snoring in his heaven, and Bleischtiffe found very little to argue with in his cosy circle of hell.

'Perhaps I could have the honour of buying you a margarita?' said Bean, puffing neat little rings of smoke.

'Perhaps you could,' said The Phoenix, sending a fine smoke tendril through one of the rings. 'I was toying with the idea of asking that man to mix margaritas, but I felt it would be a bit too cruel.'

Bean relished a challenge, and shoved Dino to one side. 'This is your first cocktail lesson, Dino boy,' she told him. 'Improve your image. Call it a cocktail lounge and you'll have ladies like me and my friends here all the time.'

'That's what I was, uh, hopin' for,' said Dino weakly. 'No offence?'

Funny how many barmen said 'no offence' to her.

'Crush me some ice,' said Reen the Bean.

Dino crushed.

'Now, lemme see, triple sec,' she reached down a dusty bottle, 'Tequila Gold – yeah!'

She stripped the rind from one half of a lime and caressed the lip of the glass with it, and then twirled it in salt. 'You don't have a cocktail shaker?'

'Ah, uh, I do believe I recall seein' one under the counter, ma'am.'

'Wash it,' said Bean. You can't offer a Phoenix neanderthal grime.

Dino washed it. Funny how he'd never used it . . . but then, yuh din' never need to mix nothin' in Normal. Must be the damn rodeo. Bean shook her head over the absence of frozen strawberries, and splooshed strawberry liqueur, tequila, triple sec. She shook the cocktail shaker like the demented rhythm section of a Mauritian sega band, scooped crushed ice into the glass, and drowned it in perfection up to the salt line. She tossed a clean cloth over her arm as if it was finest cambric, and presented the margarita to The Phoenix with a flourish.

The Phoenix's fine lips sipped, and she fixed her eyes on Bean's.

'What's your line of business?'

'Ah'm a bouncer, honeybun. Ah git rid of unwanted people.'

'I may have work for you,' said The Phoenix with soft menace, thinking of the letter in her bag. Every line was oozing with maudlin reproach: Ruth was on a bender, and had wrecked the Steinway. She sipped a little more. 'If you get rid of people with half the elegance with which you mix margaritas, precious, we are talking.'

Bean raised her free hand to her lips and kissed it. On Hauizi this was the first step in a ritual courting dance. The Phoenix began to feel at home. On Hauizi, too, Bean would have been one of the most sought after, her powerful bulk a sign of peace and prosperity: One Whose Bones Are Couched in Bliss, they would have called her. No-one in the States liked to couch their bones in anything, and at first, The Phoenix had been repulsed – the display of bones so near the surface of the skin was an omen of sickness and imminent death; a nightmare story whispered around the late-night fires: *'You could count every bone in their bodies . . .'* She rested her hand on Bean's ample arm and smiled.

'Let's dance,' she said.

Tables and Dino's mild protests were swept aside, and Reen the Bean tried to find some music on Whipcrack Ah-Weh's video jukebox.

'Ain't nuthin' much here, treasure,' she said. She chuckled as she saw the misspelt name, Patsy Klein, and made up her mind she'd have to meet that crazy guy who's in love with Patsy Cline, and don't even know she's dead.

'I'll fly a band in,' said The Phoenix. 'Join me in another margarita.'

'Surely,' said Bean. 'Dino, boy, you sure are truly privileged today. Peel your eyes, and *learn.*'

Rotary Spokes walked in with Carolee. The Phoenix looked at the tall figure, and the boots of Spanish leather. What a tragedy that people wore clothes in this country. Ah, well. And what was the little girl doing here – surely not?

'Sit,' she said. 'Sit, drink with us.'

And The Phoenix toasted their health until the setting sun was the colour of a tequila sunrise and a black russian night started to cloak the sky.

'Rotary Spokes!' Bean called through the curtained window 'Git yuh lazy ass outa bed, and come over here!'

Rotary Spokes stuck her head out of the workshop door. 'We Normal people don't lay abed,' she said. 'Hell, I been working three hours already.'

'You wanna come and have breakfast with me? Shee-it!' snorted Bean, 'This ain't a invite. I'm tellin' you!' Bean waved a telegram.

'Jo-Marie,' she said. 'Good thing us gals stick together. Where's Carolee?'

'Aw, sleepin'. Damn kid sleeps all day.'

'You ain't –?' asked Bean accusingly.

'Aw, no, Bean. You know how it was, you and me sleepin' together? Sleepin'? Waaall, just as pure and innercent as driven snow.'

'Wipe that sickenin' sainted grin offa your face.'

Dino served coffee, waffles and syrup, eggs over easy, minute steaks and hash browns.

'What's in the wire?'

Bean pushed the paper over:

'GET BABY BACK NOW. PARENTS WANT SCALPS, ASSES, BLOOD. ABDUCTION CHARGE. JESUS AND MARY.'

'Aw, sheee-it,' said Rotary Spokes. 'She said her parents didn't give a poodle-shit about her, that her daddy was a wino, and her ma was a schizo.'

'Waaall, let me tell you, pumpkin. Seems her wino pop's only the principal of that Habakkuk Moral Majority shitheap college. Those guys got a network all over the States; they'd find her anywhere, almost, even here, give it time. There's a description out, state to state, and the police are havin' their fat asses whupped, and the god-fearin' momma and poppa are gonna crucify 'the vile seducer'. One good thing – they're convinced it's a man – seems women don't git thought of when it comes to somethin' like this. It's a mess. Real serious.'

'Waaall,' said Rotary Spokes. She'd run away from home so many times herself, and got dragged back again, she didn't see as it was too serious. She lavished chilli sauce over her hash browns.

'You don't see it, do you, space-cadet? This is your ass and mine in

Alcatraz! Who the hell's gonna pay any mind to a couple of freak dykes?'

'Waaall,' Rotary Spokes frowned. She didn't really – Jesus! She recalled the naked hatred and fear on Mar'Ann's face. 'Hell, let's put her on the bus.'

'You think, of course, with that scrambled egg brain you got, sweet Carolee's just gonna wave you good-bye?'

Rotary Spokes shook her head. Carolee promised her undying love, heart, body and soul at least eight times a day.

'If we was guys, it'd be easier,' fumed Bean. 'The great brotherhood of the wayward prick. Nidge, wink, you silly boys, aw, we din' know she was so young, sir, you know how these young girls do lead a man on. Five hours' community service, and a slap on the wrists. Sheee-it!'

'Waaall, calm down there, Bean. Eat your eggs. What can they charge us with?'

'I don't believe you! What can they charge us with? I'll tell you! Abduction, corruption of a minor, seekin' to undermine the fabric of The Family, striking at the taproot of the American Way of Life. They wouldn't even have to say much in court; they could get us murdered on the streets, mickey-mousin' around with press coverage alone.'

'Aw, come on, Bean, we could say she was hitch-hikin'.'

'Yeah, and her pop would say *his* little girl didn't never hitch-hike. *Our* only way out would be to assassinate her character . . . dig up a sordid past . . . make out she was crazy, which I personally am not prepared to do.'

'There ain't no question,' said Rotary Spokes.

Bean pushed her cold steak round the plate.

'The only way outta this shit is to slide her back home without no-one noticing how she gets there. She's got six weeks till she's eighteen, and then she can git out and do whatever the hell she wants.'

'There has to be some boy involved,' shouted Abner J. Hodges full into the face of Dr. Astler. 'You tell us who – tell us the name, or I swear you'll be lookin' for a job elsewhere – and you won't get one!'

Dr. Astler had been sweating into the oxblood Naugahide couch eight or ten hours a day for a week, ever since Carolee had disappeared. He wiped his face and neck. He had lurched along comfortably enough for years now, doing a little harm here and a big harm there. He was idle, he was ill-read; the pioneering enthusiasm of his East Coast Alma Mater had not touched him; where his professor had wanted to light a flame truer and taller than the great trio of Freud, Jung, Adler, Norman Astler had realized that his best asset was his Austrian-sounding name. He cultivated a deadpan seriousness and slow speech to mask his ignorance and had fooled most of the people most of the time ever since. However, the last few days had been hell.

At his door had been laid every rehashed garble of TV psychiatry that had filtered through to Corah or Abner J. Hodges. He was being called to account for every cinematic representation of the disturbed mind, and inwardly cursed both Laing and Lang, R.D. and Fritz, Hitchcock, radio phone-ins, and every Agony Aunt column. He'd never explained anything to anyone, even at eighty bucks an hour, and realized that time was running out on the protective shield of client confidentiality.

Abner J. was paddling around the parquet floor, trouser-suspenders slapping the floor behind him, crumpled shirt-tails escaping from his trousers. Corah, who knew the signs, was hunched up in her housecoat, watching him. She was accustomed to the morning rituals of her husband. He would first of all yawn, then stretch, peck her cheek so as not to wake her, heave out of bed, kneel and pray, shower, sing as he shaved, and, beaming at her hoist his clothes around him, inch his belt tight, hook his suspenders over his shoulders, and knot his tie. Thus he approached the world. A genial big man, in total control. Praise the Lord! But when Carolee had failed to come home, the first day he had struggled with his belt, and flung it to the floor; the next day his tie and belt; and today, he had tugged absently at his trouser suspenders and left them trailing, and wandered about the house in slippers . . . and he had neither pecked her cheek, nor shaved.

'I thought girls were supposed to love their poppas!' roared Abner J. 'Ain't that what all you people come up with? Edderpiss complex?'

'I never could talk to my father,' said Corah, placatingly.

'Well, the good Lord forgive you, Corah,' said Abner. 'This here doctor don't wish to hear about all your problems.'

Never was a problem to me, though Corah, outwardly smiling apologetically, and patiently and saintedly rising to make more tea.

'Milk and sugar, Dr. Astler?' she asked.

'Thank you,' said Dr. Astler. 'Thank you, Mrs. Hodges.'

Abner watched her serene progress into the kitchen. Then he sat heavily next to Astler.

'Man to man, Doc, what did the little tra– God forgive me, what did my confused little girl say to you that would make her leave the bosom of her loving family?'

Astler drew away from the sweating grey-haired bosom thrusting from Abner's shirt.

'Mr. Hodges,' he said, 'I have told you, I have to respect the confidences of my clients. The confessional couch. It was all adolescent fantasy. She was a child desperately seeking love and direction and the mind takes many strange paths in that search.'

'My little girl? Seekin' love and direction? When we've made her home and life in the Heart of the Almighty? What greater love could we have given her? What kind of love does a young girl need outside her natural family?'

'Mr. Hodges, Abner, I,' Astler fumbled for the right platitude, somewhere between the psychiatric and the sanctimonious. 'We all, in our own way, must simply pray that the wilderness of our confused modern age . . . um, that the path for young people in today's world . . . is stony and rocky. And it is strengthening too. Carolee, in her own way, is looking for the right way.'

'Mm,' growled Abner, mollified by the tone rather than the garbage sentiments.

'You . . . we, mustn't blame ourselves, Mr. and Mrs. Hodges.'

'The Lord will blame us,' said Abner J. darkly. 'The Lord casts us down when we grow unmindful of him.'

Corah poured tea, poured milk, dropped sugar cubes, sipped and spilled, mopped and apologized.

The telephone rang in its onyx cradle.

Corah was on it in a flash.

'Darling! Baby! Where are you? What? Oh, sweetheart! Your pop and I have been so . . . what? Hello?'

She turned with shining face, clutching the dead receiver to her housecoat:

'It was Carolee. She says not to worry. She says she'll be home soon. She says everything's going to be back to normal.'

'Normal, huh,' said Abner grimly. 'We'll see.'

He padded to his study and motioned Astler to follow him.

The next evening, Carolee slipped from under the seat of Bean's truck in a dark street and flitted home through the shadows to the agonized bosom of her family. And the presence of the Lord must have been there, for has He not said:

'I am come to set father against child?'

Astler felt the guillotine blade rise from his fat neck, flipped a coin mentally, and decided that justice must be seen to be done.

'Well, young lady,' he said, putting one hand on the thin shoulder. 'I think it may be time for that little trip we were talking about.'

'Trip?' said Carolee, heart thumping, pushing the moist fingers off her.

Astler stood beside her.

'Mr. and Mrs. Hodges,' he announced in the voice of a used-car salesman: I-know-something-you-don't. 'When I was counselling Carolee, I suggested to her that it might be appropriate some time for her to come into the, um, hospital for a few days. Now is the time.'

'NO!' screamed Carolee.

'In view of what she has told me,' menaced Astler, replacing his hand firmly. 'In view of the confusion raging within, and the influences which abound . . . I feel, as a professional, that this would be the best – the only solution.'

Carolee eeled away and tore towards the door.

Abner J. lunged and brought her to the floor.

'You bastard!' she hurled at him. 'You lousy bastard – let me go!'

Astler tt-tt-ed and drew a syringe from his bag. He spurted a little fluid from the needle.

'It's for the best,' he said, and the last thing Carolee saw was her father's face distorted with holy rage and the impartial smile hanging under Astler's dead eyes. She tried to knock the syringe from his hand, she kicked, bit, and screamed, but the needle went home, the drug flowed round her body and darkness came.

When she woke, swimming through nightmare, she was on a high flat bed under a dim light. It was a room with no windows; there was a door shape with no handle; she was wearing a nightgown with a gap down the back of it. There was a dull orange light over a recessed buzzer and she stared at it wondering whether to ring. Furiously, her mind tried to shake off the eerie tendrils of the drug, and think straight again. Bean had told her to go along with her parents, play them along, be Pollyanna for the few weeks until she was eighteen, and then the police would merely shrug at her disappearance. Cultivate the inner life, Bean had said grimly. Not long to go. Think free and act dumb.

Think free? Even in here? Wherever it was?

She realized it was some kind of nuthouse. And the thought made her heart race with panic. They didn't just let you up and walk out of these places. What had Rotary Spokes said to her?

'Say nothin' to them. Just keep thinkin': I'm O.K., it's all of you got somethin' wrong with you. Your pop, your shrink, your mom, even – they're the sickos. Believe me, Carolee, I spent most of my life thinkin' I was a freak, and now that I know I ain't . . . boy, those wasted years worryin' about all *their* shit!'

Carolee sat up and fixed the memory of that face and that smile right at the front of her eyes – her silver bullet carved with a cross, to kill all the vampires.

She lapsed back into sleep. Dreamt Rotary Spokes punched clear through the walls, held her in her arms and took her clean away, flying through the night sky, the moonlight etching her fabulous face. High above the clouds, beyond the moon, beyond the stars.

Far, far away.

CHAPTER TEN

"I'm in the mood for love,
Simply because you're near me
Funny but when you're near me
I'm in the mood for love"
(Luis Prima)

Bean dealt cards and slugged a little tequila.

'Gimme another card,' said Rotary Spokes. 'Shit. Bust again.'

'You owe me thirteen million and seventy-one bucks,' said Bean flatly.

The room was a restless gray as dawn seeped in. The air stank of a night of cigarettes and drinking without getting drunk.

They had parked up near the Hodges' house, heard the screams and shouts and then silence.

'You cain't bust the door down,' Bean had told Rotary Spokes. 'If she just eats shit for a few days and plays it like we told her, she can git out in a month and a half. Then we'll party.'

But as she eased the Ford down the street, there was a banshee wailing in the distance which materialized as an ambulance, and ploughed through the Hodges' lawn. Four white-coated figures leapt out, the front door opened, and they saw a limp body manhandled into the reinforced ambulance.

'None of those guys is less than six foot eight,' said Bean.

'What the hell's happenin'? You think her pop's killed her'

'We'll see,' said Bean, and roared after the flashing light. It stopped. Not at the hospital.

It stopped at the Middlesville Clinic For Family Life And Learning, known parochially as the booby-hatch. The limp body was bundled onto a stretcher; the steel-plated doors clanged shut.

'It ain't as bad as it seems, Rodry,' said Jo-Marie the next evening. 'If she plays her cards right and don't shout and scream or nothing, she'll be on an open ward in a week or so and kin have visitors. Then she'll be out in two weeks. Mental health is expensive. You poor baby.'

'ME? Fuck *me*!' said Rotary Spokes. The idea of being locked up made her head pound. 'It ain't *me*. It's her, Carolee. She was just beginnin' to think well of herself, and I persuaded her to go home. I thought it would be best. My maw used ta whip me, kick my ass into bed, and that was the end of it. I oughtta go and talk to them god-fearin' parents.'

Jo-Marie shook her head.

'They're out for blood, Rodry. That's the only reason she had to go back. Seems they had the whole psalm-wailin' school in the auditorium for two hours every mornin' this week, and her pop seein' every student alone in his office. He wants to know where she went, who with and why. Heads gonna roll, sure as shit.'

Rotary Spokes grunted, then said, 'She never talked to no-one in that sermonizing sanctified *sewer*. There was one Jesus boy who used to ask her out all the time. Real fun dates – prayer-meetin's, confession sessions and such. He said he could see her soul shinin' like a lost star, and it was his space-mission to save her.'

'Aw, did he now?' said Jo-Marie. 'You wouldn't recall his name? I know a woman cleans there, and deals a little dope.'

'Whut the hell was it, now? Aw, yiz. Sam-u-e-l Uncle. One of them boys born with a Bible in his mouth and a halo round his diapers.'

'Samuel Uncle,' said Jo-Marie. 'Well, flower, all you gotta do is wait. Pick the fluff outta your bellybutton. You really in love?' she finished wistfully.

'Jo-Marie, pin your ears back. N-O. Got it? I ain't *in love*. I like Carolee. We got to be friends. And I feel responsible for this shit. Carolee don't have no-one rootin' for her, y'see, except me and Bean.'

'She's doin' pretty good, then,' said Jo-Marie. 'I got another friend at the booby-hatch. Works there. She ain't management, y'unnerstand – she caters there. Damned if I don't got friends in low places. I'll find out when Carolee gits onto the open ward, and you can visit, and I'll tell my friend to tell Carolee to hang onto herself in there.'

'You'd better move in here,' said Bean, a few days later. 'If only we could just talk about somethin' other than the goddawful booby-hatch?'

'Yiz,' said Rotary Spokes. 'I'm real sorry. Jo-Marie, are you sure there ain't one more thing we can do right now?'

Jo-Marie smiled, and patted her.

'Just quit frettin',' she said. 'We cain't do nothin' else now. Patience is a virtue, virtue is a grace. Grace is a little girl who doesn't wash her face. What we gotta do is keep strong and happy.'

'Trouble is,' said Bean, 'my friend here has an inclination to rip them steel doors in two, and git Carolee out NOW. Forget that She-Hulk stuff, Rodry. This ain't a barroom brawl. You gotta keep yourself well and happy. It don't seem like it, but it'll be O.K. in the end. Right? This is the Angel Gabriel talkin'. Hey, Jo-Marie, there is one good thing, already; Rodry ain't mentioned Diz Darlin' in five days now.'

'Aw, Diz? That's how you say the name? Diz *who?*' said Jo-Marie.

'Who the hell's that?' said Rotary Spokes with venom, surprising herself by meaning it.

'Atta girl,' approved Bean. 'Anyway, can I take it the Middlesville Dykiatric convention has adjourned?'

'Yeah, Bean.'

'Yiz.'

'Well, settle your buns here awhile,' said Bean. 'I'm goin' shoppin'. Might even see Diz on some business. You wanna come?'

Rotary Spokes stirred around the ashes of passion, trying to find a spark.

There wasn't one.

The Bean went out with a particular smile sitting pretty on her face. Seems to me, she thought, we gotta compose us a little leaflet called 'One Hundred and One Ways to Pass The Time While Your Dear Friend Is In The Nuthouse'. Number 1: Get Drunk. Number 2: Stay Drunk. Number 3: Improve Your Basic Poker Skills. Number 4: Sacrifice Your Finer Feelings and Visit The Best Dealer In Town. Number 5: Get Stoned. She drove the truck across town to Diz's.

A Bean is never blue for long, *if* there's nothing for her free fists and fertile mind to engage. Besides, this was a Bean-with-a-Secret. A Bean who had found a manna of ecstasy in the trailers of Normal. A

Bean to whom welcome and long overdue court was being paid. In one pocket she had a wad of paper covered with unique and flatterin' praises of a Bean.

As she parked, she was singing loud and lusty:

'I got Ford Engine movements in my hips
Ten thousand miles guaranteed.
A Ford is a car everybody wants to ride –
Step in – you will see!'

The phone rang. Jo-Marie picked it up.

'Oh, hi, Diz,' she said, winking at Rotary Spokes. 'Naw, the Big Bean ain't presently at home, I don't think.' She covered the mouthpiece. 'You wanna talk to Diz? She's asked for you.'

Rotary Spokes made an 'I-have-been-taught-by-masters' face in the style of Olivia de Havilland, and held the newspaper upside down in front of her.

'No, she's out, too. She's a real popular girl these days. So it's just little ol' me,' Jo-Marie fibbed. 'I'll tell 'em you called . . . O.K., I won't tell 'em you called . . . Me? . . . No, I'm real busy these days, you know how it is . . . I'll call you up sometime. Bye . . . right, you take care, too. Have a nice one!'

'Sheee-it!' she said. 'She must be desperate. She asked for Bean, for you, and then she asked *me* out!'

'Yeah? You goin'?'

'Am I fuck! I, really, you know, cain't git my head around close encounters of the painful kind,' she parodied Diz. 'It really, you know, just ain't my, uh, wow, *you* know.'

But it was true. Diz was desperate. Acid reality was pissing through Diz's fragile parasol with an unerring accuracy she usually reserved for other people. And a true fact of this painful and turbulent life is that even barracudas get the blues. It was a Saturday, for Chrissake, and Diz was alone. Diz never spent Saturdays alone – even if it means playing hard-to-get with a nameless Friday fuck. Her little black loose-leaf book had come up with zilch by way of diversion. To call someone as ex as Reen the Bean! To risk the Niagara of Rotary Spokes' instability! To put herself on the line with Jo-Marie – the definition of a no-one going nowhere! Life does not do this to Diz Darling.

Oh yes I do, smirked Life, cackling like Baby Jane. What had brought it on, wondered Diz, tossing her hennaed mane. It was Simeon, asking the forbidden question: 'Do you really love me?'

REALLY?

It was an outrage.

LOVE?

Simeon had to go. He went, his tattered coat of many colours flopping down the steps behind him.

Love? *She* knew what Love was. She paced her room, crunching myriad marijuana seeds beneath her Kurdistan sandals. Then sat, palms upturned, inviting peace of mind and self-confirmation. It eluded her.

Since then, her karma, on a one-to-ten scale, had been hanging out at around two . . . two point five. Love!

In Diz's emotional centre, in some miniscule netting of brain cells, she knew all about Love. Over the years, a steady intake of hallucinogens and mystical horse-shit had lasered a blueprint of Love into her mind. She saw herself as a high priestess in Love's temple.

Love was tall; Love was muscular; Love was slim; Love sometimes had a moustache; Love was a man; Love had a slow smile and glittering eyes that crinkled at the corners; Love had an earring or two; Love said little, but huskily; Love scorned commitments; Love acknowledged no tomorrows; Love had an insatiable desire for her body; Love discussed nothing; Love smoked dope like it was the elixir of life. That was Love, affirmed Diz's memory, loud and clear.

Love had always been that way.

Love would always be that way.

Of course, along life's journey, there had to be the occasional compromise. You couldn't have everything all of the time, she conceded, after a week's unbearable celibacy. But all her fellow worshippers at the shrine of Love had at least one of the archetypal characteristics, if only a passion for fucking or dope.

There had been a few challenges over the years. When she had deigned to stray into the big warm bed and loving arms of Reen the Bean, she had felt so safe, so warm she had almost let go of the elusive kite tugging at her. But cold daylight and a gentle snore from the cherub lips had distanced her back to arid moondust, and she wrote off the Bean as her 'lesbian experience', to be eternally treasured but explored no further. Like the Floating Gardens of Mexico, it was a territory for which she had no coordinates, and Diz was terrified of getting lost, or relinquishing any increment of total control.

And when Rotary Spokes had swaggered into the hotel lounge, she had displayed at least seven of Love's features. She was also terrific in bed, and Diz had zillions to compare her with. But Rotary Spokes' joyous confidence in tomorrow – a tomorrow shared with Diz – her literal and detailed plans for a Life's Journey – Leave me out! thought Diz. Had Rotary Spokes stayed pre-verbal, and blown in and out of town with that cowboy cool and no thought for the future, she could have had Diz spellbound for years, madly in love with less than half of herself. Rotary Spokes' painstaking letter and satin-stuffed card had sealed her fate. Her reality jarred so with Diz's miasmic unreality that Love turned to ashes over breakfast, and her assurances of Love everlasting were as welcome in Diz's court as the Star-Spangled Banner would have been in Red Square. And the more Diz raved superficially, or withdrew into silence, the more fervent Rotary Spokes had become. The crystal perfection of her first love lay between them on the ice-lake, glittering shards, painful to touch.

Even though Diz knew all this in a hazy way, every time it became a reality, she would gulp great draughts of wine, tequila, bourbon, rum and light smoke screens of dope, trying to fake wild abandon in the arms of some tall, muscular, slim, moustachioed etcetera thrusting away towards his own satisfaction.

She found that faking everything doesn't make it fine. She paced the hectic flowers of her emotional Hiroshima.

Mercifully, there was a knock at the door. In the lakes of Hell, there was cool water, and justice. She pasted on her most inviting smile. It would be Simeon come back to beg a reprieve.

It was the Bean, with a celestial grin and obscene song on her lips.

'Hi-yii!' said Diz, with open-ended warmth.

'Hi, Diz,' said Bean, briskly.

'Come *in*,' said Diz, dragging her eyelids as high as a whore's garters.

'Waaall, ah cain't stop for too long, Diz. Just wanted to score.'

Diz sparkled, brittle as a chandelier. Damned if anyone was going to see *her*, desperate. She weighed the purchase expertly, tucked the bills into her embroidered waist, and it was only when she grabbed Bean's shoulders and planted an insistent kiss on her lips did Bean get any idea she was needy.

'You having a party?' Bambi-ed Diz, lightly as she could manage.

'Yup. Sorta celebration,' said Bean. 'Thanks for the weed.'

'It's a pleasure,' said Diz.

The word ricochetted round her mind as she stared at the closed door.

What next?

Fuck it – she would *not* be alone!

Would she?

On the other side of Middlesville, there was love unfettered with no curfew, love so sweet.

'We're eatin' Mexican,' puffed Bean an hour later, spilling tostadas, enchiladas, sour cream, avocados, jalapcño chillies, ground beef, refried beans, tacos, and enough tequila to float a dream.

'Goddam it, you are a secretive Bean,' said Jo-Marie.

'You know what this unseemly display is all about, Rodry?'

'Naw.'

'Mexican is the C.I.A. of lovin' awareness. Mexican means the Bean is in love.'

'Goddam! Yeah?'

'Mexican means the Bean is in love and that some lucky woman is in love with the Bean. Hot damn!'

Jo-Marie grinned wide as a well-fed cat yawning. 'Ah love you, Bean. And ah love it when you're in love. Trouble at the bank, trouble at the job, and joy and sunshine in the heart of my greatest friend.'

Rotary Spokes smiled. Goddam it, she was so wrapped up in her own shit, she hadn't even noticed it.

'C'mon, who is it?' she demanded.

Bean flourished her French cooking knife around a lime, and blended margaritas. The stove simmered exotically on every burner. The Bean started her Rumillajta tape and dimmed the lights. The zest of the Andes bathed them in its clear stream.

'A toast,' she said reverently. 'And don't you raise those glasses to your ungrateful lips till I'm finished here.' Her eyes glinted with fire.

'We are toastin' Hope Eternal, Love and the unlikely turns Life does toss us, when we have almost given up.' She raised one rosy pinkie.

'We are toastin' a new mattress, and the road testin' of bedsprings like they never been tested before. Here's to joy between the sheets, here's to dancin' along the freeway of Life hand in hand, here's to eyes gazin' the same way, and lovin' the same craziness, here's to a fat old cynical dyke bein' born again in the springs of love.' Bean paused.

'Here's to the fact that there is some people so beautiful you wanna kiss their feet, and they want you to do just that thing! Drain your glasses, girls.' Bean slopped more icy pink delight to the salted rim of each glass.

'My dear friends,' she pulled crumpled sheets from her pocket and cleared her throat.

'Lemme read you Holy Writ. Writ here, holy mother – listen!: "I love you, Reen the Bean, I love you with my whole heart, like I love the Pacific moon rising. I love every one of the square inches of your wonderful body and the trackless miles of your immortal soul, and the unsounded fathoms of your heart" – you like it so far?' Jo-Marie swayed.

'Amen, Bean,' she said.

Rotary Spokes' grin split her face. Life was good.

'I give you girls, I wish for you what life has given to me, the love of a beautiful, mean, wicked, godforsook, unrepenting sinner: I give you The Phoenix of Texas! Rotary Spokes choked – Jesus Christ on a raft, so that's what the 'bidniss' had been in Normal!

'Bless you, Bean,' she said. 'May it last forever.'

'May it last as long as it's good,' said the Bean firmly. 'Screw forever – and I don't mind if I do, but I'll settle for here and now.'

'Ah'll drink to that,' slurred Jo-Marie. 'Where is she?'

Some days and some nights are perfect. And some people have small white planes.

'Here I am,' said a voice from the door, then, 'AAAAAAAAH!'

The wind was knocked out of her as 257 pounds of radiant love seized her, drew her into the pools of light and for a moment in Middlesville, incandescent Apocalypse silenced all questions, and silence was more precious than gold.

'We'll go and fix supper,' said Jo-Marie, and yanked Rotary Spokes and her silly grin into the kitchen.

'You see,' she said, 'It don't matter a whole leap if we don't eat this feast of love till three in the mornin'. Git down them fire escape stairs. You gotta be tactful.'

At three in the morning, true enough, they shared the feast of love, Bean and The Phoenix resplendent in kimonos. Jo-Marie took Rotary Spokes home with her.

'You see,' she said, 'I do think it would be tactful, and I do have a bottle of tequila at my place.'

She put Rotary Spokes into a chair.

No good. That glowing grin required another resting place. She put Rotary Spokes to bed. Got in with her. Hmmmmm?

'Hmmmm—mm,' said Rotary Spokes, returning a bone-crushing hug.

Why the hell not. Touched by the love . . . who wouldn't?

'In case you was wonderin',' breathed Jo-Marie, 'I know we ain't in love and may never do this again. And frankly, my dear, I don't give a damn.'

CHAPTER
ELEVEN

*"The only difference between the crazies they git to lock
up and the crazies wanderin' round the streets is carin'
relatives. Care so dam much they gotta keep them outta
sight so as not to offend the neighbours."*
(Karen Ingall. 'Reflections', 1986)

'Jesus Christ!' panted Reen, shaking water from her hair and stripping
off her shirt. 'Ah never seen rain like this before . . . damn! We
supposed to be desert here . . . shit!' she snorted, peeling off her
sodden Levis, and towelling down with the curled cotton strands of an
Elena von Hechtenstein towel.

Rain? Rotary Spokes looked up from *Motor Cycle Classics*. She'd
been road-dreaming a Harley Electraglide for twenty minutes.

'Rain, Bean? What gives?'

'Ah dunno, dearheart.' Bean swept the curtains aside from the
window.

Rain. To be sure. Rain as blesses the Emerald Isle, and steams the
torrid heart of an undiscovered jungle; rain that kisses the unseen
desert into a myriad psychedelic blooms – fragile, frantically
self-fertilizing once in a hundred years; rain that peasant farmers toast
with fiery spirits, swelling the back-breaking rice fields; rain that the
ducks in a million parks scorn with raucous quacks; the spirits and
gods of a thousand different names are blessed for such a gift of rain;
rain for which Middlesville, Middle America has no precedent.

There are cracks of lightning that Gooseneck Squash just misses
standing in the middle of the plain, mouth gaping open, waiting for the
clouds to roll by and reveal his adored and misspelt Patsy Cline.

'SHEEEEEEE-IIIIIT!' yelled Reen the Bean. 'They's never been

140

nothin' like this before! This is what our foundin' fathers woulda called A Sign of the end!'

High in the California hills, The Phoenix dialled her darling, terrified that lightning would tear the life out of the woman who, for her, stood higher than an Alpine peak.

'Hey, darlin',' shouted Bean, as waterlogged wires crackled in astonishment, 'hey, darlin', it's o.k.'

This is the thunderbolted lightning that sends frail old people stumbling under their stairs, slamming a cupboard door in a cascade of brooms and dusters.

Carolee Phoebe Hodges stared with forced calm out of the reinforced windows in the madhouse lounge. In her heart she knew that Superwoman was not dead, just misrepresented; she had kept her cool for ten days now, and four more would bring her deliverance: the open ward, a step nearer the door, and only a month until she would be eighteen. She had heard a deadpan mumble from one of the orderlies that there would be a visitor, and to hang on. She walked unsteadily away from the food line, Librium rocking her balance, and even ate the pre-digested muck deemed fit for the mentally unstable. A visitor. She fixed her mind on the one light she had found in her seventeen years, ten months and twenty-six days of life.

In the housing project, Moses Jeremiah Fitzgerald clung to a chair back. He thought the rain was one of the best movie special effects he had ever seen. When the lightning struck a glancing blow at the brickwork naked of any lightning rod, he grinned and laughed aloud. Sensurround! In your own home! He sat watching the window, waiting for the main feature to start.

The rain sent Gozo and Darlene and Shirley-Anne and Beau around the fallen arches, squelching slippers and litanizing mouths of Lorie-Kay and Mar'Ann.

The rain swelled the heart of Abner J. Hodges with righteousness: had he not been preaching An End To All Our Wicked Ways all week? Praise the Lord! It seemed there was justice after all. He felt the rain wash away his guilt and obliterate the picture of a collapsed, pale body strong-armed into an ambulance.

The rain sparked death to telephone cables; fear and ecstasy into the hearts of the Chosen; and an unholy joy into the soul of one misplaced European emigré. She had been starving brain and body on a diet of Margaret Drabble and Slimline yoghurt in a rented room in the poorer part of Middlesville. When she had seen the room, she'd eyed the table, judged she could get under it easily, and moved in. In a trance, like a Pavlov dog, Leonora Hendriksen pulled out her perished Wellingtons, unfurled her frayed umbrella, donned her sub-Bogart mac and positively skipped out, into the plashing, dashing, record-smashing rain.

Cataclysmic inundation! How she adored it! A few grimy tenements festering with rat-netted bedsit windows, and it would be home! Home? The word forced an eldritch *cri de coeur* to her pale lips. She ran, leggily awkward, and jumped calf-like through the puddles that the town drainage system had not the guts to handle. She skipped along for twelve blocks, hooting nursery rhymes, on and off the side-walk, spinning like a damaged top. Eight telephone calls sent the police department into switchboard overload.

'There's a crazy woman in the street!'

'Officer – we pay our taxes and live decent: git that goddam woman offa the streets'!

'I raised my kids up right; they don't want to git damaged seein' people like this wanderin' loose!'

'There's a place for people like that, Officer, and you damned well better git this one to it!'

Dust-choked windscreen wipers cope ill with rain, and the unwilling officers of the law, cringing at every lightning flash, crawled along the streaming boulevards, trying to make out a likely direction for this crazy woman through the crackling on the radios. There was no-one on the streets; even a near-bankrupt hat emporium was flooded with customers embarassed into buying a dusty toque, a fedora garish with flowers and fruit.

'Waaall,' said Car 53, 'if we can capture this crazy woman, it's gonna be good for us . . . after all that crap when we din' find that Hodges kid. If we don' find this one, our asses gonna git flayed.'

But the happy crazy woman had taken another unexpected turn, this time down an alley from Soquel Boulevard. She headed, ungainly and terrifying as all crazies are, towards Wounded Knee Drive where Reen and Rotary Spokes were glued to the window. Suddenly, Leonora realized where she was: America! She slowed between sopping gallumphs, raised her fine face and its mad staring eyes to the celestial downpour, and made her tribute in song to the land of the free:

I'm singing in the rain!
Just singing in the rain!
Oh, what a glorious feeling!
I'm hap-hap-happy again!

Her voice, well-trained for the amateur *Messiah* in the Royal Albert Hall, cut through the pagan torrent.

'Oh, Jesus,' yelled Bean, through the strident water, 'oh, Jesus, it's that English weirdo, um, Delia Schreiver!'

Rotary peered through the cascading distortion. Sure enough, a tall, gaunt figure, carolling way off tune – you'd know the mac anywhere outside of an MGM lot – Delia.

'They're gonna pick her up,' said Bean, and belted down the lung-crippling eight flights. She hauled the drenched figure back up to the apartment.

'JUST SINGING . . . SINGING . . . IN THE RAIN!' squawked Delia/Leonora.

'You can sing in here' soothed Bean as the patrol cars throttled down the street, slower than molasses.

'Hello,' fluted Leonora, 'Bean, Rhoda, hello. Isn't it wonderful? I never thought we'd have rain here, in the desert of my exile!'

She burst into *Stormy Weather* as a cursing and muttering Bean engaged the coffee pot with its threatened electricity supply.

'Can't keep my poor heart together!' wailed Leonora, back on her fragile edge of survival, beaming fanatically, and eyeing the low table.

'This is terrible,' said Rotary Spokes, *sotto voce*.

'No, no, never say that,' pleaded Leonora, 'This is like home.'

'Huh?'

'That's the reason I'm here. He always wanted Indian food when it was raining, to keep off the flu. And it rained at least three times a week. I'm allergic to turmeric, and I suddenly couldn't bear to hear him say "The Vindaloo's wet" again. So I took the tube to Heathrow, got a stand-by ticket to L. A. then took a Greyhound to here.

'Do you know what it's like when it rains three, four, five – seven days a week? You forget what colour the sky is, and you start bending to the rain. The number 45 bus never comes and everyone stands there moaning, and saying how it used to be different, and when the bus comes, suddenly the camaraderie of the queue's broken and they'd push you in the gutter rather than let you get on first. And when you do get on, it stops at Trafalgar Square and you get off and the friendly moaning starts again. I used to go to the National Gallery. There are robots guarding the paintings and when you want to get close and sniff the canvas and touch the brush strokes, they flex automatically and move towards you so you move away. I used to spend hours with Monet, he painted in the rain – he watched his wife die of starvation and neglect – and you can't touch for fear of contaminating the paint with your mortality. You might get a flake on your finger. A million flakes is one picture. I had a friend who had a grant for copying the pictures. She could go as close as she liked.'

Leonora was panting, clutching a cushion. Reen was cautious, Rotary Spokes didn't understand a word. Well, she did. Every word. But not in the order they were coming out.

'It's the pigeons I feel sorry for,' said Leonora, by way of explanation. 'They have nowhere to go. But he'd never let me keep them in the flat. Because of rabies.' Bean considered. She poured bourbon for everyone.

'Tell us about it, Delia,'she said.

Delia? Leonora waited for someone to appear. No-one did.

'Delia?' she said. 'Oh, yes. Delia – can I have a cigarette, please?' Reen lit her one.

'Call me Delia,' said Leonora, 'it really doesn't matter to me. Tell you about it? My early life – why not?

'My father was a professor of Invertebrate Behaviour. He loved invertebrates. He admired their simplicity. He would often say to me, "Leonora, I can't see why we were raised from primordial slime to all these complications." He wanted to be filleted and polarized and forgotten in the teeming mud of a celestial pond. He brought me up to have no character, no looks, no opinions save his own, no muscle tone, and a calcium deficiency. He said the world's evil stemmed from endo-skeletal structure and that eventually we could breed ourselves boneless. Do you follow me?'

'Yup,' said Bean politely.

'He had this career because his father had wanted him to be a boxer, and in a fit of rage, had called him a spineless little worm. He looked it up and decided that it was not such a bad thing to be little and spineless, and after a while, that it was the best thing to be. I loved him very much. We ate slops – jelly, pureed soup, mashed vegetables, blancmange. For years we ate Heinz Baby Foods – ham and spinach, prunes and custard. And pond water. "Just because we aren't at their stage, Leonora," he would say, "does not mean that the ambrosia that keeps them pure should not be filtered through our digestive systems." When I had my first period, he was delighted: "The breaking down of cells!" he said. "How I envy women." Then, when I was nineteen, he died. It was tragic – he got a wasting disease, and could feel all his bones. He clutched my hand and gave me some advice I've never forgotten – or understood. "Emulate the protoplasm, Leonora," he said.'

'Emulate the protoplasm' said Rotary Spokes, respectfully. 'Waaall. Waaall I never.'

'No,' said Leonora mournfully, 'You never. I never. No-one ever has, you see, and here we are.'

'What did you do when he died?' asked Bean.

'Well, I wandered round the house for a few days. He wanted to be buried in the pond in our back garden, and I couldn't lift him. So I telephoned his lab assistant eventually, and he told me people didn't get buried like that and there was a lot of fuss with the death certificate – they thought I'd killed him at first, when I told them what we ate. Then they took me to some hospital and started to give me mineral injections and physiotherapy, and in six months, they'd undone all his years of work, and they were so pleased with themselves! They'd built up my bones, you see, and my nails were a funny pink colour, and I had to start cutting them. They gave me dentures too, because I hadn't really got any teeth, but after a few months, these grew.'

She pulled her lips back, and gnashed her fine white teeth.

'Oh, take no notice,' she said, dismissing a lachrymose spatter down her cheeks onto the table. 'They flow any time I speak of my father. Odd, really. I don't think I have anything to do with them. Then – it was strange – people started saying I had marvellous posture, and that I was really quite pretty, and someone to be proud of. My father would have found me repulsive. I felt I lived only in my soft tissues. Everything was so hard-edged, so loud. Everybody chewing and biting and brushing their teeth. The thing I never really could believe was when they said my father had been a monster. I don't know why. We were so peaceful. He never raised his voice; there were curtains over all the windows ... we had a lovely sepia world of shadows. No matter.'

Scrambled eggs, thought Bean. Scrambled eggs and mashed spinach. Jello.

'You wanna eat with us?' she asked Leonora.

'Yes. Yes. I think that would be pleasant,' said Leonora.

'It will be,' said Bean.

She went into the kitchen, and used plastic bowls and wooden spoons so as not to clatter.

But Leonora was relaxed, letting the chair hold her upright, looking out at the rain. She let the soft food flow into her. Bean dimmed all the lights and went through her records. Classical shit, she decided. She'd got a free record with a Kitchen Mistress set of appliances a few years back. Moze-art. She ripped the cellophane off, and the gentle liquid Clarinet Quintet made the day complete for Leonora. She walked home, calm, dragging the toes of her wellies through the puddles. The rain had stopped. Bean had given her the blender on permanent loan. She gazed at the sky. She was just a collection of cells on the pond floor of the universe. She slept long and deep.

Rotary Spokes' firm-fleshed skeleton strode down the deadpan clinic corridor. Dim lights flush with the ceiling drained the colour from the walls and buffed floor tile to a uniform gray. The same lights gave Rotary Spokes the silhouette of an avenging angel; the silhouette silenced the institutional barrage of officiousness from the reinforced glass nurses' station.

There was Carolee, in street clothes, hunched in a chair, looking through the silent cartoon antics on the TV screen. She was sitting in a jagged outcrop of old ladies silently working their gums, bright magazines dolloped on their day-dressed laps. There were three fabrics to choose from; cerise and soot crimplene; turquoise-spattered lime polyester; navy-blue and battleship gray squared serge. The dress style was a half-sleeved sack in two sizes: scrawny and shapeless.

'My son has come,' Mrs. Biffi Burger, aged sixty-nine, announced. 'My boy, from Pittsburgh.'

'You got no natural kin,' quavered Mrs. Edna Krawitz, aged seventy and meaner than a skunk.

'Look, look,' hooted Mrs. Biffi Burger. 'He's here!' she waved an arthritic hand towards Rotary Spokes.

'Biffi Burger, you ain't got the sense you was born with. You ain't got your teeth in, even. This here's my husband, ain't you, Eldridge?' coo-ed Mrs. Edna Krawitz.

Mrs. Jolene Mayerburg heaved out of her chair and charged ox-like at Rotary Spokes' midriff.

'My baby,' she crooned, stretching up to press two scarlet streaks of lipstick onto Rotary Spokes' chin. Mrs. Burger wrangled shrilly at Mrs. Krawitz. A nurse, shaking her half-painted apricot frosted nails, bore down on the group.

'Burger, Krawitz, Mayerburg, SIT! Watch the goddam TV. What's with you? You got no gratitude. Who've you come to see, young man?'

Rotary Spokes looked at her.

'Carolee,' she said, gruffly.

'So, go see her. Don't interrupt the therapy in future, young man.' She wheeled back to the station, and continued to paint her nails, one eye on her *True Confessions* magazine.

Carolee smiled slowly.

'Perhaps we should sit at a table, Orville,' she enunciated carefully and glided away from the grumbling group.

'How are you?' she said politely.

'What's the matter?' hissed Rotary Spokes. 'You drugged up?'

'Really?' said Carolee, with measured enthusiasm. 'The doctor says I am making good, steady progress and that my attitude to life is much more normal.' She made a Blaaaauugh! face.

'And how are your studies, Orville?'

'Waaall, I guess I'm pickin' things up real quick,' drawled Rotary Spokes. 'I do miss you helpin' me with my assignments, and Professor Bean is lookin' forward to your return to the class.'

'Oh, I should be O.K. to join you soon,' said Carolee, 'So long as I can maintain rehabilitation at the proper rate.'

Rotary Spokes stared at her. Jesus, what had they done to her? She wished like hell Bean could be there, but true love and a private plane had spirited the great heart to the dizzy heights of rapture in California.

Rotary Spokes felt that the face on the front of her head was doing a damn good cover-up job.

Instinct: grab Carolee's hand and run.

Instinct: lead Carolee to saying she wanted to discharge herself. Apparently, unless you were committed, you could get out of the place, but God knows what papers her parents had been persuaded to sign. She felt that a day in this place would make her mad.

Instinct: smack the apricot frost façade of normality off the impassive face of the nurse, and ask her: Who's crazy?

Don't interrupt the therapy! She had a vague idea of what therapy meant and it sure as hell wasn't TV with the sound switched off.

So she said with forced cheerfulness:

'Whatcha been doin'?'

Carolee's sunless Renaissance Madonna smile drifted onto her face.

'I did some art therapy yesterday.'

'Yeah? No shit. Whatcha paint?'

'Well, I just painted abstracts. Mayerburg told me if you paint people they analyse it and if any of the people seem odd they increase your medication . . . or send you upstairs. She did a crucifixion once, around Easter time, and it took her six months to get off a locked ward.'

Rotary Spokes felt The Hug begin to lash its feline tail and flex its claws.

'You be damn careful,' she said. 'You wanna cigarette?'

'Nah. It puts you back a week. Also, they start rewarding you with it, and taking it away when you don't fit in. Burger says any reward is like a rattlesnake in a silk purse.'

Reen had impressed on Rotary Spokes that no matter what, she must not tell Carolee what to do: 'Damn kid'll do anything you say, Rodry, and with you being such a impetuous dingbat, the both of you'll git locked up.'

So she chained The Hug and swallowed her thoughts.

'Kin we git coffee anyplace?'

'Yes. There's a machine that works with tokens. I'll ask the nurse.'

Carolee glided serenely across the floor, assuming an attitude of humility, and padded her knuckles against the wiremeshed glass in the station door.

'. . . and so I swung the cleaver through the air and brought it down on the blonde head of my first-born . . .'

The nurse finished the paragraph and doled out tokens, waving the winter sunset spikes on her other hand like a warning. She fixed Rotary Spokes' eyes with her own. Something not quite right with that young man, she thought. Jesus, how she hated these spoilt princess-types like Carolee. Come in when Mom and Pop can't take the shit anymore. She liked her geriatric crazies, you could have a joke and a laugh with them. But when there was a kid like this on the ward – damn private shrinks were buzzing in and out all day, making notes about all of them. She liked to put on all the old jazz tunes the old girls liked dancing to, and having a crazies disco. She liked to feed the machine with tokens, and give coffee out in return for colluding grins and giggles. But that sick fake Astler had been in every day this week. His fat ass must be in the sling for something. Nurse Rowena Neill walked deliberately and stood between the row of her old ladies and the princess and her weird boyfriend. Mrs. Biffi Burger clasped her hand. Mayerburg grinned and rocked. Maybe she'd put on Cole Porter, maybe she wouldn't. It was all a question of time, and they had all the time in the ward.

Rotary Spokes lit a cigarette. Sixteen ancient nostrils twitched.

'Nurse,' she said.

Neill raised her eyebrows and swivelled her pupils his way.

'Could I offer your people a cigarette?'

Neill almost smiled.

'Try it,' she mocked gently.

Each old lady asked for her O.K. with her eyes. To them she thinly smiled.

'Yourself?' said Rotary Spokes.

'Surely,' said Rowena Neill. 'Thank you, young man.'

'Coffee, Orville?' said Carolee.

'Thank you darlin',' said Rotary Spokes. Orville? Ah well.

'I suppose,' wheezed Biffi Burger, greedily mouthing rich Virginia smoke, 'I suppose you don't never heard of Nat King Cole?'

She gleamed wickedly at Nurse Neill.

'Waaall, I guess I have,' said Rotary Spokes warily. 'Kinda unforgettable, ain't he?'

'Well? Well?' Burger demanded of the nurse.

Rowena Neill smiled and turned off the TV. The old ladies walked the chairs back against the walls. The nurse unlocked a steel door in the wall and put on a record.

'The girls like to dance,' she said, hoping to God that Astler the Ass-kisser wouldn't come in. Wednesday. Golf. Unlikely. The music smoothed roundness into the sharp angled room. The old ladies clutched each other's shoulders with pale veined hands.

Mayerburg considered. What the hell. Fed up with dancing with silly old women! She hobbled over to Rotary Spokes before Neill could stop her.

'Excuse me,' she crowed, 'excuse me, this is a ladies-excuse-me!'

'She wants you to dance with her,' said Neill.

'I'd be honoured,' said Rotary Spokes gently, and took one ancient hand in hers.

'What a grip, baby,' muttered Mayerburg lecherously, thinking scornfully of the flabby white husband hands that held hers every other Sunday.

'Go, baby, go!' she hissed, whirling Rotary Spokes across the lino tiled floor.

Neill stood next to Carolee.

'Nice boy,' she said.

'Orville has hidden depths,' said Carolee bright as an ox-eye daisy.

Biffi Burger tapped Mayerburg's shoulder.

'Excuse *me*,' she said, passing on Mrs. Adrian's shaking hand. She leaned her white head against Rotary Spokes' jacket and crooned along, slowing down to her own rhythm.

'You dance,' said Neill, hospitably to Carolee. 'It'll be fine. Deniece'll be on the next shift.'

Deniece was the booby-hatch lush and Neill kept a bottle of sour mash in the safe for her. Neill protected her; she wrote her morning reports in advance; she arranged the medication tray so that Mayerburg could deal it out; she gave Biffi Burger coffee tokens so she could feed Deniece coffees every half hour from 2.00 a.m., so that the morning shift would find her apparently normally tired; Neill read the riot act to Mrs. Adrian, Mrs. Van Weyden and Mrs. Jenesaisquoi before she left Deniece slumped at the desk and went home. Neill arranged the rota as far as she could to fit in with Deniece; Neill was in love with Deniece; this had kept her from applying for promotion. Deniece knew none of this.

Biffi Burger steered Rotary Spokes up to Rowena Neill.

'You have a turn, dear,' she said generously. 'Git your juices goin'!'
Rotary Spokes smiled. They moved into a dance.

Neill kept her hips away from what she was sure would be a phallic bulge. Hmm. She felt an unexpected pressure on her breasts. Hmm. She put her hand on one leathered shoulder, testing with her forearm.

'Why, *Orville*,' she whispered, dancing with the circumspection she had learnt at the Convent of the Rose of Sharon. She changed her mind about the princess. She smiled and passed Rotary Spokes to the tiny Mrs. Van Weyden, who twirled oblivious.

'Nice *boy*,' said Neill, passing Carolee a pack of cigarettes.

'He's cute,' said Carolee, acknowledging the game. The door swung. Astler hustled in, at his heels Abner J. Hodges, at his heels, Corah. Neill cursed herself for being human.

The dance paused, the record hissed. Nat King Cole started to sing *Unforgettable*. Neill sweated; Rotary Spokes sweated; Carolee sweated; Abner J. sweated ... the temperature in the airless room shifted uneasily higher. Corah's eyes fixed on Rotary Spokes: just like that pagan hoodlum they had chased away in California? Mayerburg twisted out her favourite mad grin and grabbed at Corah's arm. Corah had the idea that madness was infectious, or genetic, and shrank away.

'My boy came to see me!' she shrieked at Astler.

'My son come to see me,' she hissed in Corah's face.

'My son, the lawyer, is paying me a visit,' she told Abner. Then smiled at Neill who had started to breathe again.

'Waaall, Maw,' said Rotary Spokes, 'I better be gettin' along. You mind you don't give the nurse no trouble, and Norma-Sue and me'll be along with the kids to see you soon.' She pecked Mayerburg's wrinkled cheek.

'Nice and wet and on the lips next time,' leered the old lady.

Rotary Spokes winked at Carolee over parental and psychiatric heads and made her escape through the dull therapeutic grey back to the outside world.

'Don't go every day,' Bean had told her.

Rotary Spokes slammed the black off the cushion at a perfect angle and it plopped solidly into the centre pocket. Jesus, she'd played every loser in the damn poolhall, and she had to admit it, the drongo Lemmie, so idolized by Diz, was the best player here. And she still thrashed him every time. Idly, she wondered about the rodeo and Normal. Seemed The Phoenix had blown out of there completely, leaving Bleischtiffe the number of her most hard-nosed accountant. Love is blind, but it doesn't have to go bankrupt. Rotary Spokes wanted to go back to Normal, really, to slam Doris Day on the turntable, and sit, bare feet on the wolf skin, fix a few bikes, order some hand-crafted accessories for the Harley, jaw a little with Dino, rip some more shit outta Dragnet Hornwinder . . .

But she had become a visitor in her own town. From what Dor had said, so had Dragnet. He had gone off after the Caravanserai, leaving his keys with Dino and a bleaching 'For Sale' sign out front.

She, the big fish, living by breathing shallow for years, found her town like a pool of little more than mud, stifling to her expanded lungs. Shit, she didn't belong nowhere. Living in a borrowed apartment. Shunned outta Normal by the fanatic ignorant fervour of her 'friends'.

The only place she felt wanted was that damn ward with those crazy old ladies: Biffi Burger had started knitting her a lumpy abstract sweater; Mayerburg stored up coffee tokens for her; Neill gave her a knowing smile; Carolee treated her like an oxygen cylinder.

Je-sus! thought Rotary Spokes. There's gotta be more than this. Her hands itched for the mind-consuming workshop. She chalked her cue and her eyes travelled morosely round the pool hall. She became aware of a heated discussion over by the wall, and glances in her direction. Her arms tensed, her legs welded into a fighting stance. One of the living dead peeled himself off the wall and more or less shuffled up to her. His T-shirt said Killer. He pushed coins into the pool table.

'Yuh wanna break?' he threatened.

'Flip for it,' she said.

She broke, potted two spots.

'Damn,' he said, 'you're alright.'

It was clear he was the last hope of the boys; he played well. She played better.

'That your bike?' he jerked his head towards the door.

'Uhhuh,' she said carefully.

'You wanna beer?'

'O.K.'

'You, uh, who fixes your bike?' said the shifty lips.

'I fix my bike.'

He lost four more games.

Greenbacks changed hands by the wall.

'Aw, shit,' he hesitated. 'I got a bike like that. It's under tarps by my house. I wrecked it. Motherfuckin' shame. You wanna look at it?'

Blood coursed free in her veins.

'Tomorrow,' she said. 'I gotta go see a friend in the um, hospital in th'afternoon.'

He wrote an address on a cigarette packet.

'9.00 a.m.?'

He nodded and dragged his bod back to the good old boys by the wall.

Rotary Spokes called California collect.

'Hello, baby,' purred The Phoenix, 'she's right here.'

'Hi, doll,' said Bean, breathlessly. 'You sure pick your moments.'

'Any moment I pick with you two's gonna be a wrong moment. Hey, seems like I'm gettin' a job here. Better start seekin' out a workshop.'

'Hey, great! How's the baby?'

'She's fine. I'm gettin' so's I can deal with that place. There's one nurse in there who's O.K. – Neill. She's got me figured for a dyke, only it don' appear to bother her none.'

'You look in any caring profession, you gonna find it's ninety percent bent. Shit, that rhymes, don't it. I'm a poet!'

A thrilling laugh in the background assured her that this was so.

'Anyhow,' said Rotary Spokes. 'We got a invite today. The Magdalena Ladies Society, uh, lemme see, the Magdalena Janus, aw shit, you recall that motel? It's tomorrer. I guess I'll go and see what the ladies is doin'.'

'Hey,' said Bean, 'When's that damn rodeo?'

'Two weeks,' said Rotary Spokes.

'We gonna pick you up and go down there,' said Bean, 'Fuck 'em all. We're gonna have an anniversary of the meetin' of our bad attitudes . . .'

'Anniversary, Reen?'

'Yup. Two weeks. Or three if you count the day I set my eyes on her Gucci Cadillac. Goddam, honey, I'm gonna have to go. Seems there's a lady urgently wishin' to interview my bad attitude. Hey, you call again. Anytime! RIGHT?'

The line clicked dead. Rotary Spokes sat for a while. Maybe she would go to the dog-silly meetin'. Only this time it would be different. She would not grease her hair and shine the leather. She would not be Rhoda E. Spokes. She would not have no damn ex-hippie crucifyin' her gears all the way back to her place. Would Diz be there? She felt a painful heart-thump, and her lips set into a grim half smile; she flipped open a bottle of chilled Dos Equis and put on her favourite video: *Polyester*.

She hoped Dor was keepin' Fluffy in the style to which she had become accustomed. Damned if she wasn't feelin' homesick!

She blew a little smoke.

CHAPTER
TWELVE

"I don't need no city life
I don't need no town
Stay home with the one I love
Watch the sun go down,
Watch the sun go down, sweet baby,
Watch the sun go down."

(Buffy St. Marie)

Once every couple of months, Jessimer Dominie would be surprised by the Mother Hubbard state of her larder. Surely she had only just stocked up. Surprise would turn to wondering amazement as she tuned the radio, and looked for this year's calendar. She would reverse her converted Aston Martin out of the pines, use every centimetre's advantage of four-wheel drive along the pitted roller-coaster track to the road, then coast the empty forty-mile incline to the untidy cats-cradle around the outskirts of Middlesville: how she hated conurbations! Her thick tyres scored dusty snake-skin ruts in the municipal parking lot. She would tidal-wave through the necessary grocery shopping, reward herself with a manhattan in the mall, and roar back to her mountain.

Jessimer Dominie was a self-imposed hermit. God knows she had tried. For thirty years she had tried to live among people. For seven years she had even tried to be married to one. Finally the squandering of time and babble that passed for living had driven her to sell up and move to the highest point she could find. The air was clean, the view was uninterrupted, and "folks" didn't visit. For the past five years this had suited her perfectly. And there was no reason why it should not continue to suit her indefinitely.

She painted glorious pictures, took glorious walks. She tended her garden. She read luxuriously, rambling through acres of rich print, her mind grown gazelle-like. She woke sometimes with the sunrise; sometimes she went to bed at dawn. She ate when she was hungry, sang aloud to no special tune. She could not regret that it was a series of deaths and inheritances that allowed her to live as she wished. There were days when she delighted in cooking deliciously for herself; days when she ripped absent-mindedly into a stale loaf; days when she forgot to eat at all. Time stopped being years, months, days and so on to the trivia of minutes and seconds, and serenely became the time of her life. Completely alone at first, she had acquired three semi-feral cats who deigned to share her fire, or sprawl near her easel in return for milk and meat. They kept the house and barn free of mice and rats; they posed for sketches. Their wordless arrogance satisfied her.

She was a tall slender woman who walked erect. Her hair was a silvering mane, sweeping up from her brow: she had trimmed it herself for years with a concentration no salon would have bestowed. She gave overalls an elegance Christian Dior had missed by a million dollars; designer clothes, the one legacy of her twin-garage marriage, acquired a unique excellence on her immaculate frame. She was a woman who commanded attention, and repelled it vigorously.

She was irritated at having to go into town for supplies, but had realistically dismissed self-sufficiency. She hated watching the shopping trolleys, the aching stilettoed legs, the lost wanderings of unfamilied old people. Her Middlesville trips took a day or two to recover from, and she postponed going as long as possible.

Ah, well, she thought, at least they make a manhattan here as well as I do.

Karen Schuchter, going about the business of Magdalena Janus, paused. Her evangelistic fingers twitched. Finally, she overcame natural caution and stepped inside the circle around Jessimer Dominie.

'Excuse me,' she said.

Her breath was knocked out of her fervent heart by the truest blue gaze she had ever seen.

'Perhaps you'd care to read this?'

She thrust a leaflet into the relaxed hand on the table. Jessimer was amused. A pleasant and unusual sensation.

'Do sit down,' she said, with a regal gesture. Fingers waved over the slack afternoon waiter.

'A manhattan,' said Jessimer Dominie, and directed her eyebrows at Karen.

'I don't imbibe in the afternoon,' she flustered. 'A manhattan! Goodness!'

Jessimer condescended searing blue on the leaflet. She mentally redesigned the logo, dismissed the typeface, inwardly shuddered at the mawkish sentiments therein.

'Well?' she challenged Karen to explain herself. Karen babbled, bubbled nonsense, but amusing nonsense. Jessimer decided to alter the habits of five – seven? – years and go to the meeting. At worst it would confirm her life-style. She pictured Karen as a miasmic pastel blue dwarfed by the dull concrete metropolis: *Middlesville p.m.*. As soon, she dismissed Karen.

A night on a street with traffic? Breakfast at eight in an anonymous dining room? There was always room service, she decided, and checked in at the Middlesville *Alhambra*. She stretched out on a bed Rotary Spokes had slept in just three months before, and bided her time.

In her three-part biography, Magdalena Janus, the founder of the Ladies Society, had written: 'In pursuit of our vision, *Virtue is its own reward*.' After days of leafletting, and click-clacking along the pavements of Middlesville, Karen Schuchter's aching soles began to feel the profound truth of this. The biography had become her Bible, and the platitudes, clichés and plagiarism provided a comfort, a spur, milestones along The Way.

But Magdalena Janus was nothing if not realistic, and kept the feet of her flock well and truly on the path by doling out tangible rewards at psychologically effective moments. The enthusiasm of Karen's first report had earned her a diamante parrot pin which came with a letter designed to sound personal and look handwritten. And the letter told her to wear the pin with Pride. It also alluded to the glorious day when Karen Schuchter would be a regional coordinator and have her picture in the internationally circulated magazine.

Magdalena's aim was to swell the materialistic egos and nascent capitalism of her followers; but at each step of The Way, she shrewdly hinted at just how much they needed *her* to succeed and grow. They were the pastel blooms in her garden: she was the blue-rosetted gardener.

The ultimate accolade, recorded in full-page color in the monthly *See Your Way with Magdalena Janus* magazine, was to be commanded to The Presence at the Magdalena Janus Podium of Joy and Awareness in Dallas. There, bosom swelling under the sparkling trophies she had already collected – parrot, peacock, hummingbird, eagle, seagull, bird of paradise – the acolyte would be crowned with a silver-gilt wreath and honoured with The Gift of The Key. To be precise, the keys to one of a fleet of peach automatic Pontiacs: *wheels for the willing*.

Magdalena Janus had trained as an Avon Lady, and when she had trebled and quadrupled all previous sales records in as many weeks, she had consulted all her favourite saints and accountants, and struck out on her own.

Every pot of rouge, vanishing cream, vari-vein balm; each tube of Mrs. America mascara, eyelid pencil; all the brushes and bubble jars; all the spatulas and tweezers flourished the squat initials *M J* in thick gold.

'Give me a woman of any age, and I will show you a sales expert!' boasted Magdalena Janus. Eat your heart out, Ignace de Loyola: four centuries after your sinister reign, Magdalena Janus was dollar-resplendent from the ignorance and blind loyalty of *her* Order.

The secret of her recruiting success was not to let people know that the magniloquent promises in the first leaflet were to lead to salesmanship. (The Janus Empire had no time for 'persons'.) She inspired each reader with the thrilling certainty that she was *uniquely* gifted, and with *her*, potentially successful.

Live your dreams!

A token twenty dollars brought to their door the well-packaged quest on which they would succeed. Magdalena Janus employed a team of psychologists and ad men to authenticate her canny intuition that people acted best from self-interest and fear.

'Wrap it up a little!' she instructed them. 'Lotsa big woids.'

They wrapped it expensively and well.

People, Magdalena Janus knew, were afraid of three main realities: ugliness, not being loved, and growing old. So she promised them beauty, love and youth eternal. And the promise came with a wordy guarantee, from the heart. To make them beautiful, she sold them market-tested cosmetics.

If they were unloved, she told them that there was a deficiency amongst those who did not love them.

When age was the issue, a judicious application of the euphemistic words *wisdom* and *life-experience*, should temper the situation.

In a culture given to the adulation of youth, Magdalena Janus' ermine tentacles reached out and drew in the jaded neuroses blighting those between twenty-five and an undefined middle age.

Her own age was unknown: she had three middle-aged sons in accountancy, law and medicine. She headed an organization with a team of experts from every field to douse any flame of disaffection with the well-salaried waters of truth.

Karen Schuchter had completed the first stage of her initiation with the first motel meeting. For a midwestern town, the turn-out had not been bad. The first step had been taken – they had heard that there was a Way. In the second meeting, she would subtly introduce The Nature Of The Way. The word Nature would be imperceptibly blended into the word Natural – an envied quality. *It is our duty to look our best, naturally.*

Karen prepared for the second meeting. She stroked her eyelids with Growing Glo-green; brushed her cheeks with Positive Pink; outlined her lips with Caring Carmine. She selected Pure Inspiration Pale Indigo for her ascot and accessory bangles; her handbag was two shades lighter than her shoes; she smoothed her Business Magnate suit, with its brown and mauve flecks.

In a fit of post-coital bliss, Al had redecorated the lounge, and the comfortable chairs and homey decor gave way to the Magdalena Janus Total-Look Environment.

Her postulants drifted in. Karen looked them over. Some of their lives had been touched by the Magdalena Janus experience, she decided. That freak had stopped wearing grease in her hair, for a start. And there was no sign of Maureen – that ridiculous "Bean", as she called herself. Some people are irredeemable. The idea of Bean ever sporting a parrot pin would have destroyed the whole ethos. And the actress type – Diz? another nonsensical name – had clearly found something more suitable.

Lilli-O had actually left her violin behind. She now busked with a hat beside a portable stereo. The girls were there, Leslie, Trixie and Belinda. Clarabelle sat apart. Delia Schreiver seemed to have a new calm, although she wås dunking taco chips in her drink. And there was that new woman, the blue-eyed manhattan from the mall. Excellent. Karen spoke from the script in her mind.

'Let us re-introduce, and introduce our beings,' she said.

'I'm Rotary Spokes. That's R, O, T, A, R, Y, Spokes. I'm fixin' bikes here in Middlesville.'

Another idiotic name! Karen smiled brightly at the rest of it – it sounded like business.

'I'm Leonora Mudd,' said Delia softly, drowning another taco chip in her lukewarm snowball.

'I'm Claire,' announced Clarabelle. 'I'm Senior Typist at The Research Institute.'

The girls giggled. Finally, Claire's brain cells had mutinied and were now angling for the post of manager – she had trained the last two.

'I'm Jessimer Dominie,' said the new woman, with a sardonic smile. And what are *you?* Karen was dying to pry. But clearly, all Jessimer Dominie was, at this time, was a beautiful woman drinking manhattans.

Karen looked around at all of them. Eye contact.

'Do you notice anything different about me?' she asked. She gave them a challenging minute.

'You look, gosh, well, *younger,*' tweeted Trixie.

'You got some new drapes,' said Rotary Spokes, shifting in a chair designed to be bracing rather than comfortable.

'Friends, fellow-voyagers,' trilled Karen, 'I am a different person! Fulfilled. Happy. Essentially *myself* . . . look into my face.'

Rotary Spokes looked. Damn, if she'd wipe off the paint you might see what she did look like. Claire looked. Hmm—where did she get that make-up? Jessimer looked, with distaste. The colours were all wrong.

'Oooooh!' squealed Trixie, Leslie and Belinda: 'You look *great!*'

'Yes,' said Karen. 'I look great. I look *me.* I am wearing a true reflection of the inner me: this is the Magdalena Janus range for my skin type, star sign, ambitions and social expectations: this is my *being.*'

'Jesus,' thought Jessimer Dominie, 'an Avon-lady training session with karma on the side.'

Rotary Spokes switched off, her mind wandering to the Family Life and Learning Institute. Eight o'clock. The lush, Deniece, would be installed now, and Mayerburg would be taking bribes for the wrong drugs. Carolee had about a week to go, and a few more to eighteen. She lit another cigarette.

'Could you make me a roll-up?' said a voice.

Rotary Spokes turned to look into eyes the blue of a high summer sky. The calmest face she'd ever come across.

The Hug awoke, unreasonably vibrant, and started to purr down its jungle-fed muscles. Rotary Spokes rolled a cigarette above the volcano of her heart, lit it, and passed it over. Jessimer blew smoke rings through rings – Rotary Spokes' head throbbed a message of blood and sinew-strength. Again? Just when she'd settled for bein' a good ol' boy for the old ladies? She groaned inwardly at the power The Hug wished on her, flexing its claws, itching for someone to tangle with its thick fur – the eyes, the hair – Jesus, she thought, half-ecstatic, does it never stop? Karen burbled on according to the book, oblivious to the two great cats circling each other in one corner of the lounge.

Hmmmmm, thought Jessimer, anchoring herself with the cigarette. For the first time in years, actually interested in another human being. Rotary Spokes' eyes were a tantalizingly otherwise-engaged sea-gray. There were fine lines around them. Her hair tangled to an abrupt two inches around her fine-boned face. Her leather jacket was firm and full on her muscles; her boots were tight on long strong legs.

Sexist bitch, Jessimer accused herself, inwardly thrilled. And why the hell not. Life had been so lonely, so long. So the wisdom of Magdalena Janus fell on two sets of ears deaf with the tom-tom of their own mighty pulse.

Leonora – she congratulated herself on using her own name – was entranced. Make-up was so squidgy! Blessed word! She had been thriving on blended everything for nearly two weeks now; she had made a bonfire of Margaret Drabble and all her university texts; she had become an addict to Marvel's *Swamp Thing*. She had bought an Ouija board and had definite protoplasmic intimations from Beyond: bubbles of mud, as in a hot spring. She was well, nay, oozing pleasure in the cosmic pond. She had noticed with delight that one of her teeth had definite signs of decay.

At 9.00 Karen broke the meeting into decorous groups, to reconvene *for further exploration* at 9.30 Rotary Spokes found herself sitting on her own, blushingly aware of an amused azure gaze somewhere to her left.

'Can I get you a beer?' she managed as coolly as a girl can who has a deep purr churning through her guts.

'Do you run to a manhattan?'

For you, I'd run to Manhattan and back again, thought Rotary Spokes.

'Sure, yeah,' she said.

'How's your bidniss?' asked Al. 'Doin' good sales?'

Rotary Spokes crushed an empty can in one hand, casually.

'Yiz,' she said.

Not like my baby, thought Al, arms jerking arcs with the cocktail shaker. No small talk. None of them ladylike ways about this one. But Al made an excellent manhattan. Jessimer appreciated the right glass, an unexpected pleasure in the soulless decor of the Al Marquisa Motel.

'I ain't much fu--, uh, good at all this here Ladies Way stuff,' said Rotary Spokes.

Jessimer shrugged the Magdalena Janus experience off her magnificent shoulders.

'It seems we're not quite the thing,' she said, smiling wickedly.

'I cain't place your accent,' said Rotary Spokes. 'You ain't from around these here parts?'

'No,' said Jessimer, and became absorbed in the middle distance.

So, don't talk to me, thought Rotary Spokes. Truth to tell, she had hoped Diz would be there, just so she could show her how much she didn't need her. She had played a scenario of cool all the way to the Al Marquisa. Only the audience wasn't there.

Karen's pattering hands drew them all together again. She had set up a small stage: a chair under a bright light, a table heaped with multi-coloured fabrics, boxes and pots initialled *M J*.

She exclaimed over a pot of pale pink goo. This was the Foundation for the New You. She flicked around the room, and chose Leonora as her first victim. But the thought of putting the stuff on her skin was too much.

' I like to touch it,' said Leonora, intensely. 'I like to rub it through my fingers . . . but I don't like it to dry.'

There was nothing in *See Your Way With Magdalena Janus* to prepare Karen for this aberration. She paled, patted Leonora's shoulder – don't we have places for these people? – and beckoned Claire over.

'Now, ladies,' she said, archly, 'you will witness The Transformation.

'And when the Foundation is laid, ladies, we outline a shadow under the cheekbones. With *this* brush . . never mix your brushes, ladies, it is the sign of a disordered life.' She underlined Claire's cheekbones, and blended – *with the forefinger, the fleshy pad assures no abruptness, and maintains subtle gradations.* Now! She stepped back, to admire.

'Wow, *yes*, gosh, I never,' said Trixie, Belinda, Leslie.

'Now we smooth on the blusher. A natural, healthy glow is so attractive, isn't it, ladies?'

She hid Claire's eyelids under Big-Scene Blue, Garden-of-Eden Green, and Grande-Dame Gray.

'This way we bring out the depths in her eyes. And the lights in her hair. Do you bleach?' The question whip-lashed at Claire. She admitted that she did. Karen shrouded her hair in a Magdalena Janus hair towel.

'Now,' she said, 'our lips are our most intimate part. *You* put on your lip pencil, Claire, honey, just around the edges, mind. "Assertion in our most gentle areas is of the essence."' she quoted.

Claire pencilled her perfectly nice mouth with magenta. Karen came close and filled in with Pleasing Peony. She flicked expertly at both lips.

'Finally, ladies, we need to emphasize the brows. I trim mine, *naturally*. Girls, let's face it, we weren't intended to have thick brows. Let's leave that to our menfolk!' She plucked and fine-lined Claire's unique dark brows into bland conformity.

Then she stood aside modestly, fielding the oohs and ahs.

'Even the most unlikely of us can improve the quality of our lives with a little effort. It becomes second nature. And that means choice. *And choice is our privilege as women.*' Cruelly, she smiled right into Rotary Spokes' face.

'I like a challenge!' she trilled merrily. 'Let me transform *you!*'

Rotary Spokes stood up as bidden, and walked over under the spotlight. She sat with eyes closed. It was like the goddam high school prom. She remembered her mother grimly zipping a frilly dress across her broad shoulders and savagely pinning a silk flower on the cloth. 'You're goin'', and you're gonna look like a *girl* for one time in your wicked life,' her mother had told her through a mouthful of straight pins. Her feet had screamed disbelief in the high-heeled and pointed-toed flimsy shoes her mother had bought on the installment plan at the five-and-dime, her legs had itched with nylon. At the dance she had wound up punching out the Homecoming Queen who had tittered at her, high and hysterically.

Under the light she sweated and balled her fists in her pockets.

'Now, don't be shy!' goaded Karen. 'I dare say you too have to charm the boys in your business.'

Charm the boys! Rotary Spokes did not charm no boys. She fixed the shit-trash messes they made of bikes too damn good for them. What the hell had she let herself in for, here?

No low-life streetwalkin' suspect hauled in for questioning could have felt worse than she did, with the bright light on her face, the strange fluids and powders on her skin. Damn! She always washed her face, didn't she? Even wore that damn perfume of Reen's when the occasion called for it. What the hell was she doin' here?

'Do you bleach, Rhoda?' needled Karen.

'Nah,' she growled miserably. 'I don't.' Dammit to hell, blow-drying her hair was bad enough!

Jessimer watched, sickened. She remembered one of the Eastern countries where she had spent her nomadic childhood, the diplomat's daughter. Some moral degenerate member of the cocktail set had grabbed a big, amiable dog, and dressed it in a silk negligé and tied ribbons around its ears. She remembered the bewilderment in the clean brown eyes and the hesitant tail wag, as if to say, do I please you? Then some sherry-swilling colonial parakeet of a woman had grabbed the gentle head and painted blood red lipstick around the shrinking mouth, and finally the dog had jerked away, whimpering, and torn her blouse. They had shot it on the spot, amid Jessimer's screams of outrage, a dog's life is cheap, and she had watched its good red blood seep into the Paris silk negligé as it twitched, then was still.

Rotary Spokes was 'finished.' She didn't look bad, just ordinary, whereas before she had been spectacular.

'Now, is this a transformation, girls?' tweeted Karen. And the room murmured its astonishment and approval.

'Gimme some a that cream,' said Rotary Spokes, 'I gotta get this shit offa my face.'

'*Well*!' said Karen flushing. 'Well, I am mortified. Rhoda could be such a pretty girl, am I right? Magdalena Janus products can do the impossible!'

Jessimer Dominie followed Rotary Spokes into the ladies toilet. No doubt Karen would have called it the little girls room ... screw her, raged Jessimer.

Rotary Spokes was lathering her face and globs of orange, gray, blue, pink, mud, splattered into the sink. She dashed cold water over her face and looked in the mirror wildly. Was the shit off? Still some traces in her hairline ... gaaaah! She felt contaminated.

Jessimer washed her hands. Rotary Spokes' clean tanned face blushed scarlet.

'Would you like to go for a walk?' asked Jessimer.

'O.K.,' said Rotary Spokes, off-hand.

'I assume you don't have a clutch purse to pick up from the Chamber of Horrors?'

' Only kinda clutch I got is on my Harley.'

'You all come back soon, y' hear?' called Al. The door slammed.

The fresh night air cooled Rotary Spokes' cheeks. Above them, the stars shone clear and clean in the sloe-eyed night above the forget-me-not horizon. They walked a little way into the desert. So this was what was meant by a companionable silence, thought Rotary Spokes.

'I'm cold,' said Jessimer. 'I'd better get back to my hotel.'

'Would you care to have a drink with me?' said Rotary Spokes. 'I've borrowed my, uh, best friend's apartment, for a while.'

'I'd like that,' said Jessimer.

It was odd, thought Rotary Spokes. She felt so calm. She could talk or not. There wasn't any pseudo shit goin' on. Have a drink. She liked this woman. And neither of them, clinging close on the flanks of the Harley, was aware of the witches brew of two Hugs confounded into shyness by meeting an equal.

At Reen's, Rotary Spokes looked through the icebox. Goddam sneaky Bean! Stashed beside a quart of red-pepper sauce was a bottle of French champagne. It had a note wrapped round it.

'ROTARY SPOKES, THIS HERE FRENCH CHAMPAGNE'S FROM FRANCE, DON'T WASTE IT ON NO SCUMBAGS. ELSE YOU SAVE IT TILL I'M HOME. ENJOY!'

Waaall, if there was one thing Jessimer Dominie was not, that thing was a scumbag. Rotary Spokes grinned at the thought.

'This O.K.?' she asked, waving the bottle, to Jessimer's alarm.

'That would be grand,' she said. 'An excellent alcoholic beverage.'

'Whut?'

'Alcoholic beverage.'

'I never heard no-one call it that before. Why d'you call it that, Jessimer?'

'Call me Jess. I don't know . . . that's just what they always said on the aeroplanes I spent half my young life on. Following my father around the planet. "Those persons requiring alcoholic beverages please pass forward."'

Rotary Spokes laughed and popped the cork. Foam shot everywhere, until Jess leapt forward with a glass and stemmed the flow. Rotary Spokes topped the glasses full and put the bottle on the carpet.

'Put it back in the refrigerator,' said Jess. 'Let's keep it cool.' There followed a conversation effortless and flowing. She felt she'd known Jess all her life. Rotary Spokes knew that was a cliché. All their questions summed up as 'Where have you been all my life?' It seemed incredible to be so at ease and not to have met before. It seemed doubly incredible that they had finally met.

Where were you born (not that it matters). What do you do for a living (who cares?)

It turned out that Jess had lived in most countries for a few months and even years here and there. She didn't feel that she belonged to any one nation. She felt that where she lived now was only incidentally in America.

Her father had been one of those impeccable British diplomats, whose upper lip, in its rigidity, massacres every vowel. His knees had never bent when he walked, he wore starched white ducks. He drank pink gin at lunchtime and Pimm's in the evening. He rose, washed and breakfasted at the same time every morning of his life. A backbone of the Empire.

'Which means nothing to you, of course,' said Jess. 'You're the empire of today, you Americans, you breakaways of the Boston Tea Party. I was brought up during the sunset of the British Empire. And it did not go gentle into that good night.'

Rotary Spokes had never thought much about Europe. To hear that piddling little Italy considered itself the greatest lover in the world! That France grew haughty at the excellence of its cooking! That Greece affected a swagger over its philosophers. That the Texas ranch-size England thought of the United States as an upstart colony!

Rotary Spokes made Jess laugh with her descriptions of Normal and the people there.

Finally, the champagne and the words were exhausted.

'Well, Rotary Spokes, I must leave. Sleep off this champagne overnight and go back home. Here's my address.'

Jess hesitated over the paper. She had never given that address to anyone and wasn't sure she could get it right.

'Here.' She smiled, veiled her intoxicating eyes, and left. As her footsteps echoed down the stairs, Rotary Spokes almost sprung to the door. Jesus, Mary and all the angels! She suddenly recognized the same feline power of The Hug that was now one with her body. God double dammit! She had spent the evening with a live panther curled up across the hearth from her! No wonder she felt she was purring inside! A live panther with a notion of civilized behaviour, and sheathed claws, but unmistakably, a panther! She read the untidy handwriting and folded the paper into her jacket pocket. What had Jess said, apropos of nothing in particular? *'There's always time.'*

Hah! Rotary Spokes had an urgency that doubted the likelihood of any tomorrow. But tomorrow would come. She would visit Carolee, cheer her through the last two days of Family Life and Learning purgatory. It would be awhile before she could take a trip to the mountains. She zipped up her jacket and slept, sprawled all over Bean's squashy bed, one pillow cuddled in her arms.

CHAPTER
THIRTEEN

*"Sacred Family!... where innocent children are
tortured into their first falsehoods, where wills are
broken by parental tyranny, and self-respect smothered
..."*
(Strindberg. The Son of a Servant, 1886)

Along one wall of the ward there was a dull silver mirror, and the
group was herded there for therapy sessions. Something unnatural
about that mirror, thought Carolee. It was like the eye of a metal
monster in a Sam Wannamaker movie.

Carolee expected the dull walls to blink over it, and maybe they did
when she wasn't looking. And the floor would yawn open like a mouth
and the room would become the body of the monster. Only the nurses
in their thick rubber-soled shoes would be able to keep upright on the
dull smooth flesh, and the patients in their paper slippers would slide,
clutch at nothing and fall into some abyss. Then the monster would
shake itself again and resume the guise of an institute. It was simple,
really. If you disguise something that's big enough, people won't see it.
Disguise a military take over as third world aid; disguise nuclear
warheads as Missiles For Peace; disguise mind-domination as
teaching and everyone gets taken in.

'Maybe I am cracking up,' thought Carolee.

Mrs. Biffi Burger sat a few chairs away from her for an undetectable
conversation masked as the ramblings of a crazy old lady.

'You gettin' the horrors, kid?'

Carolee nodded slightly.

'Keep it to yourself. Rowena'll be here tomorrow.'

It was true: one nurse, Rowena Neill, turned the beast back into a
building. For as long as she was there, anyway. Carolee had begged

her not to go, last time, and Rowena had said:

'I can't take you with me, can I?'

But Carolee had flung a part of herself like a squirrel monkey to clutch and cling at Rowena's street clothes, breathe outside air, pick scraps from her patterned plates. When Rowena came back, the tiny creature would scurry back to Carolee and tell her stories about the world, the parks, Neill's apartment, chatter her into calm.

'Anyway, your boy, Orville – he'll be here today.' That was true. Her boy Orville, who made the building cower and protected her from the unreal mechanisms of its vampire life with a snarl. Orville – Rotary Spokes – made the walls of the corridors retreat, and threatened the wire-meshed glass. Rotary Spokes made the hermetically-sealed windows seem to open, and brought with her the scent of flowers and trees. She confounded the purified air belched from the grilled pores of the monster.

And there were only two days to go. Two days to getting out of the door and three weeks and a little to being eighteen. Carolee breathed deeply. She had almost found herself praying these last couple of nights:

'God, make me a good girl and I'll never . . .'

But what had she ever done, to strike bargains with a rather suspect Eternal Creator who, by anyone's reckoning, had totally fucked up her life, when she had simply been herself.

It was time to put on the act. She shuffled humbly over to a chair next to the rectangular eye. And stiffened. Voices! One: certainly Astler. Two: certainly her mom and pop.

'Doctor, I want her cleaned out, so we can have our baby back.'

'Doctor, we want her normal and healthy.'

'Mr. Hodges, I am not sure that any further therapy in the ward setting will benefit her. I recommend weekly, or bi-weekly, follow-ups with myself.'

'Doctor, the house has been real nice while she's been here. I even managed to do her room, and we got rid of the black ceiling. So she can make a new start,' whined Corah.

'Of course we will be *guided* by you, Doctor. You certainly done her a power of good already. See how she got us coffee last Visitin' Day?'

'If she was to stay here, I'd have to run some further tests on her,' smoothed Astler, thinking how he could really rake it in. Electronic brain scans, tissue samples, chemical therapy, perhaps a series of E.C.T. – 'she is functioning normally at the moment, but who is to say what, um, deviance, may be masked? The damaged personality has many ways of protecting itself from revealing its true nature, and we'll need to peel apart all the layers.'

Abner was impressed.

'Whatever you think, Doc,' he said.

'Shouldn't we talk with Carolee?' quavered Corah.

'Does a seventeen-year-old know her own mind?' orated Astler.

'Of course not,' boomed Abner.

'I was seventeen when I married you,' said Corah.

'Times were different then,' her husband solemnly told her.

'I'll need your permission for anything further,' said Astler.

'Doctor, we'll sign for whatever you think is needful,' Abner promised.

Chairs scraped. Carolee glided back near Biffi Burger.

'Biffi,' she said, without moving her lips. 'Getting out of here. Do I need to let my parents in on it?'

Biffi nodded and her toothless gums engulfed her thin lips and the butt of a precious cigarette. Her wrinkled cheeks sucked in and then puffed out smooth, and a stream of blue smoke settled a little cloud in front of her eyes. One long thin hand waved it away.

She turned to Carolee, almost with animation. This was O.K. – a crazy-old-lady rap. Permitted social intercourse.

'Now take me, kid,' she said. 'Take me. For example. Everybody else has. This is Mrs. Burger. A fine example of Delusiona Paranoica, complicated with Illusiona Viventiae. I been took for a ride. For a fool. I been took for everything I got. Which wasn't much to start with. It was my sister. No, before that. We had a farm, tenant farmin' y'unnerstan' – work yourself into a tired grave too young. But we ate O.K. and there was barn dances from time to time. And my sister. I had a sister, kid, fair as a cornstalk, and believe me, though I don't wish to speak ill of the dead ... ha! the disappeared – this cornsilk-fair sister of mine was nuts. Bananas. Crazy. Not so's you'd notice most of the time; only she took to walkin' around without her clothes on when it was rainin'. Said it made her feel clean. Waaall, y'unnerstan', in the middle of a plain, without no neighbours fer forty miles or so ... waaall, it was what she did. And God knows, we needed the rain real bad, and we was happy when she got that look in her eyes. When we got on the Ma Bell telephone, we'all could call up ever'body to tell 'em. She could smell rain a day off; and she'd get real twitchy. Then – the shirt would go! Right in the middle of the yard. The skirt would go around about the barn . . . and she'd be runnin', runnin', runnin', through the rain. Then home again and she'd sleep and be just fine. Waaall, finally the rain came less and less and she jest said she felt dirty all the time. And then we had to move offa the land. Dust, y'unnerstan', dust and no rain. Dust and no rain and no crops.

'We din' wanna move, but we did and we'd clean forgot about my sister and the rain, and I do believe, so had she.

'A few months after we was in town, the rain came again, and you can well see, the neighbours din' take too good to this raggedy bunch a hicks anyway, and now here's one a them runnin' down the street without a stitch on.

'So we ree-seeved a delegation from the Community Awareness Association. Maw swore she'd keep her in after that, due to a law suit bein' threatened on us if the incident was to be repeated. She cried all the time. Said her tears were clean anyhow. Then a couple years later, the rain came again, and it was all too much for her, and she threw herself outta a window. Lemme explain. The window was closed. Waaall, there was blood and glass and screamin' and cryin', and a ambulance, and she was took to the hospital, and they bandaged her all over. The rest of us went home – y'unnerstand, there was no facilities for us to stay nearby.

'So I went in to see her next day, and they said: "There is no person of that name in our care."

'Waaall, y'unnerstand, I began to panic a little. Never was a good deal of sense in our family and what there was had come to me. So I kept polite and asked 'em again, and they told me again, and then they said due to my enquirin', I'd have to sign a form. To continue care. Waaall, I thought it would be right and I did my best to sign, and then they said she was over at the Family Life and Learning Institute where she'd be better took care of.

'So I walked over to the other side of the town and found the booby-hatch, and they said: "There is no person of that name in our care."

'Waaall, I'd had three hours' sleep and that long walk, so I sat and waited and then this doctor come out and seen me, and said my sister wasn't there, and asked to see the form of admission. Which I didn' know what it was, Carolee.'

Biffi Burger had sat there for most of the day asking everybody had they seen her sister, and no-one had. She had trailed back across town and then asked for the paper she'd signed and they said no, that paper was just to certify that her sister had left their hospital in a satisfactory condition. And why had she signed it, if it wasn't true?

And so back to the booby-hatch.

And so back home.

And back to the booby-hatch, only this time she was to see a doctor, only he didn't seem to understand that somewhere in the building was her sister, and instead, asked her a lot of questions. How long have you feared your sister is missing? Have you reported it to the police? You signed a paper saying she was released – now, why would you do that if it wasn't true? Which hospital did you think she was in? This is serious official business, Mrs. Burger, and a poor view is taken of those who waste valuable professional time.

Finally, deaf with questions she didn't understand, dumb with terror and confusion, and blinded by science and tears, she had said:

'I just want to see my sister and make sure she's O.K. She don't have no idea of lookin' after herself with these spells of hers.'

'Transference is no solution,' said the doctor.

'Do what?' said Biffi Burger.

The doctor gave a sort of terminal smile and Biffi left his office. To hell with it! She dived as soon as possible down a little corridor. She would search the whole goddam building.

'Y'unnerstand, Carolee,' she said, 'I was like one of them white rats you see in those mad scientist's laboratory horror movies.'

They charted her progress as well as if they had put an electrode under her skin. She had scurried down a blind walled corridor, and found two or three recessed buttons in the wall.

Red – danger? Alarm?

Green – safe? Go? Walk?

Gray – nothing she could imagine, except a continuation of the dull corridor.

Shrewd little mouse, she had pressed green, and the whole body of the clinic knew immediately that they had a wanderer who was travelling into the central circuits of its being.

When a panel in the wall opened onto another corridor of the same dead dull light seeping from everywhere and nowhere, Biffi hesitated. But some way she would find the wards and her sister.

The next test had been a series of four doors, identical but for their handles. She chose the round handle – this fed a charge of self-satisfaction to the brain of the monster, and she was lulled deeper and deeper from the day outside.

An unnerving half hour later, she was spilled from the unpeopled scientific circuits of the maze and was back in the foyer, with its fake palm trees and plashing fountain. There was the main entrance, and all her quivering instincts told her to take it. She would get the law in here.

But then a voice stopped her.

'Mrs. Burger.'

The voice held authority, apology, urgency – that fat bastard doctor had found her sister – ha!

'And that's when the rat trap closed, Carolee. I'd been smelling cold steel jaws all over that place and was too much of a damned fool to listen to my nose.

'Suddenly, my feet are high as my head and my arms are crammed against me, and there's three six-foot-nine gorillas and a stretcher, and the doctor saying: "You mustn't distress yourself, Mrs. Burger, this is for the best, you must trust us."

'So I'm howlin' and hollerin' down them corridors faster than a greased snake and then into a room and then there's a needle. Instant sleep.'

'When the hell was this, Biffi?'

'Thirty years back. Long before you was a lighted candle in your sainted daddy's eyes.'

'But can't you get out now?'

'Ah, maybe so. Yes, I guess so, if I said I really believed she was never here. But she was. Is, for all I know. For all I know, the whole damn family is here. Me lookin' for her, my ma lookin' for me, only she'd likely be dead now, my pa lookin' for her, only I 'spect he'd be dead now, too.'

Biffi Burger nodded and shambled away to resume her role of restless old crazy. Enough wanderin' and they'd give her those little mauve pills, the ones that give you a real buzz with coffee, and then would come a day's dreamless sleep. She wrung her hands and mumbled fretfully. Good. The nurse in the station had seen and was making the right notes.

'Burger, you goddamed junkie,' snorted Rowena Neill, her heels drumming submission into the flesh of the beast. 'What is this crap? Restless wandering? Disturbed behaviour? Regressive patterns? Enjoying it, are you?'

Biffi Burger nodded.

'Sure as shit sucks,' she said, 'must be on Venus now, Nurse.'

'A Burger triple cocktail,' snorted Rowena Neill. 'You old faker.'

Her eyes flicked over yesterday's notes; there was an envelope clipped in for the a.m. staff. She sat back in the station to read it.

Goddam it. Poor kid. And she was doing so well, too. Neill looked into the dayroom. Carolee was sitting alone, listlessly staring at the observation mirror. The note said that she was to go upstairs the next day. Neill had worked upstairs two years before. It had sickened her and only by asking for geriatrics had she got out. She had been an animal rights campaigner at college and to see human experimentation was repellent to her. But she had never yet stuck her neck out: she'd never had to. If she lost the letter, it would give Carolee another day. Her mind flicked over the possibilities. Dammit, Deniece was going to a cure in Pasadena to dry out in a couple of months anyhow. She'd miss the old ladies, but they had their own ways of coping.

'Hodges,' said Rowena Neill.

Carolee abased herself in the nurses' station.

'You know they want to transfer you?'

Carolee looked as gray as the floor, walls and ceiling. Her eyes swivelled towards the metallic mirror.

'I heard them,' she said. 'Can't I discharge myself? Burger said . . .'

'Kid, you're six weeks short of autonomy. I'd like you to deliver a letter for me this evening. I'll give you a pass out.'

'A letter? Where to?'

'I'd suggest Mexico,' said Neill, filling in the pass. 'Get your young man to take you there.'

'He's not a young man,' said Carolee.

'Kid, I don't give a flying fuck,' said Neill. 'You find your happiness where you can.'

She handed Carolee an envelope, a pass and her own day coat.

'Camouflage,' said Neill. 'Get out of my sight.'

Came a frantic knock on Reen's doorway.

'Carolee!'

Carolee dived through the opened door and slammed it behind her.

'I'm sorry,' she said. 'I couldn't stand it. They're going to do something awful to me. Neill let me out and she said get to Mexico. Now.'

'Mexico it is,' said Rotary Spokes, switching off the TV.

At eleven they wolfed a burger. The sign by the stand said Evansville 5 miles. The night flowed over the hot metal and chill leather. Carolee clung, freezing under layers of clothes and a thick jacket. Rotary Spokes' sweat was icy.

The darkest of the night was over. A deep navy swept upwards from the horizon. They shook warmth into their bodies chewing pizza. A vast river flowed somewhere away to the left.

'The Mississippi,' said Rotary Spokes tonelessly. And the sign said: 'Little Rock thanks you for driving safely.' The Harley roared along the freeway like a banshee fleeing the cold white then pink of the dawn.

It was 8.00 a.m. when the signs said San Angelo, San Antonio, 280 miles.

And 'Have you checked your brakes?' said the next.

'What about if we stop and sleep?' said Carolee, scraping dust from her face. 'I can't hang on much longer.'

'You think it's safe?' said Rotary Spokes.

'I don't know. Shit, it has to be. No-one saw me leave.'

'I dunno,' said Rotary Spokes. 'I'm tuckered out, but I can push it a bit.'

Carolee swayed where she stood.

'Cain't think,' Rotary Spokes said. 'Let's get a motel room and sleep, huh?'

Truth to tell, she needed to check the bike anyhow. It had a long way to go. That and ring Bean. They drove into a motel with little gardens outside each dwarf chalet. Carolee touched one of the flowers and laughed hysterically.

'Plastic,' she gasped. 'Plastic flowers and astro-turf.'

'We find it keeps much longer than the real stuff down here,' said the lady motel owner. 'You sleep good, you kids. Where was you goin'?'

'Wichita,' said Rotary Spokes. 'Our maw's real sick. Thank you kindly.'

They flopped on the queen-size bed and Carolee snuggled up to Rotary Spokes' aching shoulders. After a while she flopped asleep. Rotary Spokes lit a cigarette and wished desperately that Bean was there. She'd know what to do. She slung her clothes on the floor, and undressed Carolee limp as a rag doll.

She plunged into exhausted sleep.

Glass shattered; an axe splintered through the door.

'What the hell?' bellowed Rotary Spokes.

Six figures stood in the doorway, silhouetted against the livingroom light.

'My baby!' screamed Corah.

'Satan, Satan,' frothed Abner.

'Wait in the other room,' Astler told the three institute orderlies.

'Corrupter of innocent youth!' howled Abner, ripping the covers from the bed.

'God save the soul of my child!' Corah moaned to the heavens, falling to her knees.

Astler took in the scene. So this was the woman. He had only seen this sort of thing in blue movies from the *Thrill of the Month Club*. 'Nice body,' he thought to himself.

Rotary Spokes put one strong arm around Carolee.

'God damn you bastards,' she said. 'Why don't you leave her alone? What do you care, anyway?'

'Get dressed,' said Corah, averting her eyes from this personification of evil.

'I won't,' said Carolee. 'Get away from me, you hear? Get out of my life!'

'Get dressed,' snapped Abner, throwing Carolee's jeans and T-shirt at her.

'If you don't come voluntarily . . .' menaced Astler, 'I thought this might happen. These depraved personalities will do anything. I brought help.'

Rotary Spokes stood in front of the bed.

'Get the fuck out of here,' she said, bunching her fists. 'GIT!'

'Whore of Babylon! Cover your nakedness!' orated Abner.

'Screw my nakedness, walking shit! I got more decency naked than you got clothed! What the hell do you expect, bustin' into folks' places in the middle of the night! Get out!'

The orderlies hung around the doorway. Nice titties, nice ass. And they were getting overtime.

'I better go,' said Carolee, tears streaming down her face. 'They'll only hurt you.'

'Stay where you are, darlin',' said Rotary Spokes. She yanked her jeans on and her T-shirt and stood with ready fists.

The orderlies moved in at Astler's signal. Rotary Spokes turned into a human dynamo, winding one with a cracking sound and knocking the other two to the floor.

Abner hustled Corah into the other room. Not a pretty sight for a woman. Astler gripped Carolee's arm, avoided the hard kick aimed at his groin, and dragged her next door to her everloving parents. In the bedroom, chairs splintered, the curtain rail ripped from the window sash, and finally Rotary Spokes crumpled to the floor. She dragged herself onto all fours; a kick in the stomach felled her again, a boot in her face blacked her out and the orderlies muscled into the livingroom.

'Who's goin' to pay for all this?' whined the motel owner. 'I didn't know they was lunatics.'

One of the orderlies, spitting teeth, bundled Carolee into a canvas strait-jacket.

'Surely that ain't needful?' whimpered Corah. 'It's that, that other one who's the animal.'

The orderlies tightened straps, one cursing his cracked ribs, and hauled the trussed-rigid body out of the motel room. Carolee flung her head back, and a primal howl hurtled over the dry plain. She bit the muffling hand on her mouth and jerked herself from side to side until she hit the floor of the ambulance face first.

'Not the clinic,' said Abner, sweating with relief. The Lord had deigned to grace him with a plan. 'Not the clinic. Take us home. We gotta do somethin' final here, somethin' to remove her from these influences. Somethin' real drastic.'

Carolee's screams ricochetted around the metal confines. In the driver's cab, one of the orderlies winced as he sloshed beer around his bleeding mouth.

Rotary Spokes tried to focus. Fuck. Every bone in her body ached and her lips were stuck together with blood. She focused finally on a pair of flowered slippers and looked up into the face of the motel owner.

'What did ya have to pick my place for? You filthy pervert! Launderin' them sheets ain't gonna clean up my memory of this evil day! And who's gonna pay for my fixtures and fittin's? You? It better be you, them other folks are gone now! I hope you got money, else you gonna be lookin' at four walls down here. My brother-in-law's the sheriff!'

Rotary Spokes closed her eyes. The voice tore on. And on, like a chainsaw. She slipped into unconsciousness again.

When the wrecked room swung into focus once more, Rotary Spokes was staring up the double barrels of a shotgun.

'You ain't takin' no advantage of me and me a widow woman,' cackled the motel owner triumphantly.

'Lady,' said Rotary Spokes. 'Lady, can I wash up a bit? Then I'll give you the money and get outta here.'

'You ain't abusin' my wash-stand. You ain't usin' my towels. You ain't filthyin' my soap with your wicked hands. Git up!'

Rotary Spokes stumbled upright. The room reeled and the woman jabbed her in the ribs with the gun.

'Lemme just git my things,' mumbled Rotary Spokes. The woman stood in the doorway, sweating onto the black metal. Rotary Spokes pulled her socks on over the dried blood on her toes. Bastards had stomped her. She pulled on her jacket – bastards had half-shredded the left sleeve.

'Let me wash my face, Lady,' she said, catching sight of the blood patches and bruises.

'Neither rest nor water nor food do you and your kind find among decent folks,' shrilled the woman. 'Git out in the daylight.'

Rotary Spokes got. The woman stood between her and the bike.

'Greenbacks, pervert,' she demanded.

Rotary Spokes emptied one pocket with her throbbing hand. The woman's eyes glittered and she snatched the notes.

Rotary Spokes dived at her and then grabbed the gun.

'You go no bidniss treatin' folks like this,' she said, and she bent the barrels backwards.

'Now you can shoot who really oughtta be shot,' she said and flung the twisted gun to the ground.

She lifted one leg painfully over the bike and kicked it alive. Agony stabbed up her thigh. She stared at the horrified face above the wad of bills, the stupid mouth wide on a silent scream. She revved the bike and rode deliberately at the woman, swerving at the last second. She flattened the flowers and the astro-turf into tyre-mashed trash, and flung herself back onto the highway.

Which way?

Who the hell cares? There was no going back, not to Normal, nor to Middlesville.

She drew up at the next gas station. It was deserted. She paddled dusty water on her face from a scummy seep in the cracked wash basin. A phone booth. Call the Guardian Angel. She'd know what to do.

CHAPTER
FOURTEEN

"Philip is a living example of natural selection. He was as fitted to survive in this world as a tapeworm in an intestine."
(William Golding. Free Fall)

Samuel Uncle was clean as an angel's asshole; his unshaven cheeks glowed with modest health and fervour. His shoes were chamois-buffed leather; his fraternity pin shone with scholastic promise. His teeth were dentally irrigated thrice daily; his hair was cut above his ears: he was the boy every mom and dad wanted their girl to walk home with.

But Samuel Uncle did not walk girls home. In due course, the Lord would show him the one who was to share his life, and meanwhile he kept himself pure. He had tried to talk to Carolee Hodges, and invited her to a pray-in, but the Lord had not seen fit to let it happen, and he blessed the Name of the Lord when he heard the rumours after her sudden disappearance. Nevertheless, he prayed for her daily: there was a virginal freshness about her, and of course that was why the world was so eager to besmirch her with its slander. He was a young man who never looked down while he showered and never looked up as girls walked past. He chewed his lunch-time sandwich, running his pared fingernails under the blessed Word.

'Pssst! Samuel!'

He looked up. No-one was there.

'Samuel!' It was a hissed stage whisper, but unmistakable. He tried to quieten his pounding heart. *Here I am, Lord*!

One of the immigrant cleaners jerked her head at him.

'*Samuel*,' she said, scarcely moving her lips.

'God forgive me for my presumption,' thought Samuel and went over to her.

'Can I ask you something, Mr. Samuel?' whispered the woman.

'Surely, ma'am.'

'It's my boy, Mr. Samuel. He's gettin' himself into a lot of trouble. Bad company, and what's a mother to do? I was hopin' – seein' as you're such a good, clean-livin' young man, would you talk to him for me? He just needs prayers and a good word from you, Mr. Samuel, would you help a poor mother who's just driven to distraction?'

Samuel Uncle took her hand. He looked straight into her troubled eyes.

'Ma'am,' he said softly. 'I would be honoured to do the Lord's work.'

The woman bobbed and blessed him. She arranged to meet him after school, and blessed him again, pressed his hand to her lips and shuffled out of the room.

She pushed in coins and punched a number on the phone.

'You better get ready,' she said into the mouthpiece. 'Yeah, he'll be there, and I swear, it's just what you need.'

At 5.30, Samuel Uncle chivalrously picked up the woman's two bulging shopping bags and shortened his stride. They soon left the green lawns and white-walled mansions around the college and a series of zig-zag alleys took them towards the poorer part of town.

'Gittin' dark early,' said the woman.

'Yes, ma'am,' said Samuel, onions and pilfered potatoes banging against his knees. Indeed, the sun was down by the time they hit the long road of Old Main Street. Samuel Uncle had thought that no-one lived here: the windows were broken or boarded up; many houses had no doors.

'You see how it is for me?' whined the woman. 'How can I hope for my boy to grow up a decent Christian?' There were shadowy figures slumped on the sidewalk here and there.

'This is it,' announced the woman, and started to haul herself up an iron staircase on the outside of one of the buildings. The handrail shook and the whole structure creaked. After every flight, the woman stopped, coughing, and then dragged herself up higher. Samuel Uncle was sweating from vertigo: fortunately it was so dark he couldn't look down.

Finally, the woman stopped and rattled through her pockets for a key.

'Here we are,' she said.

'I just realized,' said Samuel. 'I don't know your name – not that we have to have names, in the Lord's work.'

'You betcha,' said the woman. 'Anyhow, dearie, my name: Jael Mercedes.'

Jael? Samuel felt the spirit within him. Lo, I am with thee in the valley of the shadow. Jael flicked by the door and a dim bulb dulled the broken furniture and cracked flooring in a squalid kitchen. There were smells here that had never met the nostrils of Samuel Uncle before. He couldn't identify them, and was glad.

'Sister Jael,' he said, 'God has many different paths for us. May he bless you in yours.'

Jael gave his pure-white Lacoste sports shirt and creased chinos a long look.

'You better come in,' she said. 'I don't know if he's home.'

She kicked a door sagging on one hinge and led him through. She shut and locked the door.

'It falls down else,' she said.

There was a TV screen distorting a dog food commercial and a broken old sofa with two heads and sets of shoulders silhouetted dark against the cold TV light.

'I'm switchin' on the light,' she warned.

'Leave it off,' snarled one of the heads without turning. 'Come and sit here with us, Jesus boy.'

'There's no call to be uncivil,' snivelled Jael, wringing her hands. 'We got a visitor, we should show him some manners. Switch off the TV.'

'I ain't switchin' off no TV,' rasped the same voice.

'Siddown and have a beer,' said the other head.

'I don't use alcohol,' said Samuel, trying to keep calm.

'No-one's askin' you to *use alcohol*,' mocked the silhouette. 'Have a beer!'

Samuel fielded a can tossed in his direction and put it on the floor. He turned to Mrs. Mercedes. She had gone.

'Siddown, why don't you.'

Samuel sat on the edge of the broken sofa. There were no chairs. There was no carpet on the floor. Over his head, a bare bulb dangled on cobwebbed wire. This was surely hell, and these people on the sofa the lost, the damned. One was a sulky-looking boy with thick black hair in his eyes. Even with his smooth cheeks – too young to shave – he looked a desperate type. The other was a mountainous woman with dark glasses on, twitching a toothpick round in one corner of her mouth. An aunt? A wife? Samuel Uncle tried to find some bearings.

'So,' said the woman, spitting the toothpick suddenly to the floor. 'You come to evangelize my friend here?'

'Well, yes, ma'am, in a manner of speaking.'

'What manner's that?' growled the uncouth youth, leering.

'Your dear mother has asked me to talk to you. I gather you're having some doubts about the good Lord and his purpose in life for you?'

The youth kicked the TV button and there was a blue flash at the plug – language which Samuel had never heard before exploded from the boy's hard mouth.

'What purpose in life?' snarled the youth. 'They got my woman, Jesus boy, and what the fuck can you an' Jesus do about that?'

'Waaall,' said the woman mountain, placatingly. 'This here boy is from the college, Orville.'

Ah, he had a name. Orville.

'Oh, he's from the college, huh?'

'Yes,' said Samuel Uncle.

'My old lady's from the college,' said Orville, threateningly. 'Carolee – you know her?'

Samuel Uncle blushed. The very girl he thought God had directed him to. Yes, he admitted to himself, he had felt lust, God forgive him. And she had been the 'old lady' of this lost spawn of Satan. He prayed inwardly.

'She's not at the college anymore,' he said.

'We *know* she's not at the college anymore,' Orville mimicked his cheerful tones. 'What we *want* to know is – where is she?'

He stood over Samuel. Cheap aftershave and lager polluted the air. Orville wore a fringed and filthy suede jacket and jeans as torn as they were patched. His shoes were heeled snakeskin. He had a death's-head ring on one hand and heavy metal chains around each wrist.

'Orville, I don't know where she is. You can rest assured her dear parents have done the best thing for her in her confused state of mind. Leave her alone, Orville.'

'Suppose I don't want to leave her alone,' said Orville, popping another can of cheap lager, swigging and belching. 'Suppose I am in love, L-O-V-E, baby boy?'

'Orville, the love of a parent knows best. This is something you must realize. Why, that's why I'm here now. The love of your mother has brought me here. Her love for God and her love for her son.'

'Waaall, hot dog!' grimaced Orville, 'You know what I say to that? I say shit, Jesus-boy, S-H-I-T.'

'Now, Orville, honey,' said the woman mountain. 'Calm yourself. The boy's tryin' to help. He just don't know how yet, and you cussin' him ain't gonna help.' She turned to Samuel Uncle. 'Y'see, I been tryin' to help the boy, kinda bein' his guardian angel.'

'Fuck you!' slurred Orville.

Samuel blanched at the blasphemy. Guardian angel!

A door opened. Mrs. Mercedes! Samuel turned gratefully to his ally – *Mrs. Mercedes?*

The woman in the doorway didn't look anything like the worry-laden overalled figure who had trudged along beside him. For a start she had lost at least fifty pounds. Her graying perm had become a hennaed upsweep above striking brows, and a large cigar lay easy between her scarlet lips. For the rest, a skin-tight black jumpsuit had replaced the saggy overall, and she wore black spurred boots instead of down-at-the-heel mules.

'Fer God's sake!' spluttered the woman mountain.

'Jael – Mrs. Mercedes,' whimpered Samuel.

'How can you be a outlaw if you look like a in-law?' camped none other than The Phoenix of Texas.

'Mrs. Mercedes!' Orville laughed, and crushed his beer can.

'To business,' said The Phoenix. 'Sit down, Sammy boy.'

'I don't know what you people are up to,' said Samuel. 'But I really think I'd better be getting home.' He dived for the door and then remembered it was locked.

'Sit down,' barked Orville.

Samuel sat.

'As you may be aware,' said The Phoenix. 'The parents – Carolee's parents – aren't likely to talk to us.'

'That's where you come in,' said Orville, tapping one toe against Samuel's shaking knees.

'I don't want anything to do with this!' gabbled Samuel.

'One phone call,' said the woman mountain. 'One little phone call. You are concerned about her. You're an A student. You wanted to date her once. You wanna send her some sorta moral uplift, boy. You git the address where she's at. Simple.'

'I'll never do it,' said Samuel. 'Deliver her into your hands? May God forgive you.'

'Take your pants off,' said The Phoenix.

'Is that necessary?' said Orville with distaste.

'I'm glad you see the foolishness of this, Orville,' said Samuel desperately.

'I don't see no foolishness,' said Orville. 'I just got a delicate stomach.'

'Trust me, sonny,' said The Phoenix.

Samuel sat in his boxer shorts, sandwiched between the bulk of the woman mountain and the taut black thighs of . . . Mrs. Mercedes? Jesus help me, he thought.

The TV flickered back on. J.R. was unbuttoning his shirt while Sue-Ellen looked sultry and pained.

Orville hissed at the screen.

'Leave the bastard! Makes me sick to see a good woman wasted on that asshole!'

'Have a beer, Samuel,' said The Phoenix. 'Just while you're making up your mind.'

Orville grinned.

'I'll get a glass, Maw,' he said, 'seein' as he's company.' Rotary Spokes – Orville – poured a slug of vodka into the glass and topped it with beer, unseen behind the sofa.

'Drink it.'

Samuel sipped, grimacing. The Lord forgive him – he'd broken his vow.

Sue-Ellen looked over J.R.'s shoulder, biting her lip.

'Ain't that good?' J.R. told her.

Orville spat.

'You want me to introduce you?' said The Phoenix. 'I know her.'

'Sure would, Maw!' enthused Orville.

'For my baby boy, anything,' said The Phoenix, drifting a flock of smoke rings past Samuel's pale face.

'Let me have my pants back.'

'Good. Here's the phone. Here's the number.'

'I'm not going to do it!'

'The boy bores me,' said The Phoenix, flicking a scalpel blade from her sleeve. She waved it nonchalantly around Samuel.

'Gimme that,' said Orville. He leant over Samuel and the blade hovered in front of his eyes. Finally he rested his hand above Samuel's heart, a half inch from the small green crocodile on his shirt.

'Kinda preppy, ain't he?' said the woman mountain. Orville nicked the stitching with the blade.

'Shame to lose your *crocodile*, Samuel,' he menaced.

Samuel gasped as the tiny green creature flipped off the fabric. Orville held his cigarette against it, and it writhed to ashes. The ashes floated to the floor. These people are capable of anything, thought Samuel. What a bunch of sickies. But no way would he deliver that girl into their evil clutches.

'Give it time,' said the woman mountain. 'I wanna watch the Addams family.'

'Hey, move over,' said Orville. 'I like this.'

'Drink your beer,' snarled The Phoenix.

Samuel felt sick to his stomach as he gulped the alien fluid. These people were crazy. The sofa shook with glee as Uncle Fester lit up a Christmas tree with the plug he'd popped into his mouth.

'Well?' inquired The Phoenix as the credits came up.

'You're evil,' he told them all. 'I will never collude with Statan.'

'One phone call?'

'Never!'

Orville unpinned his fraternity pin and swaggered over to one of the doors in the hellhole. He opened it. It was a toilet so filthy that Samuel gulped back vomit. Orville grinned widely and dangled the pin over the cracked toilet bowl.

Cling not to the trappings of this world, his conscience told him . . .

'But that's my fraternity pin!' he wailed.

'You gonna call?'

'No!'

The pin clattered and splashed. The ancient plumbing sent it into the municipal sewerage system.

Samuel started to sweat and tremble.

'Boy's gonna be sick,' said the woman mountain maternally, pulling a grimy plastic bowl from under the rusted, sprung springs.

'No,' he said. 'Please, let me go home.'

The Phoenix picked up his folded pants. She started to razor off the label. Samuel was horrified. Of course, as a good student he always wore Calvins and a Lacoste shirt.

What more would they be capable of? Orville started pacing the floor, muttering: a fair imitation of a drug-hungry Biffi Burger, thought Rotary Spokes.

'Orville,' said The Phoenix, with a note of alarm. 'Orville, dear, give Maw the blade.'

She flicked it back up her sleeve.

'Orville's very impatient, Samuel. And a little unpredictable. It doesn't do to antagonize him. Orville, take your pills,' she nagged at him.

Rotary Spokes lurched to the other door and disappeared. She smoked one of the joints lying in a neat row, and emerged with an overdone calm.

'You just co-operate with me, and you'll be fine,' she told Samuel.

'Take your shirt off,' said The Phoenix. 'It's O.K. I'm taking mine off too.'

She smiled invitingly and unbuttoned the top half of her suit. Samuel covered his eyes against the voluptuous nakedness. The woman mountain took him by the throat with one hand and with the other peeled off his shirt. Orville folded it with psychotic precision, fixing his glittering eyes on Samuel Uncle.

The Phoenix draped herself along the pale sweating body, one hand on his inner thigh, the other gripping his hair by the root. She drew his face to hers. There was a flash.

She sat, kittenish, on his lap. There was another flash.

She pushed him to his knees and spread her thighs. Another flash. She pushed him away from her, with an expression of distaste.

'Think they'll come out?' inquired the woman mountain.

'Sure, honey,' purred The Phoenix. 'I'll need to trash this suit and have a shower, though.'

'I guess those prints'll fit into a envelope six-by-eight,' said the woman mountain. 'I guess the envelope'll be delivered personally. I guess Mr Abner J. Hodges is going to be mighty interested in what his ace student does with his spare time.'

'You wouldn't. You would.' said Samuel Uncle, clasping his arms over his naked chest.

'Sammy boy, we don't want to do nothin',' said the woman mountain, gently. 'I guess we been watchin' too much TV, right, Orville?'

'Guess we have,' said Orville. 'Or I guess some people don't take the chance of helpin' people when they can. Save my immortal soul, huh? But shit when it comes to my happiness. Or Carolee's. Get that little creep outta here. Before I do somethin' I'll regret.'

Orville threw the pants and desecrated shirt at Samuel. He buttoned and zipped, shaking.

'I'll make your phone call. But you have to give me those negatives.'

'First we'll have to see how *positive* your phone call turns out,' smirked Orville.

Samuel took the phone in his sweating hands. This wasn't happening. Where were the angels, the police sirens, where was the cavalry? He'd warn Mr Hodges. Somehow.

Orville picked up another receiver across the room.

'Just in case you was havin' any smart ideas, boy,' he said.

Samuel stuttered through to Abner J. Hodges. Whose heart was humbled that an A student would bother with the trash his wife's daughter had turned out to be.

'I know you'll do her nothing but good, Sam, my boy,' he enthused. 'What she needs is the influence of a Christian young man. God knows we've tried, and we've failed.' He became confidential.

'There was a pervert involved, Samuel. Forgive me for tampering with your pure-hearted innocence. A stark-raving-mad pervert. You wouldn't believe it, would you?'

Samuel looked at the horrifying trio gazing at him– The Phoenix tapping her wrist with the dull side of the scalpel, the soft-faced, hard-mouthed Orville, listening in, the woman mountain cracking open another beer.

'Y. . .no, sir,' he said. 'I'm real sorry for the distress you and Mrs. Hodges have had to endure. These people are animals, God forgive me for saying it.'

'Now, boy, here's her address. You got a pen?'

The Phoenix handed him a gold pen and a piece of paper.

His writing spilled shakily over it. Hanging up the phone, Orville dragged deep on a cigarette, choked him with a stream of smoke and folded the paper into a pocket.

'You can go now, preppy Jesus boy,' he whispered.

'What about the negatives?' he whimpered.

'Just keep your ass wiped and your nose clean, boy, and you'll never hear another word,' said The Phoenix. 'Get. No – wait!'

She swaggered over to him and kissed his white shirt with her scarlet lipstick. She pushed her face at his neck, once, twice, three times.

'Your first hickeys,' she told him. 'Now. Off with you. Move it.'

Orville high-kicked the door to the kitchen. The rotten wood splintered, the lock hung from the frame.

Samuel clawed his way down the outside stair and nearly fell several times along the awful street. There were still the shapeless derelicts on the doorsteps, clinking bottles and laughing like fiends. An occasional candle guttered through rags at cracked windows.

The Phoenix flipped out her pocket transmitter.

'Move in as soon as the kid makes the third block,' she said.

A bus rolled in and the derelicts piled into it.

The Phoenix waved them off. It's always useful to know a man like Seamus O'Gallagher, head of the largest extras agency in the world.

The Phoenix, Bean and Rotary Spokes walked into the desert as huge machines moved in and took the street apart, crunching the bricks to dust.

'That was real nice of you,' said Rotary Spokes.

'It was my pleasure,' said The Phoenix.

'*Mrs.* Jael Mercedes,' sniggered Bean.

A small plane landed a hundred yards ahead.

'Can I give you girls a ride?' asked The Phoenix.

'I think we've blown Middlesville,' said Rotary Spokes.

'I think we better avoid Normal, too.' said Bean.

'Shucks,' said The Phoenix. 'And I do like a rodeo.'

The ground fell from under them as the plane took off into the night.

'Where is she?' asked Bean.

Rotary Spokes unfolded the paper.

'"The Fellowship of the Risen Saviour Hostel,
  Balls Pond Road,
  London,
  England,
  Europe."'

'Yurrrup,' said Bean. 'Waaall?'

'Is that good?' said Rotary Spokes.

'I been to London once,' said Bean. 'They're as crazy as a herd a steer on loco weed over there. If it's economic, convenient or comfortable, they don't got it. And they got the shits for weather. But – Jesus, I got a friend there. She could look out for Carolee. I'll get onto it.'

'Use the phone', said The Phoenix. 'No, don't. It's three in the morning there. We'll call later.'

The plane purred toward the coast, tiny towns like piles of junk jewellery glittering below them.

CHAPTER
FIFTEEN

"Did you say I've got a lot to learn ?
Well don't think I'm tryin' not to learn
Since this is the perfect spot to learn
Come over to my place and teach me, teach me tonight !"
(Phoebe Snow, Teach me Tonight)

Dor sat in the stands, red dust clotting the sweat on her rouged cheeks. Another steer was goaded out into the ring; another cowboy bouncing in the air; the crowd surged, whooped and poured beer down its throat, over its head. Dor recognised another pair of mushroom pants, only the last time she had seen them, they were crumpled at the end of her pink polyester quilt. She knew the faces, too: sweating, laughing through misshapen teeth. She knew every bit of stubble on those boys' leathery cheeks.

But lately, she just couldn't put no joy in it. The mattress creaked, the sheets rustled, the boys banged away and sighed, the greasy bills lay on her table. But her thoughts were with a body she had never managed to lure into her bed: the tall, unattainable Rotary Spokes. *Shit!* She'd known her for years, and could only think of all the wasted days when they had drunk beer, watched TV, all the good-nights and the hi-there's: days and nights and days and days and nights. Normal was empty without her and Dor blamed herself; if she hadn't told Lorie-Kay and Mar'Ann – but it hadn't seemed like nothing strange to her, and that's why she'd told. She'd gotten to like, even love the idea. How could she have known they'd be so high and mighty about it, and now they'd driven Rotary Spokes away. She slugged brandy from her paper-bagged bottle. Shit. She felt a hot hand knead her thigh and looked at him wearily.

'Screw you,' she sighed.

He smiled with delight.

'That's what I was hopin' you'd say, darlin',' he murmured.

She gathered a rhinestoned cardigan, cigarettes, bag and brandy and stumbled away from him along the row. Asshole. The stand below looked like they was having more fun anyway. Yee-ha-in' and all that jazz. She squeezed into a row there.

'Git 'im!' yelled someone next to her, surging upright. The clock dinged, the boy was still on, and dollar bills scrabbled from hand to hand.

'Who's yer boy?' yelled the woman beside her, behind dark glasses.

'Do what?' said Dor, her head beginning to ache.

'Who's yer boy? Where you got yer money, then?'

'I'm just spectatin',' said Dor.

'You oughtta gamble,' she told her, then screamed, '*kill 'im!*' She sweated off pounds as she stood hollering and thumping one hand with the other, then sat down again.

'You wanna beer?' she asked Dor.

Dor shook her head and passed over her brown paper bag.

The woman swigged, coughed and handed it back.

'Damn good stuff!' She looked at Dor. She was a woman who hated to see people sad.

'I'm Toots,' she said unconvincingly, and then roared with laughter.

'I'm Dor.'

'Hey now, that's a real pretty name. Dor, huh? Well. Well.' She checked her programme.

'My boys ain't on for a while,' she said. 'You wanna go have a beer?'

'O.K.,' said Dor and they stumbled over feet and popcorn cartons up the stands and down into 1st Street.

'There's Dino's,' said Dor. They walked in together, shoulders touching briefly at the door.

'Goddam,' said Toots. 'They got some mighty fine records on this jukebox.' She ladled handfuls of nickels out of her tight jeans.

It turned out that Toots was a trucker; she called her rig Mabel. She had been diverted from a cross-country haul by the rodeo signs on the distant freeway.

'I'd go anywhere for a rodeo,' she said. 'Second-best thing in the world.' She dug Dor in the ribs and hooted. Dor didn't get it. Then she did. She thought of the half-hearted fucking of the last few weeks and shrugged.

'I'll git another beer,' she said.

'She a friend of Rodry's?' asked Dino.

'No. Just met up at the rodeo, Dino.'

What had made him say that? Sure, Toots did have a loud mouth and strode around like she owned the place. Dor walked back to the table, thinking fast. She noticed a dark line curling on Toots' throat.

'What's that? Scar?' she said.

Toots grinned wall-to-wall.

'I just might show you some time,' she said, and slipped the top button of her blouse undone. The line turned into a flame burst.

'That there's the tail of the dragon of summer,' said Toots. 'I got the dragon of spring on my back, and the other two, well, the other two, honey, you gotta seek them out.' She put one ankle on the other knee and sat back.

'You live here? Uh-huh. You work here? Uh-huh. You don't like it much, do you?'

Dor had to admit Normal was losing its charm.

'But you, honey, you ain't. Aw, I'm sorry, tell me if I'm spouting off, will you, Dor? I just got a main line from my little brain to my big mouth and it all comes out real plain. I don't mean no offence.'

'You can search my fuckin' soul,' said Dor. 'And that's what I do for my living. Fuckin'.'

'Damn,' said Toots admiringly. 'You must be a real forbearin' woman. They ain't got no work here, right?'

'Waaall,' said Dor, 'there used to be a cannin' factory and a couple of farms. I used to go pickin' in the season. Used to be a sewin' factory here. Fine machine work. Two years. I never worked there. Fuck of a sight easier to lay on your back and say "Do it again, big boy."'

Toots laughed. Dor began to feel witty.

'I mean, come up an' see me sometime,' she camped. 'Mmm, thatta big bankroll in your pocket, or are you just pleased to see me? All that shit. Kinda gettin' tired of it now.'

'Fancy a change, huh?' said Toots.

'I do believe I do,' said Dor quietly. 'Come on over to my place and I'll give you them knittin' patterns,' she said loudly for Dino's benefit.

'God, Dor, you have a real smart place,' Toots walked round the room, bounced on the bed.

'What sort of place you live in, then?' asked Dor, sitting on the chair and slipping off one stiletto.

'Damn. I got half a trailer in Michigan and a bed or two here and there. I never fixed a place up proper like you done. I always wanted to.'

Princess Henrietta Maria II walked stiffly across the floor and sat in front of Dor.

'So, feed me, you ape,' she said with her deep green eyes hypnotizing Dor.

'That your cat?'

'Nah, my friend's. She's gone away for a while. Hey, Fluffy, here, Fluffy – shit!'

The Princess dived out of Dor's fat arms, unravelling scarlet silk threads, and vanished, stiff-tailed and spitting.

'I always wanted a cat,' said Toots. 'Your – friend, you say?'

Eyes met again.

'I gotta level with you, Dor. I wanna hit the sack with you. If you don't want to, that's fine, if your friend's comin' back. We can git rat-assed anyway.'

Dor screeched a laugh.

'It ain't like that,' she said. 'Not for want of me tryin' I might add.'

'I *thought* you was a dyke,' Toots crowed happily.

Dor shook her head.

'I ain't never done it with a woman,' she said.

Toots smiled and opened her arms.

'Come to Toots, darlin',' she said.

The first kiss sent all the blood pouring into Dor's head. The kiss went on and on and on, and the blood and the brandy shivered down every tiny vein and flooded through every artery. Toots finally drew her face away.

'You're some kisser,' she said and plonked her lips on Dor's nose.

'Shit, you're the kisser,' said Dor, blushing like a high school kid.

'Well, shall we try that again?'

And again? And again?

'So that's where you keep the dragon of autumn,' said Dor, tracing the magnificent Chinese creature over Toots' navel. 'Why a dragon?'

'Ah, I dunno. I guess the tattooist only did dragons. I don't remember: he told a whole lot of stories about dragons, you know, they used to worship them in China. They used to fly and everything.'

Dor's lips worshipped, Dor's heart soared.

'Hey, darlin',' said Toots. 'Why don't you get your clothes right off, and get in this bed? I ain't done it in a bed for years.'

'Where the hell d'you usually do it, Toots?'

'I usually do it in Mabel – my truck. Like all the good boys. Only I guess I have a whole lot better a time than they do. I never had no complaints.'

'Me neither,' said Dor. 'Only I regard this as a real challenge.'

The mattress sagged under their bodies.

'I don't know where to begin, truth to tell,' said Dor. 'I seen all them pictures, but, shit, we ain't posin' for no cameras.'

'They should be so lucky,' said Toots, leaning on one elbow, and stroking Dor's face, neck, shoulders, breasts. 'I met a guy at the rodeo today,' said Toots. 'Wanted to photo my tattoos. Said he was nuts about tattoos and photography. I told him to piss off. Shame, really, he looked like a nice Jewish boy.'

Dor smoothed her hand over Toots' body.

'Mine,' she said. 'All mine. At least for now.'

Ah, the beauty of another woman.

'You ever see that Bruce Lee film?' gasped Dor.

'Shit, woman, no, I never seen that Bruce Lee film – that's *so* nice. What the hell – oh, Dor . . . – what the hell we talkin' about Bruce Lee for – oh, yes.'

'Cuz . . . ah, *Toots* I don't believe – what the hell's happenin' to me?'

Night drew a discreet veil over Normal.

'What the hell movie was you goin' on about?' said Toots into Dor's neck.

'*Enter The Dragon*', whispered Dor. 'I guess they got real hot winters in China?'

The bed shook and shook. And only a part of it was laughing.

Sweat poured into the white starched collar around the Reverend Thomas Pateman's neck.

'For he has written, my weak and feeble friends: "*Since they did not see fit to honour God, God gave them up to a base mind and improper conduct*!'" Let us stamp out this unnatural passion from the blood of our chosen nation! In the new kingdom of the risen Christ, he will consign them all to the flames of his wrath! Commies, faggots, lesbohemes, hippies, weirdos, junkies – the trash of the earth will rot on the garbage heaps of Eternal Righteousness!'

'AMEN!' thundered the salvated hordes of Middle America.

'I could get used to this,' said Dor. 'Do you die if you have too many orgasms?'

'You start livin',' said Toots. 'Hey, you know why dykes ain't never changed the world?'

'No. The feelin' I got could move mountains,' said Dor.

'They – we – ain't never changed the world cuz we don't never git out of bed for long enough.'

'That I believe,' said Dor fluttering her eyelashes against Toots' cheek.

'Hey,' said Dor from the tub. 'Hey, if I come on the road with you, and believe me, I'm comin', what the hell do I do with Rodry's cat?'

Princess Henrietta Maria looked coy. She preferred Dor au naturelle, and this Toots person, well . . .

'It seems zat she iss a substitute for ze brandy quarts, and ze lakes of evil schtink vat Dor hass bin usink,' thought the cat.

'Reckon she'd travel good? I got a fur rug in the truck.' Eight feet above the ground, stretched out on sheepskin, sun beating warmth, air-cooler on . . . 'So, I haff a mobile palace callt Mabel,' thought the Princess. 'So.'

She bided her time and Mabel roared out of Normal, two happy hearts heavier.

Eighty miles along the freeway, Dor sold her house to a destitute family sitting in the shade while their engine cooled. She sold it for fifty bucks, and then, feeling bad, stowed the bills in the baby's ragged undershirt.

'You really mean this, don't you?' said Toots. She couldn't believe her luck.

'I sure as hell do. I ain't fool enough to let the best thing I ever met roar out of my life.'

The truck chugged sweetly into the setting sun.

CHAPTER
SIXTEEN

"I'm gonna sit right down and write myself a letter
And make believe it came from you . . ."
(Fats Waller)

Rotary Spokes waved through the dawn at a small white plane bound for Hauizi, bearing The Phoenix and the Big Bean. She lit a cigarette, blew smoke through the pre-dawn mist and walked back past the silent airport sheds.

She kicked the turquoise-flake Electraglide into growling life and took the coast road to the beach house. Ruth had blown out a month before with a canine coiffurist, leaving splatters of ketchup, blood stains of red wine, and splinters of glossy black Steinway concert grand.

The three of them had spent a week clearing out and two weeks of good living to get rid of the *hgrillis*: the bad spirits The Phoenix felt Ruth had surely left behind her. On the island, anyone casting *hgrilliss* would have been consigned to a raft with thirty-seven days' worth of food and water: a small island cannot afford *hgrilliss* stalking about where things must live and grow. Ruth might last thirty-seven days with Indra Lacombe, the poodle-groomer, or even thirty-seven weeks. Her *hgrilliss* would wreak havoc among the yapping and the clipping, the snapping and the scented shampoo.

Sure, The Phoenix and Bean had asked her to go with them, but Rotary Spokes was no tag-along. And a certain Hug had been roaring round her heart the last few weeks, pawing impatiently, as she became expert at twirling martini glasses, relaxing her powerful stomach muscles all day in the sun. You couldn't deny it: Sea-Island cotton sheets are the best sleep in the universe, but any kind of sheets are fine, on one condition. You have to have a someone to curl around, to curl around you. The elusive Ms. Right. Hot damn! She could have been happy in Normal with Ms. Right. Except Normal would have turned on her and turned her out. And there was no way of going back to Middlesville: that would have meant another change of hair colour and a new disguise for her distinctive frame. She couldn't risk being Orville again. Besides, Carolee was out of it, and from what Bean had remembered: anything goes in Ball's Pond Road. Rotary Spokes had written Carolee a letter to that address in her best script and signed it Harletta Davidson.

She grinned at her reflection in the hall mirror:

'*Do you bleach, Rhoda*?' echoed Karen Schuchter.

No, asshole, I just lay in the sun.

Goddam, she was some dude these days! The Phoenix had showered her absently with gifts: the custom Electraglide Harley for a start – gleaming seamless tubing and monoshock suspension. She could carve 140 m.p.h. out of the revamped engine. And a new leather jacket. Gucci boots? The Phoenix never let anything else cross her doorstep.

But a certain feline paw batted her shoulder with impatience, a certain sleek tail lashed along her spine; The Hug snarled at her, MOVE! GET UP AND GO! Which was all very well. It was fine for a Hug to bound around the universe and stalk up mountain ravines. But where to?

To be more specific, Rotary Spokes was cussing herself for a careless idiot. Peace and profound relief had flowed round her when she learnt that Carolee was safe. It kind of let her off the hook. She had felt so goddam responsible. And so helpless, which was a rare emotion for Rotary Spokes.

With exultation she had basked in the memory of a particular shade of blue eyes, a feline warmth and power, a thrilling European voice. A hundred dreams had taken her this far. But the episode in the astro-turfed motel had destroyed a number of things. As well as giving her a white thread of scar tissue down her once smooth neck, the booby-hatch orderlies had torn open her jacket sleeve pocket, and unnoticed, the folded piece of paper holding Jess's address had fluttered away.

Rotary Spokes realized she couldn't even do a Gooseneck Squash and haunt the library: she couldn't recall Jess's second name, goddam it! She had only looked at the address once through a haze of champagne and couldn't remember one damn word of it.

Jess. Jess. Jess.

The hills near Middlesville were a lacework of dirt tracks, unnamed, unnumbered.

No house was in spitting distance of another.

And, anyway, what if she had misjudged the whole thing?

Rotary Spokes sighed. With The Hug mad and mean as hell, and her mind a foolish tangle, she ran down the beach and into the sea.

Later in the week, a red, blue and white van crunched to a halt on the gravelled drive at the beach house.

'Ms. Spokes? I got a package for you. You sign here.' As she did, the mailman leeringly took in her deep-tanned muscular body in its lilac hastily-draped towel. Her eyes lifted him two feet into the air and hurtled him into his driving seat. He was a mile up the road before he realized he hadn't even switched the engine on – or had he? He clutched the wheel and wondered about sunstroke.

Now, that was neat, thought Rotary Spokes.

'*Neat*!' roared The Hug. 'It was fucking BRILLIANT!'

Inside the package were four envelopes and a loose sheet of paper. Rotary Spokes dropped the towel as she strolled through the house and went to sit naked on the bleached boards of the deck. The surf pounded in her ears. She flipped the piece of paper flat.

'So, finally I got a address for you! This here shit's been piling up where Bean used to live. Either you are one popular girl or else real unpopular! Save the mauve envelope till last! There I was, wondering whether I should skip town and banzai off to Hauizi with that insane Bean, and there is a knock at the door. Picture it, Rotary, me, Jo-Marie Lesenbrecht, glued to the TV as per fucking usual, and comes a knock at the door. Figuring it's too late for any repo-man to pay a call, and my momma never comes without she writes first – I opened it.

'GOOD LORD JESUS! And me with blood pressure! Where the hell do you find them? Six-foot-twenty of gorgeous woman . . . looking for *you*! Jess? You must remember her. *I* ain't forgot her since. So she sultries in, sort of concealing a bottle of champagne, and gives this aw-shucks smile when I explain the reasons you ain't in town, or likely to be. And as yet, no address for you.

'To cut it short, I reckon she really wants to see you. I don't speculate none about what you feel, being as you are a woman of taste and discretion, even when it comes to one-night stands. (Nice, wasn't it?) I don't know about what the rest of this shit is, but I'm telling you, get your glass cooled, the icebox bursting with sparkling libations, and read the mauve one late on the beach.

'Anyways, dearheart, I know I'll see you some time, although I doubt it will be in Middlesville. I can feel a cross-country trip coming on.

Jo-Marie (remember *me*?)'

Sure enough, one envelope was mauve. Rotary Spokes moved mechanically to the icebox, put in a Marie Antoinette glass and a bottle of Veuve Cliquot Rosé. The mauve envelope she put to one side.

She slit the top of a dun envelope, on which the address looked like a mix of lipstick and mascara. Cheap lined paper and a Polaroid fell out.

'Well, god*dam*! BABY! You should a told me sooner. Where in the hell are you? We are at: Trailer 7, Blissful Contentment Trailer Park, Crazy Woman's Fork, Wyoming. So you don't know who *we* are, huh? I enclose a Polaroid.' The photograph was of Dor. In lurex dungarees, satin scarf twisted into a bra-top, her bare shoulders smudged and crimson lips parted on a huge laugh. Her arm was round the waist of another woman in faded shorts and the same silly grin. And goddamighty! There was Fluffy, staring in Egyptian profile at a pink flamingo anchored in vivid plasti-grass. Beside them, there was an enormous chrome baby carriage. Over the woman's head, Dor had scribbled in felt-tip "TOOTS", and over the baby carriage "??!!!"

'Now you got no excuse for not visiting us. We got a big big bed and a spare one in case you're feeling uppitty. You just wait, and assume that me and Toots got the kind of miracle them salvation assholes ain't never going to find. I ain't saying nothing else about it in the U.S. mail, being as how I guess a certain wanted poster in the Crazy Woman's Fork post office does bear a certain resemblance to one of the people I hold most dear! Fluffy is fine too, only she don't appear to like Flapdoodle (the flamingo) none. Toots is a trucker, only she's given up all the coast-to-coast hauls. She only does local stuff, till certain people are old enough to travel. I ain't shit at these letters. Git here!
your everlovin'
Dor.'

Across the bottom of the page was a row of X's and O's.

Well, I'll be damned, thought Rotary Spokes. Dor and Toots. She thought wryly of Diz. Life's journey? She'd have to go to Crazy Woman's Fork.

She looked again at the mauve letter, then she slit open one of the others. It was postmarked London. Of course, Carolee!

'WELL! Dear Auntie Harletta! I am well and trust you are. Finally I left the holy hostel. They were so busy praying one night I just walked out of the door, and no-one saw me leave. I went straight to the nearest pub, and *guess what*? It was women's night. Almost had to bar me and my Yankee enthusiasm, I was so happy. Need I say more? Shit, I will anyway. Her name's Marj, with a j, else she thinks of margarine. She's like this really high-powered civil servant, really important. She has a monogrammed dispatch-case. I never seen anyone drink vodka like she does! She's got this big Jap bike, 900, you'd die, it's all Jap bikes over here, and British bikes. And she's got ME! Everybody here is real broke, and real tough. Marj sends her love. God, Rotary, you shoulda heard her grind her teeth when I told her about my parents and the booby-hatch. She sends her love, but you can only borrow it, cuz I want it for keeps. I have to fly – we're picketing the Gillick Centre – she's like Anita Bryant, only *she's* got it in for teenage kids. WRITE TO ME!
love, and thank you, thank you, thank you – for everything
Carolee!!!'

Rotary Spokes stretched in the sun. Life was good. Maybe she might even make it to London.

One more to go before the mauve one. Postmarked Normal. Well, who the hell?

The paper was creased sharply in four, and had a heading: *Repent, ye foolish*. The letter was splattered in black ink.

'Rotary Spokes,

It is more than a God-fearing person can stand. God will judge you, when Death reaps his promised rewards, but it ain't right you should go through life breathing, like none of your kind has any right to. So here is what I think of you.

You have despoiled a good Christian marriage. Not in the way of most Evil women, most of them trash-mongers who content their blasted flesh with Adulterous Corruption. You are even lower than them snakes. You couldn't break up the marriage yourself, could you! Oh, no, nothing ordinary like that!

You will be gloating in your sulphur heart to hear that Gooseneck Squash has left all his dependents for the Unholy mockery of Love of some reprobate singer. How those poor mouths will manage to feed themselves, God knows I got enough to worry about, without picking up the messes you leave behind on your Hellbent journey through this Vale of Tears. May the Good Lord damn you eternally, and may your evil soul shrivel and burn in endless torment. My lips pale when I speak your name, but I pray for you, although I fear me it's a waste of Christian breath,

MAR'ANN SPRINGER

P.S. No use for you to send letters here, I will burn them as soon as they hit the mat, in a fire you will know all too soon for you and too late for the rest of us.'

Well, what the hell was all that about? So, Gooseneck had moved out. You could never pretend he was any kind of support. And Lorie-Kay would be better without him. But how the hell had he found Patsy Cline? With her name spelled wrong and her being dead, besides?

Rotary Spokes flung the letter on the sand. She stared at the vindictive words and two small circles of the paper began to char. She concentrated until flames burst out and ashed the lot, and breathed deep till the ashes fled, howling cinders across the evening-cooled sands. No goddam *hgrilliss* here, not even from God so-called Almighty.

Ha! She suddenly thought of the mailman. And now the letter. What the hell? The Hug materialized, giving a modest lick to its sheathed claws.

'You can do anything,' it told her. 'Anything you want.' She cleared the porch, save for the mauve letter. Beside it she placed the Veuve Cliqout in a silver bucket, her frosted glass tinkling against the ice She stretched mightily and breathed in salt-clean air; the wind whipped every trace of ash from the sand.

She popped the cork and poured.

She slit the envelope with a knife of mother of pearl.

She smoothed the paper out on her knees.

The handwriting was hard to read, the punctuation eccentric.

'Dear Rotary,

Well, the bird has flown, I see, I, couldn't, see. You – staying around too long. Here. Love on this mountain top. I have been in love with this mountain top for OH SO MANY years. To say, I'm happily out of this frying pan. And headed happily. Maybe a year or so in the fire. Where are you? That is to say, I'm going. To Hyperburg. Somewhere so sterile will need real tough concrete-cracking dandelions. Hyperburg isn't on. Old maps. So I will discover it. And I will enjoy it when you come and see me. I want to hear, I am not clear, although Jo-Marie has told me, quite how you left. A rose is a rose is a rose is a rose.
Till then
Jess.
P.S. Do you read Gertrude Stein?
I have lost my marbles, but maybe they're in my pocket.
J.'

Rotary Spokes read through it several times.

A rose is a rose is a rose is a rose is a rose.

Well, you couldn't argue with that!

Hyperburg?

She turned the paper over. Blank. She looked back at the top of the letter. No address. Jesus.

'So, go to Hyperburg,' said The Hug, twitching its tail.

'But I can't just ride there on a dream!' protested Rotary Spokes.

The Hug raised one eyelid.

'Can't you?'

CHAPTER
SEVENTEEN

*"Everyone has different ideas on just what Baby needs.
Naturally, you will want to have everything as
charming as possible for the Baby and the details will
be your choice."*
(Frankly Feminine. Eileen McCarthy, The Gro-
lier Society 1965)

She spread a map on the floor. Crazy Woman's Fork, Wyoming?
Sheee-it! There it was – clear through Nevada, Utah and Idaho, crazy
little roads wriggling like cracks in the glaze of an old china plate.

And Hyperburg? Boojwah County? No sign of it, as Jess had said.

Hyperburg was a new city, planned and conceived by magnates,
born on a drawing board and executed all in one go. A businessman's
dream: edifices of steel and glass hurtling as high as they dared, staffed
by ambitious inhabitants of the new suburbs: suburbs planned and not
sprawling. It was a respectable commute in this year's car along
boulevards flanked by serried ranks of imported trees. A city with no
slums, carefully-graded neighbourhoods – eminent social psychologists had given expensive consultations about the lure for each social
bracket and useful ethnic type. A city with the lowest policing ratio in
the United States, full employment and a high coronary rate. A
demonstration model of a city through which to stroll with
international V.I.P.s and the modest smiles of the ones to whom
Prosperity is guaranteed.

Hyperburg was all these things, but to Rotary Spokes it was nothing
but the haystack in which she would find her pearl of great price.
Somewhere in the urbanologists' triumph, there would be Jess.

For this trip, she could take a little time. Pace herself. And so, over
four days, she cruised towards Crazy Woman's Fork.

She stopped to fill up at a gas station.

'Do you know the way to San Jose?' she asked the lanky youth dabbing at the shiny chrome on the bike.

'Sure,' he said, 'I got lotsa friends down there.'

'I don't wanna stay there or nothing. It's on my way.'

'I guess you're smart,' he said. 'All my friends are pumping gas or selling cars. I guess you don't need a car?' She stared at him, and at her bike. She peeled off bills for the gas.

He waved vaguely along the road. She left him standing there, singing down a tuneless scale: 'boom, boom, boom, boom, boom, boom, boom-a-boom.'

She did a ton through Chowchilla, and burned through to Soledad, Gonzalea, Salina; Huevos Rancheros and Dos Equis iced to claw your breath away.

Sacramento, Roseville, Auburn, and she dived away from the dusty road at Truckee and drank to the health of Dor and Toots and ??!!! in a bleached roadside shack.

Reno, Sparks, Nixon, Carson Sinks.

At Lovelock, she stopped again and doused her lovely locks under an ancient pump. In Winnemucca, she bought a russet and navy-blue blanket from a silent and aloof Indian woman.

It was colder than a witch's tit in the desert at night. Dusk saw her through Elko and Wells. She stopped the snorting bike: Contact or Cobre? She looked back at the sky seeping rose over the Ruby Mountains, and fled the long shadows till just past Cobre. A mile or so off the road, she steered the bike under a dessicated quartet of dark trees.

The silence rose as the dust powdered down along the track. She roamed around her camp, picking up bleached wood debris. Just like any old cowboy, she thought, full length under the rough blanket, her boots propped on a stone by the flame-veined branches crackling in the fire. Too warm to move. But she dragged herself up and heaped high the fire circle and curled around the stones at the edge.

The sky went black. She slept.

The morning was cold gray when she woke. And then the sun came to the desert, pink, gold, orange streaks in the sky; the sand shifted under the hot rainbow.

She passed great clumps of orange rocks, fire-bright and crackling in the heat of the day.

Garland, Malad City, Downes, Inkom, Pocatello, Alameda, Rigby, St. Anthony, Grand Teton, Moron.

She pulled the bike onto its stand, hauled off her helmet, and looked up and then down the street. Moron could have been Normal. The only difference was, instead of Dino's, there was a sagging porch in front of a place called 'Dead Lou's uncheonette', and a nail rusting where maybe once there had been a capital L.

She moseyed on in. It was the only way to get inside a place like this.

Behind the counter was a woman whose face was the colour of a newly-laid tombstone. She was dressed in funereal black, with a respectably yellowing lace collar. Her hands were waxen with startling veins of indigo.

Rotary Spokes ordered steak and eggs, hash browns, coffee. 'How come they call this place Dead Lou's?' she asked, through a mouthful.

The woman swivelled her polished marble eyes.

'Funny you should ask that.'

A long pause.

'I'll tell you, however.'

The woman lit a cigarette. She appeared neither to inhale nor exhale the smoke. But the ash grew longer.

'Many years ago it was, they started calling me Dead Lou. Far back as I can remember.'

She flattened a buzzing fly with one pale slab hand.

'Yaaaaaz. It's an odd thing. And ever since then, that's what they call me. I guess they always will. Y'see, they always have.'

The silence went on longer than any pause.

Rotary Spokes paid her bill and passed the change back across the counter. As she left, Dead Lou was crooning:

'Always have, always will,' like a lullaby.

The Wind river almost lapped the road to Shoshon. A clean breeze blew sharp towards the Wind River Mountains.

She snaked through Shoshon, and at Thermopolis, stopped.

'Y'all able to direct me to Crazy Woman's Fork?'

'You just gotta take the road,' a youth told her, through a drooping straw. 'The road'll take you there. Left up-aways, and y'all just make your continuation.'

The road wriggled a little left, a little right. Sort of unsure. A little right, a little left. The big bike ducked and weaved, scudding through the dust. And so on for many miles. Any crow flying would have said ten. The slow-flicking digits on the dial said twenty, thirty, forty-seven.

Suddenly, the road switchbacked through fields of corn as tall as a truck. The sign for Crazy Woman's Fork was charred onto wood.

'Can y'all tell me where I'll find Blissful Contentment Trailer Park?' she asked an unshaven, toothless man in a three-button vest and flapping pants hung from frayed elastic braces.

Tobacco spit went in one direction, his outstretched arm trembled in the other.

'Ya go right past where they're puttin' up the new parkin' lot, left along by the new warehouse. And then, just keep yourself straight there.'

Well, thought Rotary Spokes, this must be the place. To her right, scarlet girders and gray ricks of breeze blocks; petrified cascades of tan rock-textured cement; sooty plasti-timber; a phalanx of faded blue overalls squinting professionally around the deafening drum of a big yellow dump truck.

A high bridge arched over a creek: a blue sign said that the bridge had come from Ashby de la Zouche, England. Rotary Spokes soared over the creast of the bridge and helter-skeltered under the vermilion sign: *Blissful Contentment, Crazy Woman's Fork*.

Dor was sitting on the step of Trailer 7, leafing through *E-Z Cordon Bleu*. She dropped it and ran over to the bike, squashed Rotary Spokes against her, pulled her helmet off, and kissed her loud, laughing.

'Lemme get ya a beer to wash the dust down, honey,' she said. 'Jesus, am I glad to see you!'

Rotary Spokes grinned at her. At the trailer. At Flapdoodle. At Fluffy, who ignored her.

'Zo, she hass come back?'

'So you just up and went and come here? How the hell long can you stay?'

'Waaall, a little while. I'm goin' to Hyperburg,' she said, blushing. Dor hooted.

'What's her name?'

'Well, an't you come to be a sly thing – Jess.'

'That's my girl,' said Dor approvingly. 'Just get up and go. I'd of never got here no other way.'

'Where's Toots? And that goddam baby carriage? Tell me!'

'Well, Toots' just gone out with – you wait and see!'

'Hey there!'

Toots sprinted towards them, the baby carriage bouncing in front of her.

'Rotary Spokes, I can only presume,' she said and gripped Rotary Spokes' arm. 'I sure am glad to meet you, honey; I figure you made my life a whole lot easier.'

She gazed adoringly at Dor, who sparkled like a lit-up Christmas tree.

Dor scooped a small person from the baby carriage. A small brown-gold person with dark straight hair. She plopped it on Rotary Spokes' lap.

'Well, shoot! A damn baby!' Rotary Spokes felt her arms go gentle and protective. 'How the hell did you two manage this?'

Toots smiled.

'A miracle, dear. A wheelin'-dealin' goddam expensive miracle. I figure it to be the best move I ever made, aside from gettin' hold of this one here.'

Rotary Spokes brushed the baby's silky head with her lips. It stretched, yawned and wriggled its tiny tongue at her.

'What d'you call it?'

'Her, darlin', *her*. We call her Little Eva, Little Britches; anythin' really.'

'Well, hello there, Little Britches,' said Rotary Spokes to the deep brown unblinking stare. 'Sheee-it, she's so little. Look at them fingernails.'

'I'm gonna go fight with some cans,' said Dor, and went into the trailer.

Toots grinned.

'She's makin' supper for y'all,' she said. 'Hold your hats. Last time, she didn't realize you gotta open the cans. Time before, she din put no water in the pressure cooker. We got more new windows than y'all would credit. Anyways, there's a good steak house up the road.'

Toots lay back on the grass, and the baby crawled and flopped over her. The aim seemed to be a complete survey of her chin and nostrils and eyes and mouth. Curses and crashes spilt from the trailer.

'Your friend cookin' her another meal?' called a woman from across the path. She shook her head, pegging out shirts and diapers.

'Yup. I do apologize,' said Toots.

'It's your windows, not mine.'

The day turned to warm evening. Toots put a baby sling on one hip.

'Let's have a fire,' she said. They strolled up to the woods for armfuls of dry branches.

'Used to call me Firefingers in girl scouts,' she said, as flames crackled.

'And they still do,' announced Dor triumphantly from the steps 'Goddam broad always fishin' for compliments. Rotary Spokes, I wanna tell you, this is history. I ain't burned nor blowed up nothin' for this here meal. It's got a name too – lemme see – Poweel ay Payrose Gwireck. Look.' The magazine had a full-page glossy picture, luscious with sauce and bright vegetables: Poule à Perros Guirec. French!

'Here's to y'all,' said Rotary Spokes, raising her can.

'Waaall, you better stay a few days, anyway, one a your old friends is comin' here.'

'Who?'

'Lorie-Kay Squash with Gooseneck Junior and little Darlene.'

Rotary Spokes told them about Mar'Ann's letter, leaving out the part about how, afterwards, her gaze had flash-burned it and blown it clean away.

'Waaaall,' said Dor, I'll fill you in. Y'all recall that dingbat Gooseneck, and him looking for Patsy Cline? You said he wouldn't never find her, being as she was C-L-I-N-E, and dead besides. Waaall, seems he called about a million numbers or more, and bingo, this lady says, "Sure, honey, I'm Patsy Kline," She said she didn't sing no more, due to she's had a accident and lost her sight, and a body cain't sing without no eyes. And she don't have the confidence to get up on the stage no more. She lives in Soda Springs. So, where do you think Gooseneck goes?'

'Soda Springs?'

'Darn tootin'! She cain't see him, being as she don't have no sight, and he moves in with her, does for her. Whiles away the evenings playing her greatest hits. Lorie-Kay wrote me about the whole mess . . . her and the kids went over for a visit and now she figures it's the best for all of 'em as is.'

'I never did think she'd ever leave Normal, truth to tell ya, Dor.'

'Waaall, what's to keep her there? Mar'Ann's gone crazy with Jesus, bats the hell outta her kids if they cuss a little, and prays aloud to the Lord ever' time Lucas comes anywheres near her. So Lorie-Kay's comin' up here. We figgered she'd need somebody to keep a eye out for her. Anyhow, the air's better round these parts.' Dor wriggled her fat toes in the dust.

'Little Britches don't seem to cry none,' said Rotary Spokes. 'I thought babies was always hollerin' and whinin'.'

'Th' only time she hollers is when we put her down. So we don't. She lives in a hug, that one. And damn right too. She didn't never ask to come into the world, after all,' said Toots proudly.

In the middle of the night, Princess Henrietta Maria II skulked through the sleeping trailer. She sniffed silently at Rotary Spokes, padded over her hip, and curled aginst the wall. Morning found her in full possession of the bed and Rotary Spokes on the floor. And the cat was indignant that a Cat should be expected to share six-by-three feet of bed with a lower species.

'You ain't changed,' grunted Rotary Spokes, pushing her over.

'And neizzers heff you,' thought the cat, consenting warily.

'Rodry, you got that twitchy look,' said Dor over breakfast. She stood up and whipped the baby's bottle from under her cardigan. 'If she sees this, she goes bananas,' she explained. 'I don't know where the hell she gets that from!' The baby guzzled away, snuggled up to Dor's beautiful breasts.

'Makes me feel I'm feeding her,' said Dor reverently.

'Ain't you never thought of havin' one yourself, Dor?'

'Honey, I had my tubes tied at twenty-three, when I saw the way things was goin' with me. Who the hell wants a baby off some five-buck fuck? Not me.'

Rotary Spokes thought about having a baby. Couldn't see it somehow. Sure, she liked kids, but you cain't pretend it's gonna be as easy as that. She wouldn't mind inheriting kids with someone. Kids with sci-fi blue eyes and an English accent. Jess didn't seem the type.

What was she doing? Here she was, damn near good as married to Jess in her mind. What if Jess wasn't interested?

'Dor, I'm gonna have to go, honey,' she said. 'I gotta find out what the hell is goin' on in my life. Else I'll just sit around here sayin' what-if for a few years, and gettin' broody with Little Britches here.'

'If it works out, bring her here,' urged Dor. 'If it don't work out, she don't know what the hell she's missin'. Not that I do either, but I got me a fair idea it's pretty hot.'

Dor gave her a hug and a big wet kiss.

'Steal my woman,' said Toots. 'Go on – take her away – I cain't afford her anyhow.'

She bear-hugged Rotary Spokes and then the two stood, waving, rosy with love and contentment. Rotary Spokes paused at the flying zenith of the bridge, and flung one arm up in a salute.

A soda in Saskatchewan, a burger in Bighorn. The miles flew by.

She found a motel in Rampling, Nebraska. One gorgeous city, houses sprinkled on the smooth flanks of the hills.

A pizza in Podunk, a beer at Bent's Fork, hot sweet corn in Sweetwater.

Times the road lazed by a big and nameless river, times the desert stretched to the skyline.

Near Independence, she pulled off the freeway, found a room in Bancroft, a sepia-tint town with a false-front general store and raised wooden sidewalks.

Pancakes and maple syrup in Poughkeepsie. Hot dogs in Hickory.

Finally there were signs to Hyperburg in screaming hot pink and day-glo orange: there were three in a row. The first announced:
"HYPERBURG!"
The second said: "If You Lived Here . . ."
The third reassured: "You'd Be Home Now."
Wherever it was, it surely thought it was one hell of a place, in fact:
The Only Place
The Right Place
and so forth.
The signs said:
'In Hyperburg, You Will Find Everything You've Always Wanted.'
This message stretched out, word by word, mile by mile. By the 'd' of 'Wanted', Rotary Spokes' grin was wider than a full set of piano keys. She stopped and looked at the glossy white creation ahead of her in the plain. Hyperburg. She looked at her watch: yup, just like Toots had said: it was only twenty-four hours from Tulsa.

She cruised down to the plain.

CHAPTER EIGHTEEN

*"In the Big City a person will disappear with the
suddenness and completeness of a candle that is blown
out."*
(O. Henry. The Sleuths. Sixes and Sevens)

In Hyperburg, she chose a furnished apartment over a workshop in a
loud street with flashing neon lights, a casino, a happy cosmopolitan
market that spilled over the sidewalks and throbbed with salsa, reggae,
blues, flamenco, country, jazz. All this and a bar for women too:
Jeannie's Chilli Beanie.

It was fine to be quiet by the sea, but Rotary Spokes' heart hummed
with the thundering, spitting tools and machines. She unlocked the
door after she had signed the lease.

Home at last.

Well, not home, but a damn good base for the quest of Jess. She
made coffee and sat down with Gertrude Stein.

She woke at three in the morning as a voice with the quality of a
welding torch hurtled from the bar up the street.

'I run a WOMEN's bar, asshole, cuz I don't want no dicks hanging
around! Go strut that pathetic gristle elsewhere!' Glass shattered and
some novel curses followed. Jeannie was having a hard time, but no
more than she could handle.

In the weeks that followed, she made herself known at Jeannie's, and
even started flirting a bit in a half-hearted way. She expected to see
Jess everywhere. Anyone wearing a flight jacket caught her eye, and
then they would turn with their perfectly nice or perfectly awful face
and fail to be Jess. What the hell.

She was having a hard time with Gertrude Stein. It had got through to her that Gertrude Stein had been a dyke years before the likes of *Dyke's Delight* and Women's Nights and lived with one woman happily all of her life. This she would toast as she tried another page.

'A bike is a bike is a bike is a bike is a ... Harley!' she thought daringly one day and switched off the blowtorch to write it down.

Damn! she thought admiringly. I might be an authoress.

One night, things being a little quiet at Jeannie's, Rotary Spokes ventured to offer the proprietress a drink – which was graciously accepted. Jeannie, when not serving or throwing out the rowdies, was always knitting. She used brilliantly-coloured wool of many textures, with a predominance of fluffy hectic purple, and flung the finished garment across the bar at, it seemed, whoever happened to be there. Rotary Spokes didn't realize that she had been measured for a sweater and Jeannie was only waiting to finish a chunky original for Big Bertha, her favourite bush pilot, before she launched into a Rotary Spokes Special.

Jeannie asked very little of life. Having won the Santa Barbara Chilli Beanie Bonanza Gold five years in a row, she had moved over and opened the bar. She demanded: a steady income, the odd passionate affair; a cream-coloured Karmann Ghia with a tan leather interior and a cat on the back window ledge whose eyes blinked neon when she touched the brakes; and total dedication from her customers. She would win this by flirting, wooing, confiding, listening – anything – once she had decided she wanted you as a regular. Every year, she held a private birthday party, and glowed amid the rainbow-sweatered and sweating crew she had chosen.

Women! She loved them.

Women! They drove her crazy!

Women!

Said Rotary Spokes that evening:

'Jeannie, what do you know about the Rawhide Palace?'

'Well,' said Jeannie, 'you thinkin' of changin' bars?'

'Naw, Jeannie, no way, but my friends said I'd kinda like trying it out – once. Shit, you run the best bar I ever been in.'

Mollified, Jeannie became expansive.

'You find all sorts there, *darr*ling. Crosses, t.v.'s, benders, – the one thing they all have in common is a love of the leather. You love the leather, eh?'

Rotary Spokes had to admit a certain fondness for leather.

'You better go. And enjoy! Go careful, though.'

Rotary Spokes felt too humble to admit that she had no idea what a t.v. was. She thought of a huge screen. Couldn't be. Jeannie groped under the bar to find the *Hyper Hyper Hype: The Magazine for You*. It listed all the alternative goings-on in a city that was puffing and blowing with Newness, trying to challenge Broadway (without success), and generally become the Sun-Belt Mecca. They called their theatres names like: The Fast-Lane Drury Lane, The Super Shakespeare, The Only O'Neill. The significance of these names was lost on most Hyper Hyperburgers as the citizens defensively named themselves. Seemed to mean that they could get flummoxed and confused any night of the week with self-conscious Yurrpean culture and gems of American thespianism.

'Here it is,' said Jeannie. '"Leather or bizarre dress only." Hey, Rotary, you'd like next Thursday – they got Eugenie Lafayette.'

'Whut?'

'Damn your backwoods hide – she's only the greatest blues singer this decade. Where you been all your life?'

Rotary Spokes thought a bit.

'I been around a little,' she admitted.

'Well, go to this one. Get a surprise. But just don't make it a regular thing.'

Rotary Spokes dutifully donned the leather and tore down to the Rawhide Palace, a building covered with Plasti-Timber and neon signs whirling over the entrance. She parked the Harley and noted with satisfaction that it was the best bike there. Nonchalantly, she paid twenty bucks to get in and strolled on through the black doors. She found a mirrored pillar and leaned there as if she had never done anything else.

The Phoenix smoked only Mahawat cheroots and, of course, joints. Ever the chameleon, Rotary Spokes took well to these manifestations of a champagne income, and flipped the slim dark 'little elephants' as expertly to her lips as if she had been born with one idly hanging there.

Out of the darkness came a light. A flame from a tailored gold slim lighter. She lit and inhaled, and dragged her eyes along the hand, past chunky diamante, or probably, diamond rings, past a six-tier spangly bracelet, up along a netted arm to a muscled shoulder, a slender neck, and a pallid face with intense kohled eyes, vampire-red lips, and a pile of ash-blonde hair sparkling in the light. The lips parted in a smile, eyes met and looked away.

Jesus.

The woman was the bizarre dress advertised alongside the leather on the bill. Her tunic had black, glittering panels slashed up fish-netted thighs.

More – there was a tattoo of a long-tailed butterfly at the base of her throat, curving down to the glittering orchid brooch pinned to her bosom. It was Joan Crawford, Bette Davis, a real Hollywood queen. Rotary Spokes sipped her Harvey Wallbanger and looked around the room.

Primarily, the decor was black: black velvet walls, thick black carpet, deep black and silver couches offering an illusion of intimacy in the deafening, blood-throbbing disco beat; the glasses were smoked black, the scattered ashtrays were dull steel and black.

Everywhere, mirrors. Rotary Spokes stared at herself with interest for a moment and as she moved a shoulder to light this fascinating person's cigarette, so the fascinating creature did the same. Rotary Spokes blushed.

The Phoenix had given Rotary a pair of mirror shades which had clear glass underneath and Rotary smiled at the disguise. Then the ceiling began to fall – what the? Panels glided down towards the lit dance floor and commenced a sedate revolution or two. They floated like spaceships, and neon tubes glided from their hearts. Then they whirled, whirled, and the dancers were bombarded with ultra-violet ... the mass of glossy leather, velvet, satin, silk, became scarlet, purple, green ... the lights burned rainbow paths through the crowd. Rotary Spokes sipped a little more. Sheee-it, the goddam cheroot had gone out, and even as she thought it, a slim gold lighter flew through the dark and kissed the tip with flame. This time, she allowed herself a half smile.

All at once, laser-blue beams bore through the dark, immortalizing the studied faces, the swirl of smoke. '*Could you be loved*?' asked Bob Marley, and the beat became Rotary Spokes' heartbeat. She was ready for anything.

All the posters had said was "Eugenie Lafayette – your very own!" But she wouldn't appear till the morning was born, and there were a few hours to throb through till then. Behind the maëlstrom of laser-blue, an immense screen glided to hover a foot or so above the jerking, pulsing dance animal on the floor.

Rotary Spokes felt a ringed and netted arm through her own. Oh, yeah? *She* was supposed to make the moves, wasn't she? Aw, what the hell. The lady of the nets and spangles hollered something into her ear. She couldn't hear, but pushed through the crowd, guided by the arm, onto the dance floor. Damn, could the woman dance! It was so junior-high sexy, The Hug surged through her body, about to give her a good time . . .

She thought back to the dances at school where she had sat paralysed, fists balled against her thighs. Cigarettes had given her something to do while the other girls coo-ed and simpered and had their spines bent into unlikely positions by the high school jocks.

Until she got barred.

She had finally gotten sick of sitting there and asked her girl friend to dance. Which clearly her girl friend hadn't wanted to do, seein' as she was panting after some football hero. It was that and Rotary wearing trousers.

What had Calamity Jane said?

'You see, I wear pants so I can get around while those petticoated females are screaming for help.'

'Your attitood is alarming,' the principal had told her, steel-gray among his filing cabinets. 'You seem to think you're a special case. You seem to think you have the right not to conform.'

Here, in the Rawhide Palace, she saw a man in black velvet, some kind of historical costume, with little bloomers and gold braid everywhere, topped by a black leather cap, heavy with chains. She saw a sinuous embrace between two men who had used the same stencil for a moustache. She saw an old man boogie-ing gently with another old man, their easy caress speaking the pleasure of their love.

I do have the right not to conform! She thought of the broken spines and listless drudgery of Lorie-Kay and Mar'Ann . . . for this she should change? She swung into the beat, feeling the exquisite leather stroke her hard thighs.

Damned if I ain't a woman! she thought. And happy with it. Two women were dancing near her – who said grease was out? And a blonde muscle-boy swaying in the arms of a black muscle-boy bestowing kisses like velvet butterflies on the blonde boy's face and neck.

She saw two other women dancing, one with an open waistcoat over her bare breasts, the other in white silk and an elegant bow-tie, who was leaning over, drawing her partner near, entreating closeness. She lost them in the crowd as Ms. Satin-and-Glitter welded herself to Rotary Spokes' body; when she saw them again, the taller silk shirt was drawing away and the open waistcoat was positively pursuing her. Dizzy with the lights and the cocktaills, she thought of the stop, go, come *here* – don't leave – I *love* you – what *me* – love *you*? of Diz: shit, Diz.

The loud music gave her pause to think and the ardent closeness of the dancing made any conversation unlikely. There would never be any love with Diz again, of that she was as sure of as the sunrise. But being a woman who hated emotional messes, she hoped they'd clear it up.

There was Diz. There was Lorie-Kay and Mar'Ann; there was her mother – unfinished business, jagged edges of pain that she couldn't blunt with the best intentions in the world, if the intentions were only her own.

Meanwhile, there was an interesting business going on somewhere below her chin. Damn: kinda promiscuous. What the hell.

And so she danced. Danced; the videos flashed over her head, the men kissed the men, and the women kissed the women. And it all seemed pretty alright to Rotary Spokes.

Backstage, the thrill of the night.

Eugenie Lafayette.

This is who she was and this is how she got there. This is a flashback. The music fades, the picture shivers like a reflection in a lake, and we are way back in the Midwest, several years before.

Before Rotary Spokes saw *Feast Your Eyes*.

Before Dor saw Toots.

Before the Bean saw The Phoenix.

Before Diz had an orgasm.

Oh, my friends! What things do go on in a few short years. For Eugenie Lafayette, things had altered a good deal, too. A few years back, she had been billed as Lady Jezebel, touting around any dive that her lousy manager could get her into. Sometimes doing three shows a night – no life for a dog, let alone a good woman.

Leroy the Count had billed her as 'Mystery Guest'. Her name was too hot.

Backstage, 'I'll give 'em *mystery*!' seethed Lady Jezebel, swirling her vermilion satin train behind her as she paced the dressing room.

'YES!' she snapped at the soft tap on the door. Leroy the Count shimmered into the room, swept off rhinestone shades and almost lost his balance as she side-stepped his kiss.

'You may be black, baby,' she told him, 'but nothing gives you the right to touch me.'

'Didn't I get you this gig, baby?'

She bunched his lurexed lapel in one slim fist and fixed his eyes with her own.

'Goodness!' he said ineffectually. 'My, my, Jezebel, you are mad at me, aren't you?'

'THIS SHIT!' she hissed, dragging him to the poster on the wall. 'MYSTERY GUEST! Ain't my name good enough? Why don't you use my name?'

'Well, Jezebel,' he said, placatingly, 'this is going to help, don't you see?'

Jezebel had blown so many dates that the clubs were wary of booking her. She had fists as free and powerful as her breathtaking voice and a disinclination to share the bill with anyone else. Count Leroy was the latest, and soon to be the last of her business managers. She had started with Wallace Sheekey, an upgraded pimp and then her husband. Five years later, sick to her guts of his thieving and beating her, she had lashed back, and Wallace had sprawled five floors below in the street.

There were several things that made Jezebel see red.

One was the phrase: '*Be nice to me, baby.*'

Another was: '*Ain't I good to you, baby?*'

And another was: '*Baby.*'

'I'm thirty-six years old, asshole, and meaner than a cobra – don't give me this "Baby" bullshit.'

'Sure, ba – sure, Jezebel.'

She knew she was good, dammit. She had a suspicion, which was true, that she might be one of the best, along with Lady Day and Bessie Smith. She had also decided that she was going to work her ass off and make it and neither pills nor booze nor men were going to drag her down.

It was hard to decide which was worse – some black guy putting her down and robbing her blind, or some white guy putting her down and robbing her blind. She was thinking of managing her own career – if Millie Jackson could . . . Meanwhile she was stuck with pasting the shreds of a career together and Count Leroy's idea of building up a following through Middle America to wow them with once they hit Vegas, had sounded like the best thing. But she had just about had it with rednecks and good old boys. Their cheers and apreciation came in a series of phrases so deep-rooted in bigotry and male superiority that she was revolted.

Jesus, she was doing them a favour. They were benefitting from the fact that they just happened to have ten bucks, and she just happened to have had all this bad management. Jezebel was rattled. To prove to this bunch of freaks that you were good! To woo this pile of shit-eaters!

'I believe I'll have a little bourbon,' she growled at Count Leroy. 'So's I know what's running through the veins of them ole boys.'

Count Leroy passed her his hip-flask. She stared at him with contempt.

'Your lips don't touch mine,' she yelled. 'And my lips don't go round no hip-flask. Cheap! Goddam it, you are so cheap. Get me a glass. And get it fast.'

He hurried away. Cunts was so temperamental.

She looked in the mirror.

Babe. Lady. Baby. Gypsy Queen.

Lady Jezebel.

Ha! Elephant. Monkey. Tangerine.

Black Amazon. Panther. Empress.

Lady Jezebel. 'The only singer today who could inherit the gardenia.'

Ha!

There was another knock at the door.

'COME!'

It was Blind Ellen Eternity, the piano player.

'Jezebel, honey, I brought you a drink. Lulu was stumblin' around like a three-legged dog out there. Here.'

'What's the crowd like?' asked Jezebel, sipping bourbon.

'Aw, you know. Mr. and Mrs. Middle America of U.S.A. Looks like they're casting a Clint Eastwood movie out there. And there's big speculation going down: who's this Mystery Guest? Odds ten-to-one it's Dolly Parton.'

'You think they're gonna take what I dish out?'

'If they don't, they can eat shit.'

'For sure, for sure . . . that's your career and mine out there, sugar.'

'You just take a look at them. You don't need 'em no more'n what you flush away every day.'

'They'd better keep their redneck traps shut.'

Blind Ellen got up and patted Jezebel's smooth cheek.

'Chin up, beautiful,' she said. 'I'll give you five, and you give 'em hell.'

Blind Ellen sat at the piano. Blind had nothing to do with her sight. It was a nickname she had given herself when she had let the love of her life walk out of the door. She looked around. Plenty of plaid in the audience; plenty of studded belts topped by well-cultivated beer guts. Plenty of ten-gallon hats and crimplene. She made a wish that they'd appreciate. Just a few good gigs and Jezebel and she would stand a chance of something decent.

She crooked the microphone and rapped through the rippling chords:

'Howdy folks, as y'all would say down here. Looks like we have a beautiful audience tonight.'

She slipped her gold rings onto the piano top.

'Tonight, folks, prepare to be amazed, astonished and delighted. You are in the presence of history in the making, ladies and gentlemen.'

'Gotta be Dolly Parton!' whooped a ginger moustache.

In the wings, Jezebel cursed.

'Who? Who?' asked Blind Ellen. 'Dolly WHO?' I give you a lady that's been all the way there and back again . . . I give you . . . Lady Jezebel.'

The audience muttered:

'Who the hell?'

'Ain't that the coloured woman smashed up the County Hall of

Fame?'

'Ain't she dead?'

'Sure as hell ain't country, boy.'

Blind Ellen played the whole keyboard in a dazzling crescendo. Milt Hepplewhite started sweating over the bass, and Luscious Chippendale breathed into his spine-tingling tenor sax. The lights went right down and came up again in a ceiling swirl of red, blue, yellow, pink, orange, whirling faster and faster along the silk curtains. The spotlight fixed onto a figure in silhouette, standing, head slightly bowed.

Ellen went straight into *Paper Moon*, *The Tender Trap*, and *Don't Let Me Be Misunderstood*, without a pause. That way, as Jezebel said, 'They's gonna have to holler their redneck heads off to get rid of me.'

But they were sold, entranced. They whooped, yee-ha-ed, clapped, stomped, whistled and cheered.

'Pray to Heaven they don't say nothing,' thought Blind Ellen.

'You kin make me breakfast anytime,' leered a thonged Stetson.

'WHAAAAT!' yelled Jezebel.

'I'll be real sweet to you!' yelled a bandana-ed neck.

'Strut your stuff, baby!'

'Hey, baby, you sing real sweet for a nigger-lady!'

'Come over here, baby, and sit on this!'

Blind Ellen closed her eyes.

Hyperburg two years later and Lady Jezebel was riding high on the tidal wave of her comeback.

Since she had wrecked that joint, she had spent a good deal of time staring at four walls and pacing unrecorded miles of concrete. At first, planning how to make egg salad out of the man who called himself a Count. Manager? He had cut his losses, taking her to court for everything she'd got. He had produced a document he called a contract, which she could swear, in vain, she had never signed. He had wept crocodile tears for the death of a great partnership. But he had blanched when she got just the two years. He knew she would count the days until she was free and he would be the first to know it when she got out. But then she had heard from Blind Ellen: 'Count the days, but there's nothing else to count. I'm keeping the ivory dusted just for you.'

She had been able to say truthfully to her lawyer that she knew nothing of a severed brake cable on the stretch Cadillac driven by Leroy the Count: driven for the last time on the hills of San Francisco. How could she? Black magic from behind bars?

After that, although she had wanted to see his eyes as he squirmed, lied and died, she became peaceful and purposeful. She saw the chaplain frequently, joined the prison choir, and embroidered as beautifully as a nun. When she walked through the gates, having shaken hands with the head warden, the chaplain, the chief guard, Blind Ellen had almost missed her.

'Where's your swagger, honey?'

'Up my ass,' said Jezebel sweetly.

The Mary Magdalene act had got her out two months early, and she and Blind Ellen ate, slept and breathed music, making the rounds of booking agents with a persistence that fixed them a tour, coast-to-coast – mainly in gay places. Jezebel had shrugged and renamed herself Eugenie Lafayette. She had re-worked the greats to blood-chilling perfection. When she sang *Strange Fruit*, a legend was born: her costumes ranged from the flamboyant to the outrageous. She belted out disco numbers like they'd only just been invented.

'Always add one more boa than you think you can handle,' grunted Blind Ellen, tacking impossible tucks and satin pleats. 'The name of the game is Over The Top, Eugenie, O.T.T.'

Blind Ellen created a lavender sheath of beads and pearly sequins, and one time tried out a tiara:

'Heard'a the Queen of England?'

It was a wow. She added rhinestone bracelets twelve luscious layers deep, and a series of gargantuan glittering rings, and composed a tune to remove them by, while the dykes and the queens whooped, wowed and swooned.

Eugenie added peacock feathers, satin roses, six-inch heels encrusted with sparkle, and at Christmas wore green antlers on her head, strung with scarlet bulbs that flashed on and off.

'Divine!' murmured the queens.

'We love you, Eugenie!' screamed the dykes.

At last, Eugenie Lafayette was Big. The empress of her patch. And her patch spread from coast to coast, in the gin mills, gay bars, night clubs and after-hour joints in every town.

She took to leaning on Blind Ellen's piano and coo-ing her

incredibly powerful voice straight from the heart into those eyes. After a year or so, she started loving Blind Ellen, who was surprised at first. She had felt maternal towards Jezebel, and protected her as far as anyone could in the world of down-market showbiz. But she worshipped, adored and enjoyed this newly-risen Eugenie Lafayette. When she slid into her bed one night, she was soon delighted. And the act got better and better: it was a love thing and all the so-called trash of society celebrated their love, fell in love with the love, strutted its stuff to the gutsy disco beat. The crowds parted for them as they swanned to the bar; leather, suede, satin and silk competed to ply them with champagne.

Blind Ellen and Eugenie were saving. Sometimes it was for a farm, then they both fell about laughing at the idea of picks and hoes. Sometimes it was for a ranch.

'Though, I swear, hell, I'm going to have to ride side-saddle, honey,' purred Eugenie, twitching her eight-foot train. Sometimes it was a beach house at Malibu.

'Though, landsakes, Miz Eugenie,' drawled Blind Ellen. 'You think them white folks'd sell to us po' blacks?'

'You think I'd buy from white trash?' cackled Eugenie. 'Not this girl. I'm lookin' for a black real estate dealer. And she better be a dyke.'

Sometimes it was a geodesic dome in the Ojai Valley.

'Though I want a dome with rocket engines, so's I can fly in the air and watch the world turning.'

Whatever it was, it was getting to be a big comfortable balance. No men, no agents, no managers.

'*Our* money, Ellen, yours and mine. Our work, our sweat, our love.'

They had come to the Rawhide Palace in Hyperburg fresh from the glories of a carnival float for the proud and the gay in Baltimore. It was an honour shared with the Divine megastar – Eugenie in leopard-skin satin, Divine in tiger-skin polyester.

'This is a fuck of a sight better than the barge they put me on in London in '85,' Divine told them.

Early next day, the celestial body left the all-night party.

'I'm on location, Eugenie,' he camped. His lips made Mohawk stripes on both their cheeks.

And so Hyperburg.

A young man, Queen Christina of North Carolina, in white tie and tails, hair slicked over premature baldness, snaked onto the stage and whipped the mike lead around him.

'Back, you scum, you rabble! Back! You know the drill, fellow creatures of this earthly darkness . . . this paradise! Back beyond the lights – or we'll never get it up! Princes and queens, and believe me, I know royalty . . .' he smirked and moued to the audience, 'and queens have flocked to lay their . . . CROWNS at the feet of the next guest . . . the only guest . . . the lady beyond all known mystery . . . the lady of – oh, it's more than SOUL!'

He mopped his high brow with Valenciennes lace.

'It's more than my life's worth to try and encompass her charms in mere oral ejaculations –' the audience screeched. 'So I'll just drag my ass off the stage and leave you to some *real* class: Eugenie Lafayette and Blind Ellen Eternity!' The stage rose to a heart-stopping fanfare.

It was empty save for a simple black piano at which presided a shimmering Blind Ellen.

'That mother finished his shit?' she demanded.

The audience roared and stamped. Rotary Spokes found herself howling with high, High, HIGHER!

A hand plucked at her elbow. Ms. Glitter-Baby was certainly persistent. Rotary Spokes slipped an arm around her waist.

'Waaall,' said Blind Ellen, shuffling delicately across the stage. 'We got any quality here tonight? Any crowned heads?' She peered into the throbbing darkness.

'Hmmm, plenty a heads and plenty a queens. Any good women here? Eugenie don't like bein' without good women . . .'

Rotary Spokes threw her fist into the air. SHEEE-IT! She was a good woman. Her new friend screeched a little uncertainly. Rotary Spokes began to feel immortal and protective.

'Eugenie!' hollered Blind Ellen. 'You kin come out now. We got the quality!'

Eugenie tottered onto the stage, bearing a few thousand sequins ('Just opened my own factory') and a charisma which flung the lights straight back at themselves. Suddenly she snapped upright.

'Y'all was thinkin' I'd had a few too many, huh? Thinkin' this gal cain't hold her liquor?'

She nodded at Blind Ellen who plashed perfection from the

keyboard. The sound engineer poised over a switch bearing the sigh of saxophone and the groan of bass. Milt Hepplewhite and Luscious Chippendale had done all of the backing tapes.

'They're part of the furniture,' giggled Eugenie.

'Y'all got to hang onto each other here . . . y'all only got each other. AS I KNOW!' Eugenie told the audience as she moved swirling to the piano and planted a kiss on Blind Ellen's electric hair. 'Y'all only got yourselves and the person you wake up next to at three in the morning. SO I TELL YOU . . . hang on in there, do it, and do it good, there ain't nothing else for you, my friends, because of what you ARE! And this is how it will always be, unless we get a RRRadical change here. And we are ALIVE! And seeing as how this is the age of the living dead . . . (don't we got a corpse in the White House?) Papa Doc, you oughtta come back here – don't we have such a love for zombies, and you could be our first black president. If Jesse Jackson was a walking corpse, he'd sweep the states! They'll love you when you're dead!'

She paused in her magnificent tirade, and her face softened. 'This here song I'm gonna sing you is from a lady who's been better loved since she passed on. What a sad sick truth we got . . . you don't know what you got till it's gone, beyond the grave. So hang onto the person in your arms . . . this here's your song.'

The switch flicked; Blind Ellen milked the keys of all their tragedy; Eugenie's lips parted:

'*Strange fruit . . .*'

But whistles and cheers drowned the phrase.

'LISTEN TO ME!' hollered Eugenie. 'I'M GONNA RUN THAT BY YOU ONCE AGAIN AND YOU HAD BETTER LISTEN GOOD THIS TIME!'

Strange Fruit began again in awed silence.

Rotary Spokes felt her blood stir mightily. She felt: if I die this day, I have been lifted into another dimension. Her cells would carry the memory of that voice, that song, the lights, the eager grasp of the nameless person at her side. Keep your heaven, milk-white Jesus. This earth is pretty damn good. She kissed the head beside her.

Who thought, alas, dear me, to himself:

'I've done it!'

He'd had his eye out for something long and lean, cool and powerful as a polar bear, and Rotary Spokes had moved in, like a pillar of fire parting the Red Sea.

Beeline? Gloria Goodtime had shot to Rotary Spokes' side like a north-to-south magnet. He'd always been a pushover for that physique and the leather, and thank God, this one smoked. His slim gold lighter lighter had been the passkey to many a bed of wondrous delight, and tonight, judging by the anonymous hunk of talent on his arm, would be no exception. Gloria relaxed. The night was his.

And goodness gracious, Rotary Spokes was happy to be pulled by such a smart woman. She had this thing for hippies, after Diz and the even more ludicrous interlude with Fender Rhodes. But she also liked women who looked smart. And women in jeans. And in overalls. And in – shit, she couldn't, come to think of it, make no generalizations. Hmm. She liked every kind of woman. Waaall. There did have to be a certain kind of warmth about them.

She would never have made a move towards someone like Gloria, though. It took someone with unique style to set her pulse crazy. Someone like Jess. Unattainable on the surface. What had happened to her, wondered Rotary Spokes. She might even be here now, bathed in the glory that was Eugenie Lafayette. Her ears were ringing as they left the Rawhide Palace.

'I only got a bike,' she grunted at Gloria, 'I ain't got no little roadster.'

'What?' screamed Gloria, Queen of Heaven. And then rapturized over the sea-blue, jewel-bright bike. Gloria perched daintily on the saddle and Rotary Spokes kicked the beast into life. To Gloria's place. For coffee. Ha! Damn fine *coffee* they make in Hyperburg, she thought, grinning into the teeth of the wind.

She drained her cup sitting on the gold moquette sofa and flipped another Mahawat between her lips. The conversation was a little slow, a reluctant prelude to the delights both anticipated.

'I'll change,' lisped Gloria. Rotary Spokes sat back. Maybe this was what they meant by role-playing?

Gloria clearly had shares in the feather and silk industry. Gloria started teasing.

She swirled her pale pink gown and let it slither to the floor.

Rotary Spokes choked.

Gloria, in a silver G-string, flaunted his body, luring Rotary Spokes on.

Well, what's a girl to do?

Rotary Spokes stood up. The lightly muscled body in front of her paused in mid-gyration.

'Is there something wrong?' said Gloria.

'There ain't but two things wrong' said Rotary Spokes.

'Tell me,' said Gloria, perching on the sofa.

Rotary Spokes slugged bourbon and put the record back to the beginning. Real loud. She unzipped her jacket and tossed it to the floor. She turned to Gloria.

'Breasts, dear,' she said. 'And the rest of it.' She blew smoke.

Gloria slipped his gown on again.

'Oh, heavens,' he said, 'you must think I'm a very naughty girl.'

'Truth to tell,' said Rotary Spokes. 'Truth to tell, I've been taken for a man before.'

She thought of Samuel Uncle and grinned.

Gloria flicked his painted eyes to the ceiling.

'There's only one thing to do,' he said and flipped through his records.

He put one on.

The disco beat broke the embarassed silence.

You think you're a man

You are only a boy . . .!

Gloria giggled.

'I thought you were the best-looking man I ever saw.'

'And I thought you were a pretty classy-looking woman.'

'Well, I regard that as a real compliment,' said Gloria, and flung back his head and laughed.

'Shit, honey,' he said. 'Anyone can make a mistake, right?'

'Sure as hell can,' said Rotary Spokes.

Oh well, she could make up something to tell Jeannie the next time she saw her.

Damn, but wasn't life strange?

CHAPTER
NINETEEN

Precious Baby blew a fuse.
(Gertrude Stein)

Aurelia Bontemps could have been any age between eighteen and thirty-eight and probably was. Barely five foot and slender as an elf, she gave the impression of condensed power, through some expensively-acquired muscles and a handmade leather jacket which she had designed herself. The shoulders were built up and out in glossy folds, the sleeves and body were leather crushed and ruched to magnify the particular glories of Aurelia Bontemps.

She spent so much time in the gym that she soon became a partner and then sole owner. She was nearly ready to make the next leap: a Women's Gym, solely and exclusively. With palm trees. With a juice bar. With a jacuzzi and hot tubs in a sensurround studio which perfectly faked a Californian midnight. With a hand-picked clientele. She lay awake at night, plotting.

Like a bat out of hell, she had hurled into the city some years before with nothing. Nothing except a determination fit to fell a sequoia redwood, the Walls of Jericho, the Tower of Babel, or any other landmark that didn't please her.

There were an enormous number of things that did not please her, and she reacted in varying degrees – from a slight clenching of teeth through a facial tic, through a scathing comment and so to a burn of adrenalin that coiled every muscle in her body, ripped down her arms like a forest fire and balled her deadly fists into fury. Then look out world.

Her favourite character in literature was the She-Hulk, and she cursed the day they had taken her out of her own comic book and bundled her in with *The Fantastic Four*. Fantastic? *Fantastic*? Ask

Aurelia Bontemps: three shit-sucking goons and the greatest green woman who ever lived.

Do not question the 'lived'. Oh, no.

Do not question!

Her parents had raised her as a cutsie-tootsie sweetie-pie, in roses of lace and ribbons and bows. She had been religiously swatted if any mud found its way onto her clothes, or any tangle crept into her hair, or any dirty word tripped off her tiny pink tongue. She learnt fast, and curtseyed, lisped and simpered, and batted her eyelashes like fans. And her parents were pleased. Proud, delighted and so on.

'I want you always to be my princess,' her daddy had told her, perching her on his knee like a piece of china, and beaming fondly at her lemon and white, or pink and white, or mint and white frothing beribboned perfection: her ringlets topped with co-ordinating pastel satin bows.

Her pink and white manicured fingers tinkled the minor classics from the richly polished piano, and her sateen pumps twinkled over the pedals.

Loud, soft, loud, soft. She quivered, demanding fortissimo, and played *Für Elise*. At school she conducted a reign of terror in the playground, extorting money and candy, and later, overalls and running shoes from a girl two years her senior.

This was on pain of mutilation.

'Death would be too quick, Belle-Sue, and I wouldn't get as much fun out of it,' she hissed, her daddy's scout knife quivering at the other girl's throat.

Then she was free to roam and explore: free and wholly unrecognizable. Her own loathed frippery she bundled into a plastic bag and hid in a tree hole, while she galivanted around the entertainment arcade. At the whorehouse, she picked up a boogie-woogie beat, a love of fighting, a taste for corn liquor and a total contempt for most adults and most men in particular.

All of which took her a year or so, and after that she was ready for pastures new and wide. All that stuff was so much chickenshit to the empire-building instincts beginning to flex their monomaniac muscles in her furious heart and fertile mind.

Mentally, she spat at the small town and its hypocrisies, and took to heart the words of advice of Big Red Rosa, the madam of the biggest whorehouse in the cheapest street in town:

'Git out and git. And don't take no wooden nickels.' From then on, she always bit into every coin plopped into her tiny hand. You never knew.

At twelve, she realized that her days were numbered: she was the boss of the entire playground, making a few good bucks playing jazz at the bar: at home she was still her mom and dad's peaches-and-cream babe. But you can't fool all the people all the time, and this truth she dreaded.

She started a savings account and her extortion became intense and purposeful. Winsomely, she charmed larger and larger weekly allowances from her daddy's adoring hands. Any Christmas, Easter or birthday gifts she sold. Her parents thought she gave the money to the Little Sisters of Sorrow. So did the Little Sisters of Sorrow, being unacquainted with the skill of palming bills.

At fourteen she had a satchel permanently packed and grabbable. She still lisped and curtseyed in the drawing room; bore off an indecent number of prizes at school: for Elocution; for Ladylike Deportment; for Being A True Friend To Those Less Fortunate. She sat in on adult conversations, her head bobbing as if at a tennis match, and would present a suitably modest reluctance when asked to play the piano.

One evening, as she was smoothing down her lacy skirts and patting ringlets into place, having just stuffed her overalls and sneakers back into the tree hole, it was no surprise to her when she was circled by a group of kids from school; a group large enough to menace and not be menaced. Fourteen of them. They were good, decent kids, who had smarted and sweated too long on the wrong end of her fists and threats. They required of her that she give back all of the money, the jewellery, the playthings; that she made a full confession at the morning assembly, and mend her ways forthwith. This living Baby Jane had to change.

And seeing no other choice, Aurelia took it with panache. She even snivelled a little to buy herself a day or two. They gave her untill the end of the week. Monday had to be the Day of Justice. They even told her she would feel better afterwards. She agreed, agreed, thanked them for pointing out the error of her ways, she atoned, she grovelled. There were only five days to plan.

She ran through the bus timetable which she knew by heart. She knew that a dash of lipstick, a cheap suit and an air of big-city seeking would render her anonymous among the white trash at the station. The station was twelve miles distant: no problem. She had a favour or two she could trade in exchange for a sworn-secret lift.

But her sense of drama would not let her leave without a finale.

Her parents were having a dinner party that Saturday night to celebrate some religious feast or other. The bus left at four a.m. on Sunday morning. So far so good. She stashed her suitcase in the trunk of Al Merino's studebacker on pain of revealing just what he did on Thursday afternoons between Big Rosa's scarlet sheets. Rosa gave her a lipstick for luck.

Saturday evening she primped in front of the mirror in her deliciously white bedroom, tying full white chiffon bows in her hair like ghostly butterflies. She smoothed the tiers of her net-petticoated dress with its two hundred rosebuds, and buckled the white patent-leather sandals over her pink-ruffled white cotton bobby socks. She fluttered down the sweep of the staircase and pecked Father and Mother.

'A fine, purdy girl you raised, Abe,' said Josiah MacMiller. 'And a good little saver too.'

Mr MacMiller, the banker, was unaware of the total withdrawal of dollars from her account at closing time the day before.

'You're quite a belle now, Aurelia. I've always been curious, dear, what does your pretty name mean?'

'Why, Mrs MacMiller,' she enthused, 'did my momma never tell you? It means there's a new day rising.'

'Waaall, now, ain't she just as cute?'

The dinner was eaten. The coffee was served. Cigars filled the room. They might have asked me, thought the little cherub, who preferred a good cigar to most everything bar winning at poker.

'Would you play us a little something, dear? Would you? She plays so prettily!'

Aurelia made her customary demurral, then tippy-toed over to the keys. She turned as if a thought had just struck her.

'I've learnt a new piece at school ... I think they call it jazz. Momma, Poppa, shall I try to remember it?'

'Why, you little rogue,' said her delighted poppa. 'Angel, you play.'

Aurelia wished she had a drink. Made it go better. No matter, there were only a few hours to go.

What she had chosen was *Who Put The Benzedrine In Mrs Murphy's Ovaltine?* This went down real sweet in the blue smoke of the bar under Big Red Rosa's. She walloped it out, to gasps of surprise, and as the last anarchic chords died out, a smatter of applause.

'Does the song have any words, darling?' coo-ed her mother. 'Aurelia has such a melodious voice!'

'Well, Momma, I don't know as I'll recall them right . . . oh, I'll try.'

Let 'em have it! Unfortunately neither her momma nor her poppa, nor Mr and Mrs Josiah Mac Miller had ever heard of Benzedrine or Nembutal. The effect was hardly a ripple. And she had wanted an explosion.

Shit.

Denied her finale, no chance of a paternal: *Out into the storm*!, eleven o'clock found her bestowing chaste kisses round the company, and flittering up to her candy-pink quilt in her vestal bedroom.

'Don't they grow up fast?'

'Abe, I do reckon that our Jeremiah's got a sweet eye on her. Mark my words.'

The parents dozed in the dream of marrying their one-and-only treasures and the unbeatable combination of bank and land, unaware that Jeremiah had, a few days earlier, headed the outraged assembly of extortionees.

Aurelia waited till the house was quiet, then eeled out the window onto the verandah roof, and after one prodigious leap, dashed for the waiting car of Al Merino.

'Sugar,' he said. 'Are you sure you know what you're doing?'

'Shut it and drive,' she told him.

And so she came to the anonymity of Hyperburg, whose faceless masses ensured that any police search would be fruitless. She ditched her surname: Sansauffe, and became Ms Bontemps. God, she could use a good time!

Her momma prayed for her, her poppa prayed. The children who maligned the memory of a 'gen-u-ine little saint' were thrashed soundly, and Mr MacMiller wondered what commie white-slavin' threat could have made the darlin' child pull out every cent of her cash from his bank. She must have been in mortal terror, poor soul. After a year, a plaque went up at her school, commemorating her. She was held up as an example of truth, purity and modesty to all future scholars.

Having had the creek dragged, the woods scoured, the state police badgered, her parents resorted to private detectives and began to sell their land piece by piece. They would not hear of a memorial service or a tombstone even after two years, and in their hearts, she was always as she had been on that last night: a darling child of fifteen, her life ahead of her.

In Hyperburg, Aurelia was drawn downtown, and was soon playing spots in five bars. Finally she got sick of being hassled and gawped at for her fresh country complexion, and decided that a woman needs protection. Then began the second ruling passion in her life: pumping iron.

As to the first Aurelia had tried a succession of men, and then, realizing that you have but the one life, gravitated to women's bars where she acquired a series of lovers and a reputation for violence that ensured her respect.

She developed a walk with the rhythm of her blood and had a theme song she was working on. Thus far, it went:

I'm so cool, I'm no one's fool,
I came to the city and I know I'm real pretty
If you don't it's a pity
For you.

I came to the city and I'm one and twenty
If you want talent then I've got plenty.
Don't even start to look for a heart
Cuz you'll find it's empty
And I've thrown away the key.

Well, I'm looking for a woman who's a natural queen
She's ten feet tall and cool and mean
I'll make one move and I'll strut my stuff
And she's gonna know I got enough . . .

New verses would occur to her as she burned the leather down the boulevards, or sweated yet more glory into her sculpted arms and rippling back.

> *The minute you walked in the joint*
> *I could tell*
> *You were a gal*
> *Of distinction*
> *A real big spender.*

The one who walked in the joint being Rotary Spokes, flaunting a designer leather. The joint being Jeannie's Chilli Beanie. The brain through which the rhythm richocheted seething in the skull was of one Ms. Aurelia Bontemps.

She threw a look at Rotary Spokes.

'Spend a little time with *me*?'

Rotary Spokes looked down. Kinda cute kid.

'O.K.,' she said amiably. It being a women's bar, she was unlikely to be a re-run of Gloria Goodtime.

'Drink?'

'Screwdriver,' said Aurelia Bontemps.

'I'm Rotary Spokes.'

'I'm Aurelia Bontemps.'

'Goddam. What's that mean?'

'It means there's a new day rising and I'm out for a good time.'

The gauntlet hovered between them.

'A good time. Yeah,' said Rotary Spokes, picking it up.

'What does Rotary Spokes mean?'

'Means? Ah, I dunno. Means . . . I'm here, I suppose. Or maybe, I got good strong wheels and they're rollin', if you wanna get fancy.'

Rotary Spokes flashed a wolfish smile. The temperature rose. Aurelia Bontemps slugged her screwdriver down and ordered another. Rotary Spokes drained her can of Red Stripe.

'Women,' thought Jeannie, expertly mixing a third screwdriver. It was O.K. – she'd seen Rotary Spokes lap up a whole lagoon and not even stagger, but this one? Aw, well, Rotary Spokes could handle herself and was the unofficial bouncer anyhow. Jeannie picked up her multi-coloured knitting and started to whip in a scarlet thread. She perched behind the bar, needles flying while she tuned in to the wrestling match on the other side of the bar. Jeannie liked wrestling and these two were experts.

Rotary Spokes was sounding the glories of a good bike. No, an excellent bike. Her bike. The Harley Electraglide. The pair left briefly to burn around the block and hurtle back in.

'Some bike,' grudged Aurelia. She cracked her knuckles. 'You ever work out?'

'Nah,' said Rotary Spokes. 'I never found it needful, workin' with the bikes. I guess an eighty-pound engine is pretty good for ... exercise.'

A fall. A count. One, two, three ...

'Maybe you should call by the gym.'

Some faltering footwork.

'Take a look at the ultra-bike' (jab), 'twenty-seven gears', (jab), 'or the Simulo Water Slalom ... row yourself up Niagara Falls.' (JAB).'

'Well, maybe I will.'

A submission?

'Sounds kinda entertaining,' finished Rotary Spokes.

DING!

Each of Aurelia Bontemps' screwdrivers sounded the bell for a fresh round.

'What do you do, like apart from the gym?' led Rotary Spokes.

'*Well, what time of the day are you talking about?*'

Rotary Spokes hard against the ropes.

'Now?'

Aurelia Bontemps sagged against the ropes this time. This woman was outrageous, dancing just beyond her eager reach.

'I have a few drinks with you,' she said, finding her feet. Rotary Spokes bipped her down again.

'And?'

'Well, that's ... very ... much ... up ... to ... you.'

DING!

'Right, now I get the next drinks,' said Aurelia Bontemps.

What the hell am I doing? thought Rotary Spokes. It was all kind of amusing, but she felt, um, imposed on. Hell, she was lookin' for Jess.

'You wanna eat?'

Damn, there she was again. Pesky as a mosquito. Couldn't even say that without sounding like a sting.

'Yeah, I wanna eat. But I also require a little tranquillity to digest.'

'Tranquillity, huh?' said Aurelia Bontemps , nervously. Tranquillity started the facial tic. All her life had been a wildfire rush from tranquillity.

'So I can boogie later on,' said Rotary Spokes.

'*Alright!*'

In the Capital T Bone, the temptation to order raw steak was strong, but Aurelia paid lip-service to the truce and settled for rare. Rotary Spokes ordered hers well-done, and changed it to charred. She liked it that way. But she had never eaten food while she was arm-wrestling before.

Clearly Aurelia had, her sharp little teeth tearing meat while her rosy lips chatted at a ferocious rate.

As Aurelia flung verbal grenades over her Caesar's salad, machine-gunned through strawberry shortcake, and bazook-ed over black coffee, Rotary Spokes began to understand Diz's murmurs of:

'*Wow, you're so hostile.*'

Goddam Californians – a phrase to cushion every situation.

Finally, Rotary Spokes grinned at Aurelia, mid-minefield, and pulled a white silk handkerchief from her pocket. She waved it exaggeratedly slow.

Aurelia Bontemps' smile flickered nervously.

'OK, OK, I guess I come on a little strong. If you had to punch your way outta life like me . . .' Aurelia flexed her extraordinary neck muscles.

'I had to twist a shotgun barrel back once,' Rotary Spokes threw in. 'Kinda . . . humiliatin' defeat.' She told Aurelia about Carolee.

'Them places oughtta be razed to the ground,' fired Aurelia, and dented the hardwood table top – by way of illustration.

'Sure. But as it happens, it all worked out. She's got her Marj with a 'j' and I got my independence. I never figured to bein' nobody's mother, anyways.'

They sat, as two exhausted swimmers who have slapped the side at the same split second.

'I don't wanna boogie,' said Aurelia, suddenly a fire of allure.

Rotary Spokes thought rapidly. What had Bean said? *If you gotta stop and think . . . you kin clearly skip it . . . it's bedtime, pumpkin.*

She was stopping and thinking. Sure, she was interested in the cliff-jumping wiry person on the other side of the table. But. There was a but.

As much as it could in a joint blaring with videos, music, baseball scores and the thunder of a self-delighted clientele, silence fell between them.

'OK,' said Aurelia Bontemps. 'I'll see y'around, huh?' She winded Rotary Spokes with a final curt body-blow bow, and the crowds were scythed apart as she hacked her way to the next challenge.

CHAPTER
TWENTY

*"Of all the gin joints in all the towns all over the
world, she walks into mine."*
(Casablanca)

It had been relatively easy for Jess to find herself a studio in
Hyperburg: there was an awed respect for a Real Artist. The
urbanologist committee which had met frequently and expensively
over the Hyperburg project, had cannily recommended a deliberately
downmarket feel to Area 15 on the town plans. It was felt that a certain
type would gravitate there and be unaware of the lower standard of
household amenities. What they had not anticipated was Jess striding
ahead of the realtor, sweeping into one of the attic apartments, still
totally unfurnished and fitted, and declaiming:
'I'll take it.'
Consternation. Telephone numbers of interior designers, colour
co-ordinators, carpenters, electricians, plumbers. Jess smiled, took the
numbers and used them to test out the trash-compactor gleaming
under a chrome dome in the twin-sink fantasy food unit.
The realtor gained instant kudos: A Real Artist, and just where they
had wanted her, too. The contractors were less delighted as it became
clear that this one would design and execute her own environment.
The realtor bought one of her paintings and hung it in his
air-conditioned office among the glass, steel and simulosilk plants.
Real Art with a capital A.
Jess's idea was to fit out the studio so that she could find everything,
store everything and explore everything with the minimum effort. She
fitted deep shelves and dividers from one end of the room to the other,
on which to drape fabric and fascinating debris from the streets
nearby. Hyperburg was a city of consumer coneheads who junked at
least 50 percent of everything they bought, on principle.

She dropped into Jeannie's Chilli Beanie from time to time: she loved chilli, and Jeannie had her five Santa Barbara gold trophies over the bar. You could get chilli on three kinds of rice, chilli in baked potatoes, chilli tacos, chilli tortillas, chilli chapattis, chilli salami salads, red chilli, green chilli: hot, hotter, scalding.

Each time she had been in she missed Rotary Spokes by an hour, or five minutes. Often she would wonder what had happened to Rotary, why she had never replied. Jess seldom wrote letters herself; it didn't occur to her that she had left her own return address off the letter to Rotary Spokes. She was mildly surprised that she had heard nothing from her . . . she had mulled over their meeting for a few months, and decided she'd like some more.

But she was much sought after, and even said yes to the odd night here and there, although dawn would find her striding an unfamiliar sidewalk and cursing that the best hours of daylight had been lost.

Recently, she had been into Jeannie's more frequently, for two reasons: there was a lumberyard nearby which specialized in interesting woods from all over planet earth; the other reason was that she was being pursued by a young poetess who had developed the habit of declaiming her blank verse on Jess's doorstep incessantly, and spending the rest of the time filling up Jess's telephone message recorder with her experimental genius. Leaving the phone off the hook brought a Donald Duck indignation into the pre-recorded message: 'Kindly replace your telephone receiver . . . Kindly replace your telephone receiver . . .'

When she had stuffed it into a drawer, a telephone engineer had been round in half an hour. Hoping she and the poetess would find plenty to talk about, Jess slipped out of the back window.

And so, later that day, with a plank of obeche wood culled from some nameless forest in West Africa tilting over her spectacular shoulder, she had sloped into Jeannie's, ordered a chilli tacos and a manhattan.

Aurelia Bontemps had just signed the lease to *her* gym. It was celebration time, but there was just one small problem: with whom should she celebrate?

Her lifestyle had become one of 'If it's Tuesday it must be Tallulah', 'If it's Wednesday, it must be Wendy', and so on. This added up to a real difficulty when you wanted to have a group celebration. She could invite them all (and Saturday and Sunday had three sections each: morning, afternoon and evening) and risk losing a very gratifying harem setting. She could, since it was Friday, invite just Francesca. But her ego needed something better, bigger, more. Wait a minute! There was an 'r' in the month, so she decided with a vulpine leer that today would be Rotary Spokes' lucky day. Not everyone got a second chance. It never crossed her mind that no might mean no. Not if it had been said to her.

So she splashed on the Eau Sauvage Extreme, dressed fit to kill, and swanked the streets to Jeannie's Chilli Beanie. Excellent, Rotary Spokes was there in a booth, back to the bar. She downed a screwdriver, and sipped at another. Rotary Spokes was there alright. Present and correct. She had in fact given the spitting fireball a good deal of (albeit confused) thought.

'Do I really want a tag match in my bed? Maybe. But what if I was dallyin' with that one, and Ms Right – probably Jess . . . Perish the thought – I don't believe life can be that good. And if Jess don't turn up, and I have kept myself clear from what was sure to be an athletic experience, aw . . . I don't mind lookin' for Ms Right, but it could be years, and I sure as hell ain't wastin' my nights sleepin' on my own . . . then again . . . maybe. Maybe not.'

She could not pretend she would fall into bed with Aurelia Bontemps like an innocent newborn lamb – as, say, when she had met Diz. Ha!

Along the shooting gallery that passed for conversation, Aurelia had let slip that *sex* was her favourite pastime. And that she worked out before leaping into bed. Rotary Spokes had guardedly agreed that sex was pretty much the best . . . Only she had reservations about who you did it with and what it might mean to them. These thoughts were met with hostility by Aurelia Bontemps – although she pathologically despised hippies, she seemed to personify the loose-fitting philosophy: 'If it feels good, do it.'

An alarm bell rang in Jeannie's mind. She dropped a stitch. A bell clanged in Aurelia's mind as she began her High Noon stalk to the booth. The black-leathered self-styled champ. Primed to floor – rather, bed Rotary Spokes in one round.

But, oh my friends, the chance factor intervened.

Rotary Spokes turned and saw a tall figure spooning chilli at the bar with one hand, the other casually balancing a plank over one shoulder.

As she hollered: 'JESS!' The figure swung in surprise and the edge of the plank caught a determined little jaw full on and sent Aurelia Bontemps and all her intentions sprawling unnoticed to the floor.

'Jess!' Rotary Spokes half stood up, confused, delighted.

'I'll be damned,' said Jess, propping her plank at the edge of the booth, scooping up her chilli bowl and swinging into the seat opposite. 'Why didn't you write to me?'

'Why didn't you leave your address?'

'What?'

'No return address on your letter, Jess.'

'Ah. I guess I always forget these things. How have you been?'

'All the better for seeing you, my dear,' Rotary Spokes grinned. 'Y'all wanna celebrate?'

'A libation?' smiled Jess.

'An alcoholic beverage?'

'You betcha!'

Jeannie sashayed over to the booth with a chilled bottle of champagne.

'French champagne from France?' twinkled Jess.

'You think I serve shit in this bar?'

Jeannie turned away a moment and her face twisted into rage.

As the cork popped she blew a fuse:

'I WILL NOT HAVE NO DRUNKS IN MY PLACE! GIT HER OUT OF HERE!'

'Wow, and I thought Aurelia could hold her liquor,' said Rotary Spokes. 'Hey, Jeannie, maybe she just fainted.'

'Fainted? Fainted at seven o'clock at night? Bullshit. Git her out.'

Rotary Spokes scooped up the body and propped her in the booth. Her head lolled onto the table.

'She looks unwell,' said Jess.

'Give her a minute or two,' said Rotary Spokes. 'We'll take her home later.'

Blackness filled the fertile brain, dribbling across the table-top.

As the bubbles danced through the champagne, Rotary Spokes' heart felt it was fizzing, and the glow in Jess's eyes said the same thing. A loving exchange of a subtle intimacy that would have knocked the wind out of Aurelia Bontemps. A tenderness which would have eluded the steel fist.

'Anyone else,' said Rotary Spokes, 'and I'd be saying my place or yours?'

'Well?'

'Well, sheee-it,' protested Rotary Spokes, blushing. 'OK, seeing it's you – my place or yours?'

'Which is nearer?'

'I'm a block up the street.'

'I'm four blocks across. Sounds like it'll be your place this time.'

With little hope, Aurelia's parents had commissioned yet another private dick to search for their one and only child. By now, her mother had passed from fantasies of kidnapping to a near certainty of drugs, white slavery, death. This latest search meant the loss of the last acre of their land. After this, there'd be nothing to sell. This private dick pleased her. He had the hat brim and cigarette of Bogart's Philip Marlowe, and a single syllable vocabulary which encouraged her confidence. Her father was less hopeful. In the last few years he had taken solace at the hands of Big Red Rosa, and one afternoon, committed coitus interruptus as the strains of *Who Put The Benzedrine In Mrs Murphy's Ovaltine?* punched through the floorboards under the well-used bed.

'Don't I please ya, honey?'

'What's that tune?'

She told him. He had speculated with flinching heart. Surely not, not Aurelia, his angel, she couldn't have.

But Big Red Rosa cradled his head and reminisced to comfort him.

'We useta have a kid in here playin' the piano. Couldn't have been more than fourteen, but damn if she didn't have a feel for the keys. She used ta play herself fit to beat the band and that was her best tune . . .'

He left Big Red Rosa with dread beating through his heart. Surely not, not his princess. But his mind staggered towards the truth.

He really didn't want to know. He only wanted his little princess back again, but it had been eight years and he realized that she, if not dead, would be unrecognizable. He started surreptitiously to buy corn liquor and drink it at home, and after a while his wife would join him.

Meanwhile, the flatfoot had come up with a shrewd assessment of the situation, and slouched into Hyperburg, determined to solve the riddle. He had got as far as the new gym, although the new owner was in hospital with concussion and a fractured jaw, and this afternoon he was about to do a hospital visit. He bought some flowers and noted the three bucks in his dog-eared expenses book. He fixed another toothpick in his nicotine-stained teeth, and took the lift to the seventh floor.

Aurelia Bontemps was lying in bed, having just performed her daily work-out on the traction wires over the bed. She was sweating profusely and trying to remember what had happened. Last thing was Rotary Spokes' hunched shoulder. And then nothing. Had they fought? Had *she* been beaten? Well, something had beaten her.

'Hi, Ms Bontemps.'

She looked up. Some guy with flowers.

'I think you got the wrong bed, asshole,' she tried to say, but the wire in her jaws made it come out as:

'MMMPFOOOOOPPPTTTRRRUUUNNNGGGGGUDDDD.'

'Or should I say, Ms Sansauffe?'

'JJJJJZZZKKKKKRRR!'

'I come from your mom and pop.'

'GRRRRNNNNNNFFFFSSSSTUNGGFFFKKKOOOFFFFF!'

'They're real worried 'bout you.'

'UUUUUUUUUdddnnnuunngnnffk.'

'I'm paid ta find ya and bring ya home.'

'Nuuffffddffuuurrr.'

'They jist wanna know what happened and see that you're well.'

'Guuuuuuuwuuuufffmmmuu.'

'I kin say you're daid, but they gonna wanna have your remains to bury in the fam'ly plot.'

'LLLLSSSSYYYUUUUUGRRRVVVFST!'

'Ms Bontemps is exhausted. You can call in and see her tomorrow.' A nurse ushered him out.

'Aren't you a dark horse and a half!' the nurse lilted at Aurelia. 'That your young man?'

'NNNNNNNNNNNNNNNNGGGGGG!'

CHAPTER
TWENTY-ONE

"Bless you, for being an angel
Just when I thought heaven was not for me."
(Fats Waller)

Rotary Spokes peeled crushed foil from the neck of the bottle.

'Let me do that,' said Jess.

She put the bottle on the low table and stared at it. The wire untwisted slowly and flipped onto the floor.

'Get the glasses ready,' said Jess.

She stared again and the cork suddenly flew from the neck; the champagne foamed to the brim of each glass.

'Damn, that's somethin' else!' said Rotary Spokes admiringly.

'Only works when it's really important,' said Jess with a lazy smile. She gazed at Rotary Spokes, unblinking like a cat.

'This is perfect,' said Rotary Spokes.

Jess took her hand.

'Be ambitious,' she said.

Down the street, a bottle smashed against a wall, a garbage can clanged and rolled in the gutter.

'We can be anywhere,' said Jess. 'Anywhere we want. Trust me?'

Rotary Spokes nodded.

Their brows touched over closed eyes.

There was a rush of cool night air. Dots of brilliant colour danced behind Rotary Spokes' eyelids.

'Open your eyes now,' said Jess. 'We're here.'

EPILOGUE

And in the hearth burns applewood, and on the wall the firelight dances. And the moments laze by, fire-dreaming, and up the stairs lies a wide low bed, covered in green linen. And the window-ledge is full of roses.

Rotary Spokes' face was an inch or so from Jess's. The firelight gave their skin the ancient beauty of golden clay statues: an ikon of anticipation.

Rotary Spokes broke the silence:

'Will you be my Lauren Bacall?'

Rotary Spokes broke the spell.

'Jesus Christ!'

Jess flung herself upright from the rug and went out into the cool darkness. Rotary Spokes stumbled after her. What had she done! What had she said that for! She felt that a door had slammed on her: a door which had been slowly opening on a tantalizing glimpse of somewhere she had known all her life. The night air slammed her sober.

Jess sat on the bench and patted the seat beside her.

'Listen to me. Me. Jess.'

And Jess thought:

I will not be your Lauren Bacall. I will not be your Greta Garbo; I will not be anyone but me and I will not be yours. All my life I've had men wanting me to be everyone from Bette Davis to Marilyn Monroe, depending on who was to be the sadist. Saying it as if they were conferring an honour, a starring role in their fantasy. "Will you star in my movie?" And I have left. In the middle of the night, in the middle of a meal, in the middle of a marriage, clutching my integrity and my identity. I have left their houses never to return.

But this is one house I don't want to leave. And one person I don't want to leave. But it has to be *me* she loves, really me, as I love her. I couldn't bear to feel I was appearing in glorious black and white with full Hollywood orchestral backing. It would be like kissing someone while watching a movie over their shoulder.

Jess picked up Rotary Spokes' hand.

'Listen,' she said, 'you don't have to pay three bucks and queue up to see me. You don't have to clip a speaker onto your car to hear me. Come on.'

She drew Rotary Spokes across the hilltop.

'This world is our screen, our movie, our lives, and we've got better than front-row seats. We've got *our* life, Rotary . . . continuous performance, sensurround . . . and no-one else writing the script. So how about if I'm just Jess, huh?'

She put her arm across Rotary Spokes' shoulder.

They looked into the blue-black dome of the night, studded with ice-white stars. A sliver of moon hung there, beautiful. The pine scent rose around them and the chill green scent of grass at night.

Their kiss was slow, deep and needy. Their kiss bore them indoors to the huge warm bed.

From time to time in the night, she woke. Jess was there, hot, asleep, warm and soft, and always there was some part of them touching: toe to calf, thigh to bum, hand to breast, lips parted against a bare shoulder.

'I am sleeping. With you. All night,' thought Rotary Spokes.

Finally she woke and the Chinese paper blind was fallen from the window. She was astonished, both by Jess and the clear morning light. She inched her body to the edge of the bed. At the window, she pulled on a T-shirt and leaned out into the day.

Already it was hot. The sun poured over the field in front of the house, sheets of sparkle, making the green a colour of light. The stone was white and gold on the barn along the track.

And the sun poured all down the valley, the tangles of bushes held great bursts of light on the dew. There was almost a haze on the ground. The hill shadows crept back along the valley, and the mist tinged rose and vanished. The trees held shadows and highlights; before the dawn they had been a flat dull promise of green, lumped against a sky of gray, in a light which drains everything of colour and form. Now there was no way you could call them just green: they were every shade and more.

Rotary Spokes put on her jeans and bent to kiss Jess – gently – so as

not to wake her. But also to say, 'I must go out there.' A feeling . . .
how thrilling! . . . tripped over the grasses; a breeze calling 'Come on
out!' had touched her face from a sky of vaulted light. And she had to
go.

Jess held onto her from out of her sleep, then turned, curling the
bedclothes around her. Rotary Spokes pinned the blind back up: sleep
a while, darling.

Downstairs, one cat was delighted that someone was up. Another cat
slept in a box by the stove, and a fat little mouse lay dead on the
flagstones.

Outside, the air was moving cool, moving warm, moving into the
new day.

'Hey, beautiful,' called Jess, naked-gold at the upstairs window,
'Come up and see me some time.'

Rotary Spokes swivelled with a ridiculous grin.